WENDELL BLACK, MD

WENDELL

BLACK, MD

GERALD IMBER

BOURBON
STREET
BOOKS

HarperCollins books may be purchased for educational, business, or sales promotional use. For information, please e-mail the Special Markets Department at SPsales@harpercollins.com.

FIRST EDITION

Designed by Janet M. Evans

Library of Congress Cataloging-in-Publication Data is available upon request.

ISBN 978-0-06-224685-1

14 15 16 17 18   OV/RRD   10 9 8 7 6 5 4 3

1

Airline pilots sound like old-time radio announcers over the PA system. This one had a voice near the bottom of the baritone register, with a pleasant cadence and flat regional accent. The kind that didn't jump out and grab you by the throat. I figured him to be from somewhere west of the Mississippi, and maybe just north of a Southern drawl. He had interrupted the soundtrack of the film with the usual series of annoying pings, and illuminated the seat-belt icon before he spoke. There wasn't much need to tell passengers to buckle up; anyone with any sense at all had already strapped in. According to the captain, the rough ride was due to temporary clear-air turbulence, whatever that meant. He didn't sound disturbed. When things got worse ten minutes later, he delivered another bit of pilot balm, which did even less to reassure me. The sky was clear, that was obvious, and an occasional white puff against the endless blue made a beautiful picture when it was possible to focus.

We had been tossed around for an unpleasant twenty minutes, when the cabin staff was ordered to give up trying to serve lunch and take their seats. It was rough. My Côtes du Rhône would have spilled all over the place if I hadn't had the common sense to chug it down. I stuffed the empty glass into the seat pocket and made it my business not to glance out the window at the waving and shaking of the flimsy-looking wing. It scared the shit out of me. Other than that, I'm a pretty good flier.

The physical principle of wind over airfoil generating lift is basic stuff, and I understand it. It all goes back to Bernoulli: air flowing over the convex upper aspect of the wing has farther to go than the air under the wing, so it flows faster, creating lower pressure on top of the wing, higher pressure under it. Enough lift to overcome gravity, and away we go. I also know that the wing box attaching it to the fuselage, as well as the wings themselves, are incredibly over-engineered and wings simply do not come off aircraft. Planes can lose speed in rapid wind shear and stall, but wings don't come off. I get it. I studied all this stuff in college and I get it, but it still scares the shit out of me.

A distinguished-looking man in full pilot dress sat across the wide aisle in the business/first section. He was tall and thin, with straight-edge posture, airline-issue black hair streaked with gray, and enough squint lines alongside his eyes to be taken seriously. He was probably deadheading back home or scheduled to pick up a plane in New York. I kept sneaking looks over there as he read quietly through most of the turbulence. Then he tilted back his glass of Coke for the last few sips and put it, and the paperback, into the seat pocket just as I caught his eye.

"It doesn't get much worse than this," he said, in a voice not unlike the captain's, and not quite smiling. And then it did.

The 747-400 hit an air pocket and dropped what seemed like a thousand feet, launching all sorts of objects. Plates and drinks hit the overhead, passengers screamed, luggage compartments sprang open, bags and clothing were everywhere, oxygen masks dangled and bounced on their plastic leads, interior panels rattled and shook, and all hell broke loose. Flight attendants held on to seat backs, scrambling hand over hand, and people were mumbling prayers. Then, quick as it started, it stopped.

Smiles of relief replaced white-lipped terror and most of us were unembarrassed about congratulating ourselves on surviving. Cheering from a group of high school kids in the back of the plane finally made me laugh, and I was starting to settle back and chat with my new friend across the aisle when a new voice came across the PA system.

"If there is a doctor on board would you please identify yourself."

This happens now and again, and much as I would like to hide under my blanket, I do my duty. In-flight emergencies are rarely significant. When they are, I do what little I can until we land; mostly it's just treating anxiety. I unbuckled and stood and identified myself, feeling a bit self-conscious. But at the end of the day it usually adds up to extra drinks and a lot of attention from the flight attendants. One time I actually got lucky enough to end up with someone nice, and that lasted for a few months. But flight

attendants were stewardesses then, and seriously attractive. The one that came up to my seat didn't do much for
me. He was dressed in dark blue trousers, shirt, tie, and
vest, none of which contained a single natural fiber. He was
about my height, just about six feet, rail-thin and doused
with cologne that snapped my head back. With all of that,
he was efficient.

"I'm the purser, are you a medical doctor, sir?"

"I am."

"Can you show me some identification please?"

Now I was getting annoyed, and I guess he read my
glance.

"We have to be sure you are a physician."

I fumbled with the button on my left hip pocket and finally fished out the battered wallet. The New York State
Physician ID got an approving glance, but my NYPD card
earned a second look I wasn't comfortable with. Anyway,
he was right. There are all sorts of doctors, and there's no
limit to the stupidity and ego of people when it comes to
titles. It's a rare in-flight emergency that requires a PhD in
philosophy or a podiatrist.

"Now you know my secret. What's the problem?"

"Could you follow me, please?" He hadn't answered my
question, but I hadn't expected him to. He knew his job.
The heads cranked toward us withdrew in disappointment
as we made our way past the over-wing exit to the back of
the plane. Other flight attendants were reorganizing the
galley, and passengers were rearranging clothing and baggage that had been uprooted. Most eyes were on us, and I

could feel the intense scrutiny until we were stopped a dozen rows from the rear by a flight attendant kneeling in the aisle. She was busy adjusting a wet towel on the head of a young woman stretched across three seats with the armrests raised. The scene immediately commanded all my attention.

"Marjorie, this is the doctor."

I smiled at the solid, middle-aged woman when she looked up at me over half-glasses, with obvious relief. Her glasses were secured around her neck on a long gold chain that looped lazily down either side of her neck. It looked like the tasting cup worn by sommeliers in fancy restaurants, and I smiled.

"Thank you, doctor," she said, pointing her nose at the woman beneath her. "Just a minute ago she was sobbing and babbling nonsense. Then suddenly she stopped . . . and now she's quiet, but she doesn't look so good."

That was an understatement.

"Excuse me." I eased Marjorie out of the way, lifted the wet towel from the stricken woman's eyes, and saw a young, pale face with a broad, high forehead, small nose with a wide tip, and flaring cheekbones. Her color was more than pale, a kind of odd, pasty look of pigmented skin gone white. I brought the tips of my right index and long fingers to the middle of her neck, feeling for a carotid pulse. It was there, but it was faint and rapid and irregular. The skin of her neck and cheek was wet with sweat and unhealthily cold to the touch. From habit, I asked where it hurt, but there was no response. I didn't expect one, but I asked again, this time louder, "Where does it hurt?" She was beyond conversation. There wasn't enough blood getting to her brain and she was drifting away. Far away. Struggling with the inert weight, I managed to pull her onto the floor and laid her flat in the aisle. The move wasn't graceful, and she hit the carpet hard. She didn't seem to care, and it got her into a position where emergency measures were possible. I lifted her chin, turned her head to me, and felt for her breath against my cheek and ear. She was breathing, but her breaths came shallow and rapidly. Not normal, and barely effective enough to keep her alive. What the hell was going on?

Crewmembers arrived with a small oxygen tank and plastic mask and laid them on the floor beside her. The control wheel on the tank was tight, and I struggled for a few seconds to get the flow started. I put the mask over her mouth and strung the elastic band over her head. She didn't help at all and occasionally threw her head from side to side.

The woman looked to be twenty-five, maybe thirty, fairly tall, and dressed like most everyone else around her, in blue jeans and sneakers. She wore a black cotton T-shirt under a zipped sweatshirt. My mind was spinning as I tried to run through the possibilities. Some sort of abdominal crisis: ruptured ovarian cyst, ectopic pregnancy, perforated appendix. What else could make a young woman so sick so quickly? I loosened her belt and pulled the shirts up to touch her abdomen. If my guess was right, her belly would be hard as a board and tender to touch. Laying my hand lightly on her mid-abdomen, I felt that it, too, was soaked in perspiration. I pushed against the muscles. Her belly was soft, and she didn't respond. I looked into her eyes, hoping to see some sign, but her pupils were closed down to a pinpoint even in the low light of the cabin. She began to shake. Three seconds later, the shudder became a full-blown seizure, and she lost control, throwing her head from side to side, kicking and moving her body oddly and without purpose. In twenty seconds it was over. I reached for her face to see if any damage had been done just as she began to vomit up clear liquid and bile. Instinctively, I pulled away. She made no effort to clean herself and I began to wipe her face with a wad of cocktail napkins someone had handed me. I felt moisture through the knees of my pants as she lost control of her bladder. I looked at her face, and in that instant her wide eyes went blank and she died.

Airlines now carry automated defibrillators that are easy to use and have saved many lives. There was one on the floor beside us. Marjorie had already anticipated the need. She held the two big electrode pads, ready to pass them to me, and activated the unit. There was little doubt in my mind about whether our patient was dead or alive, but experience had taught differently. The machine would determine whether there was a dangerous irregular rhythm that wouldn't circulate blood or a normal condition that demanded to be left alone. It was better than any doctor's finger on the pulse, and I welcomed the help.

I struggled to get the woman's arms out of the sweatshirt, which I managed with Marjorie's help; then I pulled her T-shirt up to her neck and Marjorie unhooked the clasp on the front of the white lace bra, which looked unusually feminine and out of place with the rest of her clothing. All this couldn't have taken more than fifteen seconds. There was still time. I attached the electrodes according to the diagram clearly printed on the back of each pad. It didn't call for precision. One went below the lower right chest, the other high on the left chest. A computerized voice from the machine instructed what a half-blind person could easily see, but I guess that was the purpose. The point was to keep cool and do it right. Thirty seconds had passed. The AED told us to stand away from the patient, which we did. It computed the information it was receiving and diagnosed no cardiac activity. She had straight-lined. The defibrillator advised SHOCK. We stood away from the patient and I pushed the SHOCK button, as instructed. The jolt and the patient movement shouldn't have surprised me, but I reacted like the others and jumped back. The machine failed to restart her heart. I shocked her again, and again, and again. We were getting nowhere. Every year the ACLS guidelines seem to change. The rule is external cardiac massage right from the start. Artificial respiration has been abandoned. That had been the worst part of trying to help. Mouth-to-mouth contact with someone from God knows where, with God knows what disease, who had recently vomited, strains the will to serve. We had the oxygen and now a breathing bag, and I gave her a few breaths before handing it off to Marjorie as I straddled the patient, preparing for external massage. Almost two minutes. There was still time to save her.

When I settled on my knees and started to position my hands at the bottom of her sternum, I noticed strips of adhesive dressing under both breasts. I hadn't registered the flesh-colored tape before, but there were matching wounds or, more accurately, matching dressings under both breasts. I set the heels of my hands and started massage. Fifteen pumps and I signaled Marjorie to squeeze the oxygen bag; then I started the cycle again. I was sure the woman beneath me had had recent breast implants and I made every effort to avoid them, though in all likelihood it wasn't going to matter if my body weight crushed them or not.

Three more tries at jump-starting her heart failed, and after nearly thirty minutes of massage and artificial respiration she was more obviously dead than when we started. Time to accept the ugly reality. I nodded and mouthed a sad "no" to the young flight attendant who had replaced Marjorie, vigorously pumping the breathing bag, and she seemed to sag. Her heavy makeup was a mess and I noticed for the first time that she had been quietly weeping during our futile exercise. I felt like crying myself. Sitting up and stretching before attempting to straighten my knees, I stared at the firm, round breasts and the skin that seemed enflamed, particularly against the dead pallor around them. I got up slowly, thinking, but the information didn't compute. Nothing made sense. Still staring at her breasts, I pulled the T-shirt down to cover her and got to my feet. I had no idea what the people around me were saying, but they seemed to be offering condolences. I must have looked like I lost the big fight. I guess I had.

The captain, or first officer, I don't know which, then took control of the situation and the passengers were ordered back to their seats. I don't remember walking the aisle, but there I was, strapped in the seat with a large glass of scotch in my hand. My knees were shaking, and my shirt felt uncomfortably wet in the cool air. I turned off the overhead ventilation duct, pulled the blanket around my chest, and took a sip of whiskey. The whole thing was weird. But I had no idea how weird.

2

The flight from Heathrow was overbooked, as it usually is around the weekend, and the prospect of a body in the aisle didn't exactly thrill the passengers. The crew had covered and moved her to the tail between the lavatories, but the thin blankets could not hide the outline of a body, and the sight of feet frozen in a V position was disturbing. Passengers were divided between those whose eyes were locked forward to erase evidence of a life having been dramatically lost, and those who kept glancing back over their shoulders at the motionless mound under the blue blankets. For my part, I was too far forward to have to make that decision, and I tried to put the whole episode out of my mind by quickly sipping down what had to be four ounces of pretty good Scotch whiskey. The captain and the crew were my new best friends, and after listening to the guy in uniform across the aisle I knew more than I wanted to about airline procedures for on-board deaths. Probably the single fact of this conversation that will stay with me is that only Singapore Airlines has a corpse cabinet built into their planes; otherwise, it's the aisle, a seat, or the head.

Since the woman in question was already dead, there was no cause for diverting the flight, and we arrived at JFK on time. An EMS team met the plane and rushed down the aisle, further disrupting an already disorderly disembarkation. It seemed an unnecessary exercise, since I had officially declared the woman dead and released the crew from further action or diverting. But those are the rules.

I stayed back, identified myself, and answered the few questions they asked. There didn't seem to be much else to do, so I waited for my bags with everyone else on VS045. A good number of my fellow passengers made their way over to me with a comment or question, and I could feel the sense of community that the shared tragedy brought on. It does that to people, brings the humanity out. I was among the last stragglers around the carousel in terminal 4 by the time my black Tumi bag finally slipped down the chute. I upended it, grabbed the handle, and hefted it over the metal lip. The red, white, and blue ribbons on the grip made it distinctive enough, but I snuck a look at the name tag before making my way to the customs inspectors. I chose the line being inspected by a very attractive, slim black woman with a lively bit of attitude in her body language. I always choose the women, and they are invariably the most difficult. This time it was more than a pass-through, but not difficult.

"How long have you been out of the country?"

"Four days."

"Have you been anywhere other than England?"

"No."

"You only spent ninety dollars?"

"No. I made a ninety-dollar purchase. I spent a lot more than that."

That made her smile. "Right. I'll have to look through your bag."

I didn't really care, although all the dirty underwear and soiled shirts weren't going to make a good impression. "Have a go. The purchase is right on top in the DR Roberts bag. It's a shaving brush." I watched while she rummaged through my things with her gloved hands. She looked at my new shaving brush, tossed it back into the bag, signed my declaration, and said, "Welcome home." Apparently, the intelligence grapevine wasn't concerned with the story of the deceased.

New York was surprisingly cold for an early-fall evening. A wind-driven rain snapped at my hands and cheeks. I pulled up the collar of my quilted jacket against the rain and waited. The taxi queue wasn't long. I was directed to the far lane, where a trunk lid popped as if to signal me. The driver cheerfully helped me with my bag, and I slipped into the cramped backseat. The cab interior was poorly maintained, like the rest of the cabs, but the accommodating driver switched from lane to lane trying to make headway in barely moving traffic. The television news loop kept restarting itself after each attempt to silence it. I finally admitted defeat and lowered the volume. There was plenty of time to answer text messages and e-mails, and I cleared the deck. I made no calls. I was glad to be home and had no interest in telling the tale of my flight. Sometimes living alone is a good thing.

3

*Monday morning at the police academy is always a disori-*enting experience for me. The old building is a mixed-function nightmare, filled with sour-faced, coffee-carrying uniforms and civilians packing the halls and elevators. But mixed in among the crowd are the bright young faces of cadets in novice gray shirts and trousers, buzzing happily to one another and seemingly afraid to speak to anyone outside their ranks. The hopeful young recruits, the academy teaching personnel, and the ancillary function units made it feel lighter than the usual police grind, and almost separate from the human tragedy that drives the police world.

Most of the time, being a police surgeon redefines routine. Seeing sick call is not how I would choose to spend every morning, but increasingly I find it an interesting exercise in understanding the police mentality. Don't get me wrong about the department. I'm in it, but much as I consider myself part of it, I'm not. I'm still an outsider after eighteen years on the job. Not just me, probably all of us. When we do something brilliant, which happens once in a while, like save a life at a scene or get the best medical team to a bedside, the officer and the family appreciate us, and even the PBA acknowledges our worth. Personally, we feel like heroes. Most of the time, we're gold badges poking into the private lives of the blue line. Cops don't like that. The good ones, the ones who want to be left alone to do their job, and that's most cops, see us as a necessary evil. The others—well, the others are trying to beat the system, and when the job contract allows for unlimited sick leave, you can guess the rest.

At eight thirty, there was a pot of green tea steaming gracefully on a black lacquered tray, which sat on the only clear spot on my huge, messy, old city-issue desk. I knew it would be there and could see it through the open door as I approached.

"How was your trip?"

"It was good, Mrs. Black. An odd end to it, but good." I could have called my secretary Joyce, but we play a little game. My name is Black as well. No relation. She's Japanese-American, married to a black cop named, strangely enough, Black. I'm second-generation American Jew with deep German roots on both sides. Over there, our name was Schwartz. Somebody—the immigration officer at Ellis Island, or maybe my grandfather himself—thought the English translation, "black," sounded more New World or less Jewish. So Black I am. Wendell Black. Sounds American enough. How many Jews were named for the 1940 Republican presidential candidate?

There are a number of my ethnic brothers on the job, but not nearly enough to equal the demographics of the city. Except among the doctors, that is. A good number of police surgeons are Jewish, and every once in a while there's an anti-Semitic murmur when a cop or two is pissed at us. Despite directives and sensitivity training, it's not a particularly enlightened atmosphere. Mrs. Black and I do our best to ignore it.

"I'm glad you got away for a few days, doctor. You deserve it. I have tea for you."

I made my attempt at a bow. "How lovely. What a pleasant surprise."

Now, all of this may sound dumb to you, but we both are punctual creatures of habit, and the little dance gets the day off to a nice start. The tea is always on my desk at eight thirty.

"You have a message from the medical examiner, and the clinic is already half-full," she said, following me into my office. Mrs. Black grew up in Flushing, Queens, and by the time she finished Queens College, she was a sociologist and about as Japanese as a candy apple. She was forty-five, five-six, tall for a Japanese woman, and both slim and curvy, with great legs when she showed them. Very elegant. I really liked her. I liked to work with her, I liked to look at her, and under different circumstances, I might have gone the next step. But neither of us wanted that. We had come close to it once and realized it would have broken up a good thing. So we left it alone. A few months later she went back to Billy, and things are more comfortable now.

"What did the ME want?"

"He wants you to call him."

"Which one?" I asked.

"The chief. Benson."

"I suppose it's about the woman that died on the plane."

"What woman?" she asked, drawing her head up and lifting her eyebrows in question, causing horizontal folds in her beautiful, smooth expanse of forehead.

"Ah, word hasn't circulated about my airborne heroics." And I proceeded to tell the story. Rather than acting surprised, she listened closely, all the while standing in front of my desk.

"And I can't figure out what killed her. I'm sure the ME is making the courtesy call, knowing I'd be interested."

I circled behind my desk, took a quick look at the stars and stripes by the window, as I always do, and plopped into the beaten-up, old-fashioned leather chair. I watched Mrs. Black pour out green tea for me and thanked her again as she looked down and stepped backward in traditional Japanese fashion. Then she turned, shook her ass in her tight jeans and heels, and said, "I'll get the ME."

4

"*Dr. Benson, sir, I'm honored that the chief medical examiner of the City of New York has seen fit to call me. Deeply honored.*" I had known Benson from medical school. He was a year behind me. Always devoted to his goal, very ambitious and very smart. Not surprisingly, his rise was direct and meteoric. He had his curmudgeon professor act down pat, but in his own way he was a good guy.

"Fuck you, wise ass." There was a slight echo from the Bluetooth speakerphone Benson used during autopsies.

"Ah."

"Interesting flight you had, Wendell. Is there anything you can add to the report to help point us in the right direction?"

I had the feeling I was getting set up, but I answered seriously. "Well, I'm not sure what's in the report. It was the usual failed resuscitation. She was agitated, and then she tanked. There was a rapid, thready pulse before her pressure dropped through the floor and she flatlined. Two unusual things, though, pinpoint pupils and bilateral inframammary dressings, like from breast implants. Could be an OD, but otherwise I'm in the dark. Did I miss something?"

"You got most of the fine points, but perhaps you didn't notice that she is a he."

As my face reddened, I could imagine the assistant MEs around the chief getting ready for the big laugh. "Shit. Don't tell me that. Why do you say that?"

"Why? Simple, big boy, he's got that thing dangling between his legs."

What can you say when you feel like a fool. There was no reason to pull her . . . his pants down during CPR, but still I felt well beyond foolish. I said nothing. Defending myself would feed the laughter I could already hear over the speaker. I suffered through ten or fifteen seconds of snickers until Benson spoke again.

"You were half-right, at least."

"What does that mean?"

"Your patient was a genetic and partially anatomic male with a normal penis and almost no body hair. His testicles have been surgically removed. You were right about the breast implants, three hundred cc silicone bags, but then it gets strange. The implants were in old surgical pockets. The only thing fresh about the site was the healing skin incision. The pockets were lined with a mature capsule, the kind you see with the presence of long-standing implants."

"Interesting." We were stepping away from making me feel foolish and I wanted to maintain that trajectory. "But why did she die?"

"He. Why did he die. Looks like an OD. You got that one right. The implants were filled with crystalline heroin. The left one broke and I assume the pocket absorbed it like a dry sponge in a hot tub. We don't have blood levels yet, but they're going to be high, very high. Interesting. Want to come down here and have a look? This is an odd one, and it's your case."

"My case? It's not my case," I answered.

"Scientific interest, doctor."

I was afraid Benson would pull that. I really get creeped out by the morgue. I did my time in pathology, even assisted at autopsies. You learn a lot about disease that way, but everything from the first smell to the casual disregard of the attendants is unpleasant. It's worse than unpleasant, but you never say no. That's the whole macho bullshit. You don't like it, and unless you're a trained forensic pathologist, you add nothing to the experience, but you go. It's an old routine pulled on new Homicide detectives all the time. What the hell is a thirty-year-old cop with two years of college going to get from watching a postmortem examination besides acute nausea and losing his lunch? Or even better, her lunch. But that was part of the initiation, another stupid rite of passage.

So I went. My office at the police academy is on Twentieth Street, about ten short blocks from the medical examiner's office. The weather had improved greatly. It was cool and very sunny, so I opted to walk. That section of First Avenue is a really boring stretch of Manhattan for the sightseer, the east side of the street primarily occupied by Bellevue Hospital and the west dotted with medical-center buildings, the old dental school building, convenience stores, a few apartment buildings, and generally not much to look at. It took me twenty minutes to reach the tile anteroom of the Office of the Chief Medical Examiner of the City of New York, at 520 First Avenue. The city morgue. It's not quite as gruesome as television shows might make you believe, but it's sad and foul. Most of the civilians milling about were in small, sorrowful groups, and were managed nicely by understanding intermediaries. Downstairs, in the business end of the building, it was cold and quiet. The place smelled of death and chemicals and futile attempts to freshen the air. Metal doors separated the working areas from the halls, and I followed the directions I had been given to the autopsy room where Benson held court.

The deceased was definitely a man, and it wouldn't have shocked me if Benson and company had tied a ribbon around his organ, but they'd resisted. I had anticipated him working me over, but he never mentioned it again. The anticipation was bad enough. Giving the office of the ME its due, the proceedings were fully professional and, as Benson had predicted, very interesting.

There were three other men in the room. The oldest man was substantial, but not obese. He had huge hands and a bit of a belly that made a soft curve out of his green rubber apron. He stood close by Benson and seemed to pay no attention to what was being said. Benson referred to him by name, Raymond, when addressing him, which he often did, alternating between Raymond and myself as he spoke. Raymond said nothing. The other two gloved and rubber-aproned men were appreciably younger and seemed not to exist to Benson. I assumed they were residents, but I didn't ask. Benson did all the work, dissecting and dictating as he went along. Raymond tidied up after him, moving organs, weighing them, and swabbing and hosing as necessary.

Close examination of Azul Capinpin's face—that was the name on his passport—showed no evidence of a beard. His cheeks were smooth and free of the telltale enlarged pores where hairs had been removed. These days laser hair removal does the job without the ugly side effects of elec-trolysis. This was smooth, female-looking skin. There were traces of hair follicles on the upper lip that had previously been hidden by makeup. The body was clean. No hair. The pubis had been shaved, or waxed, or lasered clean. The rest of the body was hairless as well. Generally, Asian males don't have pelts like their Western counterparts. But Capinpin's body was totally hairless.

Benson talked me through his findings, and doctor or not, I would have missed the boat. The distribution of body fat was feminine, with a fairly soft belly and hips. Even without the implants, which had been removed to a stainless-steel pan hanging from a scale over the table, there were hints of breasts.

"Most of what you see now is hormone supplements at work. It's a good bet that our man was taking an androgen blocker, probably Aldactone. It's cheap and it's been around for decades as a diuretic. That's the drug of choice for male-to-female transsexuals outside Western Europe and the States. Some use finasteride with it. The trade name is Propecia, more commonly used to treat male-pattern baldness. It does something to block testosterone, but it's expensive. Then a year of estrogen supplements to grow small breasts and redistribute body fat. Facial hair and body hair is reduced; shape changes, even the timbre of the voice raises a bit. But the pelvis never changes to the wider female configuration."

He pointed to the pelvic area, but measurements and observation of the skeleton would be necessary to make his point. At least, I couldn't see it.

"And the hands are a giveaway . . . so is the penis." There was delayed, restrained laughter following Benson's levity. He caught us off guard. We all had been listening intently to his lecture and hadn't expected it. I took it like a man and chuckled.

"Whether or not our victim discontinued the use of testosterone blockers after castration is hard to tell without the chemical assays, but it doesn't matter. Scars from the surgical castration are mature, and it looks like scrotal skin may have been preserved in place for future vaginal construction." Here he paused and held the empty, shriveled skin of the scrotal sac in his gloved hand for our inspection. I got the picture without needing closer scrutiny of the evidence.

"And last, the implant pockets." Here Benson insisted we move in closely to see the smooth, lined pocket between the underside of the breast and the muscles of the chest wall. Benson had separated the skin and breast along the sternum and folded it back for observation. "This smooth capsule is something the modern pathologist has seen a thousand times; our colleagues of a few generations ago would have no idea what to make of it. Under the microscope the white lining you see is made up of a thin fibrous tissue layer spotted with foreign-body giant cells and silicone residue. It effectively separates the implants from the body. That's its job. It develops quickly and matures over time. Take the implants out and after a time it disappears, or at least dissipates, but as long as implants are in-situ, it remains."

"What are you telling me? The implants were there until you removed them, weren't they?" I asked, pointing to the tissue scale alongside the autopsy table.

"Maybe."

"Maybe? Maybe what?"

"Maybe they were there all the while, and maybe they had been replaced. The old capsule and the new scar don't go together."

I know the light bulb should have lit up like Times Square, but it didn't. Benson kept looking at me like I was thick. And then, finally, the power came on. "You think these implants . . . these bags of heroin . . . were put into an old surgical pocket where other implants used to be. I get it. So that makes our person a professional mule. Is that what you're saying?"

"Not quite. That's more of a leap than I'd like to make, but it's a thought. I can say that the vulcanized silicone sacs of heroin were in old pockets that had held implants in the past. The foreign-body giant cells and the silicone residue make that clear. Whether those prior implants were filled with heroin, I can't say."

"Well, one trip or a routine, this is no longer our turf," I said. "Will your guys call Customs and DEA, or do you pass it on to Narcotics and let them worry? Either way, this is definitely outside my job description."

5

By the time I hit the street at four twenty, the afternoon had turned colder. I saw no point in going back to the office for an hour, and there was nothing much to do anyway. The way it works is I do sick call in the morning, hospital visits to inpatients from our command, suffer through piles of bureaucracy in the form of meetings and paperwork, and listen to the ranting union reps when a bad apple has been caught out malingering. The reps are good guys just doing their jobs. The fervor and emotion of their pitch often brings a bit of hydrophobic spittle at the corner of the mouth before they look you in the eye and crack the tiniest smile. We're all on the same page about this stuff and they have to do what they have to do. I just don't have to buy it. Deep down, the reps know better than their clients that I'd go to the wall for the good guys—and that's most of them.

So, barring emergencies, my day was over. I felt lighter being out of the ME building and checked my phone for messages while I walked over to Second Avenue. At the corner, the smell of old beer and frying grease preceded the door to the Waterfront Ale House and beckoned to me. The sun was already low in the west and flooded the entry and the first few feet of the room with a dazzling light that revealed every seedy detail. Beyond that, the room was dark and welcoming. The lunch crowd was long gone and it was too early for after-work socializing. A few sad-looking guys sat at the bar. I found a spot halfway down, where it was dark and empty and wouldn't encourage conversation. The girl behind the bar greeted me pleasantly and pulled a Sam Adams and a smile after I pointed to the tap. I lifted the glass to her and sipped off the foam, set the glass down on the bar, and stepped over to the carnival machine behind me to scoop a bowl of hot air-popped corn. It managed to have no taste other than salt, and if you're drinking beer after a confusing hour at the autopsy table, that's good enough.

What did it mean? The girl was a guy, and the breast implants were a vehicle for transporting heroin. She——it was hard for me to think he——had implants in the pockets before, maybe drug-filled implants, and this time the string ran out, killing the mule. But this was only a disturbance on the surface. The big stuff was deep underwater, and I didn't have a clue if it was a whale or a flounder. I didn't even know where to look. That wasn't my job. But I was curious enough to ask some questions. I knew I wouldn't get more than a greeting out of the DEA or Customs guys—unless they needed something from me, which was not likely. Even if I could help, they wouldn't admit it outright. That's how close they are to the NYPD, and I'm not even a real cop.

I drained my beer and used a fingertip, wet from the condensation on the mug, to mop up the salty dregs of the popcorn. I was tempted to wash it down with another beer, but even one on a work afternoon was breaking with precedent. You work with enough middle-aged alcoholics and it becomes easy to see how it creeps up on you. A beer or two at lunch, a few drinks after a trying day—share the pain with people who understand—and who knows how many with dinner or after. You think you get used to the headache, the edge, the irritability, and it eases a bit with a cold one or a shot in hot black coffee. I'm probably overreacting, but these guys aren't all genetic alcoholics sliding down the slippery family path. You can do it to yourself. It was too easy to fall into the trap and it was too hard to get out, and I wasn't going there. I was already an NYPD statistic with a failed marriage, and that was enough belonging for me. I paid for the beer and left a generous tip for the smile. I got my jacket off the hook, pulled the collar up around my neck, and snuggled in for the walk back to my car at the academy.

By the time I drove across town, parked, and picked up my mail, it was nearly six. It only took a quick glance to reveal that most of the mail was junk and not worth the trouble. Before I reached for my apartment keys, I could hear my pal stomping and snorting, banging his tail on the door and whining at the threshold. Naturally, I ratcheted up his excitement with some throaty encouragement. "Yes, Tonto . . . yes, baby . . . yeah." By now I knew the

big Lab was spinning in circles. It was always a nice welcome. "Don't jump" doesn't work with Tonto, and I let
him bounce a few times before scratching his neck. I bent
down and took the obligatory slurps, tossed the mail on
the entry table, and said, "Get the leash, Tonto," but he
was in mid-fetch mode before I started talking. Routine.

Having a dog in New York is a pain, and it's expensive.
There's no guilt about leaving him at home because he's
never at home. Tonto has more playdates than a five-year-
old. The dog-walker and the doggie gym wear him out, and
I'm sure he's putting on this show so I'll know I'm loved.
So, out we go for a quick turn and some sniffing. He did his
business quickly. I cleaned up after him, that's the law, and
we headed home. The late-night walk is a game changer,
and much more of a chore.

We settled in. I switched on the news and stretched out
on the sofa. Tonto took the club chair. It was Monday, and
I could feel smart winging through the *Times* crossword
puzzle. Later in the week it got progressively more difficult
and took too much time. I had planned my evening no further. Back home after five days away, and the only person I
was anxious to see was otherwise engaged. Sad. I had no
work to catch up with and I'd been reading constantly, so
there was no book I was dying to dig into. Order in, and
waste the night in front of the tube.

Dinner arrived about half an hour after I had called it
in, and by eight forty-five I was looking at pork soup dumplings, fried rice laced with unidentifiable morsels, and
braised tofu over spinach. A feast I would barely make a

dent in, and all for twenty-four dollars. One of the rough parts of living alone is trying to maintain a reasonable level of civility. Tonight that meant eating from real dishes instead of the paper cartons and Styrofoam plates that came with the food. I set up a tray with a pair of pretty, ebonized chopsticks left over from my marriage, a large bowl for the rice, on top of which I doled out dumplings and tofu. The spinach didn't do much for me. I folded a cloth napkin onto the tray instead of the more sensible paper toweling I usually favored, poured a glass of water and another of Sancerre, and carried the feast to the coffee table in front of the television. An hour, a sip of Sancerre, and I was fast asleep fully dressed.

6

I slept the sleep of the innocent but still woke up feeling like hell. I'm a fairly solid six feet, with regular features, a nicely shaped broken nose that turns a bit to the right, and more smile lines than the average fifty-year-old. Most women think I'm attractive . . . maybe handsome, but staring at my face in that mirror was enough to make anyone lose their appetite. My eyes were puffy and my cheeks had sleep folds like knife wounds. My short-cut salt-and-pepper hair stood like a punk rocker's in an acid dream, and my mouth tasted like the inside of a trash can. I'm probably too old for salted popcorn and Chinese food in the same day.

In an hour I was alive again. I took Tonto for a trot, did forty minutes in the barely functional gym that occupied part of the building's lower level, had coffee, showered, and dressed. Then down to my car in the garage that took up most of the building's basement. I liked the privacy of driving to work. Manhattan traffic was no picnic. Subways were definitely faster than the streets, but I liked my co-coon. I listened to the news and some music and spaced out. Parking was not an issue. The official NYPD vehicle placard was a major perk of the job. I hadn't spent a second thinking about Azul Capinpin since returning home last night, and he was the furthest thing from my thoughts when I arrived at the office.

That changed quickly. As usual, Mrs. Black timed her tea service perfectly. "Two detectives from Narcotics are in the waiting room," she said, as I entered the office. "When can you see them?"

"At nine when clinic starts," I answered ever so slightly curtly.

Mrs. Black shot me a glare and headed for her desk before I could apologize.

She turned back to me. "They are not patients, doctor. They want to interview you." I knew better than to ask why.

"Okay, show them in, but let me have a sip of tea first."

Mrs. Black poured out a cup of properly brewed, not quite steaming, sencha, a simple green tea that we both liked. I thanked her, sipped my tea, and admired her as unobtrusively as possible as she left the room.

The two detectives from Narcotics Division looked about as official as a pair of muggers. Blue jeans, ugly high-top sneakers, hooded sweatshirts, and scruffy hair. One wore a goatee; and the other, two or three days of sparsely distributed bristle. Both had IDs and gold badges on chains around their necks and, I assumed, holstered pistols in the waistbands of their jeans. That was the Narcotics drill.

They introduced themselves. John Griffin was the big guy with the goatee. He was about forty, and a sergeant.

His partner, Michael Rodriguez, was a good five inches shorter than Griffin, wiry and twitchy, with olive skin. Rodriguez was a sergeant as well. They were both friendly. Everyone was friendly to the surgeons; you never knew when the goodwill might come in handy. Griffin did most of the talking, and it wasn't long before he said, "Either these yo-yos got their plan straight from the movies, or they were doing it first."

"Is this something you guys look for?" I asked. I wasn't questioning their systems, just curious.

"No, not really, but a few cases have been reported over the years. We consider them in the same category as mules that swallow condoms filled with cocaine, or shove them in their anus or vagina, which is much more common and doesn't need surgical assistance for recovery." Griffin seemed awkward using anatomic terminology. They weren't even testifying. Street talk would come a lot more naturally, but I wasn't one of them. I nodded and encouraged him to go on. "Mostly, the dogs don't find these people, so we work backward from tips, CIs, or undercover info."

Most of Narcotics worked that way. There was very little sleuthing. These guys had their eyes and ears open and were on the firing line all the time. You had to respect them, except when you didn't. The temptation was always there. And the job couldn't help but screw up your perspective on behavior and reward. It was a hard day's work . . . and for most of them, definitely not a life's work. Mostly, only the feds made a career of it, and they weren't on the streets.

The conversation continued in that inside-baseball way for a while. They asked a few questions about the situation on the plane, any traveling companion with the victim, anything else I might have noticed, that kind of stuff. Then Rodriguez asked, "Any idea who the receiving surgeon might be, doc?"

I hate when people call me doc. It happens too often to take a stand, but in my edgy way I think of it as a kind of sloppy disrespect. Most people use the term as a measure of friendly respect, maybe even endearment. I'm sure it's meant that way, but I wouldn't call them cop. Yes cop, no cop, sorry cop. If I took the trouble to call him Sergeant Rodriguez, he could call me Dr. Black. I let it pass and thought about the meaning of what he said. That pissed me off more. Why would they think I had any idea who could be involved? I was a Good Samaritan in all this. Nothing more. A few seconds passed silently. I hadn't actually been considering the question, and I snapped back into the present.

"No, no idea at all. Why would you expect that I would?"

"Just routine. You were there and you're a doctor and all."

"Sorry, guys, no dice. I have to work now . . . so if you will excuse me." I walked toward the door and opened it, not bothering to shake hands with the two detectives as they left.

The rest of the day passed normally. That is to say, dull. I saw twenty-two officers at sick call in less than three hours.

Not exactly high-end medicine, but neither were the complaints. There was the usual autumn flu going around New York, and some of the guys looked like hell. Pale, lethargic, dehydrated, dull eyes, and others were florid-faced from fever, with upper respiratory symptoms. As far as diagnosis was concerned, it was all part of the same disease. Early phase, late phase, different manifestations of the same virus, or maybe different viruses. They would all pass. These were young, healthy guys. Bed rest and fluids for everyone, aspirin or Tylenol for fever, and call me if it got worse. Sometimes antibiotics were appropriate when bacterial pneumonia seemed near, but for the most part there was nothing to do but let the virus run its course.

Then there were guys injured on the job. Before your imagination runs away with you, most were injured from tripping, falling, twisting an ankle, and an occasional bruise from physical interaction in the line of duty. Never a gunshot wound. Those were emergencies treated at hospitals. We always came by to oversee care and follow the officer's progress. Maybe oversee is an exaggeration. Observe was more like it. That was my afternoon. Two bedside visits. Perusing the charts, chatting a bit, and asking the officers if they needed anything. I felt more like a priest than a doctor, but I got home early.

There was an eight-hour shift coming up in the emergency room where I did my moonlighting. It was sanctioned, and I had been at it for years. I have been a certified emergency physician since my residency, and I like to ply my trade. Sometimes I wish I had continued on my original course as a surgical resident, but it was a bad time for me and I took the easy way out. The era of long days and longer nights didn't do much to stabilize an insecure young wife. I opted for regular hours and a regular life, but a decade later, the marriage died on its own, as it should have. It just took a while for us to realize that.

A couple of times a week I work the overnight shift in the emergency room in an affluent community just over the border in Westchester County. Not too much happens there, and you practically need a platinum American Express card to be admitted to the ER. It wasn't very taxing and they paid well. With two salaries and a healthy family endowment, I really had no money worries. I'd never be rich, but I never bargained for that anyway. That level of comfort probably stifled my career ambitions, but I liked what I did, and I liked my life. I also really liked the people I worked with, particularly Dr. Sheppard.

Alice Sheppard had been working occasional shifts at the hospital for nearly a year. For a lot of reasons, I made it my business to try to work the same schedule as Alice whenever I could swing it. Tonight we were both on, and I hadn't seen her for a week. We had been going out for a few months now. It'd been fun, and I thought she liked me almost as much as I liked her, which was an issue for both of us. Still, it always gave me a thrill to see her, and working together was a bonus. Alice and I had planned to spend the long weekend together in London. We each had two jobs to juggle, and when her schedule changed at the last minute, I couldn't accommodate. But now I was back.

Alice was a pretty good example of what patients wanted their plastic surgeon to look like. She was five-eight, weighed in at a hot one-twenty-five, tops, and was almost head-spinning gorgeous, in a nonchalant, casual way. Alice didn't need short skirts, paint and powder and ploys to command men's attention. You could feel it . . . smell it. She was finishing up yet another fellowship before hanging out her shingle. Alice was going to knock 'em dead—which may not be exactly the best choice of words to apply to a medical practice. She had a fabulous English accent, and on top of it all, she was a very good surgeon.

It was serendipity that we ended up working in the same place and kind of falling in together. She had only just gotten over being dumped by her husband, a London investment banker who, she said, considered himself single. Hubby took up with an airhead model that earned even more than he did, which was a lot. Alice took it hard. She was way down and had reached the stage where she was blaming herself. She needed to vent, which was my good fortune. I'm a good listener and a pretty sensible friend. Alice did it for me from the first second, but it took a bunch of friendly dinners, a zillion e-mails, and a few hesitant gropes before two consenting adults fell together. I was the happiest guy in the world; she cried and I loved her for it. Not immediately—in the moment it was confusing—but when I thought it through. This was a serious person. The real deal, and I had a shot. I wasn't going to blow it. It was the first time in years that I had calculated my behavior with a woman. I was almost fifty-one and found myself desperate to get serious. What goes around comes around.

"Hello, lovely," she said. That should have been my line. We kissed chastely, like friends. I hoped we were more than that, but I was never certain. She wasn't at all cold, just the opposite, and she was treating me the way she treated all her friends. I was jealous. I know that's crazy, but it's the truth.

7

The bullpen, where doctors sit to write up charts or drink coffee before the onslaught of patients, is a feature common to most emergency departments. It is usually a glassed-in cubicle that makes it possible for the staff inside to have eye contact with the ever-changing emergency scene. It also puts you on display. I brought in two containers of black coffee from the machine in the back of the ER. It was brewed freshly to each complicated, computerized order, and once you understood the directions, it was pretty good stuff. Despite that, I made the simplest choice and brought back two black coffees.

"Thank you," said Alice, smiling up at me through delicious, angelic lips, flashing natural, white teeth as uniform as the spines of the Harvard Classics. She had a stack of charts in front of her and tossed another onto the pile, picking up the paper cup. The after-dinner rush had diminished to a trickle. As usual, it consisted of people with lingering complaints not important enough to disturb their daily routines with a scheduled doctor visit. Most of the real emergencies happened later. Even automobile accidents had a predictable time frame. When heavy traffic made it impossible to do much more than crawl the streets and highways, the ER was quiet, as it was now. It would last another hour at most. I rolled one of the hideous blue-green plastic chairs beside Alice and sipped my coffee.

"Ever hear of people smuggling drugs into the country in breast implants?"

Her head snapped around. "Excuse me. I think I missed what you said."

I repeated myself.

"Hear of it, yes," she answered.

"Well, that puts you and everybody else a step ahead of me. I never heard of it until yesterday." I retold an encapsulated version of my story, carefully setting up the punch line.

"A man! Wow. You couldn't tell? There are lots of clues, you know."

"Don't say it. It all happened so fast; there was no time to evaluate physical characteristics. It was try to save her . . . his . . . life and go back to my seat." I had ceased being embarrassed, or at least I had an excuse I believed in. I continued talking. "Would you have to be a plastic surgeon to do the operation?"

"Which operation?"

"Removing the implants."

"No, not at all. Anyone familiar with simple surgical technique could remove the implants and get away with it. Inserting new implants would require a greater level of skill."

"Why?"

"Well, the first time around, a pocket for the implant has to be developed either between the breast and pectoralis muscle or under the muscle itself. In a man it would be a tougher, bloodier dissection than in a woman. It would be easiest in a woman who had nursed children . . . the fibrous tissue is looser. Either way, one needs to know the anatomy. You know, control bleeding and use good sterile technique or it's asking for disaster. Inserting a foreign body, even an inert material like silicone, is a setup for infection. It's something we take really seriously."

"Got it. So, whoever put the heroin into the implants had to do it under sterile conditions. That should limit the field."

If the mule was part of a drug-smuggling ring, which had to be the case, considering the value of the heroin and the sophistication of the device, there was a surgeon at both ends, maybe even a plastic surgeon. I thought about that for a while. There were hundreds of plastic surgeons in New York, and a thousand general surgeons capable of removing the implants and closing the incision. And how many general doctors or operating-room nurses could possibly do it? But I had to keep reminding myself that it wasn't my problem.

The phone rang in the bullpen. Across from me a sleepy young guy with a silly-looking haircut answered it. "Save it, Dr. Sheppard is right here." He pressed hold and nodded toward Alice without saying a word. She picked up the receiver and he looked to me and stage-whispered, "Fucking car wreck on the interstate."

And so it goes. The next four hours were hell. Well, not so much for me as for the surgical people. Technically, Alice and I were equals. Outsiders, working as ER receiving doctors. Mercenaries. We saw everything that crossed the threshold, treated what we were capable of treating, and palmed the rest off on the specialists. In a teaching hospital like this, that meant action for the residents. Great for me, but Alice was their fairy godmother. She was the idol of the surgery residents, a grown-up vision of themselves. She had been there, she knew, she helped, and she was the de-facto team leader.

By the time the last of the drop-ins were treated and gone—runny noses, infected pimples, and other great challenges—it was nearly one a.m. I dragged myself to the on-call room and flopped facedown onto the itchy wool blanket stretched military-style on the rock-hard single bed. I might have slept for ten or fifteen minutes before I dragged myself up and undressed. I used the head, found my toothbrush and a tiny airline-size tube of Colgate in the Dopp kit at the bottom of my father's leather carry-on, brushed, showered, and might already have been snoring when I crawled under the covers. I left the door unlocked so Alice could slip in beside me when she finished. Or at least I meant to.

On-call rooms are the heart of hospital social life. Before residents successfully agitated for a forty-, or fifty-, or sixty-hour week, it was routine to spend every other night, or every third night, on call at the hospital. You didn't work all night, but you had to be there. You can imagine the rest. Even now, working per diem in the ER, we had on-call rooms provided for catnaps. They weren't luxurious, but we made do. I was hoping for a pleasant few hours. Dream on.

Turns out that even though I remembered not to throw the dead bolt, the door locked automatically, and I had the key. Worse still, I didn't hear Alice rapping on the door at three. We didn't discuss it in the morning because we didn't see each other, but her e-mail was not warm. The path to the doghouse is paved with good intentions.

8

The New York Times *ran a small piece about the smuggling* episode in the morning crime blotter.

> . . . A spokesman for the medical examiner's office said the deceased, identified as Azul Capinpin, succumbed to an overdose of heroin when a drug-filled breast implant ruptured during a flight from London's Heathrow Airport to John F. Kennedy International Airport in New York.

They neglected to mention that the victim was male. They also didn't mention me. I was happy for the second and didn't understand the first. Mostly, I couldn't understand how, or why, the breast implant information was released.

By the time Alice returned my call, it was early afternoon. We had taken to mostly e-mailing or texting during the day, but I felt like talking. Knowing she would not pick up messages until the morning's surgery was completed, I left a long and fairly awkward voice message. Any distance I might have imagined evaporated when I heard her voice. She was all ease and congeniality and was eager to talk about dinner plans for that evening. I had forgotten that she was joining a visiting colleague for drinks and I was window-dressing.

Farzan Byarshan had trained with Alice in England and had now, by all accounts, become a runaway success as a plastic surgeon in London, while Alice opted for fellowships and travel before signing her life away to three decades of practice. By Alice's telling, Farzan had married up within the Persian community. His wife, Alaleh, was distantly related to the late shah, Mohammad Reza Pahlavi. It seemed that every ex-pat Iranian claimed some tie to the shah, so I didn't take that very seriously. Besides, the shah was an inept fraud whose only saving grace was his willingness to be influenced by the CIA. Alaleh's father was well connected and rich as Croesus. Anyway, the Persians overthrew Croesus, and the Islamic Revolution ran Alaleh's father out of Tehran.

I had no interest in this reunion, but Alice and Farzan had been an item. She downplayed the romance in the telling, though I remained dubious, since she still needed a man by her side when she planned to see him. I was the beard, and I was a little curious about Alice's taste in men.

The King Cole bar is the centerpiece of the posh St. Regis Hotel on Fifth Avenue. Farzan and Alaleh were staying there in what must have been an insanely expensive suite.

I had once naively recommended the place to a friend who bit my head off when he got his bill. We arrived a little after six and settled in among the tourists. The lounge itself was a funny place. There was a long, comfortable bar beneath Maxfield Parrish's King Cole mural, and lots of little tables were scattered around the room, always "reserved" until one parted with a twenty—in which case they were "reserved for you, sir." I hate that, but it fuels New York. I played the game. Alice and I sat alone for a quarter of an hour, and she chattered away about Farzan and the old days, which couldn't have been more than six or seven years ago. I listened. I liked to watch her while she spoke. I watch people's lips—not just beautiful people like Alice, everybody. It's a bad habit and I have to remind myself to make eye contact, but you get pretty good at eavesdropping, and if family history plays any role, I'll be deaf as a stone by seventy and have a leg up on the other old guys.

The room was cold, probably in anticipation of a hundred or so warm bodies arriving within the next hour. It was not yet dark outside, and the low lights had to struggle with banners of sunlight through the curtains on the Fifty-fifth Street windows in order to set a sophisticated scene. Patrons were well dressed. Men wore suits and neckties, some straight from business, some dressed for an evening out. The ladies looked elegant in dresses or fashionable trouser suits, and appropriately upscale for a place where a martini and a glass of champagne ate up a fifty. Alice had her blond hair swept back, diamond stud earrings and very little makeup. She wore a basic black dress with a scooped neck that was filled with her breasts beneath an inverted V inscribed by a black cardigan buttoned only at the neck and flowing out. I wondered on whose behalf she had planned the landscape.

Farzan and his wife arrived from the lobby, and we didn't see them approach until they stood over us.

"Alice, darling."

I was immediately uncomfortable. Alice and I stood up reflexively, and she and Farzan embraced. Mrs. Byarshan and I stood by, watching. She couldn't have been any happier than I.

"I'm Wendell Black, nice to meet you," I said to the other outsider. She was an attractive woman with refined features and thick black hair, and was seriously made up and decked out. I had never seen so many jewels on so young a woman. She couldn't have been more than thirty, and she dressed like an upper-class matron. She and Alice embraced warmly, though I don't believe they had met before. Farzan offered me his hand and a lackluster grip, but he looked directly into my eyes, held my right arm with his left hand, and said enthusiastically, "So good to meet you."

Maybe so, but he could not have known enough about me to make that judgment. We sat, and after a few minutes of reminiscences we were all four included in the conversation, which was pleasant enough. Farzan was a good-looking man and spoke with a British accent that was too polished to be native. He was slim and graceful, with longish, thick black hair, heavy eyebrows, and clean-shaven cheeks. Steel-rimmed eyeglasses made his appearance more severe than his attitude. He laughed freely and was nothing of the formal Middle Easterner I had expected. He put me at ease. It is my nature to be standoffish with strangers. My own insecurity, I've been told, too many times.

The first round of drinks was consumed quickly and helped break the ice. Farzan and the two women quickly killed a bottle of criminally expensive champagne. I had two nice single malts. Whatever had gone on between Alice and Farzan was not obvious to me. The cocktail hour was painless, and we were off to dinner. Apparently I had passed the test, or maybe it was all about Alice, but something had made her more relaxed, warm, and affectionate. We walked arm in arm for three blocks to a fancy Italian restaurant set in the atrium of a nondescript Park Avenue office building. My plan was to feed our hunger and get her out of that little black dress as quickly as possible. I leaned toward Alice and began to nuzzle her hair and touch her ear with my tongue. When my hand slipped under her dress, she smiled and pushed it away.

"Later."

But not too much later. It was a needy and passionate night. Less lovemaking than clawing urgency. Which neither of us seemed to mind at all.

9

As I mentioned before, the simple act of owning a dog in New York runs your life. I wanted nothing more than to spend the night in Alice's bed. Sometime during the night, in what was clearly going to evolve into round two, I remembered Tonto sitting at home with his legs crossed.

"Honey, I have to go," I said. We were already pawing each other and she had quickly brought me back to life.

"Don't go yet—I need more."

Being weak of will, I stayed, and Alice expressed her approval loudly enough to awaken the neighbors. A thirty-second shower barely brought me back to earth; a quick kiss, and I was on my way.

It took twenty minutes to get back uptown, and by the time I reached my door, it was after two. Tonto, bless his heart, was not the least bit disapproving. No guilt trips, just the usual "nice to see you" slurps, and out we went. I was undressed again and in bed by half past two, and I managed to log nearly five hours' sleep, which would have to do.

Morning broke with a headache and I performed my routine in a fog. I skipped the gym. Mrs. Black recognized my condition with no more than a raised eyebrow and silence. Before I could sip the tea, my cell phone sounded *Eine Kleine Nachtmusik* and I fished through pockets looking for it.

"Wendell, good morning." It was Alice, in her professional voice. I knew she was surrounded by people and couldn't speak freely, and the English accent made her sound very serious. I contemplated teasing her about being a sexual predator but couldn't get myself in gear. Good thing, because it became clear she was in no mood for my sense of humor. "I need to talk to you."

"Go ahead." Just the tone of her voice made my headache worse.

"No, not now. I have to get someplace private. Can I call back in five minutes?"

"Yeah, sure. I'll be here. Want to call on the landline?" Cell reception in the office was lousy.

"No. The cell. Wait for me." I wondered why she hadn't gone someplace private before making the call to begin with, but it wasn't the time to bring it up.

"Got it."

I closed my door, picked up my teacup, and paced. Alice called back fifteen minutes later. "Sorry, I had to wait for transport to get the patient to recovery. Wendell . . ." I kept silent. "Farzan called me. He has to speak to you."

"Me? Why me?"

"I'm not exactly sure, but he knows you are with the police and that has something to do with it."

"Start from the beginning. Farzan only found out about my job last night, and it seemed to roll right past him. Why the sudden change?" I waited several seconds for an answer.

"Actually, I told him about you before, but you're right, he didn't seem particularly interested. Can you speak to him . . . please, for me?"

I hesitated. "Sure, but I'm just a doctor like you guys. I have no influence on police procedure." I didn't like where the conversation was going. It was an unnatural progression of events, and my bullshit meter was topping out. I had the sense that everyone knew what was going on but me, but I agreed to take Farzan's call. Actually, I would have taken it without Alice's intervention. There was no reason not to.

The day passed slowly. It usually does when I don't get enough sleep. My headache disappeared before lunch and I was feeling almost human. Farzan called at one forty-five, which is when I am scheduled to return to the office from lunch to clear my desk for traveling duties. Very convenient.

"Dr. Black, this is Farzan Byarshan speaking." Of course it is.

"Wendell . . . please call me Wendell. I've been expecting your call. What can I do for you?" I was just the least bit annoyed. Farzan had called me Wendell throughout cocktails and definitely in his enthusiastic farewell. Why the sudden formality?

"Wendell, I would like to meet with you." Two calls and I still didn't know what the hell was going on. I was almost willing to write it off to cultural differences, but I couldn't let it go.

"Why don't you tell me what this is about, then we can meet if we need to."

Farzan hesitated. "It's about the man who died on the plane, and I would prefer . . ."

"The person on the plane . . . what could that have to do with you?" One of the things cops and doctors have in common is that neither believe in coincidences, and I'm both. This was starting to smell like three-day-old fish.

10

Farzan Byarshan was sitting in a booth toward the back of the coffee shop when I entered. He was wearing an elegant, dark brown sport coat, blue shirt, and tan tie, and stood out like a neon sign among the cops and cadets chewing, gesturing, and laughing loudly. His expression barely qualified as a smile, and he stood to shake hands with me.

"Hello, Farzan. I assume this must be important."

If he was shocked by my lack of social grace or at all uneasy with the cop-stop coffee shop, he didn't show it. He wasn't here to make small talk, and I was betting he wanted to get whatever it was off his chest as soon as possible.

"That person who died on the airplane? I think I know something about it." I kept quiet. There was really nothing to say, and I couldn't imagine where he was going from here. "I didn't know him, not personally, but I know about people like him." He got the sex right, and he sure as hell didn't get that from the papers. They didn't know. In fact, the newspapers and television stations had already lost interest. The captivating idea of heroin-filled breast implants was worthy of a single news cycle. No one really cared about swallowed, sewn, or inserted drugs. It was old news. Images of breast implants bought the story a few salacious minutes.

Farzan held his chin between the thumb and forefinger of his right hand and rubbed it, seemingly lost in thought. "One doesn't know where to begin." As if to emphasize his confusion, he paused for several seconds. The moment tingled with expectation, and the din of the coffee shop vanished as I waited for him to continue. I felt like I was in a movie. He was definitely working me, and I was ready not to like him. Still, there weren't many upper-crust British Persians in my life, and maybe his way about things was just different, so I waited. He drew his lips back a bit as if to smile, and for some reason I focused on his large, very white teeth. There seemed to be too many for his mouth. His style of handsome was the sort that comes with centuries of good breeding.

"These people, the Asians . . . like your person from the plane . . . they are mostly Filipinos and Indonesians working in Saudi Arabia. We see some of them in the clinic. They come to the Saudis and Kuwaitis from advertisements and agencies, by the thousands. They come to earn money for families at home. They hire out as domestics, but there are construction and driving jobs as well. They take any work that the spoiled, oil-rich Bedouins don't want to do themselves. In Saudi Arabia these people earn perhaps seven—eight hundred riyals per month . . . less than a hundred and forty euros. There is nothing to save or send home, and to add insult to injury they are treated like cat-tle. Kuwaiti labor laws do not apply to foreign workers, and they are routinely abused. It is every bit as bad, perhaps worse, among the pious Saudis. Human rights groups have begun advertising campaigns quoting the words of the Prophet Mohammed, 'He who has no mercy will not receive any.' It is a very bad situation for these unfortunate people."

I didn't want to interrupt Farzan. He was on a roll, but I didn't know where he was heading. I wasn't in the mood for a lecture on human-rights infringement in the Middle East.

"How does the person from the plane fit into this?" I asked, trying not to show my impatience.

"He may have been one of them."

"Why in the world would you jump to that conclusion? These are poor people. They can't afford plastic surgery. They can barely afford to eat, and they . . ."

Farzan held up a hand. "A moment, Wendell, if you please, I am getting to the point." I stopped talking and slouched against the plastic back of the booth, feeling a bit like a chastened child. "Some of these unfortunate people are homosexual, a few are transsexual or wish for surgical gender change, just as in Western society. In fact, Muslim societies have always been tolerant of homosexuality." I started to interrupt, but Farzan headed me off at the pass. "Sodomy . . . homosexuality, these are capital offenses, but not if you look the other way. In my country, my old country, there is a thriving gay community. Our Daneshju Park is the Tehran version of the Brambles in Central Park. Gay men meet for sex and no one interferes. Even our wonderful Basij, the morality police of the Islamic revolution, look the other way. In Tehran and Riyadh it is easier for a gay couple to meet for sex than for unmarried heterosexuals. That is the way it is, whatever the law. Like any other group, a small percentage of the Asian servants are homosexual and a smaller subset have gender issues. It is not very difficult to identify them. They will do almost anything to find their surgical release from the bonds of gender misidentification. Do you see where I'm going now?" I nodded. "A lot of this surgery is performed in Thailand, but with menial work and no way to pay for the multiple procedures, they become desperate. Enter the drug traffickers. To gain control of these workers, they are known to use both threat of expo-sure . . . punishment by death is a heavy threat among the unsophisticated, and then dangling the carrot of gender-altering surgery. Your man fits into the pattern."

I listened. Most of this was new to me. The closest to transgender surgery we see in the ER is the occasional moron who puts his dick in a vacuum cleaner and skins himself. On the job . . . well, don't even think about it, we have a pretty lousy record being sympathetic to that stuff. I wished I had chosen somewhere else for this meeting. I suddenly wanted a drink. Farzan was well versed in the issue, maybe even passionate. I doubted he was homosex-ual, but he knew the subject well. His argument still didn't put the dead man on the plane in the picture until he got to his associate in practice, another Iranian-born, London-based surgeon, named Tahm Tahani.

"I think my associate is the person implanting heroin-filled breast prostheses in these transsexual men."

I didn't know what to say, and I could feel the waitress standing over the aisle end of the table before I could see her. She was a pro, and she was doing her thing, waiting to pick up the beat and get our order without listening in. That was all but impossible, but she faked boredom perfectly, pulling a dog-eared pad of checks and a pen from the pocket of her apron. Her name was embroidered across the bib, and it was soiled with the accidents and wet fingers of a long day. "Don't usually see you this late, doc. What can I get for you boys?"

I smiled. "Decaf espresso for me, Doris." Ordering anything beyond the ten-gallon tureens of coffee sitting over the flickering gas flame was definitely testing the limits of the place, but nobody ever accused me of having common sense. Farzan ordered mint tea, which earned a stare from Doris and drove her away shaking her head. I waited to see Doris's back before speaking again.

"What are you talking about? Who is your associate?"

"Tahm Tahani."

"Tahani? He's a plastic surgeon?"

"Yes, he has shared my office for some years now."

"Right. But why would you think he had something to do with this?"

"For the usual reason, Wendell, money. Tahm is gay and something of a celebrity among the chic London set. He earns a great deal of money, spends lavishly, and everyone in the hip community, gay and otherwise, knows him."

"So why did he need money? Drugs?"

"No. No, I don't think so. There's a limit to what one can earn as a plastic surgeon. Tahm had invested millions of pounds of his money, and much of his family's money, in a big property deal with some Russians, who had done quite well for him in the past. But the timing couldn't have been worse. The deflated real estate bubble and the credit crunch stopped the project cold. Super-expensive time-share resorts were the first to go. The banks foreclosed, the project sank, and the investors lost everything. Tahm risked more than he and his family could afford, and probably borrowed money to do it."

"He's not alone."

"Perhaps not. But his practice was thriving, and all in all, it wasn't quite the end of the world. I suppose his family in Iran was vulnerable once their financial position changed, and he worried for them. He was under pressure. A month or two later he began working on weekends. It seemed odd but was certainly not my business. Just out of character. Tahm for all his talent was about playing, not working, and his weekends were sacred. I thought he was putting in the extra days to accommodate more patients, but he did only a few surgeries. Each time, they were breast augmentations, and each time, he employed people to assist him who didn't ordinarily work for us. That seemed really strange."

"Did you confront him about it?"

"Yes, kind of . . . well no, not really. Then one evening I was working late at the clinic. Tahm was gone and one of his patients showed up in a panic. I calmed her down and was finally able to examine her. She had tripped and fallen chest-down, and opened one of the breast incisions. It was superficial. Not dangerous and not infected. We cleaned the wound, re-sutured it, and prescribed antibiotics. But Miss Hayes, my nurse, kept trying to catch my eye, gesturing to the patient's neck. I hadn't noticed much with all the sobbing, but the patient had a man's Adam's apple and even some hair follicles under her chin. I'm sorry to say that I didn't fully examine the patient, and I saw no need to press the issue, but I'm quite certain she was a male, or at least born a male."

Doris returned and planted our cups on the table, pulled a handful of sugar packets and Sweet'N Low from her bottomless pocket, dropped them onto the table, tossed off a "You need anything else?," didn't exactly wait for an answer, and retreated.

Farzan emptied three sugars into his tea and mixed it with a studied intensity, as though he didn't want to return to the conversation. So his buddy was doing breast implants on transgender men. Someone was going to do it. He obviously needed the business, and he might have been a bit more understanding than most. That didn't make him a criminal. It wasn't enough of a connection for me, but everything considered, it was not such a big leap from there to involvement in drug smuggling, and even connecting him to the death on the plane.

"Things seemed to turn better for him quickly. He was away from the office a lot, ran around like your, your Energizer bunny, and seemed very different, and then he disappeared."

"Disappeared? You mean totally out of touch?"

"Yes. He didn't show up at the office for weeks. He hasn't called or returned voice messages or e-mails. Tahm loves doing all that twittering, or tweeting, and that has stopped. Everyone in our office is linked on the BBM system, so I can verify that my messages were received. But not answered."

"Interesting. How long has he been missing?"

"For eleven days, until I saw him last night."

11

I had no idea what all this meant. Probably not very much.
Narcotics traffic between the UK and the U.S. is not a major
route. What's more, it isn't my field of interest, and I was
ready to turn the whole thing off.

Farzan had told a credible story. True, swallowing it required a few leaps of faith, but I believed his partner had
gotten involved with some bad folks, and his being in New
York, possibly being on the receiving end of the heroin-
filled implants, adds another level of suspicion. But I wasn't
a narcotics cop, and London was well out of our jurisdiction
anyway. The information belonged with the UK authorities
and local and federal people here. I had encouraged Farzan
to contact them. I even offered to make a call on his behalf
or hook him up with our local narcs. But our conversation
ended coolly when I pointed out my obligation to mention
the connection to local authorities. The drugs and the body
had come through Kennedy, and it was a good bet that the
doctor on the receiving end was either his friend Tahm or
the local version. Tahm showing up in New York spoke
strongly for him being on both sides of the transaction. He

had called Farzan and pressured him to meet. Apparently, that had taken place shortly after Alice and I had left his hotel. It was a quick drink with Tahm talking nonstop, offering nonspecific apologies for his erratic behavior, and begging off to make the late flight to London. So if I bought the tale, it needed to be passed on.

I went home and wasted an hour flipping through unread issues of *The New Yorker* and various medical journals that had taken over my bedside table. I tossed the throwout pile in the direction of the wastebasket and started building a smaller keep pile at the bedside. It was hard to throw the journals away. They were serious and important, and they were all available online at a moment's notice. All those leather-bound symbols of a studious physician were now just décor. I was behind the curve and running hard to catch up.

I planned to have dinner this evening with an old buddy, and I was relegating Farzan to the background and resetting my outlook to normal when my cell phone sounded. I patted the quilt, pushed the magazines and newspapers aside, and followed the music to the phone. It was Rodriguez.

"Hey, I was going to call you."

"Great, 'cause I need you to come downtown."

"Can't. I have plans. What's up?" I really didn't like this guy.

"Your little smuggling case is becoming more complicated. I think you might know more about it than you've been letting on, maybe even without realizing that you know it. We need to flesh out the details, especially now."

"Yeah, that's why I was going to call, but I can tell you about it now, if you have a few minutes."

Rodriguez waited before responding. "No. You better come down here. This is official business."

"Are you out of your mind? I tried to save someone's life, period. Do I have to lawyer up or what?"

"Whoa. Hold on there, doc. You're not under arrest. We just need to talk to you."

"Yeah, well, shove it." I ended the call and threw the phone back onto the bed. Before it even had a chance to bounce, I realized I was behaving like a jerk, but I couldn't bring myself to call him back. I stood up and paced around the room. They couldn't possibly suspect me of anything. I didn't do anything. Maybe I should have called them directly after talking to Farzan, but that's not exactly a crime. And he wasn't involved, either.

As I struggled through the maze of disjointed thoughts, the phone rang again. I knew it was Rodriguez.

This time he was almost pleasant and nonconfrontational, but very firm in his "invitation" to join him at Midtown North, over on West Fifty-fourth Street. It was narcotic/ prostitution central, and I wasn't surprised that Rodriguez was based there. Even in their new, clean family clothing, the streets fanning out from Times Square remained a magnet to the trade. That's where the marks were . . . the tourists.

All told, it took almost half an hour to cancel my dinner plan and get the car, and another twenty minutes to drive ten blocks across town near curtain time. Midtown North was at the fringe of the Theater District. It was officially the Eighteenth Police Precinct, but no one used that designation. Cops called it MTN, and it was a busy place. I angled into one of those nose-first spots reserved for "official business" alongside the private vehicles of guys out on their shift. "Official" means whatever you want it to, so long as you're in charge. The room Rodriguez told me to find was not an office. I double-checked the sliver of envelope where I had written the number. This was it. I could see light and activity through the frosted pane. It was obviously a large room, way above his grade. When I knocked on the pane, several voices answered. It wasn't exactly harmony. The "yeahs" had it, but I might have heard at least one "come in." I did. I shouldn't have. Inside the room was a nasty-looking lot sprinkled liberally with brass buttons. Seeing grungy detectives with gold shields around their necks mixed in with uniformed brass was never a good sign. The worst of it was, they were all waiting for me.

13

The short story is, no one from the medical division was in the room, so it wasn't about my job. My two friends from Narcotics were at the crummy old conference table with open folders of printouts and photos, and their pocket notebooks and cell phones in front of them. On the other metal and plastic folding chairs irregularly spaced around the table were the Homicide lieutenant Peter Secondi, two of his detectives, and C. B. Connor, commander of Midtown North. A heavy crowd. You didn't have to be a genius to figure out that someone important was murdered in midtown Manhattan, and it was somehow drug-related. What I couldn't figure out was what all this had to do with me.

Connor introduced everyone, and nodded to Rodriguez, who spoke first. "Farzan Byarshan is your friend, correct?"

Shit. This wasn't going anyplace good. "I know Farzan Byarshan. Why?"

"Mr. Byarshan is dead."

I made all the usual noises of shock and surprise. I really was shocked and surprised. Stupidly, my first words were to correct him, saying "Dr. Byarshan," and we were off on the wrong foot yet again.

Rodriguez was about to snap back, but he looked at the brass around the table and remained coolly professional. Score one for him. I poured it all out and I'm not sure whether or not they bought into my ignorance, but no one accused me of anything. They listened to my account of the afternoon without interruption, asked a few obvious questions, and filled me in on the circumstances. Apparently, Byarshan had been found dead by his wife, in their hotel room, barely an hour after our meeting. He was lying on his back in the entrance foyer, in a pool of blood. His throat had been slit from ear to ear. Mrs. Byarshan was a basket case. No surprise there; who would not have been undone by something so horrible. The last time she had seen him was at lunch. He told her he planned to see me later in the afternoon, and they went off in separate directions. He to our meeting, she for an afternoon of shopping. No one who interviewed Mrs. Byarshan had the slightest suspicion that she had anything to do with the death of her husband. Naturally, the usual investigation would have to take place, since most murders begin at home. But women were unlikely to kill large men in that manner, especially with no sign of a struggle. Alaleh sold her innocence pretty well. Most likely because she was innocent. She had receipts to substantiate her tour of the stores and a desk clerk and elevator operator to vouch for her time of arrival at the room. Being in the presence of a grieving Middle Eastern woman is enough to send the most callous Homicide detectives scrambling for the door. Anglo-Saxon restraint represses anguish and encourages a stiff upper lip. The Middle Eastern expression of grief crosses all castes. It is uninhibited, it is devastating, and it has been so for too many centuries to count.

What the cops got from interviewing Alaleh Byarshan was me. So I held my tongue, looked thoughtful, and answered their questions. It was easy to retrace my steps for those few hours. The issue was never in doubt, and the way they shared the bits and pieces of information made that fairly clear. Still, I was their only connection to the dead man . . . or now, actually, two dead men, and the facts were too weird to be coincidence. I shared that point of view. The trouble came in convincing them that I was not holding back anything that could help shed light on the situation.

"Let's go over this again. Tell us about the connection between the victim, the mule on the plane, and the missing partner?"

"Well, Farzan heard about the mule, put two and two together and wanted to discuss it."

"Right. And why do you think he chose to confide in you?"

"Because he thought I was a cop, and we had a mutual friend."

"Right. And what did he say about the fact that it was you who dealt with the mule on the plane?"

"Well, actually, nothing. And then when his missing partner showed up in New York, he made the connection and called me."

"It can't be that simple."

"I know," I said, and meant it. Over the next hour the conversation kicked the same stones but didn't change the landscape. I told them everything—well, practically everything. As much as I wanted to keep my relationship with Alice private, she was the link with Farzan Byarshan, so I included everything that I thought mattered and glossed over the private parts—no pun intended. Maybe I should have mentioned that we were lovers, but that didn't seem pertinent, and I was enough of a gentleman to keep private things private. I assumed they'd read between the lines. But looking back on it, delicacy wasn't a strong suit with Rodriguez and company.

By nine thirty we had gone over the same ground at least three times, and I was excused. There were none of the dumb admonitions that cops were supposed to say at the end of an interview, and I didn't feel like a suspect. I was confused. One of the screwed-up things about being a doctor is a feeling of omnipotence. The day after graduation you're transformed from a know-nothing medical student into a person responsible for the lives of strangers. Believe me, you still don't know a damned thing, but pretty soon you've drunk the Kool-Aid and believe the bullshit that swirls around you all day. We do actually believe we are smarter than other people, and based on school performance and objective intelligence tests, some measure of that might be true. But there's more to life than test scores, and with their heads in the books or the clouds, they become social misfits, bumping into life's pillars and generally making a mess of things that less bright people manage to negotiate gracefully. That's why doctors have an unimaginably high rate of private-pilot accidents. We're smarter than the weatherman. We can beat the thunderheads that scare most pilots out of the sky. I was confident that if I couldn't make head or tail of what had been going on, neither could the room full of detectives.

One of the Homicide cops, the lieutenant, was smarter than the average bear, and I use the term advisedly. Peter "Deuce" Secondi was six-four, easily two-fifty, with a shaved head, hard gray eyes you couldn't stare into, and a confident manner matching his appearance. He was also a really good guy. Deuce and I had been friends for years. It was one of those things that grew out of mutual respect. He was pretty much the only real cop that I socialized with on anything like a regular basis. Deuce and his wife, Amy, listened to my nonsense through the divorce and have occasionally been surrogate family. He was all business in that room, and that was as it should be. His two detective "firsts" knew we were friends, and knowing Deuce, he made sure the others learned it from him before and not after the fact. I thought about waiting for him downstairs, but that was a bad idea. Tomorrow would be soon enough to talk, and I headed out onto Fifty-fourth Street.

I was tired and hungry. For a bit, I stood between the two Art Deco green light sconces indicating the precinct house, thinking. I wanted to call Alice, and I needed someplace close for a beer and a burger. Hunger won the day, and I hopped into the car and drove eight blocks south to

Joe Allen's, an old standard on West Forty-sixth Street. I beat the after-theater crowd by an hour and snagged a seat at the bar. I'm not quite a regular, but the bartender knew his job and had a cardboard coaster in front of me before I was done wiggling into a comfortable position on the shaky stool. I dialed Alice, got her voice mail, and left a perfunctory "Call me." Two sips into my second Heineken, I was busy reading my e-mail and sending one off to Alice when a juicy, rare hamburger arrived. I can honestly say it was the best part of my day.

Forty minutes later, Tonto and I were propped up on pillows on my queen-size bed, surfing the local stations for the story. Alice still hadn't gotten back to me. I assumed she was in surgery. If she had spoken to the cops, she would have been on the horn in seconds, so I didn't bother calling again and went back to working the remote. Farzan made the tease on channel 4 with something like *Mutilated doctor found in posh midtown hotel room, details at eleven*. I sat through ads for cars, toilet cleaners, adult diapers, and erectile aids, which was a pretty good insight into the demographics of the news audience. It was the lead story, delivered on location by a good-looking blonde standing on East Fifty-fifth Street, in front of the ornate, turn-of-the-century entrance to the St. Regis. She pointed over her shoulder several times to be certain we knew where she was. Every time she turned, the buttons on her blouse looked like they were about to pop. Her delivery was breathless, falsely urgent, and said little more than the tease had. Farzan was not identified, and Lieutenant Peter Secondi indicated it was an ongoing investigation and refused further comment. Nothing there. I worked the remote and caught the end of the same on two other stations before I switched it off and tried Alice again.

13

An uninterrupted night's sleep is a great thing. Seven hours and I felt pure of mind and body, but it did nothing to clarify the previous day's events. No word from Alice. I checked my e-mail and phone. Nothing. Early morning was the busiest time of day for surgeons, and I would have to wait until later to connect with her. By seven thirty she was in another zone. I had a good workout and a leisurely walk with Tonto. I fed and watered him, roughhoused with him for a few minutes, then showered, dressed, and headed off to work.

Mrs. Black was in a talkative mood, and we chatted about the odd recent events over a cup of tea. My schedule for the day was front and center on the desk blotter, as usual, and it didn't look like a lot of laughs. I had only begun to scowl at it when the intercom interrupted.

"Your friend Rodriguez."

"Oh for Christ's sake." I waited a few seconds to reset my attitude and picked up the receiver. "Good morning, detective. Now what?"

"Good morning, doc. I think we need to talk some more."

"I think I've pretty much said everything I have to say. What is unclear? I mean other than the whole picture."

"I keep wondering where your mule was heading before her bubble burst."

It was a funny remark, but I wouldn't give Rodriguez the satisfaction of laughing. He irritated me. Instead, I countered with "His bubble."

"Right, his. Was it possible he was headed for your friend, Alice?"

"Not likely. Farzan Byarshan's partner is the first place to look, don't you think? I mean he said so himself."

"Right. But we can't find him and we can't seem to locate your girlfriend. Could be they're in it together." He was baiting me, and I wasn't biting.

"Not likely."

"Byarshan was held from behind when his throat was cut. Slashed from ear to ear. It looks like a ritual Middle Eastern sacrifice, like the hostage videos on YouTube. How long would it take for someone to bleed out after that kind of slash, doctor?"

"Minute, minute and a half."

"So he was held up while he bled out. No thrashing around. They just stood there and watched him die. Nasty stuff." I said nothing and waited for Rodriguez to fill the silence. "Considering how Byarshan was killed, there was no struggle. The killer got through the door like the victim knew him. Or her."

"Her? You think a woman killed Byarshan?"

"No, not exactly. Maybe your friend Alice went up to his room. He looked through the peephole, saw her, opened the door, and was taken from behind by a man who slipped in with her, held him and slit his throat while Alice watched him bleed out."

"Nonsense."

"Got a better explanation? He knew her, would let her in. She could be the receiving surgeon here. Maybe with the other Iranian. They could be in it together. She held and he cut. Nice friends, and they all know you. Could be you were accompanying the mule back from London. That way it all fits."

"Fuck you, Rodriguez."

"We'll see who gets fucked. Now is the time to talk. If you aren't one of them, give us Alice, and we can find the other guy."

I hung up the phone. Actually, I slammed it into the cradle. Mrs. Black opened the door and stuck her head in. "City property, Dr. Black. Easy. Anything you want to talk about?

15

The workday was distracting enough to occupy my mind once I got over being pissed at Rodriguez. I finished sick call, made a hospital visit, and headed for home. Deuce had called, asking a few more questions about Alice and her relationship to Farzan. I answered honestly, but I really didn't know any more than I had already told him. Unfortunately, the idea that Farzan knew the killer and allowed him into the room made sense. That it was Alice didn't. When I told Deuce about the call from Rodriguez, his only response was, "The guy has a hard-on for you. Sounds like he wants out of Narcotics and into Homicide. Can't blame him. Hang around with dirtbags too long and you get dirty. They all do."

Somehow it got to be six thirty, and I was starved. I called Alice twice from the car but couldn't raise her. I called the hospital page operator and waited for a return call that didn't come. At traffic lights I punched in every message I could think of: e-mail, text, BBM voice mail. The only clue to Alice's whereabouts was that she had received the BBM, or at least her BlackBerry had. There was no response, and that didn't help at all.

At least I knew that Tonto still loved me. But he'd had a hard day in the doggie gym and was too pooped to do anything but eat. Obviously, I was going to have to amuse myself. I hung my jacket on the doorknob, pulled off my tie, poured out two fingers of Jameson's, and sat with the mail. Two fingers in a shot glass isn't much . . . almost an ounce. Two fingers in one of my father's crystal tumblers can do real damage. I was well into it when I realized I couldn't fight my way through another bout of greasy Chinese take-out, and I was too hungry for popcorn. I tossed the Jameson's, washed and dried the glass, and polished it twinkling clean for next time, as I always do. It makes the drink more of an occasion. Then I thumbed through Zagat's restaurant guide. Why? I don't know why. I always end up in one of a few places where the food is good and the people make me feel at home.

I am one of those almost naturally thin people. I'm always hungry, and I don't get fat. That's not my nature to go wild. I know too much and I'm not stupid. But when I'm nervous or feeling reckless, booze and beef are on my mind. The cure for this kind of hunger was a steak, but I waffled between red meat and sushi. Sushi was healthier by far and only twice the price. So I salivated my way over to East Forty-third Street and opted for the beef, ignoring my pledge to hold down red-meat consumption to once a week. I'm good at conning myself, and I managed to feel virtuous by even considering opting out. Anyway, I eat so much sushi that my mercury level must be higher than a thermometer. You can't win.

Pietro's may be the most unattractive restaurant in New York, and the clientele doesn't help: groups of big men eating huge slabs of beef. Not the place for a delicate lady. It is an institution that dates back to Prohibition, with the Palm, Christ Cella, and a few other red-sauce steak places begun by hardworking Italian immigrant families. It was a plain-looking joint from the get-go, with simple square tables and a big communal chow-down where you couldn't help meeting interesting folks. In the old days it existed quietly on the second and third floors of a tenement building on East Forty-fifth Street. My dad loved going there with his friends, and it was a big treat to tag along. It didn't seem like a step up when they moved, thirty years ago, but you get used to anything.

I said my hellos and made my way to the back. A frosty vodka martini was in front of me before I could get comfortable and set the BlackBerry and my book on the table. My overriding Jewish guilt kicked right in and I couldn't bear to disappoint the thoughtful Bruno, so I accepted the drink, not planning to finish it. The chopped salad doesn't quite qualify as healthy filler. It's huge and delicious, glazed with olive oil, studded with Roquefort cheese, and anything but low-calorie, and by the time the very rare strip steak and potatoes arrived I was ready to call it quits. I made a slight dent in the steak, drank half the martini and a Diet Coke, and asked Bruno to bag up fifty dollars of prime beef for Tonto . . . or maybe me, and headed home.

Still no word from Alice.

By this time I couldn't sort out whether I was worried or annoyed, but it was definitely unsettling. Finally, I called the hospital and roused a plastic surgery resident. I identified myself as Alice's friend, Dr. Black—no police stuff—and asked if he had seen her today. At first the guy was hesitant to speak, but apparently he weighed the options and figured he would not be giving any secrets away. During that first quiet moment the thought that she had put me on a no-information list bounced around the paranoid spot in my brain. Finally, he said that Alice hadn't appeared at work that morning.

"It was kind of a mess. We had to postpone cases until we could get coverage, and she never called."

"Anybody hear from her later?"

"No, we paged her here, and I called her and texted her. Weird. I hope she's okay."

"Me too." Now I was worried, though I wasn't sure what I was worried about. Alice wasn't avoiding me . . . or wasn't avoiding only me. If there had been an emergency, she would have let someone know. I reversed course and headed for Alice's apartment in Tribeca, but I really didn't expect to find her there. She was tangentially connected to two people who had been murdered, and that was scary. I'm not often ruled by anxiety, but I soon found myself running yellow traffic signals and sounding the horn at taxi drivers scouting fares. It took no more than fifteen minutes to reach the ugly glass tower where she lived. The place boasted a double-height, black stone lobby and a mini porte cochere, but was otherwise indistinguishable from dozens of other buildings catering to up-and-coming young New Yorkers. I pulled into the curved drive, flipped my NYPD identification onto the dash, and hit the remote lock as I entered the lobby.

Then I went into full-bore police mode. Badge, ID, the works, and approached an unfamiliar doorman. He claimed to know nothing and referred me to the concierge. Across the lobby, the other man had been watching us, and he rose before I reached the huge, granite roadblock of a desk. With that kind of efficiency, it was a good bet that he knew everybody's business. The blue-and-gold uniform was worn with military precision. The cheap-looking metal display stand identifying the concierge as Albert was large enough to read from outside the building.

"Albert, I'm a friend of Dr. Sheppard, in 15A. Do you remember me?"

"Yes, sir, I do, black BMW with police ID. How can I help you?" I was surprised to have things begin so smoothly. I had expected Albert to ask for a writ from the Supreme Court before answering questions about his charges.

"Can you please call up to Dr. Sheppard and tell her Dr. Black is downstairs?"

"Yes, sir, but I don't think she's in." Albert looked like he knew something and was waiting for the right question before he spilled the beans. As he waited for an answer with the intercom phone to his ear, I went on.

"Did you see her leave for work this morning?"

"No, sir. The doctor leaves very early. I work four to twelve." Made sense, it was ten p.m.

"Well, did you see her leave this evening?" It was an uninspired line of questioning. I would make a lousy cop, but I couldn't think of a more productive approach.

"No, sir." He returned the receiver to its cradle and said, "No answer."

I decided to stop playing games. He wasn't on the stand, and this was just a conversation.

"Okay, Albert, how did you know she wasn't home?"

"Well, sir, the doctor left last night with two large suit-cases and a carry-on and I helped her into the taxi."

"Did she say she was going away?"

"No. But I heard her tell the driver, 'Kennedy Airport.'"

Then Albert and I went around a bit about letting me into the apartment. I lost.

So, Alice's friend is murdered, and she leaves town in a hurry. That didn't smell right. I quickly reconstructed the time line: she was probably working when Farzan bought it, and then she was gone. Why?

Why? That was the question that Rodriguez and Deuce would ask when they found out. And they would find out. This time I used my brain and struck first. I called Deuce, got his voice mail, and asked him to get back to me ASAP, which he did. That turned out to be a good move because Alice was on his short list for interviews in the morning. I told him the whole deal, short of lingerie and midnight murmuring.

"She's involved in this, doc. No question."

"You know my name, don't start that doc shit."

"Wendell, your girlfriend is involved in this."

"How? What is it that she's involved in?"

"Unclear, but two people are dead . . . and Alice took a powder. Why does the friend of a nice doctor get murdered? Was she afraid she was next? Any way you approach whatever this is, it's going to be bigger than we know. I'm getting a bad feeling that we're only seeing the tip of this particular iceberg. Tomorrow we find out all about the lovely Alice."

15

I was back at work on Thursday morning, but my head was elsewhere. Instead of trying to work out the puzzle or worrying about Alice's safety, I just couldn't get past the idea of heading off to the ER that evening and not seeing her. Some of the sadness was of my own doing; I had been there before. That's who I am. But Alice really pushed the right buttons, and I guess I cared more than I let on. We both mouthed the usual sophisticated platitudes; casual and fun shouldn't spell commitment. Apparently the rules had changed while I was looking the other way.

Just before noon Deuce called, and we agreed to meet at Alice's apartment at four. I tried to keep him on the phone and asked a lot of questions, all of which he deftly sidestepped, and then he left for our meeting. The remainder of the afternoon was interminable. I must have looked at my watch every five minutes. At three thirty I headed for my car.

Tribeca lacks the low-rise charm or lovely homes of the West Village, and it has none of the limestone elegance of the Upper East Side. The cobbled streets were old and uneven, most of the buildings are the same eyesore as turn-of-the-century factories everywhere, and the absence of trees was depressing. Canal Street traffic, the endless snake of cars in and out of the Holland Tunnel, and byzantine traffic patterns lead to "you can't get there from here" addresses. And on top of it all, it's expensive. Very expensive. The hippest neighborhood in town. A lot of the big loft apartments were spectacular, but Alice's wasn't one of them.

I don't remember having been in Alice's apartment without her or at least without being welcomed by her, and entering the building with Deuce put a whole new spin on things. The romance of early visits, and the promise of things to come, was absent. It seemed like business. It was business—maybe that was what I didn't like. Deuce presented the warrant to the building manager by slapping it dramatically onto the black stone surface of the concierge desk. The man studied it as though he had an idea of what the legal jargon meant, and then led us to the door.

At the apartment door, Deuce knocked, and said loudly, "Dr. Sheppard, NYPD, open the door." When there was no answer, he said it again. Louder this time. Then he nodded to the building manager and at the door. Deuce had his fists clenched at his side, but when the building manager began to open the standard building mortise lock, he already had his pistol out and held against his hip. That shook me. The manager turned the knob at the same time as he inserted his key into the dead bolt. The bolt had not been shot, and the door sprang open. Deuce announced himself again and waved us back. I entered a few steps behind him. The manager followed behind me, until Deuce stared down at him and said, "Thank you. We can take it from here," and turned his back on the man, dismissing him. We held our conversation until the door slammed behind the building manager and we had entered the bedroom. I was edgy about what we might find as we did a quick tour of the place. Deuce had me trail behind him until we were certain the apartment was unoccupied. Then he holstered his weapon and turned to me. I relaxed my tense shoulders, unclenched my fists, and felt the discomfort of cold sweat dripping down my sides.

"What's different? Quick. Look around and say whatever you think."

"You're an intimidating prick, Secondi."

"My job. What has changed?"

I looked around the bedroom and the bathroom and saw nothing but a few very pleasant memories. In the living room I dropped onto the sofa and saw nothing unusual except a big cop instead of Alice. Same for the open area that served as kitchen/dining room/library. The closets meant nothing to me, I had never opened them before, and they looked like a lot of girl stuff. They smelled like Alice. Coats, umbrellas, and never unpacked boxes filled the guest closet. Dresses, blouses, pants, and lots of things still in the crummy plastic bags from the dry cleaner hung closely packed. Shoeboxes were stacked one on the other, with still more shoes in a hanging contraption behind the bedroom closet door. Every inch of space was spoken for. Alice had only been in the place for a year, but no woman ever had unused closet space. I let out a deep, audible sigh, and pawed through the bureau drawers. Some of the silk and satin things were familiar, and nice, but I really had no idea what the hell I was looking for.

"Looks the way it always did," I said with little confidence. "Nothing unusual."

"Sit down on the couch and lie on the bed. I gather you now remember that you've been there before." I deserved that for having been dumb enough to let it go so far before giving up details of the relationship. I did as I was told and had a sense that something was out of place as I sat on the edge of the bed. I looked around, got up, circled, and sat again. This time on the right side. The guest spot. I felt guilty for having the sarcastic thought, but hey, that's real life. Why shouldn't Alice assign me the side of the bed that made HER comfortable? We are all creatures of habit. Then I understood. "Got it." I bounced off the bed and crossed over to the chest of drawers on Alice's side. "The picture is missing. Alice loves that picture of her nieces. It's gone."

"Good going, Wendell. Do you remember the frame? Was it one of those little silver traveling frames that folds closed?"

I knew where he was heading, but I answered anyway. "No, it was pretty big, like eight by ten, I think. Modern. Silver."

"Right. So we can rule out your Dr. Sheppard being snatched. Packing the picture means she planned to go . . . and maybe permanently. She may have left in a hurry, but it was thought out."

"What about all the stuff in the closets?"

"Disposable. Replaceable. She's gone, and so is everything that matters to her." That didn't make me feel good.

Deuce wasn't about to let go. We picked the apartment apart piece by piece. Nothing was off limits, and he questioned me about everything. It was amazing how little I knew. I did know the names of the beautiful young girls in the picture. Victoria and Elizabeth, not very imaginative for a British family, but I'd be damned if I had any idea of their surname. Never asked. Her parents. What about her parents? Well, I knew they were called Sheppard, Madeline and Edward, and they lived between London and someplace in the southwest. In Devon, or nearby. An old country house where the photo of the girls had been taken, or at least that was what Alice told me. Her sister, Clementine, was three years Alice's junior, which would make her thirty-seven, or -eight. I knew all about Alice's professional credentials. Medical school, residencies, fellowships, interests and aspirations—those things were common ground and easy points of reference that doctors shared. I spilled it all for Secondi, who bent his head into his notepad and took it down using a gray ballpoint pen with the gold logo of a midtown hotel. He rarely looked up from his notes. Detectives and reporters are the last professionals to rely on handwritten notes, and I had never known one to spring for a decent pen. I doubt it was for fear of losing them. Shitty pens are a point of honor with these guys. Deuce Secondi is a well-groomed, well-dressed behemoth, and the scrawny, throwaway pen looked ridiculous in his mitt. The only thing that seemed to bother him was losing my attention, but we had run out of things to say.

"Let's call it quits over here. I'll have the boys seal the place and you can head off to job two."

"Not so fast. How about the information you didn't want to talk about on the phone?"

Secondi thought for a moment before answering or, at least, he hesitated.

"Yeah, well, I started reaching out last night. I wanted my requests for information sitting on desktops when the London guys opened their computers. That way there was a chance of hearing something by our morning, and I did the airports, Homeland-ICE, and FBI before I fell asleep." He went back to his pad and flipped a few pages back. He was glancing from neatly numbered notes in different-colored ink. I wanted to crane my neck over to get a better look but figured that was pushing it a bit. He didn't read his notes aloud but kept glancing back at them as he decided what to share and what to omit. "Alice Sheppard left the country on the 10:40 BA flight to Heathrow, where she deplaned and passed customs. She was not flagged at either end, and the only note of her passage was routine passport clearance."

"No surprises there."

"None. Funny thing is there is no trace of her after passing through customs."

I didn't find that peculiar. In a free society one is easily lost in the crowd, and I made the point to Secondi.

"Wendell, it's not like we were looking for her to show up at Piccadilly Circus. None of the three Alice Sheppards in London are our girl. No hotel check-in, no telephone list-ing, and no National Identity Card."

"I thought the National Identity Cards were finished."

"They are. A few billion pounds down the crapper. Too much Big Brother for the Brits, but I thought it was a great idea. Anyway, no National Identity Card had ever been is-sued to your particular Alice Sheppard. As far as we can tell, her passport was first issued four years ago and has been used primarily for travel between the U.S. and the UK. Other than that, she doesn't exist."

"Give me a break. Check the hospitals and medical schools. She didn't simply appear. Check her references at Westchester Polyclinic. They didn't give her a job on her own say-so. And in case you're interested, she is good at what she does. She had to learn it someplace." I was getting annoyed at the stupid idea of Alice Sheppard falling through the cracks. "Come on, Deuce, Alice is real and you guys ought to be able to locate her. In this post-9/11 world we're supposed to know where everybody is."

"Right. According to your friends at the ACLU we have to protect the rights of the criminals. God forbid people should be forced to identify themselves."

I was about to rebut his position, but this wasn't the time. Right now I was for a national biometric ID card, GPS chips, CCTV on every corner, and anything else that would give us a clue to the story of Alice Sheppard.

Secondi continued, "No doubt we will trace her down sometime today. But, as for this moment, she has vanished."

16

On my way to work the next morning I called Deuce from the car. He was not a happy camper. The search for Alice was a bust. Nothing checked out. No one in her past had any idea who she was. The National Health had no data on her as physician or patient. Nothing on her UK driver's license checked out. Addresses, contacts, and official documents were all real but, apparently, Alice Sheppard was not.

Two other things thickened the brew. Telefónica O2 provided scans of Tahm Tahani's cell phone records, which turned up two calls to Alice's cell number and one from it, all on the day he vanished, or, very possibly, was killed. And to my surprise, there was a call to my phone as well. It was a ten-second connection, probably indicating a missed call. I remembered no message, nor had I ever spoken to him. The calls to and from Alice were all several minutes in length. Real conversations.

The full-court press was on. Within hours the network was buzzing. Sources were pressured, and a few civil rights may have been compromised in the effort. A confidential informant tip to Homeland Security initiated an antiterror raid of a Muslim Cultural Center on Atlantic Avenue in Brooklyn. It turned up a quantity of uncut heroin neatly packaged in two 300 cc breast implants, and no one to tie them to. Several individuals involved in the center had known ties to radical groups.. It was a hotbed of former associates of the late, lamented, American-born Yemeni terrorist Imam Anwar al-Awlaki. In the end, none were turned up. Electronic surveillance had tracked contacts from the Gulf of Aden to Atlantic Avenue, but now that connection was blown.

The cost of confirming the Middle East connection was high, but that was expected. Damned if I knew the significance of the news, but it must have been important. Rodriguez was on my case again. I don't believe he saw any role for me, but he used the excuse to assert his authority and try to trip me up. He was waiting, uninvited, when I arrived at my office. I was annoyed with Mrs. Black for allowing him into my private anteroom, but at least my office door was locked, or the creep would have been lifting hairs from my comb. I must have snapped at Mrs. Black because she shrugged her shoulders, turned away, and said, "The man was sitting there when I came in. What did you expect me to do?" She turned and left me with Rodriguez. He followed me into my office and took the visitor's chair without being asked. Listening to him talk trash deepened my foul mood. I didn't need any more aggravation, and I lost my temper.

"Rodriguez, arrest me or get the fuck out. Is that clear

enough?" I had been sitting on the edge of my desk. I pushed forward, walked past him to the door, opened it, and said, "Now." When he didn't move, I grabbed his left elbow to help him out. Rodriguez spun away, then slammed his left forearm into my chest. As I was falling back, he caught me with a right that was just beyond his reach. It skimmed my left cheek as I snapped my face away. His body slipped forward and I landed a good right and a left to the side of his rib cage and his kidney. He went down on the desk, knocking over the chair and clearing the desktop, and I was on him. It wasn't ten seconds before the room was filled with cops, who pulled us apart. Rodriguez was cursing mad, shouting that I was under arrest. No one paid him any mind, and I just wanted to beat the shit out of the little bastard. As it was, he would be pissing blood for a few days.

While my stock went up with the doctors, desk jockeys, and malingerers, Mrs. Black refused to speak to me. Rodriguez was hustled away, and I slowly put my office back together. I wondered about the protocol for the episode. Who was assaulting a police officer? Doubtless, there was a reg. But having gotten the best of the situation, I was cool with it. What Rodriguez did was his business . . . and, I guess, mine.

I wasn't sure how much of the new information Rodriguez was aware of. He was fixed on the heroin-filled implants, but I assumed he knew about the telephone calls. Deuce had been true to his word and kept me in the loop. But Rodriguez was part of the de facto task force, so he had to be in on everything. Whatever. It didn't change the fact that I had no idea what the hell was happening around me.

I straightened my necktie, slipped into my white lab coat, and went out to the waiting area, which was anything but normal-looking. Officers on sick call were standing in small groups, chatting and laughing. Few were seated. No one looked or acted sick. The adrenaline rush had pumped everybody up, myself included, and we were ready for anything.

"Here's the doc," a female officer said when she caught her first glimpse of me.

"Go get him, doc," another laughed. I smiled broadly and it seemed as though we all started to laugh at once.

"Thanks, everybody. Remember me when IA comes around. Innocent. Self-defense." I raised my hand and waved to the room full of happy people. "Now let's see how sick you are."

It didn't take long for me to calm down and lose myself in the work. I admit having been unusually lenient and sympathetic in the moment, and a lot of people got a long weekend who would ordinarily have been back on the job. When I finished the morning session, I made a mea culpa overture to Mrs. Black, and invited her to lunch. She brewed some hot tea while I went out and picked up two tuna fish sandwiches from the coffee shop. It would have been easier to call for delivery, but I wanted to show that I was making an effort. Ten minutes later I set napkins and the food on the coffee table in front of my sofa, and dragged a side chair over to face the sofa. Mrs. Black chose the sofa, and it didn't take long for peace to reign. The conversation centered on the bizarre events of the week behind us, and the coming weekend, a few hours away. The weather had warmed up again, and she and her husband were heading north to an inn in Columbia County to catch the last few days of leaf-peeping. I had no plans. My mother was in Los Angeles, visiting my sister and her kids. I was happy not to be a part of that. Not that I don't love them both. I do. Under the best of circumstances, Mother is difficult. To say that she is headstrong and opinionated is to gently white-wash her personality. She also has exquisite timing and says or does something outrageously endearing just as the level of frustration is about to boil over. My sister, Helen, is a saint. With infinite patience she manages her oaf of a husband, Mother, and two wonderful teenage sons, and she has enough left over to give good advice and guidance to her difficult clients. At least one would like to assume so. Entertainment law has to be an oxymoron.

In a previous life, Alice and I had planned to drive out to Montauk for the weekend. With all that had gone on, I hadn't remembered to cancel the reservation. The money was spent and maybe the change of scenery would clear my head. October was always mild at the beach. The ocean was still warm, and the onshore breeze warmed the land nicely. The crowds had scattered when the social season ended at Labor Day. Streets were strollable, the beaches were empty, and restaurant owners welcomed the business. The rich folks were already working on their winter vacations, rent-ers were out of season, and tourists had nothing to gawk at.

All in all, it was the best time to enjoy one of the most physically beautiful parts of the world. Maybe the only time.

My plan was to spend Friday night in the city, trying to track down some traces of Alice. I had to free-associate and follow the smoke. It wasn't something that lent itself to sharing. I called ahead to SushiAnn, where they knew me well enough to have my credit card on file. I was good to go with ten pieces of my favorite sushi, neatly wrapped with pickled ginger and freshly grated wasabi and sitting on the counter waiting for my arrival on East Fifty-first Street. Fifteen minutes later I dropped the container on the kitchen counter and was out and about with Tonto. Following a dog with a plastic bag strikes me as the ultimate indignity. How one gets accustomed to handling dog shit before dinner is a phenomenon of its own. But we do it. As a bow to gentility, I washed my hands thoroughly and finished with a blast of industrial-strength germ-killer. Tonto and I were both hungry, and I had the impression that he was eyeing the plastic box with the fish smell.

"Don't even think about it." Tonto knows my tough-guy tone, and he backed off and sat by his bowl. I know he was trying to say, "Okay, so feed me." So I did. Then I set the sushi on the dining table and got comfortable.

I have the odd habit of sipping whiskey when I eat at home. I can't drink anything near a whole bottle of wine, so I hate to crack a good bottle and waste it, and the whiskey buffers the food from the drinking water. The sensation of cold water solidifying a mouthful of fat makes my tongue crawl. Absent alcohol, even a Diet Coke will do.

The sushi was terrific, but I needed something sweet to finish off the meal. Elegant man about town that I am, I grabbed a Snickers bar from the freezer and nearly lost my premolars. I had another bite, and tossed it. Then I kicked off my shoes and headed for the computer. My plan was to Google the hell out of Alice Sheppard and her fictional résumé.

I started with a list of names Alice had mentioned. There was no particular order, and I sat in front of the screen and let it flow. Based simply on its comic potential, the first name that popped into my mind was Sir Peregrine Freely. Don't ask. Whenever Alice uttered even the very first syllable, Sir . . . I knew what was coming and broke down laughing. Alice seemed to find that somewhat juvenile behavior quite charming. I doubt Sir Peregrine would share that view. Freely was the dean of British reconstructive surgeons, having inherited the mantle from the legendary Sir Harold Gillies and Sir Archibald McIndoe, the two men who had, in that order, invented reconstructive surgery, treating disfigured survivors of both world wars. Freely was easy to track through his numerous scientific papers. I uploaded a Word template with the NYPD logo from the Office of the Police Surgeon. It was as official as we got. No one knew what the hell a police surgeon was, and the title carried more weight than it deserved. Hey, you use what you've got.

Dear Sir Peregrine,

The NYPD Office of the Police Surgeon is seeking information regarding Alice Sheppard, MD. Dr. Sheppard is a plastic and reconstructive surgeon. We have been led to believe that Dr. Sheppard served a fellowship in reconstructive surgery on your service at Queen Victoria Hospital, East Grinstead, during the years 2006 and 2007. Any information you provide will be treated confidentially. Thank you for your help in this matter.

Sincerely yours,

Wendell Black,
Police Surgeon NYPD

I had barely admired my handiwork when the incoming mail signal lit. It was a reply from Freely.

Dear Police Surgeon Black,

I have no knowledge of the woman called Alice Sheppard. She has not been trained by me nor, to my knowledge, been employed at this institution during the period in question, or, for that matter, in the last decade. Feel free to call me at the above telephone number if further assistance is required.

Yours truly,

Sir Peregrine Freely, CBE
Professor and Surgeon in Chief

The reply was quite definite, and since I was certain Freely was awake, I dialed the number he had provided.

"Good morning, Police Surgeon Black, I presume."

"Correct, Sir Peregrine. I hope I am not disturbing you. I understand the hour is late in the UK, but as we have been communicating in the ether, I took the liberty."

"Indeed. Please do tell me about your young lady, and why the authorities are interested in her." Not an unreasonable request, as I was seeking information from him and had no jurisdiction in the matter.

"Dr. Sheppard is employed as a plastic surgeon at Westchester Polyclinic alleging that her training was with you."

"Is that what police surgeons do? Background checks?"

"Ha. No, sir. The actual fact is not so mundane. In this case Dr. Sheppard has gone missing and another doctor, a British plastic surgeon, has been murdered."

"My goodness. And do you police suspect Dr. Sheppard?"

"Actually, we do not, but it is important to locate her."

"Hmm. Who was the unfortunate plastic surgeon?"

"Farzan Byarshan."

"Good God. I know Byarshan well. A good man. I think I may just know the girl as well."

17

I had spent hours following up even the most farfetched threads of Alice Sheppard's life and got nothing worth the effort. The Internet is great, and I learned all sorts of stuff about the history of English plastic surgery but nothing about Alice. Sir Peregrine was indeed the big fish I needed.

On Saturday morning, before nine, I called the St. Regis Hotel and asked to be connected to Mrs. Byarshan's room. It had been three days since the death of her husband, but since the body had not been released by the medical examiner, it was a fair bet she would still be in New York. The operator put the call through immediately, without asking my name. A gentleman speaking slightly accented, very proper English answered the telephone. I identified myself and asked to speak to Alaleh.

"Yes, please. Who is this?" she asked. I identified myself again, and she responded, a bit put off.

"Dr. Black, my father said you were the police."

"Sorry. I may have misled him a bit to be sure he would let me speak with you. Alaleh, I have to ask you some questions about your husband and Alice Sheppard."

"Yes, of course. They were good friends."

"I need to know more than that, if you can help."

"Of course," she answered. "I think they may have dated before Farzan and I met. He was very fond of her. I have not spoken to her in two days. How is she?"

"That's what we would like to know. Alice is missing. We have been contacting her associates here and in the UK, trying to find some direction. How well do you know her?"

"Oh, not very well at all, Dr. Black." It was time to go at it from another direction.

"Please call me Wendell. Alaleh, where did Alice and Farzan meet?"

"I think they were fellows together at Queen Victoria Hospital."

"Ah. And when Farzan opened his surgery in London did Alice work with him?"

"No, Wendell. Farzan never said that."

"Do you know if they saw each other in London?"

"Yes, I think so, or at least she called the house a few times. Farzan didn't speak about her often. I think he believed I was jealous."

"Did Alice know Tahm Tahani?"

"No, I don't think so. I actually do not know."

As a matter of family tradition, Deuce tried to spend Saturdays with his boys, and I almost felt guilty interrupting him. Whatever he had been doing, he answered his cell phone on the second ring. I took a deep breath and started from the beginning. "Alice Sheppard was never a fellow or a student at East Grinstead, where she claimed to have trained, but Farzan Byarshan was. Alice showed up at social functions as Farzan's girlfriend, and Sir Peregrine Freely . . ."

"Who?"

"Here we go. Deuce is a pretty funny name, too. Just hold on for a minute, okay? Sir Peregrine is a famous plastic surgeon in England. Alice says she trained with him. Freely says she didn't. He"—I made a point of not saying Sir Peregrine again—"remembered her from my physical description as a lovely young doctor who visited with Farzan several times. She had a London accent, and he said they knew people in common. I have the names. Maybe you can get the addresses from Scotland Yard. But I still have no idea where Alice learned her trade. She's good at it, she's definitely real, but Alice Sheppard isn't."

"They all knew one another. We already knew that, and Alice isn't Alice. At least one of the other two got himself killed the other day. What does it mean?"

"It means you were right," I admitted to Deuce. "This is bigger than we thought. We have to find out how Alice fits into the puzzle."

"I'll get the London guys on that, too. But don't expect a hell of a lot. Alice covered her tracks like a pro. She's up to no good."

I stuffed my laptop and a change of clothes into a carryall, tossed Tonto's bowls and his food into a shopping bag, which excited him no end, and headed for the car. It's about a hundred and twenty miles from Manhattan to the eastern end of Long Island. Sometimes the trip is so slow it takes the wind out of your sails. Today it was just over two hours, and actually pleasant. The humidity was gone for the year, so the sky was crisp. The morning temperature in the low sixties allowed for open windows instead of AC. A good start. I found an a.m. news station and was surprised to hear that the death of a visiting plastic surgeon was part of a war between international drug cartels. Amazing. I was afraid to read the *Post*.

By noon we were walking the beach. I was feeling a little blue and a lot confused, but melancholy doesn't hold up to an empty expanse of beach. A supercharged dog running from breaking waves, attacking on the ebb, and cajoling me to play along is just too much fun. After an hour we retired, beat and sandy, to the little motel unit on the dunes.

The furnishings of the room weren't much to speak of. Not stark or modern or really anything but beachy, comfortable, and appropriate. There was a big bed with a headboard upholstered in the same blue-and-white striped canvas as the rattan chair and ottoman and bedspread. An old tube television and cable box were about as far from the bed as possible. One of the night tables had a clunky phone on it, and immobile half-length draperies braced the big ocean window like a frame. There was a pull shade for use when privacy was necessary.

The bathroom was small and clean and of indeterminate vintage, with a tiny frosted-glass window. There were no sample plastic bottles of shampoo and body wash, and the small bars of soap wrapped in paper were actually easy to open. That was as luxurious as it got. After a quick shower I wrapped myself in a decent-sized towel, plugged in the laptop behind the headboard, and set it on my lap on the bed. I hadn't considered the issue of Internet service, and I was relieved to find myself on the Seabird Motel Network. I went right to e-mail and found a few disappointing responses from the English medical establishment. By now I wasn't surprised. I tried hard to concentrate, but my eyes shut almost immediately. Half an hour later I was ready to work, which was more than I could say for my companion. Tonto was off in dreamland, alternately snoring and wildly waving his paws. I laughed at him for a bit, and then I remembered Deuce and checked my BlackBerry. Nothing. No messages other than a single missed call from a blocked number and a voice mail, which I retrieved. I was prepared for more anonymous cop bitching when I heard Alice's voice.

18

The message was very short and very serious. No personal chitchat.

"Wendell. Sorry for running out. I need your help, and I must speak with you alone, it's important. I will ring you again at ten, your time. Please, please, don't say anything to your colleagues. Thank you love."

It was pure Alice, no doubt about that. The timbre of her voice was strained and she was all business, except maybe the "thank you love," but I had often heard her use the term addressing patients, so it was more likely habit than bond. She was out of the country. We already knew that, or at least we knew she had left via JFK and was in a different time zone. Whatever was going on, I worried for her safety and contemplated calling Deuce. It was probably the right thing to do. In the end, common sense—or maybe lack of common sense—convinced me to hear her out before calling in the cavalry.

The day finished in blue and gold and finally red. There was the beginning of a chill in the air, and the lack of humidity made the colors and shapes in the sky crisp and clear. There were no neighbors to be seen, and the slab porch was a great place to enjoy the early evening. I sat on one of the Adirondack chairs and took it all in. The seat was deeply angled and all slats, and after twenty minutes I got uncomfortable and antsy. I fed Tonto, freshened his water, and let him out to cruise the dunes and do his thing. He was back like a boomerang in less time than it took me to use the toilet, pull on a sweater, wash up, and run my fingers through my hair. I was hungry and anxious to fill up and get back for the call. I opened the door and Tonto was out in a flash and waiting at the car. That wasn't the plan, but if he wanted to sit in the car in a parking lot while I ate, it was his problem.

Deuce hadn't called and I didn't call him. I would wait to hear what Alice had to say first. Errors of omission don't feel as rotten as lies, and I didn't want to lie to Deuce. In the fading light it took all of five minutes to find the business district of Montauk and the direction of the harbor. Montauk had changed a lot over the last few years. I was amazed at the super-hip vibes everywhere. Not much was left of the fishing village I remembered. It was another couple of minutes before I was parked in the very quiet lot of a large lobster restaurant that I visited every decade or so. The place was as empty as the parking lot, and I got a nice welcome. A single at a waterside table for four would never happen in season. I ordered a dry Belvedere martini and a large bottle of bubble water.

I listened in on the bits and pieces of the few conversations around me until the frosty silver bullet arrived. I savored a sip, complimented the waitress, and ordered steamers, a boiled lobster, and a baked potato. I even took a chance on corn. That was a mistake. The first bite reminded me that the season was over. If it hadn't been yellow, I might have been hard pressed to identify it. The rest of the meal went down well. The waitress was more than cute and visited my table a bit more than necessary. The place was pretty empty, and she had plenty of time to flirt while I finished my coffee. I enjoyed the moment but let it pass.

I managed not to check my BlackBerry during dinner, but I was anxious to see what was going on. Back in the car with Tonto, I endured the obligatory doggy licks while managing to scan three texts. Two from Deuce and one from Rodriguez. It was nine fifteen.

At precisely ten my cell phone rang. It displayed an unknown number, which didn't surprise me. I had been stretched out on the bed, on top of the throw, and was lost in thought. I bolted up to a sitting position and put the phone to my ear.

"Hello."

"Wendell?" she asked, as if unsure that she recognized my voice. "It's me. Are you alone?"

"Yes. Where are you?"

"Wendell, there's a lot going on that you don't know about."

"That's for damned sure."

"Don't be angry."

Don't be angry! That threw me over the edge. I lost my self-control and let Alice know that I felt she was screwing me over.

"You haven't been straight with me about anything. Everything about you has been bullshit. Don't bother making nice. Just tell me what the hell has been going on. Whatever you're in the middle of, spell it out right now. Just don't backpedal and jerk me around." Then I was quiet for a few seconds. In the quiet, I realized that I had been shouting. The silence was jarring.

"Can I rely on you not to repeat what I'm about to tell you?"

"No, you fucking well cannot."

Alice was silent. When she spoke again, she was forceful, her manner formal and official. I got the message.

"Wendell, the drug smuggling and the murders are not really about drugs. That's the least of it. This is about terrorism. The details are still unclear to us, but the operation is being run by known terrorist cells in the Arabian Peninsula and the UK."

"Who is us? Who are you?"

"Wendell, I work for an antiterrorism unit of the British Secret Intelligence Service, and this is our business." Jesus. I didn't know whether to laugh or salute, and I still had no idea who I had been sleeping with for the last few months.

"MI6? James Bond? Give me a fucking break."

"Hardly James Bond, but yes, MI6. There's a lot to talk about. I would like to do it face-to-face and as soon as possible."

"Sweetheart, it is very unlikely that you will get back into the country. The NYPD, the feds, and the customs people have you on the BOLO list. Your pretty face is everywhere. They'll pick you up the minute you step off the plane."

"I don't think you understand. This is my world. I will be wherever you wish to meet. You needn't worry about me."

I was no longer sure I was worrying about her. "This is a big mistake . . . big mistake. You should call our authorities, clear your name, and let them help you with whatever needs to be done. I won't be of any use to you." I felt like I was talking to Farzan again.

"Unfortunately, I can't do that. Not now."

Very much against my better judgment I agreed to meet Alice the following evening. There was never any doubt that I would, and she knew it. I'd read enough detective novels to insist on a public meeting place. Alice suggested I pick her up outside the Ritz-Carlton hotel in Battery Park at seven Sunday evening. As I thought it through, that wasn't what I considered public, but at least I would be able to check out the circumstances. Whatever her level of criminal activity, the idea did not strike fear in my heart, and I agreed. The entire conversation lasted less than two minutes, and, of course, I didn't know much more then than I had before the call. What I did know was I had to avoid Deuce for the next twenty-four hours.

There wouldn't be a damned thing going on at the tip of Manhattan on a Sunday night other than a little hotel activity, and I remembered that the entrance was as visible as the steps of the Lincoln Memorial. She was either confident that I wouldn't set her up or had some plan for monitoring the scene. As far as I was concerned, there was little chance of being grabbed; the one-eighty view of the entrance would protect me. I could look for first sign of anything irregular and take off before they were on me. I thought about it a little more, then tried to push the whole thing into some recess of my mind and get some sleep.

Autumn is definitely a magical time on Eastern Long Island. Relief from crowds and traffic may be the least of it. Skies are clear, days are warm, and the evenings cool enough for sweaters. It was one of those nights that demanded to be enjoyed. I struggled a bit to jimmy the windows open in the hermetically sealed room. In a few seconds the ocean breeze lifted the curtains and blew the musty smell out of the room, replacing it with a wonderful salinity. I pulled the covers down, tossed one of the crummy foam pillows across the bed, settled my head onto the other, and reached for an old Charles McCarry novel I had been looking forward to reading. It never happened.

I woke up at first light, snuggled between the still-unopened book and a snoring dog. Not quite the romantic seaside weekend I had envisioned, but I was clear-headed and rested. I had nothing to do for the day but duck Deuce and try to figure Alice's angle. The first proved far easier than the second. Deuce called at nine and left a "call me" message. By midafternoon it became "Where the hell are you? Call me." That was it. He was likely parading around in shorts and an extra, extra-large T-shirt, surrounded by kids and laughing like one of them. That's who he is, and it won me over years ago. Deuce had a reputation as a hard-ass, as tough as he looked.

The first time we met off-duty, it was at his home to plan a retirement party for Tony Rocco. Lieutenant Tony was Deuce's mentor and the son of an old family friend of my dad's, so we were obvious candidates. The idea of drinking beer and hearing war stories before noon on a Saturday left me cold. Spending an hour with the notorious Lieutenant Secondi left me more than cold. He answered the door with a remarkably well-behaved four-year-old on his shoulders. The child sat there happily for the better part of half an hour. He smiled and fidgeted a bit, but with none of the fist-throwing hostility tolerated by so many parents. Deuce kissed the boy's leg whenever he spoke, occasionally mussed his hair, and periodically trotted over to the play-room and checked the howling group, who were having more fun than I could dig out of my own childhood memo-ries. We planned our party, had coffee, and talked about childhood. I didn't want to leave. Since then, Deuce and I have become friends. We have different lives and different styles, but we respect and like each other and have fun to-gether. I think we trust each other, but now I was pressing the issue.

Sunday morning meant not shaving, for the Black fam-ily. My dad taught us—my brother, Billy, and me—the joy of a day off, and when I didn't have to work on Sundays, I joined the club. Nothing to do with the three-day beard thing so fashionable with young guys trying to look cool. The Black family men weren't cool. For us, it was just a day of freedom when we didn't have to pull and scrape. We are easy men to please.

Tonto and I enjoyed an early run on the beach, and I was showered and in East Hampton by ten. For a town that was unlivable six weeks ago, it was strangely pastoral. I understood what drew people out here years ago. I attached the leash to Tonto's collar, which he didn't seem to mind, and tied him to an empty bench. There were a couple of people with the same idea, and it took almost ten minutes to get a coffee and half dozen powdered doughnuts. Health food. It was only a couple of times a year . . . what the hell. Tonto was out of his mind by the time I set up the newspaper, napkins, coffee, and rolled back the top of the brown paper sack already transparent with grease. I refused to think of what the doughnuts had been floating in just five minutes earlier, but they were warm and fragrant. Tonto drenched the pavement with saliva by the time he got his first hit. Once he realized he was in the game, he calmed down. He was one funny-looking pooch, sneezing from the powdered sugar on his nose and licking at it wildly. It had been a lovely, natural weekend, and I really gave no thought to what would happen tonight.

19

I found a pair of dark gray pants just back from the dry cleaner and got a fresh blue oxford shirt from the drawer. With shined loafers and a tan sport coat, I looked pretty good. Running my fingers through my hair, I realized this was not a first date . . . or any date. I had taken the hook big-time. Not only was I being worked, I was working myself as well. I tried to shake it off and laughed. I put the gray dress pants back on the hanger, threw a corduroy sport coat over the jeans I had worn all day, and changed to the clean shirt. I checked my pockets, then went to the little safe in the bedroom closet for the Beretta. I hadn't had it out in months. Mostly I use it to qualify. It wasn't part of my job, but I had a carry permit that was legal and up to date. I clipped the holster behind my right hip and tried to get comfortable. I felt like a fool, carrying to meet my girl-friend—or, rather, the person who used to be my girlfriend—but I would have been an even greater fool going bare.

I left home at six p.m. I figured it wouldn't take more than twenty-five minutes to cross the park, run down West

Street, swing around the Battery, and get into place near the hotel. By six thirty I was on Little West Street, parked south of the hotel entrance by the row of young trees that would someday soften the feel of the area. The hotel entrance was up a short, wide, stone staircase leading to dark glass doors. Uniformed hotel employees were wheeling luggage to two SUVs with Pennsylvania plates, filled with exhausted-looking families heading home after a sightseeing weekend. An occasional businessman pulled a small wheeled case up the stairs, but generally it was quiet. I had a good view of the hotel entrance, and I settled in to wait. Anyone who was interested could make me immediately. I wasn't hiding. I wanted distance between myself and whoever was approaching. Time to think and react, and maybe take off. I wasn't a cop on a stakeout. No coffee, no cigarettes, not even a bottle to pee in. I was just a nervous guy taking precautions. I chose a playlist of old rock music and had the steady company of Rod Stewart and Bob Seeger. I kept the volume low, but the driving beat helped keep me alert. Maybe not so alert during the periods when I was singing along, but not dozing.

The only women I had seen so far were holding children by the hand or in their arms. By ten of seven there was no sign of Alice; nor was there anyone loitering outside or sitting in any of the parked cars. The only repeat faces were the bellhops and parking valet, and they never even noticed me. I tried to scan the hotel windows. It wasn't fully dark yet, and the east side of the building was in the shade of the quickly setting sun. Lights were on in a few of the windows, but the angle made it difficult to make out what was going on behind the tinted glass. There were curtains moving in one of the lit rooms, and I rolled down my window to get a better look. Someone was looking out, then backing away from the window. Repeating the process every minute or so. I could have kicked myself for not bringing binoculars, as I strained to catch sight of the observer. Just then there was a loud rap on the passenger window. I swung quickly toward the sound, slamming my head on the top of the door as I pulled in, just as I saw Alice smiling at me through the glass.

"Shit," I shouted, and grabbed my head with my left hand. "Shit." I watched Alice pulling on the door handle and making an impatient, funny face at me. I tried to unlock the doors, but in the over-engineered BMW the lock release is lost in the maze on the dash, and it took a few seconds to get it done.

"Lucky it wasn't an emergency."

"You scared the hell out of me."

"Sorry," she said, but she clearly wasn't sorry. In fact, she was laughing. I looked at her angrily, and then gradually started to laugh as well.

"Not funny. My head is killing me." With that, I started massaging the lump that was growing by the second.

"Want me to kiss it?"

"I want you to talk to me." I had managed to regain my dignity and tried to be serious, but Alice had won round one. I ran the window up and turned to her. She looked great. The fading light danced off her eyes, her blond hair was pulled back and tied. She was wearing jeans and a fine, thin sweater of wool or cashmere. She could have been any good-looking, upscale New York woman. She was composed and businesslike. I wasn't.

"Do you want to talk in the room? It would be more comfortable," she said. When I didn't jump at the offer, she added, "Are you afraid I'll seduce you, or do you think my associates are waiting to take you prisoner?"

"No, I . . . I don't know what I think. I'm in a bad position even talking to you. I can't do anything but hear you out. We can take it from there. Your turn." I stared into her remarkable blue eyes. Her gaze was intense, even if there were lines at the outside of her eyes and her smile said otherwise. I felt I could look through her eyes, into her head, and see nothing.

"Okay, then. Shall we sit right here? It's a nice, quiet place and no one will bother us." She smiled more broadly.

"Fine by me. Talk."

"Where would you like me to start?"

"Start with who the hell you are." Despite my best efforts, I had raised my voice. It got her attention, but she made no comment. She was thinking. I'm sure she rehearsed her piece, but she wasn't about to blurt it out. This was her show and she was going to direct the flow. There were a million questions I wanted to ask, and I almost jumped into the silence several times. The tension in the air was jogged up a notch by the time Alice got around to starting her story.

"My name is Alison Withers . . ."

"Is that your real name?" I interrupted.

"If you will be gentleman enough! Yes, my given name, my Christian name, is truly Alison." Now I was confused, too. I always forgot which was which. Did they give you the surname, or did they give you the Christian name, and why didn't they just call it like it was and avoid the confusion. I held my tongue, and actually lost my concentration for a fleeting moment and almost smiled. "My surname is Withers. Alison Withers. I am a plastic surgeon, and I work for the Secret Intelligence Service, the Firm, MI6, the equivalent of your CIA. Don't interrupt." She must have seen the incredulous look on my face as I was about to spit out the first of many questions. "You know what they are, but you need to believe that's what I do, how I got back into the country. How I got out of the UK and through your customs. We, like your people, are practiced in these things. It's what we do."

I noticed she didn't say anything about working with the CIA or being invited back into the country.

"We have been close to this cell for almost a year, but something went off and they started killing people. We believe it was to silence those individuals. And we believe they now have to push up their schedule before either they or we are ready."

"Ready for what? They've been successfully smuggling heroin across our borders for quite a while, it seems."

"It may seem that way, Wendell, but this is a terrorist operation—it's not about drug traffic."

"Nonsense." I shook my head. "There seems to be no evidence for that."

"Sadly, you are very wrong. First, let me tell you why this isn't about drugs. The heroin that came through Kennedy was the good stuff. China White. What's the value of one mule clearing customs? What do you think?" For the first time I realized I had no idea of the magnitude of what we had seen of the smuggling operation. Nobody mentioned it. Not Rodriguez or Griffin, or even Deuce. I never even thought to ask. I shrugged.

"A lot, I would guess."

"Well, let me save you the trouble of guessing. A unit of China White is seven hundred grams, a bit under two pounds in weight. Trading is done in half-unit bricks. The bricks are five by four by two inches. A brick is worth about $2,000 in Afghanistan, about $3,000 on the Pakistani side of the border, $8,000 by the time it gets to Turkey, and $40–50,000 by the time it gets here. One breast implant filled with China White is worth $25,000 to the distributor. Two implants, $50,000 before it's cut and hits the street. A lot of money, but small-time, considering the logistics, the risk, and the fact that the trunk of a car can be lined with a hundred bricks, worth $5,000,000. It can be covered and concealed, and easily driven across the border from Canada or Mexico."

"Jesus. So why take a chance with compromised plastic surgeons who might get a touch of conscience, and multiple mules?"

"Exactly. That's why we are convinced that it is not a drug-running operation."

"We? Who's we?"

"I just told you, MI6."

"Right. James Bond." I wasn't buying the MI6 stuff.

"You have to take this seriously. A lot of people are in danger."

"How's that?"

"Wendell, don't be angry because I disappeared. I was doing my job. We are on the same side. I promise."

"I am angry, and I feel used. Whatever your part in this scheme, at least one person was murdered—maybe two, if you count the missing surgeon. Three, if you count the overdose on the plane. So far you're playing James Bond and explaining nothing."

"Except why this is not a drug operation, which is at the heart of the matter." Alice, or Alison, reached across the center console, grasped my hand, and locked her translucent agate eyes on mine. That might have worked at another time. I stared back and said, "I need more information. Now."

Alice withdrew her hand and sat back in the seat. She looked vacantly over my head and I snapped around, expecting to find someone behind me, and reached for the Beretta at my hip. Alice grabbed my wrist with her right hand before I could bring it up. She was stronger than I expected. "No, no, no. No need for that. There's no one behind you. Relax. Look around. It's just us. I promise."

I did have a good look around. The night was fully dark now, but the street was well lit and there was not a soul around us. I relaxed a bit. "Sorry. Now, get to it, please."

"I think the purpose of the heroin-filled implants was to test our recognition systems at airport security scanning stations. They are pretty much up to speed on installations in the UK, as in most other European countries. We have had a reasonable experience reviewing stored images. The images give a clear view of layers and objects beneath clothing, and clearly recognize breast implants. Better than body searches on the same individual. Implants read as dense foreign bodies on the chest wall. Implants filled with heroin read a little denser than silicone gel, but a lot more radiation is necessary to differentiate between the two substances. One of the issues of the scanning program is to limit radiation exposure. There's been a good deal of fuss about that already, and the level of emission is not going to be increased. So, mostly, they look almost the same. Knowing that a powder-filled implant looks like a gel-filled one offers the traffickers a lot of latitude." She stopped for a breath and I jumped in.

"But you already said it was a dangerous and inefficient method for drug trade."

"Yes, definitely a bad choice for smuggling heroin into the country. Not so dumb for smuggling anthrax."

20

I wasn't ready for that. "Anthrax?" *My voice must have* sounded high-pitched, at least it did to me, and I'm sure my face registered the confusion I felt.

"Correct. Anthrax or something with similar properties, whatever that might be. Same consistency, a fine white powder, and safely stored unless the implant bursts or is opened. There are enough anthrax spores in two implants to kill hundreds of thousands of people. Maybe millions."

"Is that what they are trying to do? Shit. How do you know that?"

"Well, I don't really know it, but I think it's so. It's the only thing that makes sense." Her moment of doubt seemed real, and I began to listen with a bit less hostility. "Our people have had a local cell with bioterror capabilities on our radar since shortly after the London Underground bombings in 2005. We got really serious then. We began to coordinate with the EU and the U.S., and names came up that cross-linked with money sources in the Middle East. Not at all like our homegrown radical Islam suicide bombers. For God's sake, one of ours lived in Leeds and worked in a fish-and-chip shop. This is different. These people have money and move freely across continents. They contribute to radical groups and, in at least one case, have a proven al-Qaeda connection.

"We got sucked into this drug business after two drug dog hits at Gatwick and Heathrow. Both of these guys were British Muslims with loose ties to some of the same crews. But one of them had grown up with one of the Underground bombers, the one loosely associated with al-Zawahiri. That was a red flag, a big one. Exporting heroin to finance terrorism isn't exactly new. It has kept the Taliban going for years. But the scale is grander, and that money usually stays in Afghanistan or gets shipped out to buy arms, but it's pretty much local stuff. Al-Qaeda is different. They have strong financial support from the oil countries and radical Islam supporters everywhere, even lots who don't follow the word but sympathize with the tune. That's pretty much common knowledge. This was a new twist— heroin traffic to the West with an al-Qaeda connection, that's how I got involved."

That was when she lost me. "Why you? What al-Qaeda connection?"

"Al-Zawahiri. I was recruited by the Firm right out of college. I had been toying with the idea of medicine, but just toying with it. I wanted to travel and give it a good think. My uncle, my father's eldest brother, who had been with the Firm for decades, suggested it might help me do both. I traveled for that year . . . mostly to the Middle East and Africa but also the States. I went home for medical school, did surgery here and there, wherever there was a good fellowship. The usual stuff. And I did the occasional odd job for the Firm on the side. Nothing dangerous, not even very interesting, but it kept me in touch. I finished my plastic surgery training in Canada, then hit some of the hot spots, keeping my eyes open and reporting more regularly. It was a good cover. I learned tradecraft and became pretty good at my side job. When this thing started two years ago, the first thought was that I was the right fit, being a plastic surgeon. The traffic pattern was Middle East to the UK to the U.S., and it seemed easy for me to cover this side of the pond. Then things got hot." She was very casual about her provenance, which surprised me. But I was getting accustomed to being surprised.

"Do they want you telling me this stuff? I thought it was top secret. CIA field people never admit what everybody suspects."

She smiled. "Good point. It is the Secret Intelligence Service, after all, and this is where it gets a little sticky. As I told you on the telephone, I need your help, so I'm giving it to you straight."

Alice went on and mostly I listened. I asked questions when I had to but tried not to interrupt. She told a good story. Her people, MI6—the Firm, she called it—had been exchanging information with the CIA and Homeland Security since the first shipment was followed through Kennedy. It became a jurisdiction issue when the FBI got involved. Homeland passed the drug stuff off to the FBI and the DEA, the CIA was pushed out of the loop, and in the end only the DEA was interested. The NYPD wasn't in the game until I took the wrong airplane and had the bad judgment to try to help a passenger in distress. Rodriguez and company got all hot and bothered, and then Farzan's murder put it in our laps. The international agencies hadn't considered that it might be a terrorism case, and now the turf war had greater implications. If something really bad happened while they jockeyed for position, it would really hit the fan.

"So call a meeting," I said. "Get the director of the New York office of the FBI to lay the problem on the commissioner. If New York is the target, he has to know immediately." She made a face and wiggled her nose like that smelled bad.

"Can't do it. I haven't been quite able to sell the anthrax angle. My boss thinks this remains a simple drug case until proven otherwise, which I haven't done."

"What do the feds think?"

"I . . . I haven't discussed it with them."

"So let me be sure I understand this," I said. "You are in this alone? That's crazy."

"No. Not alone. We are all involved in the case, but apparently I'm the only person who has reached what I believe is the proper conclusion. I believe the drug runs were testing airport capabilities before shipping anthrax."

"And what happened to the drugs?" I asked.

Alison hesitated before answering. "I guess they go to the street to finance part of the operation. I don't really know."

"But that doesn't just happen. It's like any other business; there are layers of intermediaries before it gets to the user. A bunch of Islamic fundamentalists won't go unnoticed."

"I don't know what they do with the heroin. That's the past. Clear your mind. Think anthrax. I am serious." And she looked quite stern making that little speech. I backed off for the moment.

"Okay, forget the heroin. Say you're right. Why go to all the trouble shipping anthrax through airports where there actually is some security? The borders can be breached easily by car or truck or shipping container—you just made that point—so why airports?"

"I'm not sure, but it's not for lack of knowing a better way, and it's not random." Alice exhaled noisily and shook her head. Suddenly she looked tired. "I'm just so sure of this. It galls me that those idiots don't get it. We should come down on every name we know, redact the leaders if necessary, and find out where the anthrax is coming from, and more to the point, find out where it's meant to go before it arrives."

I was tired of sitting in the car. It was going on two hours for me, and I wasn't convinced that we were looking at the apocalypse, so I gingerly changed the subject.

"Can we have a bite to eat while we continue our discussion?" I asked. Not only was I fidgety, but I felt like a target sitting in a parked car in that weird, deserted part of town. I still had lots of questions. At the top of my list was the role Farzan and Tahm Tahani played in this scheme. And what changed to make them enough of a liability to require eliminating them. What happened to the heroin that made it through U.S. Customs? Was it sold? And to whom? Who was watching the chain, and why weren't they watching Farzan and Tahm? Who were THEY, and what did THEY have over Tahm to make him cooperate and apparently stop cooperating? Who killed them and what did it accomplish? I was unable to get past the drug smuggling to concentrate on the bigger picture. It still didn't make sense to me, but it hadn't taken much to make me believe that Alice was one of the good guys. I wondered if that was a mistake. I kept calculating the options but kept my doubts to myself.

I cranked up the BMW and swung around onto West Street. Traffic was light, and we made it to Forty-second Street in eleven minutes. It could have been faster, but I got caught at three lights on the trip uptown. It was quiet in the car. Both of us were immersed in our thoughts, and I hadn't even cued my iPod. It amazed me that Alice felt comfortable cruising the city while every law enforcement agency in town was looking for her. But I didn't know what that should suggest. Stupid and reckless came to mind. She most definitely was not the former, and I never before considered her the latter. Some things just are.

I broke the silence by suggesting a Japanese restaurant in Midtown under the flag of hiding in plain sight. We had been there together in the past. It was one of the few decent sushi places open on Sunday, and it offered the added ben-

efit of an exclusively Japanese crowd with very little English in the air. Sunday evening driving in New York is
eerie. No traffic, easy parking, and quick commutes. Cross-
ing half the length of Manhattan south to north and west
to east had taken a total of twenty minutes, which were
spent mostly in silence. After all that talking, I was happily
mute. I found a legal parking place on East Forty-ninth
Street, just across from the restaurant. Most of the cars
parked around us were SUVs with Jersey plates. Japanese
families in town for Sunday dinner.

Finally, my curiosity got the best of me. "Alice," I said,
"why aren't you worried about being picked up? Have you
gotten a free pass?" Alice had already opened her door and
was about to step out of the car. She pulled her leg in,
closed the door, and looked across at me.

"If I'm stripping myself naked in front of you, perhaps
you should start calling me by my true name, Alison. And
no, no free pass," she continued. "My superiors know I'm
back here. They sent me here. But they have not shared my
whereabouts or my suspicions with your agencies. Much as
we all cooperate, I have never announced myself as Her
Majesty's asset in the United States. If it came down to it,
my superiors would own up, but for now, they seem to
think I can do more outside the system."

"So, all these guys looking for you have no idea you're
anything but a doctor who is not who she said she was.
Who is somehow connected to the dead men, and who, for
some reason, beat it out of town. Brilliant. What's your
plan, Sherlock?"

21

Eight thirty on a Sunday night, and the place was buzzing.
The petite hostess kept us waiting briefly in a tiny foyer
with a blond-wood lectern, well out of sight of the dining
room. We stood uncomfortably in the passageway until
two Japanese families carrying innumerable sleeping children made their way to the exit. We were led to a table in
the corner of the dining room, well removed from street
windows and other diners. It was probably the worst table
in the house, and fine for us. Talk from the tables around us
was barely audible, and there was every reason to believe
that our conversation would be private as well.

I got right down to it, but each time Alison tried to answer one of my questions, a waitress appeared. Alison
would stop speaking abruptly and smile blankly. Ordinarily I would have laughed, but this time it didn't seem funny.
During the forced silences, water glasses were filled, and
boxes of dry, cold sake and plasticized menus were placed
neatly in front of us. We continued to smile stupidly and
remained quiet until the waitress returned to take our
order. Alison looked even better in the brightly lit restau-

rant than she had in the car. Her face looked unstressed, her eyes sparkled, and she even wore a touch of fresh lipstick, which I hadn't registered before. Even the smile worked. She couldn't have looked more casual or carefree.

I ordered for both of us. Fresh tofu, lots of sushi, and a couple of cut rolls. It was plenty of food, too much food, but as I was contemplating the order, my hunger got the best of me. For the moment I forgot everything swirling around us and enjoyed the company, the drink, and mostly the thought of eating. Then I figured it was time to ruin the moment.

"Why did you disappear after Tahm Tahani went missing?" I asked, in what I thought was a neutral, dispassionate manner.

"Do you mean, did I kill him? The answer is, I am not even sure he is dead. Are you? So no, I did not kill Tahani. And while you're at it, what about Farzan? Do you want to know if I killed him?" Her words were neither sharp nor as contentious as the phrasing might imply, but she sounded a bit disappointed.

"That would help clear the air. You're going to have to answer that one for my friends from Homicide, so you might as well practice on me." I switched on the bullshit detector and waited. After so many years of "the dog ate my homework" from malingering cops, I knew the signs. Avoiding eye contact and changes in breathing rhythm were a dead giveaway, but I didn't expect to see them. I was looking for subtle changes. Alice . . . Alison was a pro, and I teed up for a contest. I needn't have.

"I was working when Farzan was killed. You know that. And I was called back to London when Tahani went missing." The time line was reasonable, if anything in this mess could be called reasonable.

"How did you find out everyone has been looking for Tahani?"

"Oh, come on, Wendell, we're in the business. Your guys told my guys. That's when they realized they couldn't leave me in the mix. Too difficult to explain without declaring myself. It seemed to make sense to pull me out and think it through."

"So, what do you need from me?" The nature of our relationship had changed precipitously, at least for the moment, and my question was businesslike. So was her answer.

"We think the details of the murders will help direct us to the players, or at least confirm who we think they are. If you could get that information, we could begin to move on them without sounding alarms and scaring them back into their holes. Having everyone in the mix is a recipe for disaster."

"This isn't *High Noon*. The marshal can't hack this one alone."

Alison looked blank. Totally. She could not make any sense of what I had said.

"It's a cowboy movie from the fifties. Gary Cooper is the marshal. And he is forced to take on the bad guys alone." She nodded and said, "It's not that way, Wendell. The Firm is pouring resources into this. We are simply being prudent about avoiding leaks." Alison was every bit as sure of herself as an MI6 person-spy as she was as a plastic surgeon. Precise, rational, and quite certain that her way was the right way.

"What about our intelligence services, the United States?"

"We are in continuous contact. We have the same goal. Though, in truth, I don't feel they are taking the threat seriously enough."

"Come on. Homeland Security has a $68 billion budget. This is what they do. There must be some reason they don't seem to take this as seriously as you."

Alison shook her head. "Any organization that large is automatically crippled by the bureaucratic logjam. As soon as they focus, they will be all over this. We just need to get them to focus. Too much is at stake to simply allow them to be proven wrong. 'I told you so' doesn't count for much." True, but I wasn't comforted.

"Wouldn't talking to them be the most expedient way to accomplish that?"

"Apparently our people have tried . . . are trying. Just think about it."

I promised to think about it. That was an understatement. I wouldn't be thinking about anything else. I was about to list the reasons for my obvious reluctance when she raised her right palm in front of my face and interrupted.

"Shhh. I know what you're thinking. I need your decision in the morning. Just promise you won't tell anyone about this conversation."

I had to think about that as well.

"I promise," I said.

I handed the waitress my AmEx card before the check was presented and waited for the paperwork. I added 20 percent to what seemed to be an arbitrary number and scribbled my name. I took Alison's hand as she slipped out of the banquette, we shared a smile, and she held on to me as we headed for the street.

22

The street was quiet. The big, glass office tower on the south side, where the car was parked, was dark, and the usually bustling sidewalk at the side entrance to Saks Fifth Avenue, on the north side, next-door to the restaurant, was deserted. We crossed casually at mid-block and walked directly to the car. I beeped the remote unlocking mechanism and handed Alison off at the passenger door. She slipped into her seat and beamed the first melting smile of the evening at me. I stopped long enough to lock onto her eyes, then walked around the front of the car and dipped to enter.

I remember only a flash of light followed by an explosive crack, and a million splinters of glass pricking my skin. I think I heard the noise fill the night only after my hands went to my face. It was too quick to be sure. There was shock but no pain, and I felt only the warm ooze between my fingers. Alison shouted something and pulled me down. A big car sped by and a series of muzzle flashes lit the street. Huge cobwebs grew around each bullet hole in the safety glass of the destroyed windscreen, and by the time I finally exhaled, I was aware of sitting on a bed of glass. I saw nothing more than orange and red, and the pain made me throw my hands at my eyes.

"Don't do that," Alison shouted. She pulled my hands from my face and held them forcibly by the wrists. "You may have glass in your eyes. Keep your eyes closed and don't touch. I'm going to come around." She released my wrists and I did as I was told.

"Who the hell was that?" Her voice came from my left. Alison had come around the car and was leading me from the driver's seat.

"Sit in the back. We have to get out of here."

I dropped onto the rear seat and blindly swept away the few shards I felt. "We have to call this in. Where did the shots come from?"

"It was a dark-colored full-size SUV. American, and it's long gone. We can't call it in. The last thing we need is to spend the night answering stupid questions. Give me the key."

"It's up front somewhere. I had it in my hand when the shooting started. Don't worry about it; the car will run as long as it's in here someplace."

"Shit." I could feel her bouncing around in the seat. "Damn, that hurts. Okay, I've got it."

She fidgeted in the seat some more and swore under her breath. Then, in one motion, she started the car and spun out of the parking space. I remember glancing at the empty street just before the roof fell in, so I wasn't shocked by Alison's rapid moves. I didn't dare open my eyes. The pain was excruciating, and I couldn't risk dragging the glass fragments across my cornea. Gently holding my lids shut brought some relief, or at least didn't make the pain worse. But even the slightest eye movements created waves of unbearable piercing sensations as the glass bits were pressed between my eyes and the inside of my lids. I sat still and stared rigidly at the inside of my closed eyes. Tears ran down my cheeks, stinging the little lacerations studding my skin. Every bounce and jerk was torture.

"Alison, we better get me to the hospital. Head over to East Sixty-eighth Street. We can be at New York Presbyterian in five minutes."

"Not smart, Wendell. I'll deal with it at your place."

"Shit, Alison, this isn't funny. Screw your fucking intrigue. I need to get to a hospital."

"No you don't. I know it hurts, but I can deal with this easily, and we can avoid unnecessary questions and the police."

"Jesus."

We were in my garage after the longest ten minutes of my life. Bumping over New York City streets was a traumatic enough experience without an eye full of broken glass. The garage ramp was east of the building on Sixty-fourth Street. The garage was quiet. Alison came around the car, helped me out, and led me gently, like an aged relative, to the passenger elevator. I stood there with my eyes glued shut. She drove the car down to the attendant. I heard some buzzing of conversation between them, but it was out of range. Alison returned to me and I handed her the keys as we waited for the elevator. We managed to get to my door without incident, and she worked the locks to the tune of Tonto circling and yelping. When the door finally opened, he could not be denied. He surveyed the scene, and his happiness quickly turned solicitous. He rubbed against my leg and let me think I was petting him. The reality was quite the reverse. Once we were inside the apartment, we headed directly to the bathroom. Tonto planted himself on the threshold and watched everything. Alison sat me on the toilet and lifted my chin. I dreaded having to open my eyes.

"Where do you keep your emergency kit?"

"On the shelf in my closet. The attaché case."

"Attaché case? Oh, right. I haven't heard the term since my father left the Foreign Service. Righto, I'll be back in a flash."

"Back in a flash. Now we're even. I haven't heard that term since my uncle Ben went out for the newspaper and never showed up again."

"Sounds like you're feeling better." I wasn't.

Alison was gone for what felt like an eternity. And then she returned. The sound of the old leather case smacking down on the sink counter was easy enough to identify, even before she snapped the clasps open. She rummaged around and set some things on the countertop. I imagined the plastic vial of tetracaine, a boat of gauze, and I definitely heard a metal instrument, which I expected to be forceps. This wasn't going to be fun.

"Okay, now, I'm going to gently open your left eye, love. You hold the right one shut. We need to get it numb so I can work."

With that, she pinched the skin of my left upper lid between her left thumb and index finger and pulled it off the globe of my eye. There was a pop as the suction released, or I may have imagined it. Sensations and sounds were more acute than usual. "Here we go now. A bit of burning."

That was an understatement. The searing lasted for eight seconds, by my count, then the pain in my eye abruptly subsided. The relief was substantial as the local anesthetic worked its magic. She repeated the process in the right eye after cautioning me, once again, not to blink. I would have been insulted if the urge to open my eyes or rub them hadn't been so great She held my left lid off the eye with what she told me was a forceps and a Q-tip and made unintelligible, clucking sounds as she worked. After another eternity, she said, "Not so bad. One shard that stuck through the upper lid caused a small, superficial corneal laceration at two o'clock. Nothing else here. I'm going to put some bacitracin in and patch it before we look at the right."

I felt nothing. The endorphins were raging, and the rest of scratches and punctures were very distant and not bothersome.

Alison repeated the process on the right eye and found only a few small lacerations of the lid and one ugly one in the lashes. It took only a moment for her to put a single fine-silk suture into that one; it wasn't worth injecting with anesthetic. The others required nothing more than re-moval of the glass splinters. She didn't patch the right eye, so I could see.

"Thank you."

"Very welcome, indeed."

"I'll see my ophthalmologist in the morning."

"No need for that," Alison snapped back. "I know what I'm doing." Before I could defend my position and explain that I trusted her but thought an ophthalmologist should have a look, she added, "And we do not want to answer any questions."

"You don't. I have nothing to hide."

Alison raised her eyebrows and looked at me question-ingly. "Sure you do. Harboring a fugitive, for one, and not reporting a shooting incident, for another. Not the stuff your superiors will look kindly upon."

Alison must have expected me to go under with her. There was no other way. It would be begging reality to expect to show up with a patched eye and not elicit questions. I didn't bother saying so, but my plan was to go to the oph-thalmologist, then to the job. After that I'd find the right ears for my story.

We spent the next half hour shaking out our clothing and picking glass splinters like a pair of chimps grooming each other. When we seemed to be finished, Alison wiped the floor down with wet paper-toweling. She volunteered to walk Tonto. He went willingly, looking back only once to see whether I was joining the party.

When Alison returned, we showered. Separately. We still hadn't had a substantive conversation about the shooting. I assumed it had been an attempt on Alison's life. I figured she had come to the same conclusion.

"What do you think that was all about? You don't even know who's involved in this . . . so why should someone want you dead? Does it make any sense to you?" It made no sense to me. None of this made any sense to me. How I got from being a Good Samaritan on an airplane to a bystander in a drive-by shooting was difficult to compute. I figured Alison was a lot closer to the answers, and she was definitely not telling me the whole story. The vision in my unpatched eye was blurred with ointment, and I tried focusing on the ceiling while I pondered the situation and waited for Alison to answer. And then I heard her gently snoring.

23

The first light nudged me from sleep at a little after six. I had been too tired to pull the shades. Actually, too disoriented by the events of the evening to even think about it. I felt like I had been through a meat grinder. I couldn't shift positions without wincing. Like Leonard Cohen says, "I ache in the places where I used to play." With some effort, I turned to Alison, or to the place where she had been when I fell asleep.

The pent-up anxiety was getting the best of me, and I angrily whispered through my teeth, "What the fuck is wrong with her," but very soon I was enveloped by great relief at being alone. Being free of her theories, the urgency, and the catastrophic implications allowed for a momentary respite, which I savored. I happily dug my head into the sand, even though I knew it wasn't going to last. My eye was still patched, and I stayed put until almost seven, when I felt a need for music. I had gotten out of the habit of awakening with radio, and the invasive idiocy of television in the early morning vanished with my former wife. I love music. The depth of my technical ability to reproduce it was limited to managing the Sonos music system all over the apartment. It had been installed against my will by a cop from the Nineteenth, who had a semi-high-tech moonlighting business, and thought he owed me for overseeing his ruptured appendix and slow recovery. The truth is, I feel really cool being a step ahead of all the other blockheads my age.

It was definitely a Mozart morning. Actually, most mornings are. I scrolled through the library and settled at *Le Nozze de Figaro*, as I knew I would. The perfect choice. All about lying and subterfuge, but at least it had comic proportions and great music. When the Metropolitan Opera Orchestra struck up the overture, all was well with the world. I was too sore to exercise, so I sat quietly on the edge of the bed for a short while before I stumbled into the bathroom to relieve myself. At least the plumbing worked. When I glanced over at the mirror, a one-eyed monster stared back and gave me a start. My face was covered with scratches and dried blood and was swollen, like a pumpkin with an eye patch. Even the good eye was puffy, but it didn't hurt. I splashed water on my face, preparing to shave. The stinging put an end to that folly, and I settled for gently cleaning away the bloody crusts with warm water. The wash may not have made me look any better, but I felt as if I did. That was half the battle. The scruffy look would have to do for the next few days. I changed the makeshift eye patch for a clean, dry one, taking care not to open the injured eye. A corneal scratch usually heals in a day, but this one may have been deeper. I planned to be cautious, and the first order of business was a professional opinion.

After showering, I dressed in gray pants, blue shirt, dark blue tie, and the soft tweed sport coat that had become part of my uniform. It was about as casual and understated as any in a college professor's closet, which helped deny its custom-tailored cashmere heritage. I made coffee, toasted a bagel that was well beyond its sell-by date, disguised it with too much butter, and shared it with Tonto, who hadn't left my side. He was unusually quiet and mindful of me, and he only came to life when I filled his bowls. Even the morning walk was at a slower, more mature pace. By the time we returned, it was eight thirty, and I had done all I could to postpone the inevitable.

My car was a goner for the time being, and I made a mental note to get it over to BMW before the day was out. Having no interest in being stared at on the subway or standing on the street flagging taxis, I figured a car service would be best for the immediate future. The cell phone in my jacket pocket began vibrating before I could pull it out to make the call.

"Hello."

"Dr. Black, this is Lieutenant Secondi, remember me?"

"Right, Deuce, you were on top of my list. We have a lot to talk about."

I fell into a soft chair, got comfortable, and told Deuce everything. He was not happy. He asked a lot of questions and was very skeptical of Alison's story, and of Alison in general, calling her "a person of interest at the very least." On the plus side, he seemed to believe that I wasn't holding back, but he didn't come out and say it. His response to my tale was something like "Are you a fucking moron, or what? You're a member of the department. You're on the job and you make nice with a suspect in two murders. You're fucked, bro, fucked." And that was the nice part. He allowed his anger to ramp up, and he read me the riot act. When the smoke cleared, we agreed to meet at the coffee shop for lunch.

With my day planned around meeting Deuce, I called Mrs. Black to tell her I wouldn't be in until the afternoon. She was cold and quiet, and I knew I had put her in an unpleasant position.

"I'm really sorry, but I'm having an eye problem and I need to have it checked out. Apologize to the other guys for me and have the sick ones come back at two."

"What happened to your eye? Can you see?" Her concern relieved me, and finessed her disapproval.

"I have a corneal laceration and the eye's swollen shut. See you later." Indeed.

My ophthalmologist bought the automobile accident story. Why shouldn't he? The patch had to stay on for another day. Damage was minor and not permanent, and the eye was anesthetized again and painless; I was out on the street in half an hour. The autumn sun was nearly overhead, and walking south on Park Avenue was pleasant. The old apartment buildings on both sides of the grand avenue helped retain the heat generated by the steam pipes in the underground world of New York City so the planted cover of the subterranean railroad tracks beneath the center island continued to look more like summer than fall. I enjoyed seeing it with my one eye.

New York is the only American city where people still walk. Like the rest of them, I had a cell phone to my ear. Everyone walks and talks. People have stopped noticing one another on the street. Pedestrians at crossings are blindly oblivious to danger and walk and talk and text. Try it. You automatically become one of them. I called the BMW dealer and arranged for the car to be picked up from the garage, called the garage and gave them a heads-up, and tried Alison's cell. She didn't answer. I hadn't expected her to, and I left a message for her to call me. By Fifty-seventh Street, my interest in walking had waned, but it was too early to meet Deuce. I grabbed a cab and headed downtown to kill some time and think about things. The only conclusion I came to was that I wanted no part of the clandestine activities of my former lover. I planned to make that clear to Deuce and, when the occasion arose, Alison.

24

Deuce had already finished a cup of black coffee when I ar-
rived. He took up a lot of the booth and stood out like the
Statue of Liberty in the harbor. His loud check sport coat
did nothing to camouflage his presence. Maybe that was
the idea. Doris greeted me before he did, and I sat. It took
him a while to acknowledge me, but then he smiled and we
were friends again.

"Where is she, Wendell?"

"No idea." Deuce raised his eyebrows and tightened his
lips.

"Really, I have no idea. She took off this morning and
hasn't answered her phone."

"That's no surprise. We have her cell number, too, and
whether she's with us or against us, we can trace the phone
as long as the battery is in place. Has she answered that
number since she took a powder the first time?"

"No."

"Right?"

"So?"

"So she's wise to cop tricks. She's either one of us or one of them." Not exactly a conclusion.

"Anything new on the dead guys?"

"Nah." Deuce shrugged his big shoulders. "Well, maybe. Rodriguez got a line on another surgeon tied into, or at least an acquaintance of, those two. Fancy Persian family, and he disappeared, too. No body yet, but he vanished."

"Wow."

"Wow is right. By the way, you need to come up to MTN for an official visit. Too many open issues." That was a conversation stopper. Then Deuce softened the blow by telling me it was simply to make a statement. I know too much not to be leery of that, but I trusted Deuce enough not to ask whether I needed a lawyer. I considered it but figured he would have been insulted. Anyway, I hadn't done anything wrong . . . other than not rushing forward with information about Alison, and the shooting. Deuce must have seen the surprise on my face.

"Not reporting an attempted murder doesn't look good for a department member. Neither does withholding information."

"I just told you . . ."

"Don't bullshit me, doc."

I agreed to meet Rodriguez and a detective from Homicide at Midtown North at five. I wasn't looking forward to it.

"Have you talked to the feds?" I asked.

"No. Not unless I have to."

Institutionalized animosity dies hard. The relationship between the federal agencies—particularly the FBI—and the NYPD has always been "town-gown," the NYPD being the local yokels. Special agents are college-educated, well-dressed, and well-funded, and have an extremely high opinion of themselves. My cousin Harold, who had been an FBI lawyer, said the only thing they could catch was a cold. The NYPD brass subscribes to that point of view, but you'd never think it hearing the feds talk. Cops see them as self-important, holier than thou, condescending, ineffective glory-grabbers. Cops believe most crimes are solved on the street level, and the bureau has no street sense. So it's hard for them to embrace working together when they feel patronized. Who knows what the feds think.

"You have to contact them," I said. "Use your connections at the bureau. Get the line on Alison. Find out if she's MI6. Find out what the hell she's doing." I may have sounded a little hysterical when I meant to sound forceful, but I pressed on. "If there's a big terror angle, someone over there should know about it. Everyone should be concerned; it can't be a secret."

"Calm down. Obviously someone has to look into that. Maybe not me, but we need to find out who we're dealing with, otherwise we're gonna get bitten on the ass. You do what you have to do; I'll get on this." After that, there wasn't all that much to say. I made a few runs at small talk, but my heart wasn't in it. We ate in silence.

Deuce left half of the second half of his turkey club sandwich on the plate when he pushed it away. I had never seen that before. I couldn't bring myself to chew and had settled on pea soup. It was pretty good, but I lost interest quickly. Neither of us had coffee. I paid the check and we went out in silence. I never saw Rodriguez at the counter.

The reception at the office ran from horror to laughter. The normal folks were solicitous and curious, but the doctors knew a minor injury when they saw one and had fun ragging on me about my swollen face and eye patch. Everyone bought the auto accident story. I told Mrs. Black the truth. She shook her head from side to side more than she really needed to, in either disbelief or contempt for my stupidity. I didn't ask which. As quickly as I could, I closed the door to my office and separated myself from the questions. I wanted to call around for information about the missing surgeon, but I didn't know his name, and asking blind questions was meddling in things that were not meant to be my business. For lack of anyone else to call, and for no good reason, I tried Alison. Before I could leave a message, my BlackBerry beeped an urgent signal from the news services. I scrolled down to a message that originated from Reuters.

"A top U.S. security official warned Europe today that it faced a serious terror threat. The U.S. official stated that British and German terror cells allied with al-Qaeda were plotting an attack, which would most likely take place in the United States or Great Britain. The information is linked to seven German militants killed by drone attacks in Pakistan, on Monday. In France, police arrested twelve men in a village near Avignon, and charged them with possession of unspecified terror-related devices and two Kalashnikov automatic weapons. Information in a confiscated cellular phone led British police to an address in Manchester where two British citizens of Pakistani origin were arrested and charged with possession of equipment to produce weapons for terrorist purposes."

The alert wasn't very different from dozens of news pieces since 9/11, and I read it through, but with my newly found sensitivity to the issue, I didn't delete it.

Festivities at Midtown North were no surprise. Another drab room, an ugly, rectangular table surrounded by four tired-looking guys in plain clothes thumbing through incident pads and manila folders. At the head of the table was the seat reserved for the guest of honor. It faced a heavy door with a metal mesh–covered window. The door clicked shut and locked loudly. The seating arrangement wasn't haphazard. The interviewee was meant to be intimidated. It was laughable . . . unless you had nothing to laugh about. I was the guest of honor. Rodriguez was confrontational, as expected, and the Homicide detectives were quietly professional. They pressured me on Alison's whereabouts, which I honestly denied any knowledge of. They asked how I came to be "involved" with the victims, and why I hadn't reported my meeting with Alison earlier. I handled the first two easily, but I was surprised that Deuce had handed me over on the Alison business. Then I figured he didn't consider it a hanging offense, and I wrote my defense off as romantic stupidity.

I felt generally good about the interview, except, of course, for Rodriguez's barely disguised hostility. But he did nothing to move the needle in the room, and there were no judgments or admonishments at the conclusion.

"Thanks for your help, Dr. Black. Sorry to have to drag you over here," said Detective Sergeant Richard Able, standing away from the table and clearly speaking to Rodriguez. I appreciated the gesture and shook hands all around.

I went home, did the dog stuff, hung my jacket and tie on the doorknob, poured myself some Jameson's, and set the heavy glass on the desk to the right of the computer. I flipped the lid of the laptop open and began a search for recent terror alerts. Scanning Google entries is great fun once you learn to let it flow. Follow the clues to the next entry. It was amazing to see how little the stories varied from paper to paper. The writing in the *New York Times* was better than most, maybe a little looser than it had been, but light-years better than the rest. The information was the same filler from the same source. No gaggle of reporters pecking one another for exclusives. No sources were cited other than government briefings and the occasional statements from Beltway sources, who didn't know very much themselves. Few reporters spoke Arabic, Farsi, or Bahasa Indonesia, and fewer still had contacts within the rigid world of Islamic terrorists. Most of the stuff had been beaten to death by the twenty-four-hour news cycle on television, but the detail in press reports gave color and perspective to the stories. I was searching for links between drugs, terrorism, the UK, Iran, Saudi Arabia, and Pakistan, and Afghanistan. In other words, a needle in a haystack.

I needed to start with what I knew. A transsexual male with heroin-filled breast implants flew from Heathrow to New York and died for his trouble. A British surgeon of Iranian ancestry was murdered in New York. His associate in London, who very likely inserted the heroin-filled implants, had gone missing. A third Iranian-born surgeon seemed to be missing as well. They were dropping like flies.

Low-backscatter X-ray scanning machines have been in operation at Heathrow for three years. The high-energy, low-penetration emissions penetrate clothing but not the body, unlike traditional diagnostic X-rays, so the scanner sees what is under the clothing, not what is inside the body. It also cannot penetrate certain kinds of plastic. A whole body wrapped in plastic would be impenetrable by this technique. Breast implants show up as breast implants. Differences in filling cannot be made by the scanner. A gun tucked into a bra lights up like a scoreboard. Anything beneath clothing is plain as day, especially body parts, and lots of people don't like it. The person reading the scan is meant to be distant from the passenger. Body parts, faces, and names are protected, and the images immediately deleted. Not everyone believes that. The Bollywood movie star Shahrukh Khan found himself badgered to autograph copies of a scan made as he passed through Heathrow, which clearly showed his naked body, dangly bits and all. So much for protecting the identity of the innocent.

If Alison was correct in linking the heroin-smuggling to terrorist activities, and if future anthrax-filled implants would elude the scanners at Heathrow, why kill the doctors? Obviously, to keep them quiet. But Farzan seemed to have had no clue about the big picture. He was alarmed about the drug smuggling and his friend Tahm. Would drug smugglers kill to protect an imaginative but minor route? Maybe this was a conversation I needed to have with Rodriguez.

25

In a week's time Rodriguez had come to occupy a central
role in my life. He was listed in my cell phone only as Rodriguez. No first name. For better or worse, he was the Rodriguez in my life. I hesitated before pressing the call button,
nervous about how to start the conversation. Like the mem-
orable opening words of the first call to a new woman.
Stumble through the call and you feel like a jerk for longer
than makes sense. Obviously Rodriguez had me spooked.

"Rodriguez."

"This is Wendell Black. Dr. Black."

"What can I do for you?"

"I was trying to figure out why the drug smugglers
killed Byarshan. What did they gain?"

"Hey, he's your friend. Why ask me?"

"Cut the shit. You know I have nothing to do with this."

"Really." He went over the same ground for the second
time in as many hours. I held the phone away from my ear
and made an exasperated face for my imaginary audience.
Why was I bothering with this jerk?

"You know that just isn't so. I'm trying to help here."

"Doctor, if you want to help, stop bullshitting me. You're trying to get me to believe that by coincidence you happen to know everyone involved in a drug-smuggling ring and one, possibly two murders. I've been doing this for thirteen years. It don't work that way. You're in this up to your ears. Look at it, doc, you make what, a buck, buck and a quarter. Another buck and a half moonlighting. Live pretty high for a guy paying 57 percent in taxes. Fancy condo, $90,000 car, expensive trips, fancy girlfriends. Where's the dough come from, doc? Get my point? I don't know what you got on the lieutenant, but I'm not buying." He cleared his throat twice. "Now, unless you want to make a statement, I gotta go."

Well, fuck you, too.

I would be lying if I didn't admit I never saw that coming. I was looking straight ahead and he slipped in an uppercut. This guy really believes I'm one of the bad guys. I was too shaken to protest, and as I thought about it, I was too pissed to defend myself. Let's see where he takes that line of reasoning. I was not going to help him. If he went as far as requesting my tax returns, he wouldn't get them casually. Let the prick make a formal request through his captain and the DA. The truth is, William Black and Co. takes good care of me. I do what I love and earn my way to a decent living. Dad was well educated by the first-generation route. City College, Columbia Law School, night jobs, day jobs, and scholarships. He left the law at twenty-nine, when Grandpa died. Someone had to run William Black, and he was it. I never heard him complain about the grind of borrowing big money to buy expensive presses just to keep up. Selling printing in a cutthroat environment and forever scrapping with the unions was not a walk in the park. He had been a young legal star, hoping to stay on at Columbia, until he couldn't. Whatever he did, he did well. That was the lesson of his life. As William Black prospered, so did our family. Dad died in 1990, just as the digital world sandbagged the printing trades. No one foresaw the wholesale change in the way information was to be transmitted, including Dad. Profits shrunk and business contracted. He had already taken care of us in his trusts. We were safe, but it would have saddened him to see two generations of work circle the drain. Lucky for him, he didn't have to. That job fell to my brother-in-law, which may be part of the reason I avoid spending time with my sister in LA. Families are complicated, and money doesn't make it any easier.

I tossed and turned through the night, unable to solve the puzzle, which I didn't really expect to do. Nor could I clear it away and lull myself to sleep. I snuck a look at the clock at two and gave up. One of the liberating things about living alone was being able to switch on the lights or the television without disturbing your partner. Turning over in bed had been enough to wake my ex and foul her mood for the day. This little bit of freedom was much appreciated. What I didn't appreciate was staring at the tube in the middle of the night. I surfed around once and, on the second turn, lucked onto a newsmagazine doing a piece on terrorist cells in Yemen. It was mostly old footage slapped together with a bunch of talking heads and a very British narrator, but it got my attention. What we were looking at was a pattern that was a perfect fit with al-Qaeda of the Arabian Peninsula, AQAP. Their routine had evolved to using mundane objects filled with powerful explosives undetectable by scanning. Why not breast implants, why not anthrax? It was exactly what Alison had postulated, but I had been infected enough by her disinformation to become resistant.

Yemen is a raw and beautiful place. It is poorly developed and known to be corrupt despite having the only semi-republican-style government in the Arab states, if you don't count Egypt. Yemen has been strongly pro-American and hadn't been on the terror map prior to the attack on the USS *Cole* in the port of Aden in 2000. After that, and then 9/11, we leaned on them hard and virtually destroyed al-Qaeda in Yemen. The terrorists seemed down for the count until 2006, when twenty-three of their operatives escaped from a Yemeni prison. Their leader, Nasser al-Wahishi vowed to rebuild al-Qaeda from the ashes, and he was as good as his word. The radical Yemeni-American cleric Anwar al-Awlaki helped the cause, and so did the dozens of Yemeni al-Qaeda members released from Guantanamo right back to their Yemeni cell. Al-Awlaki was in the thick of it. He is the guy that counseled an American major—a psychiatrist, no less—to kill thirteen comrades at Fort Hood. It was a big blow for them. But what struck me most of all was their schemes to export terror in the form of explosives concealed in other items. They had gotten more sophisticated, and they were smart. They stuck to what they knew. In the fall of 2010, good fieldwork interrupted the shipment of explosive copier cartridges destined for Chicago in the airports of Dubai and Britain. The bombs were meant to explode and take down the planes carrying them. It was close. They had become increasingly good at the task, and it was becoming their trademark. That wasn't the way Pakistani cells operated. We were looking at an AQAP operation. Then we took al-Awlaki and a couple of his deputies out. Maybe this is retribution. Let us know they hadn't gone away.

I wanted to share my epiphany, but it was four a.m.—still too early for Secret Service boys, who didn't hit the gym till near daylight.

26

When Thomas Lee bought 2,800 Northern Virginia acres from Lord Fairfax, he named his new farm Langley, after his ancestral home in England. By 1953, Allen Dulles, brother of Secretary of State John Foster Dulles and director of the CIA, had convinced the government to buy a large piece of the property to house his new security service, the Central Intelligence Agency, successor to the OSS of the war years. Langley was it. Harrison and Abramowitz, the architects of the United Nations building, were chosen for the project, which is interesting to ponder. Pretty soon the original buildings were outgrown. The facility expanded, and a visitors center and museum were added to the campus.

There are other offices now and other buildings, and Langley is almost as well known as the Pentagon, and nearly as dysfunctional. Layers of employees separate the people of the clandestine services from the Disneyland atmosphere. My contact with the agency has been zero, but I knew that an important clandestine activities office at 7 World Trade Center was destroyed during the terrorist attack. There are other, more visible offices in the city, but talking to them is a joke. I called a couple of numbers in New York and finally Langley. I learned more than I needed to about job opportunities and visitor hours, but I couldn't get through to the proper desk to get a line on Alison's story. Far too secret. It was as though their real operations were meant to be unspoken. I knew I could do it the hard way as a walk-in, but I didn't have days of interrogation to waste. The way I saw it, the country might not have much time to waste, either.

I thought about the bureau and Homeland—they were real possibilities—but going in cold is like walking up to a film star at a party and expecting to be taken seriously. I needed an introduction, a name. Of course, I had a name; I had a handful of them. I had visions of the World Trade Center. Ten years had flown by. Anyone that had been down there would never forget it. We worked, and cried, and dug, and prayed together, and then we went our separate ways. But Cranford had become a deputy director of the Secret Service, and the Secret Service is part of Homeland. He had to be a big-time insider now. He's my man. I hit the address book on my phone and found his e-mail address and phone number. It was a 202 area code, and I hoped it was his cell.

I punched send, got out of my chair, and paced while the connection cranked up. Tonto figured we were going out, and actually got off the chair. He yawned and hopped back to his spot as soon as he heard me begin a voice message.

My cell phone rang less than five minutes later.

"Wendell, Dell Cranford. How are you, man?"

"Dell, thanks for getting back to me so fast. I'm well. Don't need a Secret Service detail. How's the family, and how are you, big shot?"

Cranford laughed. "Fine. We're all fine. Liz and the kids are all at college. She's getting her master's, the twins are joining fraternities and drinking, and I'm working my ass off. All is right with our world. What gives with you? You didn't call at six thirty to say hello, not after . . . what is it, maybe five or six years?"

"I was busy."

"Asshole."

"What about you? Government doesn't have phones?"

"I have a family and a president to take care of."

"Truce."

Dell and I met an hour and thirty-two minutes after the second tower was hit on 9/11. At the time, he was assistant to the agent in charge of the New York region of the bureau. We arrived after the firefighters and the first wave of responders were trapped in the rubble. The second tower had fallen, and the air was thick as oatmeal and it was impossible to breathe. The grit between your teeth and on your tongue—sand, cement, ash—made your mouth dry and speaking a chore. It was impossible to speak anyway. Getting there was swimming upstream against the masses of people fleeing the area for safety and air. Traffic stood still. Cops were trying to unravel every intersection, and sirens were lost in an orchestra of untuned wails. We drove on the sidewalks when we had to and inched our way downtown. People scattered but understood and encouraged us. Our unmarked car was filled with doctors and nurses. We had a dome light, a siren, and a honking horn. Just like everyone else, it seemed.

Dell may have been a big wheel in the bureau, but he was as lost as the rest of us in the horror of the scene. Surgical masks helped against the toxic air and the stench of burning flesh, and everyone stopped by the ambulances and first-aid stations for a few seconds of oxygen. I was outside the NYPD command center when Dell stumbled by, coughing and unable to catch his breath. He was red-faced, choking, and drenched in perspiration beneath the dark nylon jacket emblazoned with FBI. I led him into one of the makeshift triage areas, washed out his eyes, and hooked him up to an oxygen mask until he could calm down and assume a normal color. He didn't say a word as I talked him down. Then he made a gesture at the carnage around us and began to cry. And then I did. When we regained control, we chatted for a while, then went about our jobs. Twelve hours later he came by to thank me, and we took a dinner break together. We shared a lot that week and hung out quite a bit as things settled down. Something happened to all of us that day, that week, and we were able to talk about things that men rarely discussed. I knew less about Dell's professional life than I did about his parents, his marriage, and how his religion sustained his morality and his faith in humanity. No man ever told me about his dreams before. The intrusion of . . . I guess it was mortality, and the unthinkable destruction gave us both a sense of proportion and an understanding of how little space we occupied in the big scheme. I spilled my guts out as well. We stayed in pretty close touch for a while, until he moved back to D.C., but there was a special bond between us.

"Dell, I'm sniffing around the edge of something that I think could be very serious," I said, and then I told him the story as concisely as I could, trying not to forget any details or color the events with my interpretation. I found myself switching ears, cranking my neck, moving the cell phone between my fingers, and generally fidgeting uncomfortably. I pressed on. Dell listened, interrupted a few times when I wasn't quite clear, and heard me out.

"Okay. This is out of my jurisdiction, but somebody in our shop may know something. I'm far from being on the inside, but generally speaking, it does smell like a Yemeni al-Qaeda–type operation."

I thought to caution him against spreading the word but stopped myself. I had no reason to keep the lid on anything, and I trusted his judgment. Dell Cranford was about as white-hat, and white-bread, as anyone I knew. And he was smart. He continued. "Our lines of responsibility have blurred a lot. Keeping track of foreign intelligence services, including MI6, was bureau business in the old days; now everybody does a little of everything. Secret Service is under Homeland now, so is ICE and customs. The bureau, the DEA, and Washington Interpol are still at Justice. I'll start here, then I'll try the others. My buds at the bureau are the big cheeses now. Somebody has to know something."

I thanked him and felt much relieved. We were still in the dark, but if anyone could get to the people with answers, it would be Dell Cranford. And since I wasn't dumb enough to make the same mistake twice in as many days, I called Deuce and left the quick version on his voice mail. He didn't know Dell, but I suspected that he would soon enough.

I put my cell phone down on the desk, massaged my neck, got up, and headed to the door. Tonto wasn't convinced of my intentions. He lifted his head above his crossed paws and watched until I reached the door. Then he slithered down from the chair, stretched front and back, and trotted to my side. I always assume he's thinking some wiseass thoughts about my behavior, and it made me smile.

27

I wasn't rested or refreshed. Neither a lousy night's sleep nor my conversation with Dell did anything to calm my hunger. There wasn't much on hand, but I mangled four oranges in the juicer, brewed some strong coffee, and then searched around for something to toast. I settled for another old bagel from the freezer, defrosted it in the microwave, and sliced and toasted it. It was too much work for too little bagel, but with butter and salt it satisfied my craving. I checked my e-mail, looked at the newspaper online—no terrorist attacks—walked Tonto, and headed for the garage.

"No car here, doc. I heard you had an accident or something," the morning attendant answered.

"Oh, man. Sorry, Louis. I forgot."

"Hey, I get it. You got a routine, it's hard to break." He was right. I wheeled around, waved as I turned, and climbed up the ramp. Even when I drove it, I often wondered if the angle of the ramp was steeper than the fifteen-degree max on the treadmill. Fast-walking it, my thighs were burning by the top. I caught a taxi right out front and

was planning my day when my phone rang. It was an unfamiliar 202 number with a lot of zeroes. The main switch-
board of some government agency.

"Wendell, got a minute?" I recognized Dell's voice.

"Hey. I'm in a cab. What have you got?"

"Mucho, my friend, mucho. To begin with, you are on the
money about Alison. They've had her since she showed up
here last year, though her real name may still be in doubt.
You're probably so confused already that her name doesn't
matter. But she's definitely an asset working here. Most of
what we do has been pretty much bilateral. Information-
sharing is our lifeline. We have the same international agen-
das, or at least we're targets of the same enemies. The UK has
a longer history of a sizable Muslim population than we do,
and they're more influenced by the radical cells than Muslims here. Anyway, we trade information on a daily basis,
and apparently the flow is mutual and free and at all levels.
That said, we have assets there, as in every country, and they
do the same. It's the way intelligence services work. We avert
our eyes, so do they. Not only do both sides know it goes
on, but we can usually identify the assets. There's not much
call for us to do real spying on each other. The rules have
changed. We're on the same side on about every significant
issue, and we both find our security challenged by the
same people. We are definitely in this together, and no one
wants to upset a system that works.

"Anyway, your Alison has had no presence at the Farm
or in diplomatic circles down here, but the local office of
the bureau knows her well."

"In D.C.?"

"No, New York. She was in to see them last week. My guys remember her well because what she was doing was out of protocol—and because she was hot."

"I figured. What was she seeing them about?"

"Well, she was going pretty much where you were. Threat. Terrorist cell in the UK. Target in New York. What made no sense was why it didn't come down through channels. Urgent information gets a good look. I mean, if the embassy, or the MI5, or MI6 liaison officer sent us the memo, we would have to give it a hard look, even if it was farfetched. And we would have had to take a position and answer for it."

"You mean to cover your ass."

"Correct."

"So they thought she was blowing smoke?"

"No, not really. It was just that there was no hard evidence, and she was operating out of channels. It was a little freaky."

"Yeah, but this is going down. Two people have died for it, and whatever is going to happen is going to happen soon. Very soon." As I said that, a wave of concern rushed over me as I caught the eyes of the driver locked on mine. He looked away and I glanced at his New York City Taxi and Limousine Commission license, having no idea what nationality he represented. The guilt of lumping the innocent into a large, dirty bag shamed me, but the reality of my fear made me measure my words. Which I should have done under any circumstances.

"And how do you know that?" Dell asked.

"It's obvious. The thing is coming to a head, like a cyst full of pus."

"That's disgusting."

"Doctor talk."

"Gross." He sounded like one of his teenage children.

"Really, Dell, it's now," I said, fairly evenly. The driver had already looked away, aware that his eavesdropping had not gone unnoticed.

"I understand the urgency, but there isn't enough evidence for anything but observation. I can get some people on it today, but it will be investigative, not interventional. No action. That's outside my job description."

"Jesus, Dell."

"Think clearly, man. What do we know? Who are we supposed to arrest? Agents of friendly foreign powers don't act the way Alison did. Her information came from the Firm, yet she was bypassing them. How should we respond to that? Well, let me tell you how we responded. They tried to draw her with the usual 'we will look into it' routine, but she knew it was the brush-off. She probably wasn't surprised when they called the boys in London to check."

"What was their take in London?" I asked, already pretty sure the news would not be well received.

"Good agent, mixed up. Please have her call in when next you see her. No one saw her again. Obviously, she got it."

Dell wasn't going to be a lot of help, at least not at this point. But it was important to get serious people on the job.

I was happy to get out of the taxi, and I tipped my way out of feeling like a bigot. Wondering what had gone through the driver's mind when the address I had given him was buzzing with police cars, barriers, checkpoints, and blue uniforms, I smiled my embarrassment away.

Getting back to routine has its benefits, and the day passed pleasantly, if uninterestingly. Nothing short of apocalypse seemed out of the ordinary anymore. And then Alison called.

28

My conversation with Alison was brief. She didn't need more than a mention of my call to Dell to put it all together and enter the "I can explain everything" mode. She was good. Or it was true. Governments are bureaucracies, and bureaucracies are sometimes slow as glaciers and dumb as stones. This might be one of those times. I was convinced even without hearing the passion in her voice, and we agreed to meet at the end of the day. I was sensitized enough to Alison's outsider status to avoid home, and I scrambled for someplace where observation or listening-in was unlikely. Of course, avoiding scrutiny has its disadvantages. If your cover is blown, there is no talking your way out of it. Avoiding scrutiny invites scrutiny, but hiding in plain sight wasn't an option when an intelligence service, a narcotics cop, and maybe a killing crew had made some assumptions. I only wish I understood what they assumed.

I left work at five and headed uptown. There are lots of hotel bars in New York, mostly full of out-of-towners and businessmen. That's what hotels are about. The bar of the

Carlyle is a loud, upscale version, where quiet conversation is impossible. But it has style. The Bemelmans frescoes that lent the place its name, and the eternal jazz piano, make it unlike any place else in the city, a special experience. The experience was shared with tourists in goofy outfits, drunks, and working girls. But the tearoom, just through the bar, is an oasis. Dark Chinese wallpaper, low banquettes, and seductive lighting make it perennially evening, adult, and inviting. The room is quiet, and the tables are well separated. When I settled in at five twenty-five, the tea crowd had mostly gone and the lovers hadn't yet arrived. Six minutes later, a bathtub-sized, very dry Belvedere martini appeared. I picked the salted macadamias out of the silver bowl of mixed nuts and had a few sips without making a dent in the drink. Alongside the glass was a mini-shaker seated in ice with a partial refill, which could easily render me senseless. I hit the brakes and went back to the nuts. The people in the room were well dressed, and other than a family with two preteen children, the crowd appeared to be locals. My table was too far from the others to catch much of the conversations on either side, which was a good sign. Alison was late. She was a surgeon, and that was unusual. I checked my BlackBerry a couple of times, expecting her excuse for deciding not to show up. She arrived at five forty-five, looking like one of the fashionable Madison Avenue ladies who, until a few minutes ago, had been happily sipping tea and trading gossip around me.

Alison was anything but happy. After a perfunctory kiss on the cheek, she was all business.

"They've been through my things."

"They?"

"Vauxhall Cross, the Firm, who else?"

"Alison, everyone has an eye out for you, not just your masters at the Firm. The NYPD, the smugglers or terrorists or whatever the hell they are, the FBI, the killers, and who knows whoever else. Someone searched your apartment. Is that what you're trying to tell me?"

"Don't be so smart."

"Easy, easy." I held up my hands in capitulation. "There's no reason to be angry. You're agitated, so you're not thinking clearly. That can only make things worse."

"Right. Sorry." Alison saw the waiter approaching and smiled over my shoulder. "I would love a Campari and soda in a tall glass with one ice cube, please."

When the waiter was out of earshot, we resumed. Neither of us knew what the next step should be, but we were damned sure something bad was about to happen. The most frustrating part was the inability to convey urgency to the people who might be able to do something about the situation. I recounted my conversation with Dell, as well as the hardening attitude of Rodriguez. "So, how do we get one of the agencies to act?" I asked.

"We don't. The position of the FBI and Homeland Security is clear. They have no reason to assume imminent threat. The position of my people is confusing. They have information from good sources. The same information that I have, but they have been stonewalling me and treating this as a drug issue, which isn't our area. So off it goes with a long memo and a telephone call to the appropriate drug people in the States. But it doesn't ring true."

"What doesn't ring true?"

"That this is a drug case."

"No, I mean what part of their behavior doesn't ring true? They have the information, but they may be interpreting it differently than you. Is it an honest difference of opinion . . . you might just be wrong . . . or are they hiding something, keeping you out of the loop?"

"That's possible. Shit. That's very possible. If this is as important as we think it is, they may agree and I may be overreaching my need to know. Everything in the intelligence service is separated into silos of knowledge. No one knows the whole story, just their own isolated task. But nothing changed when I reported the shooting. Their response was simply to call me in."

"Right. That wasn't stupid. This may be a small part of a bigger operation, and they don't want to foul it by chasing small potatoes."

"Small potatoes?"

"Come on, you get the picture."

"I do. But they are dead wrong, whatever their reason, for ignoring the facts."

"Maybe they are not ignoring the facts. Maybe we are."

29

Alison couldn't leave New York. Her passports—she wasn't being exactly clear about how many she had—were all official-issue and known to her superiors. She could be stopped at every port of entry or exit. She couldn't stay at her apartment. Someone was interested in it, as evidenced by the look of it that afternoon. They had been there, and they were likely to return as her absence dragged on. That is if they were the same they who tossed it. She couldn't use her credit card, and she couldn't stay at my place, that was for sure. She had gotten me in this up to my neck, and everybody knew where I lived. And there was the issue of whoever had shot at her outside the restaurant. Assuming, as I had, that the target was Alison. Not only could she not stay with me, but it was pretty dumb being seen with her anywhere at all.

What made sense was for me to take a hotel room and install Alison there. There was no reason to assume that my cards or my phone were being monitored—Rodriguez didn't have that level of pull, and no one else thought I was one of the bad guys.

Lots of weird little hotels had been springing up all over Manhattan. Some were conversions, some updates, and some new construction. What they had in common was a young staff dressed in black that had no idea what good service meant. I chose a new one on West Twenty-ninth Street. For obvious reasons, bellhops were virtually extinct in these places, and no one made a gesture toward my empty rolling bag. It was just as well. I would have been embarrassed when it took flight after the first tug. Alison would stuff it with clothes later. Her place was off-limits, and she would have to shop. The bag would be useful as she moved around. It also made me feel like a proper hotel guest. There was a time when one might even have been denied a room without luggage. Nice hotels didn't want to be seen as hot-sheets assignation places. We checked in under my name as Mr. and Mrs. and took the elevator to the tenth floor. The room was painted white. It was large and spare. Some people find polished cement floors, steel tables, and plastic chairs modern. I thought it looked uncomfortable and silly. But, hey, I'm getting old, and I was never that hip anyway.

Alison stood at the doorway and looked around. She poked at the electronic console at the bedside and checked the closet and bathroom. Then she shook her head, said "Okay," and fell onto the bed with her arms spread. She looked out of place stretched out in the stark room in a matronly teatime dress, but that was her style. As the dress rode up on her thighs and she cracked half a smile, she became a pornographic mousy librarian shaking her hair free and lifting her skirt. Alison knew it, and she knew she was not mousy. I was beside her with my hand on the softest part of her thighs and my tongue tracing her lips. She spread her thighs and pressed against my hand.

30

To be perfectly truthful, the idea of playing detective with no authority and no leads was not an inviting prospect. I would have been happy to walk away from the whole thing, but I had already passed Go and couldn't easily undo whatever involvement others perceived. And then there was Alison. It had actually been a lovely couple of hours together. Narcotics and terrorists be damned. Although the subject was never far from our collective conscious, it was kept at bay by anonymity, closed doors, a minibar, and room service.

My plan was either to head home for the evening walk or call the dog-walker. Instead, I was dozing for the second time when my phone woke me. It was Deuce.

"Your boy Tahani showed up."

"Really?"

"Really."

"Sorry, that was dumb, but it surprised me. Dead or alive?"

"Yeah, surprised me, too." Deuce didn't answer my question immediately, and I waited to hear the gory details.

He went on, "I thought our man was permanently disappeared. We got a call from the London Metro Police, who got a call from immigration when he landed in Heathrow. They found a nice room for him and had a long conversation. He was a babe in the woods. Ignorant of everything and shocked at the death of his dear friend Farzan."

"What did he have to say about the mules and the smuggling scheme?"

"Nothing. Knew nothing at all about it. Shocked to hear about it."

"So, we know nothing other than he isn't dead."

"Correct."

"Sounds like a lot of bullshit, Deuce. Tahani is the key. Maybe not exactly the key, but he's someone who might actually know something or know someone who knew something. Either way, someone who understands the bigger picture needs to talk to him. Are you going over there?"

"Are you kidding? This is New York; it's 2013. There's no money for fishing trips. We're feeling the pressure. City only has money to paint bike lanes and pray they don't have to clear the snow. We have to worry about keeping the lights on. This guy is not highest priority, at least when it comes to spending.

"We don't really know that he did anything. Byarshan suggests he might be involved with the heroin boobs business. Byarshan gets dead. Suspicious? Yeah, but Tahani claims he wasn't even in New York at the time and says he can prove it. So where's credible evidence to suspect he did the deed or anything else, and where does that leave us?

And how do I convince the brass to spring for a few thou for me to visit London to talk to some guy who isn't even a suspect? The way these situations are managed now is by e-mail and telephone. They help us; we help them."

"Point taken," I agreed, but we both knew better. As little as Tahani may know, it was definitely more than we did, and he was our only living contact with the events of the last few days. He was the lead we had, and we had to follow it. There was no other next step. I couldn't believe Deuce was giving him a pass. Problem was it was none of my business, except that it was everybody's business. If something awful was about to happen, I'd be damned if I would walk away from it just because a bunch of civil servants, even if they were my friends, refused to take it seriously. I was tempted to pressure Deuce, but he wasn't the sort to succumb to pressure. It got his back up, and that was the last thing I needed. Deuce was a good friend to have.

"So there is no place to go on Byarshan's murder?"

"Right now that's true. We're working with Narcotics on this. They have the best chance of scaring up a lead. They're shaking the trees for every CI in town. Problem is the overlap with the radical Muslim connection. If it's drug trade, narc has the contacts; if it's antiterrorism, the feds have it; and we're at apples and oranges again."

"Narcotics means that asshole Rodriguez?"

"Afraid so."

"Jesus."

"Have a nice day."

I broke the connection without telling Deuce where I was and without him asking.

I gave Alison the short version, but she had already pieced it together. We chatted for a few minutes and came up with the outline of a plan. It was not a very satisfactory plan, but it was all we had. I headed for the door, kissed Alison good-bye, and was lost in thought when I found myself on the street, staring blankly at a guy in a black outfit waving down a taxi I didn't remember requesting.

31

I didn't sleep well. No bad dreams; no dreams at all that I can remember, just turning like a chicken on a spit. Before first light I'd had two cups of coffee and finished packing. I wanted to make arrangements for Tonto and some lame excuses at the office, but normal people were still asleep. Instead, I sent e-mails and was in a cab, heading for the airport, by six. Tonto's minders were reliable, and the fallback systems made it highly unlikely that I'd find the animal cruelty people at my door when I returned. Still, I rattled chains from the cab until someone was awake enough to reassure me. That settled, I was almost able to relax. Reverse commuting has its moments, and we were at the gate at Terminal 4 at Kennedy at six forty-five. The eight a.m. Virgin flight would make Heathrow at eight p.m., and I could be eating at the bar at Le Caprice by nine thirty. I was becoming a regular. I usually splurge in London and stay at Claridge's, where I'd been a lifetime ago, just the week before last. But this wasn't about fun, and time was short. I figured the Stafford, on St. James's Place, would be a nice fallback, since it was a mini-stroll from dinner and very English. The woman in the overdesigned Virgin Atlantic uniform at the desk was efficient, and I was on my way to the lounge in what seemed like less than a minute. I made good use of the time before boarding by stocking up on newspapers and gorging myself at the breakfast buffet. Nothing like a few thousand calories before seven a.m. to bring on sleep.

I called Tahani's office from the lounge. It was just past noon in London, and damned if he didn't take my call. Alison had given me the short course on sniffing him out like a pig after autumn truffles. I was almost disappointed that it was so easy. I dialed his published office number and voilà . . . Mr. Tahm Tahani, plastic surgeon.

It caught me off guard and I was momentarily at a loss for words.

"Yes, Dr. Black, this is Mr. Tahani."

He repeated himself into the silence and I found my voice.

"Good afternoon, Dr. Tahani." Surgeons in England are referred to as mister, as in Mr. Tahani, MD. I never know what is expected of a foreigner and I use doctor, as I would for any physician. "I am with the New York City Police Department. If you can spare some time, I would like to talk to you about the death of Farzan Byarshan." I was balancing the need to play down the doctor part and emphasize the NYPD, but I knew that saying I was a doctor was the best way to get him on the line.

"Of course. What's on your mind?"

"Actually, I would like to discuss this in person. I could come by tomorrow."

"Tomorrow is Saturday—my office is closed."

"Yes, I assumed that. Perhaps we could meet in the morning. I won't take too much of your time."

"Sorry, but I have plans for the day."

"Then we'll have to do it at the Metropolitan Police Headquarters." It seemed worth a try.

"I've spoken with the police. Henceforth, my solicitor will deal with this."

"Something terrible has happened. Like it or not, you are involved. We know all about the implants, the smuggling, and your travel schedule. You can't run away from this. If you'd like to save yourself a lot of trouble, you can start by talking to me. This is going to get very bad, and you need a friend. Believe me, you need me. Farzan was my friend. He told me everything, and then they killed him. We can get you out of there. Help keep you safe."

"You didn't help Farzan," he said. His voice was breaking, and I thought he might cry. I pressed harder.

"The only way out, the only way to stay alive, is to help us. Then we can help you. If not, you're a dead man."

There was quiet, then more of the same, and in the end Tahani grudgingly agreed to see me. I hadn't thought much past that, but I had a six-hour flight to work something out. The plane was crowded with tired-looking, seasoned travelers dragging full-sized carry-on bags through the aisles. I was seated at a window about halfway into an old-fashioned business-class cabin. I tossed my small bag into the overhead, made my apologies to my stylish young seatmate in tight sweater with exposed midsection and sprayed-on jeans. She sprawled across the space and barely looked up from her cell phone to acknowledge my passing. A perfunctory attempt to draw her legs in offered no more room. In my heart of hearts I envisioned a full-body check, knocking her over the armrest. In the absence of physical violence, at the very least a caustic comment on her rudeness. The reality was I squeezed past and said nothing. I made a careful reconnoitering of the opposition. On second glance, she was older than I thought. Smile lines and softening of the jawline put her solidly in her thirties. Still young, but old enough to have better manners. The fierce morning light streaming through the windows onto her heavily painted face made her appear desperate when she could have been elegant. I would avoid making friends.

Studying my neighbor in the relentless, unfiltered, high-altitude sun, I looked around to find my own reflection. The illusion of eternal youth had long ago been dispelled, but I had the urge for a reality check. I was quite comfortable with the gray in my hair, but what did she see? No matter, my neighbor had not yet looked my way. Being over fifty is an odd place when you are healthy and feel young. For the most part, my women friends are age-appropriate, but the first time an eye-catching twenty-five-year-old called me sir, it ruined my day. I thought about that for a moment and laughed at myself. It wasn't very long ago that I was young and at loose ends in my career. I laughed out loud when I realized that "not very long ago" was twenty years. I shook it off, amused, then settled down, looked at the magazine covers, and flipped my iPad open, and began reading the thriller I had downloaded at the airport.

I was on a mission, maybe a fool's errand, but it felt right. I ought to have a plan for my confrontation with Tahani. Falling asleep with the iPad in my lap got me nowhere. By the time I had read a few pages and picked some things off the lunch tray, we were just a couple of hours out. The west-to-east flight always caught a big tail-wind and was very quick, and we touched down before eight p.m.

Not a word had been exchanged with my neighbor throughout the flight. I alternately read and laid out my plan. Once or twice I did manage short naps. I noticed she had looked my way and smiled a couple of times, but she kept her own counsel, didn't drink, and barely glanced at the magazines she had piled on her lap. When she reached for her carry-on in the locker above us, I spoke up.

"Here, let me help you with that."

She smiled. "It's okay. I can do it."

"No, please, I'm just standing here." I smiled back. She actually wasn't unattractive. I lifted the anonymous black case easily and put it in front of her. It was unusually light.

"See. I told you I could handle it. Thanks." With that, she headed for the exit door at the back of business class. Outside passport control, she was met by a pasty-faced young man with close-cropped hair. He was tall and skinny and wore a dark business suit and black cop shoes. They spoke a few words and disappeared through a door marked RESTRICTED ACCESS. He hadn't offered to help with her bag or shown any identification. She looked perfectly comfortable with the situation. I wondered whether she was intentionally seated alongside me. If so, why and by whom. There were too many possibilities. As I watched her, the line of passengers pulling bags and holding passports swarmed around me. They were professional travelers in a hurry, and I was in the way. I got my act together and was soon in a cab on the M4 headed into London for the second time in two weeks.

The M4, an archaic excuse for a highway, was every bit as awful as it was at rush hour on business days. There was some sort of exposition at Earls Court—there always was—and traffic was backed up to hell and gone. All in all, it took more than an hour and a quarter to get to St. James's Place, and it would have been worse if the driver hadn't known how to avoid the rough spots in town.

The first call I made from the cab was to Alison. I scrolled through my address book to find the number of the prepaid cell phone we had bought. The call rang through without an answer or a message. Alison called back within seconds.

"Wendell." I was very happy to hear her voice, even if she was all business, which was obvious in the single word.

"Hi there. Everything all right?"

"Unchanged. Just being cautious about answering the phone." We passed pleasantries about my flight, commiserated about London traffic, but I avoided talking business. London taxis have an efficient intercom system between driver and passenger cabins, and though the light signaling operation was not lit, I didn't want to take a chance.

"Just checking in, call you in a bit."

By the time I was installed in my room, it was well after ten—only five my time, but I was wiped out. I was too tired to go anywhere for dinner beyond the clubby little bar downstairs. A bottle of water, a single malt, and all the salty snacks on the table would have to do. I had two sips of a second drink and headed back to my room.

I called again. Alison answered on the second ring, and we got right into plans for the next morning. I had no idea what to ask Tahani or how to go about interrogating him. To my surprise, Alison claimed ignorance as well. "Wendell, my dear, I have never interrogated anyone in my life. I wouldn't know where to start."

After some laughter, it was clear that I knew more about police procedure than she, most of which rubbed off just from being on the job. Depressing. We roughed out what Tahani might be able to tell us and how to pressure him to let go. I told Alison about my seatmate and her reception at Heathrow. She was interested and asked a few questions that I couldn't answer, mostly about the man who met her and where they left the customs line. Her fear was that MI6 had made me and she had been a tail. My fear was that it was some affiliate of the NYPD or the FBI. Both of which were suspicious of our motives, to say the very least. In the end, we knew no more about mystery woman than when I mentioned her.

I fell into a deep sleep and awoke at first light. My internal alarm clock was clanging away by six a.m. It didn't matter that it was really one a.m., New York time—there was little chance for more sleep. I would catch a few hours later in the day, when I hit the wall. I didn't know if there was a gym in the hotel, but I had packed running shoes, shorts, and a T-shirt, and from the look of the sunrise, it promised to be a beautiful day. I ducked out the alley, past the tail end of the Rothschild Bank, took a right onto St. James's Street, and found my way past St. James's Palace and into Green Park. The park was just waking up. The grass was wet with dew, and the last of the fall flowers were opening to the sun. There were a few other runners enjoying the morning, and we nodded an affirmation of one-upmanship on the rest of the world as we strode past one another. I ran an unfamiliar loop that felt to be about three miles, but I didn't really have a goal. I felt good for the run and was back in my room forty minutes later. I was a little jittery after the episode with my seatmate on the plane and took care to check whether anything in the room had been disturbed. The idea of someone going through my things was a long shot, but not out of the question. These days it was pretty easy to document the layout without relying purely on memory. I pulled my cell phone out of the flapped back pocket of my running shorts and called up the picture of the room I had taken just before leaving. Nothing was out of place. I had even photographed the precise relationship of the items in my carry-on, which lay unzipped on the easel. Everything appeared to be as it had been left. That was all I could infer, but it put me enough at ease to enjoy a long, hot shower. My room-service tray was spartan and arrived exactly twenty minutes after being ordered, as promised. I wondered if the waiter had been loitering outside the door, counting down. The freshly squeezed orange juice was too cold and tasteless to have been recently produced, but the coffee was strong and hot. I diluted it with enough cold milk to make it potable and sipped it with a crusty slice of wheat bread flavored with butter and orange marmalade.

I tossed off the terry robe, got a fresh blue shirt, socks, and boxer shorts from my bag, and dressed in the same trousers and jacket I had worn on the flight over. My necktie was a bit unfashionably wide, I was a little rumpled, and I congratulated myself on the cop-like fashion statement. It was easy to find a cab on the street and avoid sharing my destination with the hotel doorman.

32

Tahani's place was in a posh area off Eaton Square. Very high-end and very uptight. I rang the appropriate bell in the small lobby of what had once been a grand house and was now several flats. Several very elegant flats, I would guess. Tahani buzzed me in and was at the second-floor landing to welcome me. There did not appear to be any staff present. Tahani was courteous, spoke without appreciable accent, well . . . an English accent, but that didn't count. Despite our prior conversation, he did not act pressed for time. I followed him and took in the surroundings. The flat was not chic or overdecorated, or whatever I imagined it would be. The only hint that the occupant was anything other than an upper-class English gentleman came from a few tiny, old-looking Persian paintings. The other pictures in the hall and sitting room included a painting of a regal horse with cropped tail, that could have been a Stubbs, some hunt scenes, and a portrait of a very unattractive old English gent. The furniture matched the art, and I wouldn't have been surprised to see an old duffer in a three-piece pinstripe suit sleeping in a leather club chair. It was that

English. Not quite shabby enough around the edges, but more English than the English, which was often the way with people proud of an adopted culture.

Tahani was slight, maybe five-five or -six, a hundred and thirty, thirty-five pounds. He was dressed for the country, or at least he wore all the gear: corduroys, tan checked field shirt, shooting vest, and paddock boots. When we were facing each other, I reached out to shake his hand, which he offered raised, as if expecting a Victorian kiss. His fingers were delicate, the nails longish and buffed and polished with clear lacquer. I stopped in mid-sentence of introducing myself and stared. His waist, under the vest, was cinched with a wide belt, and the vest itself stood away with what could not have been anything but the tenting from breasts.

My jaw hung open, and I must have looked as stupid as I felt. Tahani savored the moment.

"Dr. Black, you seem surprised. I thought you knew all about us."

I wanted to start asking questions, but Tahani seemed ready to save me the trouble of getting my thoughts together. Every interviewer says not to interrupt when they start talking. Look at them, say nothing. Let the urgent need to fill the silence take over. He invited me to sit on the overstuffed sofa by motioning with his hand, and he took a seat on a cane-and-cherrywood Sheraton chair kitty-corner from me.

"You certainly have fallen into our mess, haven't you? Farzan getting killed panicked me. I promise you, this was completely crazy. He was such a nice man. But what can I do for you? I didn't kill Farzan, you know." I stared at Tahani. I wanted to say that we checked with customs and knew he wasn't in the country, but I said nothing and waited. "So what do you want to ask me? You can have a good look. Maybe that will put you more at ease." With that, he held his vest open and began to pull his shirt out of his pants, and started to stand up.

"Not necessary, doctor, I've seen it before."

"Of course you have." He sat up straight in the hard chair, and it was clear I had lost the moment.

"There is a network smuggling heroin from the Middle East to the United States, through the UK. Breast implants filled with three or four hundred grams of high-quality heroin are implanted in mules, mostly transsexual men—or, rather, transgender men. The implantation has been performed in London and the ex-plantation in New York."

"Ex-plantation is not a word, doctor."

"I stand corrected, but you know what I mean."

"I do."

"We know you are involved, and we need your help." As soon as the words passed my lips, I realized how much like Rodriguez I sounded. I didn't feel good about it; nor did I change course. I listened.

"I know nothing about any illegal activity. I am a British subject. Born in Iran. Educated in Iran and Great Britain, and I remain a dual citizen. My loyalty is entirely British. I would do nothing detrimental to my country."

"Which country?"

"You haven't been listening. Great Britain is my country."

"Yes, I understand, but that is not what I came here to talk about." I proceeded to outline what I thought I knew about his involvement in the smuggling operation, including the recruitment of Asian mules who were virtual slaves in homes in the Arab countries. He nodded occasionally, and let me make my case. "I think the drug-smuggling is only a means to an end. Except, perhaps, for the mules. Have you ever thought about the inefficiency of bringing heroin across borders this way? It's stupid. It's high risk, high cost, for small quantities. Not a good business model." I had resorted to reason instead of intimidation, but apparently I wasn't very good at that either.

"I see." Tahani grimaced. He was not looking at all feminine. "I have nothing to do with any illegal activity."

"Bullshit."

"I may have to ask you to leave my home."

If I didn't push now, I would lose him. "Don't do that," I said. "I came a long way to talk to you. This is your way out. When we finish putting the facts together, the New York police will talk to the Metropolitan police, and MI5, and they will be on you like Velcro until you give it up. This is serious shit. If you're lucky, you'll be back trolling Daneshju Park. More than likely the Revolutionary Council will lock you away until you don't care anymore. Then there are the people that killed Farzan. Throw me out and it's a lose-lose situation for you. Help me and I can help you slip through the cracks."

There is a moment in life when everything hangs in the balance. Is the person behind you on that dark street a threat? How do you act? The warm, forceful spray of arterial blood as a vessel tears loose during surgery, demanding action. What you do next changes life forever. I felt low for bullying him the way I did, but Tahani was now at that juncture. He was there. He had his demons, he had fucked things up miserably, but he wasn't dumb. It didn't take long.

"I understand." And then he began to sob. He had dropped all pretense, and he was very feminine. "What have I done?" It was all the usual stuff. I waited it out. He took two folded tissues from his vest pocket, wiped his eyes, and blew his nose. It was dainty. I was impressed. I felt dirty. I waited.

"I'm ready. What do you want to know?"

It was a good conversation. The implant and smuggling side worked as we thought it had. Tahani did the surgery on the London end. He was furnished with sterile, heroin-filled implants. He was supplied with mules from the population of poor souls willing to do anything to finance their gender-correction surgery. The Iranian connection came from home in the form of threats to Tahani's parents. He had been contacted anonymously by telephone. Conversations were in Farsi. He received the calls on his mobile phone from blocked numbers. London or Tehran, he had no way of knowing. Casual mentions of Tehran weather and the activities of his parents made it clear only that they were under close surveillance. When one of his conversations with his mother was replayed on the phone, it was obvious that at least one side of his conversations was being recorded. From that moment he took his contact seriously.

I asked about the financial aspect of working with the smugglers and said that Farzan had mentioned that Tahani had fallen on hard times.

"Yes, that is true. I was struggling to maintain my life-style here in London and help my family in Iran. I lost a great deal of money in the financial collapse, but I blame myself for being greedy. Doing their bidding paid well and was not very arduous work. Just a few cases a month. Things were so bad that, in truth, I might have done it for the money alone, without the implied threat, but I was never given that choice."

"How did you fill the implant?"

"I had nothing to do with that part."

"So how did it work? Were they factory-pre-sealed, like silicone gel implants, or empty shells meant to be filled with saline?"

"Saline-type, but already filled and sealed."

"And how did you know they were sterile? Were they in the manufacturers' sterile containers?"

Breast implants are supplied to surgeons in sealed boxes in which sealed, sterile, bowl-like containers held the implant. The whole bowl is removed under sterile conditions by the surgeon. A tab is pulled, separating the top from the bowl, and the sterile implant is removed from the sterile container by a sterile-gloved hand. Refilling implants and resealing the container would require access to the manufacturing plant. Filling implants with heroin is another process. It does not lend itself to performance at the time of surgery, as inflating saline-filled implants, but it can easily be done through the same type of filling tube.

"They were in surgical trays wrapped in autoclave paper sealed with tape sterility indicators. I always checked." In this flood of honesty and self-incrimination, the self-serving remark flashed brightly. I guess we all need to feel good about ourselves. Tahani looked away, and I sensed embarrassment.

"Who gave you the trays?"

"The patient always brought them to the clinic on the morning of surgery."

"How were you paid?"

"Same way. Cash wrapped in autoclave paper on the morning of surgery."

"No bank deposits?"

He shook his head. "No."

"When are you scheduled to do the next case?"

"There is nothing on the schedule. I am told a day or two in advance of surgery. Usually it is a message on a Friday for Saturday or Sunday surgery. For obvious reasons I cannot use my own staff, so they provide a very competent Persian nurse. We speak in Farsi at the operating table, but she treats me like an employee, so there is no other conversation."

"Who removes the implants in New York?"

"They never told me, but I have always thought there was a Persian connection."

"But do you know?"

"No. I never asked. It was better that I didn't know, but it was time to leave London."

"Why now?"

"Too much of my life has changed. As you can see." He put his hands under his breasts, lifted them, looked at them, and smiled. "My practice has suffered and I feel too vulnerable here. That's why I went to New York." He was telling me something, but I wasn't sure I got it.

"Farzan told me you disappeared. Is that true?"

"Yes. That is true. I went to Tehran to see my family and from there to France, Cuba, Canada, and New York. I did not want my observers to know I had traveled to America. I came back home because they scheduled another operation."

"Why didn't you just stay in New York?"

"Too many reasons. I had not made arrangements for my family and I needed more money for that."

"When is the operation they called you back to do?"

"This morning."

"Great." The opportunity came out of left field. I had to compute it quickly. "I have to make some calls. Wait for me. This can help us."

"No, Dr. Black, I'm sorry. The operation was this morning before we met."

33

It was coming together quickly. Or maybe coming apart quickly, was more accurate. Too many links in the chain had weakened for the operation to go on much longer. Whatever they were going to do, it would be soon. I needed to get some direction and some help. The time for threats had passed. "Listen to me, Dr. Tahanl. I believe you have been straight with me."

He laughed. "Poor choice of terms, doctor."

He hadn't lost his sense of humor, and I was glad I hadn't either. It was a bond. I put my hand on his shoulder and said, "I will do everything possible to help you, but you have to work with us starting right now. I have to leave. I will call you later to thank you for the coffee . . . which, by the way, you never offered. When I end the call, you will find a secure public phone and call me on this number." I handed him my NYPD card with my cell number. "It's a U.S. number."

I was out on the street seconds later. There was very little automobile traffic, the odd jogger or two, and an elegant

woman in a long fur walking a dog that looked like a relative of the coat. I found a cab waiting on Eaton Square. It
was almost too easy, and my senses were heightened. I did
not use the phone and glanced behind us as unobtrusively
as possible. Everything seemed normal but the accessibility
of the cab. I had the driver drop me at the Ritz on Piccadilly. I walked around to Arlington Street and through the
elegant lobby, glancing around as though I was looking for
someone, and avoiding registration or the hall porter. After
killing enough time for the cab to leave, I slipped out and
walked over to St. James's Street and down to the Stafford.

Back in my room, I took the notepad and pen from the
bedside table and started to make a to-do list. Dell was my
best bet, and I decided to call him first. He was the one
among us with the ability to get forces in motion. Alison
was on the run from the only forces she could possibly
rally, and my own influence was zero.

It was five a.m. on the East Coast. I decided to give Dell
another hour of sleep. There were a lot of scrambled facts to
consider, but it might be critical to intercept the next mule.
The first step of what all the planning and practice runs were
leading to might have been set in motion this morning. This
morning . . . only two hours before my arrival. I was close,
but all I knew was to be on the lookout for a male posing as
a female with recent, potentially lethal, breast implants.

We would have to convince the British authorities to
redefine body search, and that wasn't going to happen, at
least not on the hunch of a New York police surgeon with
no hard evidence. But passenger-profiling could signifi-

cantly narrow the field, and we could bend the rules for a few flights. I had to talk to Tahani again. I scrolled the call log on my phone and hit his number. Tahani answered on the third ring. He hadn't added me to his contact list, which was probably smart, and he didn't recognize the number.

"Dr. Tahani, this is Dr. Black."

Silence.

"Dr. Black, from New York. I called to thank you for the coffee. I'm sorry I couldn't eat, but I am not feeling very well. Speak to you soon."

"Sorry. Yes, of course. You are quite welcome. I shall speak to you soon." I broke the connection before Tahani said anything obvious and waited for his call. He was as good as his word and returned my call within five minutes.

"Sorry I took so long. I had forgotten where call boxes were located. Mobile phones, you know." He was right. I hadn't used a pay phone in years. I'm not sure I even know how much a call costs. I took down the number of the pay phone and returned his call from the mobile.

"*A quick question,* if you don't mind, Dr. Tahani. How long after the operation do the patients fly?"

"Hmm. I am not certain. I expressly forbid it for forty-eight hours; of course, it is probably safe immediately—after recovery, of course."

Shit. That was a very small window. I thanked him and reminded him to feel free to reach me at the number he was using.

I was spinning. If the mule could fly, now he was gone. There were no rules here. No malpractice issues, and surely

no concern for the well-being of the patient, at least not the
one carrying anthrax. Expendable. If they sent out their
own people to be martyrs for the cause, what would they
care for nonbelievers? It didn't matter to the terrorists.
They were vehicles, human pack animals, mules. Some of
them, or at least the one I saw, judging by the signs of prior
implants, had probably made more than one pass. But this
wasn't their game. Just unhappy people clutching at straws
and trying to turn their lives around. Round and around
and around, I thought. It wasn't so easy getting life straight.

I wasted enough time until it was a few minutes after six
in Bethesda, and Dell should have been about to begin his
Saturday morning. He answered after a few rings and must
have had a peek at the screen.

"Wendell, give me a break."

"Sorry, Dell. This is the real thing. Couldn't wait."

I gave him the short version of my conversation with
Tahani and my conclusion. "This is it. I feel it."

"This is what, Wendell?"

"The payoff. The drug shipments were practice runs to
the target. They are going in with the anthrax or neurotox-
ins, or whatever WMDs they packed into those implants,
and New York is the target."

"Slow down, man. You're way ahead of the facts. I agree.
The heroin is a red herring. And yes, something is going
down. But we have no hard information. None. No humint,
no intercepts, nada. What we have is you and a burned
MI6 asset. Tell me how to present those facts. I mean . . . I
have to go pretty high to get action on this. I'd be hanging

out in the breeze. Things are good at home. I'm too young to retire."

"Hey, I get it. I know. But wouldn't you be a sad sack of shit if they poison the water supply or dust Grand Central with anthrax."

"You certainly have a way with words."

"Sorry about that, but I'm serious. We can't look the other way."

I continued beating Dell across the head with suppositions and hypotheses, until he gave in to what he knew he also believed to be a real threat.

"It sounds too much like the real thing to ignore. But if we go for it, we have to do it right. I'm going to take it to the top of Homeland. If I can't get to the secretary, then I'll get to whoever can get to the secretary on a Saturday. There's also ICE and CNE. It might be smart to go there first."

"What is CNE?"

"Right. Counter-Narcotics Enforcement."

"Dell, this isn't about narcotics."

"It is until it isn't. Better to jump in at the top. I hope you can put in a good word for me at the NYPD. I may need a job. Call you back."

That left me with nothing substantive to do. I had to wait. I called Alison but couldn't reach her. It was almost seven in New York, and she was probably still asleep. I didn't want to return to Tahani's flat, but I had more questions. I called and went through the "thank you" routine again, and Tahani returned my call quickly, and in turn I called the pay phone. Our conversation had taken a number of turns, and I probed the few things that seemed promising. Tahani's knowledge of the network beyond his own involvement was negligible, but I was convinced that they must be very well organized on the New York end. They were getting in and out of the airport and disposing of the product, and yet there was not a whisper about this type of trafficking. When organized crime is involved, there are always rumors. It was a business, and the new product had to hit the streets and make waves. Retail dealers were always the weakest link. They were the most exposed and the most willing to trade information for a free ride or to kill competition. It didn't take long for buzz to start. The DEA has known the intimate details of the Mexican and Columbian cartels since they elbowed the Mafia off the streets. But as far as I could tell, our guys hadn't heard a whisper of a new source or different-quality product. It was a closed circle.

"How long have you been working for these people?" I asked.

"Ten months."

"Was anyone else doing the work before you?"

"I don't think so. The system worked smoothly at my end, but it was not really organized in the beginning, like we were inventing it as we went." That wasn't the picture of an organized-crime drug operation. Still, they were awfully confident about getting through customs. Someone in the operation was very sophisticated or very well connected.

I asked some more questions but didn't learn anything worthwhile. Tahani made some noises about his own future. I listened with a sympathetic ear, but I couldn't help him. No matter what I had said, that kind of thing took place much higher up. No question, he crossed the line, but deals do get made and things are allowed to slip by. I reassured him as much as I could, which wasn't very much, and he knew it. There was a sadness about his voice and even in his choice of words. I found myself liking him and feeling sorry for the mess he had gotten himself into.

My return ticket was for Sunday, and I considered changing it and heading home later today. Given the hassle of concierges, phone calls to airlines, and the Byzantine, punishing rules governing last-minute ticket changes, it was simply too damned much trouble for too little gain. I wanted to do something useful. It seemed to make sense to connect with Scotland Yard or MI5 and get the airports covered, only I had absolutely no one to connect with. In New York, that wouldn't get in my way. You always know somebody who knows somebody. It's probably the same here, but much as I love it, I'm a visitor, a tourist. London is not my town. The connections would have to wait for Dell. Maybe, when I reached Alison, she would put me on to someone she trusts at Vauxhall Cross, who might help overcome the inertia. Meanwhile, there was nothing to do but lunch. I didn't need much convincing. As usual, I was starved. I am firmly convinced that anyone in London, with time to spare and a few extra bucks, had no choice but to head out to Hammersmith and the River Café. Simple as that. It might be the best restaurant in the city.

On the long taxi ride out to the restaurant, I began to feel guilty about fiddling with lunch while Rome burned, but what were the options? Marching around Hyde Park Corner in a sandwich board predicting the end of the world wouldn't solve anything, and I was hungry. It took thirty-five minutes to make the trip. The Hammersmith side streets were lined with rows of working-class cottages, which had been gentrified about as far as their modest dimensions would allow. Mid-level BMWs and Mercedes sedans had replaced the Civics and Fords on the street, and even the estate agents' signs were more upscale than they had been a few years ago. The day was drab and drizzling, as it always seemed to be along Thames walk, at least when I'm around, and garden seating at the restaurant was a bad joke. I was glad to shake off and be seated near the blazing fire set midway up the white wall at the end of the restaurant. It wasn't at all cold out, but the fire seemed just right. Everything about the place made it impossible to think of anything but pleasure. The food was just right as well, and I polished off more than half of the modest Brunello I had ordered. I was feeling no pain.

A mini-cab called by the restaurant brought me back to the hotel with the usual fits and starts, but I managed to doze off anyway. Unfolding myself from the backseat of the old Honda made me appreciate real London taxis all the more, but most of the phone service cars at the fringes of town were another class of transportation.

Back in the room, I brushed my teeth and threw some cold water on my face. Dell hadn't called, and I was too antsy to wait patiently. He answered before the phone had a chance for a second ring.

"Expecting somebody important?"

"Yes, I was. Not you, buddy."

"True enough. What's happening?"

"I think we're doing well. The secretary was all over it. Really surprised me. There has been enough chatter about something going down that they were considering raising the alert level. Enough of your story rang true for them to take it seriously."

"Great."

"Hard to think of a genuine terror threat being great, but I know what you mean. Now maybe something will get done. I'm waiting for word from up the chain of command. Get right back to you when I do."

"Is it okay if I tell Alison the news? She was key in all of this."

"I don't see why not." He hesitated for a split second, then continued. "But maybe just hold off until I check with the task-force leader. No need to step on toes so early in the game."

"Right. But get back to me, man. I'm on pins and needles here, and she is on the front line at home. We have to find the mule and break this thing up."

"I get it. Hang on. Be back to you ASAP."

It wasn't entirely clear what we were trying to break up, but I had the overwhelming feeling that something bad was about to happen. Something really bad, and we were all that stood in the way.

34

Alison woke me from a really lovely nap. I must have been doing some serious snoring. My head was cranked forward on two pillows. My chin was on my chest, and half the bedspread was folded back over to keep me warm. I must have been working on an insoluble psycho-dilemma when the phone rang. My neck felt frozen at ninety degrees as I sat up. I patted my pockets for the phone and tried to localize the sound. But it was lost among the bedcovers and had stopped ringing while I scrambled to find it. After orienting myself, I rubbed my eyes and concentrated on the caller ID. It registered an unfamiliar number. By the time I had a sip of water from the bedside bottle, the voice message symbol came on and Alison identified herself. I lay down again and returned her call. She sounded edgy or distant. Or maybe I was too sleepy to know the difference.

Alison listened quietly as I started to run down the day's events. I was about to mention Dell and the feds, when I remembered that he had asked me to hold off. She chimed in with an "uh-huh" or two, probably to show she was still on the line.

"I was thinking that it might make sense for me to head over to Vauxhall Cross."

"Whatever for?"

There she was again, so English. So much more impact than how come or, simply, why.

"They have to know more than they're letting on, and if I get them up to speed, we might learn something important. There is no more time to waste. Who was your contact . . . control, or whatever you call the person running your portfolio?"

"But, Wendell, Marshall won't know anything at all about this. We weren't drug enforcement people. And I couldn't breach protocol and send you in."

"Fuck protocol. This is a crisis. Who is he?"

"Oh, Wendell. You are putting me in a difficult position."

"Difficult position. You are dead smack in the middle of this. You know all the players, and unless I was hallucinating, someone looking for you shot up my car."

"Perhaps they were looking for you."

"Nonsense. I didn't know anything or anybody. You were the target. You must know something that can hurt them. We need to brainstorm with everyone. New information and a fresh point of view can make the case. Let's get on this."

"Okay. Okay. Let me think for a second." During the seconds Alison was pondering, I drifted back to the moment. I heard the tires squeal, the windshield shatter, and maybe I saw the muzzle flashes. But I didn't remember ducking, and I couldn't understand how neither of us had been hit. Amazingly good luck or lousy shooters, or was someone warning us?

"Who was trying to warn us, Alison? Think about it."

"What?"

"Sorry, I was back on Forty-ninth Street, when they shot at us."

"Warning? Why warning? We were almost killed."

"No we weren't. Any half-decent Russian hood or any gangbanger could easily have hit us both and gotten away. Think about it. I could have done a better job."

"I . . . I don't know. Who would do that? It might have been the terrorists. Amateurs."

"Not exactly amateurs. Think about Farzan."

"My God. Poor Farzan. Right. I have to think."

Alison sounded frightened, which is definitely not her natural state. Nor did vulnerability or coy dependence have anything to do with Alison. For me that was part of her allure.

"Let me make a few calls and get back to you."

"Yeah. Okay." But it wasn't okay. "The clock is ticking."

I did what circling was possible in my tiny, over-furnished room and thought it through. I didn't like the way this was going.

I did nothing but wait for people to return my calls. After an unrewarding hour and a bit of dozing, I called Alison. She didn't answer. I wasn't doing very well. I left a short message for her, and then Googled the Secret Intelligence

Service. In England, the Secret Intelligence Service, SIS or, as it has become commonly known, MI6—or the Firm, to insiders—was no longer very secret. In 2010, Sir John Sawers, the director of MI6, emerged from the shadows to offer public interviews on his professional life. It wasn't all that surprising. Few things remained secret in the information age. The British way was not ours. In the U.S., the head of the CIA is appointed by the president, testifies before Congress, and often changes with administrations. The working division heads operate in shadow. The Brits are different. Their spooks and analysts are out of sight like everyone else's. But every once in a while, when it hits the fan, we get a peek inside. Despite a generation of Cold War scandals culminating in the unmasking of the highly placed, upper-class, double agents Guy Burgess and Donald Maclean, and the notorious "third man," Kim Philby, MI6 survived and thrived, and with it a level of civility unthinkable in the United States and silly to contemplate in Russia. The "fourth man," Sir Anthony Blunt, had secretly confessed in 1964 to being a Soviet spy. He was publicly exposed by Margaret Thatcher in 1979 and finally suffered the horrendous indignity of being stripped of his knighthood by Queen Elizabeth.

I found the general information number of the Secret Intelligence Service on the website and copied it onto the bedside notepad. My call was answered promptly in the visitors center, which wasn't exactly what I had in mind but definitely what I had expected. It was Langley all over again. No surprise.

"Hello, duty desk, Marshall speaking, which spy would you like to discuss" was more what I was looking for. I stumbled and made some dopey noises and, after reaching several other public-access areas, finally got into the guts of the place. I explained my position to the operator, managed to get transferred to the duty officer, and tried to work my way to Marshall, not that I thought there was a chance in hell of that happening. Mr. Evan St. Clair, the duty officer, heard me out and seemed genuinely interested. He would pass the information along, and he invited me in for an interview. Same old story. No way I wanted to spend the next twenty-four hours being grilled like a suspect. How do you shake the trees enough for these monkeys to take the situation seriously? Small wonder so much important intelligence slips through our fingers. There were countless instances of good intelligence going unprocessed, the tragedy in Boston being a prime example. Mining all that humintel and electronic intercepts was a coup; sifting through it was an impossible task. I understood, but I was still frustrated.

To hell with it. I called Alison again. No answer. I called Dell. Same thing. I called Deuce.

"Hey, doc, what's happening?"

I told him where I was and he was surprised. Not quite annoyed but not happy with my Lone Ranger behavior. I tried to head him off by telling him exactly what had transpired over the last thirty-six hours. "The thing is, I'm convinced we're at the edge of disaster. You know me, I have no interest in stepping on toes, but I just have to open the right eyes here, or in D.C., or at home. I can't look the other way until somebody picks up the ball."

"Wendell, we are on the case."

"Yeah. Following the drugs and investigating a homicide. Speaking about that, any progress on Farzan?"

"Not a whole hell of a lot to report. No hits, no runs. Going nowhere. Same with your shooters. The brass decided it was linked to whatever is going down with the heroin and the homicide, so at least it has top priority. And Rodriguez still has a hard-on for you and your girl. I can't talk him out of thinking you're involved."

"I'm not, Deuce. I swear. I know nothing. The birds keep circling my head. I'm afraid to take my hat off. I was hoping you had something. I think the feds are coming in big-time. I called Dell, and he gets it."

"What?"

"He understands that this is bigger than drug smugglers."

"Yeah, it is. It's a murder investigation now. I'm not saying your theory is wrong, but I have to deal with what I see. What's the situation with your girlfriend? Rodriguez says she took a powder again. He and his boy Griffin have been trying to talk to her for days. I assume you know something about that."

"I do." I explained why she was lying low.

"I need her location and number. We can't withhold information. We're cops and this is police business. I'll look after her. Don't worry about Rodriguez."

I took Deuce at his word and gave him the new number.

"I think something is going to happen in the next forty-eight hours. There will be a mule heading for New York soon. Very soon. Forget about getting the dogs out. This won't be about drugs, and these won't be Mexicans or Colombians. Think some level of Islamic fanatic. Beyond suicide bomber, and think anthrax."

"Jesus, Wendell, how the hell do you get to that?"

I gave Secondi a brief rundown of my thinking.

"I'm not kidding, Deuce. We have to cover the airports here and in New York and find her or him. Whoever the carrier is."

"How? X-ray every boarding passenger and every one that disembarks at JFK? The feds won't do that on a hunch."

"Maybe not, but it has to be done."

"Good luck."

That sounded like the brush-off to me. Even Deuce. The surgery had been done, the mule was waiting to board a plane with the most dangerous cargo since the *Enola Gay* left for Hiroshima, and nothing was being done to stop it. I was a little anxious about Alison, anxious about the next few days, and at a loss for direction. I knew I wouldn't find any in the minibar, but that's where I went. I grabbed two little bottles of Oban, poured them into a tumbler, and had a few sips. I walked to the easy chair in the corner of the room and released myself into the soft cushion. I sipped and thought. Sipped and thought. I can't say that that was when it all became clear to me, but ten minutes later I understood my predicament. Then I was able to act on it.

35

The 5:15 Virgin flight from Heathrow landed at JFK a few minutes earlier than its 8:10 ETA. With only a carry-on and virtually no line at customs, I was in a cab at 8:20. I called Alison on the way in and got no answer. I was at the hotel at ten past nine. The room was in my name, I had a key card, but no one challenged me at the desk or the elevators, and it certainly wasn't because they recognized me. I took my card out of my pocket but knocked on the door anyway. When there was no response, I rang the doorbell and slipped the key card into the slot, waited for the green light, removed it, and opened the door. Before the card was back in my pocket, I knew something was wrong. I entered the room cautiously, afraid of what I would find. All the lights were on, the bed was made, and there was no sign of life. No bags, newspapers, or clothing. To the right, the bathroom was bright and clean and waiting for use. No one was about to use it. Alison was gone.

There wasn't the slightest hint of anything sinister. The room was clean as a whistle. Nothing out of place, just a nicely cleaned room ready for the next guest. Rodriguez was right. Alison had taken a powder. It was getting to be an old story.

There was no point asking the hotel staff for information. Alison was too smart for that. She didn't check out, because the room was registered in my name, and I had estimated my stay at a week. Maid service was usually in the morning, unless the DO NOT DISTURB hung on the doorknob. I could check that out and have some idea when she last used the room. Not a dent in a pillow or a tissue pulled since the room had been made up.

I wasn't at all worried; I was pissed. Alison had her own agenda, and she sandbagged me again. Like a jerk, I believed most everything she told me and definitely everything she whispered sweetly in my ear. She was working. That's all it was, and I must have been pretty easy. When you catch a woman in a good-sized lie, any reasonable man recognizes it was not an isolated incident. With Alison, they were fast and furious, one after the other. Good spy, lousy girlfriend. I was really, really pissed.

I asked around at the reception desk, in the bar, and focused on the two young guys working the door. They didn't seem to do much, but they wouldn't miss a pretty woman. They were friendly and casual and never bothered to ask who, what, or why. Both had come on at four, and neither remembered seeing anyone matching Alison's description. If she was slipping away, it was unlikely that she would set herself up to register with the doormen. More than likely Alison had made a quiet exit and found her own taxi.

I went back to the desk and checked out. The bill wasn't too complicated. No one used hotel phones anymore. The outrageous surcharges made them a just victim of cell service. The Wi-Fi was free, and room service was billed out the way it always had been. At 12:37 that afternoon, a BLT and a Diet Coke had been delivered to the room. Alison ate in the room just after noon. She knew I was on my way back from London, and she split. Looking through the rest of the room-service backup paper, I saw that she seemed to have taken most of her meals in the room. They were always orders for one—I don't know why I was so relieved by that. Her meals were the usual boring stuff. How many BLTs can a person consume?

It was Saturday night. Figuring the time change, Tahani had performed the surgery almost twenty-four hours ago. The local anesthetic in the area had an effective life of no more than four or five hours. It had long since worn off, and the mule would be feeling the pain of stretched skin and the surgical incision. This would be the most uncomfortable period, with local effect long gone, and endorphins dissipated. Strong pain relievers were necessary. Not a pleasant time to travel but not impossible. Medevac planes transfer soldiers in extremis. Cabins were pressurized. It could be done. This patient was not in any danger. But I was guessing that he wouldn't be traveling for at least seventy-two hours. Definitely not today, probably not tomorrow. Too much pain. Too great a possibility of attracting attention. Slipping through unnoticed was required.

Acting peculiarly or attracting attention was a receipt for detection. Rule number one in the mule business: don't stand out from the crowd.

It was too late to retrieve Tonto from the Dog House, where he boarded in my absence, and I wasn't sure what the next few days would bring. I would make arrangements for him to stay on. Dogs adapt quickly and live happily in all sorts of situations, but first love is first love. Like I said, for me it's about guilt. It's in my genes.

I was pretty sure I had a day or two to mobilize forces, and I headed home for a night's sleep. Alison wasn't about to return to the hotel, so there was no reason to stay there. I had one of my new pals at the door hail a cab, which wasn't easy on a Saturday night in Chelsea. I handed him a twenty-dollar tip to seal our friendship and headed home.

At the door I realized it was a mistake, not retrieving Tonto. I listened for his snorting and his little cries of excitement, and my heart dropped from the silence. Inside, there was a faint aroma of dog and a gray loneliness. It would have been nice to be in my big old chair scratching Tonto's head while I tried to figure out Alison. My mind was spinning as I flopped into the chair. Before I managed to get comfortable, I jumped up.

"Shit." They wouldn't have to worry about pain, or drugs, or making a scene if the mule was a repeat carrier. The pockets under the breasts would already be there from previous implants, and if they re-implanted within a few weeks, they would not yet have closed. It was like changing batteries. There would be no stretching of the skin, no pain. The mule could easily go from the operating room to the airport; at most they might have to wait a day to be sure there was no bleeding. A bloody shirt would make quite a scene on an airplane. Just a few Tylenol #3, or a Vicodin, and go for it. Tahani knew the details.

I scrolled to Tahani's home number and sent the call through. After four rings, a voice I did not recognize answered in foreign-inflected British English.

"Mr. Tahani's residence."

"May I speak to him, please? It's important."

"Who is this?"

"Dr. Black. He knows me."

"What is this in reference to?"

"Just get him on the phone. This is important."

"Sorry, Mr. Tahani is away."

After a few more attempts to break through the barrier, I disconnected the call. Tahani was planning a weekend in the country, and it was three a.m. in London. What the hell was his staff doing wide-awake at three a.m. Sunday morning? Then I remembered there was no staff. I called Tahani's cell phone. There was no answer, and I left a message asking him to call me.

If Tahani was in trouble, there was little I could do about it, and every instinct told me he was in deep shit. Somehow or other, it was not going to end well for him, and I liked the guy. He was sad and had screwed up his life, but there was a gentle humanity about him that made me automatically hope for his survival. I was reluctant to call Dell again, but I couldn't let this pass unnoticed. I compromised by sending him a long text message and hoped he would read it before his Sunday morning run. He was too compulsive to go blank on Sunday, and I had to grab a few minutes of his time before he and Liz and the kids were off to church. I wanted to respect those few hours and didn't want to be responsible for Dell being the only person vibrating while the pastor ran on.

At seven fifteen, Sunday morning, Dell called. He was in gear. The London Metro Police were on their way to Tahani's flat, and he had a meeting at the office of the secretary of Homeland Security at nine.

"If everything works out, we will be in New York by noon. Are you available?"

Available? Of course I would be available. I was the whistle-blower. "Of course. Where should I meet you?"

"TBD. Call you when I know more."

I thanked him and signed off. I think I may have smiled. I know I was relieved.

My sense of relief was short-lived. That's what life is like. At nine on the dot, Rodriguez and Griffin showed up at my door, unannounced. They rapped with their fists and shouted the usual intimidating phrases.

"Police. Open up. We know you're in there." It was standard operating procedure. I wasn't intimidated, but man was I annoyed. I snuck a peek through the security eye, recognized the two, and swung the door open, steaming.

"What the hell do you want? Get off my case, you two fucking dummies."

"Shut up. Back up and hug the wall." Griffin actually had his pistol drawn. Rodriguez pushed me backward, grabbed my arm with an iron grip, and spun me around too quickly for me to react. My forehead was slammed against the wall and my hands cuffed behind my back before I could lash out, which would have been a very stupid move. He turned me again and pushed me into the big overstuffed chair. It isn't comfortable, half-reclining with your hands cuffed tightly behind your back. I was happy Tonto was not at home. Something very bad would have happened, and Tonto would have been the loser. I really hated these two assholes. Now I couldn't stop thinking that they would kill my dog. My face must have been beet-red, because Rodriguez suddenly got concerned.

"Calm down, doc. Don't fight it. You're gonna have a stroke here. Cool it." Rodriguez looked over to Griffin, who had holstered his pistol and looked as sour and nasty as ever. "He looks like a candidate for it, right, partner?"

"Yeah, Rod. He does. I've seen 'em go just like that." And he snapped his fingers.

"He knows his stuff, doc. Better listen to him."

Now they were playing with me, but it wasn't a game. No questions. A few quick statements, the Miranda card came out, and I was under arrest doing my version of an innocent man kicking and screaming. I had seen it dozens of times, but when you are the perp, there's no restraining your emotions. They were enjoying it. I couldn't wait to get to Midtown North and straighten these two guys out.

In the back of the unmarked car, my whole perspective on law enforcement changed. Riding downtown on Fifth Avenue, they hit the siren at corners, and the whooping stopped traffic and brought stares from pedestrians and people in the cars we passed. I couldn't see if the flashers were on, but it was a good bet. This was a sideshow, and I was the star freak. It was easy to understand those newspaper photos of guys with their coats pulled over their faces. I would have hidden my head if I could, but that was not an option as I sat against my cuffed wrists in the backseat of the black SUV. Griffin drove and didn't say much. All the while, Rodriguez kept tossing questions at me. I didn't bite. Not a word. Although I did tell him to go fuck himself when he asked how long I had been involved in the drug ring.

We crossed town on Fifty-third Street, drove uptown for a block on Ninth Avenue, headed east on Fifty-fourth Street, and pulled into one of the nose-first spots on the south side of the street, in front of the precinct house. Not that long ago, I had entered through the office entrance. Today, the two assholes paraded me up the front steps with my hands cuffed behind my back. It was still Sunday morning, and the city was quiet. The shift had changed a couple of hours ago, and the few uniforms going in and out were kids, mostly in pairs, chattering about football and women. The one lone female looked zoned out and unhappy to be where she was. None of them seemed to recognize me, and they gave us no more than the sidelong glance to take in a perp. That was how it was done. Eye the perp parade. Good police habit. Have a look when somebody else makes the collar. It's the same faces over and over, and it's good to know the bad guys.

36

The best I could make of all the fuss was they still thought Alison was a drug trafficker and I was her accomplice. Both of which were ridiculous, but they were working me over for a reason. I stopped protesting, trying not to draw attention to myself going through the bullpen in handcuffs. Then I thought better of slinking through the room as though in shame. I scanned the room and shouted to the first familiar face, "It's me, Dr. Black. Call Lieutenant Secondi and tell him I'm here."

The two jerks led me to an interview room, undid the cuffs, and pushed me into a chair. I think I was pretty calm when I finally demanded my right to call a lawyer.

"Right. I'll get right on it," Rodriguez said with a smile, and they both left the room. I was glad for that, and I needed time to think of a lawyer. The idea of rousing my tax attorney or my divorce lawyer made me laugh. I had to think of a defense attorney. There were lots of good ones passing through our place of business, and they all knew the ropes. Murderers, thieves, and drug dealers all had the same rights, and when experienced people faced off, it was simply business as usual. I found myself thinking about who I wanted to ask for help, and in whose company I would be too embarrassed to be seen. A lot of slimeballs are in the precincts and courthouses. But mostly they are smart, upstanding people. Good lawyers and former prosecutors, people who, for their own reasons wanted to enter the private sector.

Pissed off as I was, I really couldn't get too anxious about my situation. Being innocent is for newborns, but I certainly hadn't broken any laws or done anything seriously wrong . . . that I could think of. I was part of the system. Far too well-connected to be railroaded, and I was too innocent to be worried. So what the hell was I doing here?

Best I could figure, they were working on the curious coincidence that Alison knew a victim and one of the players. And then she was nowhere to be found. That made her a suspect. It was barely even circumstantial, but you had to admit it was a starting point. That was enough to make an arrest and bring her before a judge . . . however briefly. But that was Alison, not me. So I guess they figured me for her partner in crime. As far as I knew, my only crime was sleeping with her.

More than fifty minutes had passed, and I was saved the agony of calling a lawyer by the miraculous appearance of Deuce. The big guy made the best of it, standing at the door of the interview room, laughing. I laughed as well and shrugged my shoulders. I felt like a complete dork.

"Shit, man, get me out of this zoo."

"Police Surgeon Black, this is our NYPD in action. It may seem like the monkey house in Central Park, but on the whole, the monkeys are smarter."

"You talking about me or your two gorillas?"

"Keep being a wise ass."

"Enough. Get me out of here."

"You got it. I had to pull rank on those two hotheads before they get themselves laughed out of court. What they have here is nothing but a few interesting facts about Alison's behavior."

I agreed with that, and I had a few questions of my own.

"What facts?"

Deuce had stopped talking while the duty officer went through the ritual of identifying me, opening the self-locking door to the interview room, and instructing me on where to pick up my personal items. I did the whole cliché: rubbed my wrists, shook the stiffness out of my shoulders, took a deep breath, and followed the two men out of the room. I guess the ritual did exactly what it was supposed to. I was shaken up and defensive when I actually had no reason to be. The whole thing didn't sit well and only increased my interest in getting to the bottom of whatever pit it was that I had fallen into.

Deuce had a different take on the whole thing than I, but he was warming to the possibility of anthrax and terrorism being at the center of events. Where I lost him was Alison. "I don't follow the whole MI6 part of this," he said. "Is she a foreign asset, or isn't she? If she is, then the feds should have no trouble squaring her role in this. If none of her masters owns up to her, then she has gone rogue or was never MI6 at all. In which case, she either has a lot of explaining to do or could be a person of interest, and maybe a very dangerous one."

"And?"

"And we have to find her. That's the best chance she has of telling her side of the story to friendlies. Rodriguez and Griffin won't make it easy on her."

"True. Best if we find her first."

"The other problem is the feds. Do they know she disappeared?"

"I'm not sure." I looked skyward and tried to think but couldn't remember the exact sequence of events. I shook my head. "I will fill Dell in on everything at noon."

"I take it I am not invited to this party."

"Sorry, Deuce, no can do. Dell has been pulling strings to get this together, and I can't cross him. I'll speak to Dell and deal you in as soon as I can, but obviously, I'm not in charge."

"Understood. You know the department is going to have to take action on our own unless the feds get us called off or at least establish a joint task force. It would be best for all of us to work together."

"Understood. Just give me until after we meet. I'll call your cell. Maybe we can meet with Dell later in the day." Deuce thought about that and nodded his agreement.

"Agreed. Till after your meeting. Come on, I'll drop you off. Where's Dell at?" The suggestion seemed odd, but I let it slide.

"I don't know. Dell is going to call when they touch down."

"Okay. I'll give you a ride home."

"Grcat. Lct's get the hell out of here."

"I think you already said that." Deuce smiled. We left the same way we came in, and I felt a whole lot less conspicuous. There were a few familiar faces, not the same ones from earlier. I put on a happy face, waved, and said hellos.

Twelve minutes later, I was back at my empty apartment and Deuce took off to do whatever was on his schedule.

"Thanks, Deuce. I'll call you as soon as the meeting breaks." I hoped it would be as easy as that.

37

Dell was down at 26 Federal Plaza on the honcho floor of the FBI offices. The place was new to me, and the contrast with Police Plaza was sharp—maybe shocking. Other than federal security, there were no uniforms. Everything was neat, and if not new, things were maintained in a manner well outside the mind-set and the budget of the NYPD. The suits had the day, but maybe that was just upstairs. There were none of the blue FBI windbreakers in evidence, just a lot of no-nonsense people who were a world apart from New York cops. I wasn't sure if that was good. Imperfect and screwed up as they were, New York cops were people. These guys had a different mind-set.

The check-in process at security was thorough, polite, and impersonal. My NYPD ID carried about as much weight as my driver's license. Being on the visitors list for the director of the New York field office brought a bit more snap to it, and I was upstairs at reception in a flash. Even the elevators were faster than at 1 PP, and they weren't packed like subway cars. But again, maybe that was just for the executive floors.

Dell was standing to the left of the reception desk, looking solemn. He was dressed in a lightweight gray business
suit, white shirt, and dark red necktie. He was a big,
healthy-looking, happy guy, but he barely smiled a greeting. All business. "Hi, buddy," he said, and walked forward as I entered, shook hands firmly, and ushered me
across a waiting room decorated with flags and lots of official photos. I recognized the president and the attorney
general, but I had no clue about the others. I looked around
us to see if the serious face was for company, but we were
alone in the waiting room, if you didn't count a reception-
ist, who was concentrating on something out of view on the
desktop. She paid us no mind, which set her apart from an
otherwise alert organization.

"Let's go in here," Dell said, and opened an unmarked
door behind and left of the reception desk. I walked in
first, and he closed the door behind us.

"Dr. Wendell Black, NYPD," Dell said, announcing me
to two men and a woman. They were sitting along the long
axis of a conference table with their backs to the big, bright,
west-facing windows, and I couldn't make out their faces.
They had the home court advantage. They could study me
while I had to squint to see their silhouettes. This was not
meant to be an adversarial situation. I knew the game and
I was disappointed.

"I would like to introduce you to Harriet English, director
of the New York field office of the bureau; Benjamin Marks,
assistant U.S. Attorney for the Southern District; and Constantine Panopolous, undersecretary of Homeland Security."

All three rose and reached across the table to shake hands. These were heavy-hitters with good manners and they were working on a Sunday. My annoyance dissipated and I asked Dell if he could close the blinds before he took his seat, which he did. It took a few seconds to acclimate myself to the lower light level, but I was more comfortable and could see who was across the table. Harriet English was a good-looking amalgam of austere features. Yankee to the core. She was tall and thin but definitely not skinny. Her hair was pulled back away from fine features that were slightly too prominent to be pretty. She sat board-straight and, all in all, gave the impression of strength and recti-tude. I guess those were attributes a woman needed to land on top of the most important field office of the bureau.

Marks was a really big guy. Big, like in fat. He was under six feet and over two fifty. His skin was taut, his black hair slicked back, and he looked as preppy as a Princeton freshman. His white golf shirt had a yacht club burgee on the left breast, where most people had an alliga-tor or a polo player, and he wore finely pressed chinos. No evidence of a jacket. Marks couldn't have been more than forty-five. He was going places. I classified him as a trust-fund baby doing the job because he loved it. Which, com-ing from me, wasn't an indictment—I was the same kind of guy.

The last member of the group, Constantine Panopolous, looked, acted, and talked like a cop, which he had been. He was pretty well known as the tough guy who kept the Homeland secretary on message. Panopolous's sad eyes and

Mediterranean features were regularly seen on news interviews and panels whenever issues of security in the post
9/11 world were discussed. He, too, was dressed casually.
More JC Penney civil-servant than the upper-class casual
Marks. For no concrete reason, I was happy to see him at
the table. I was happy to see them all involved. Apparently,
they saw the threat.

I was wearing a jacket and tie.

Dell joined me on the wall side of the table and we
looked at the faces across from us. An uncomfortable few
seconds of silence followed. Not interrogation silence, but a
where-do-we-go-from-here silence. Dell broke it.

"Wendell, it's your party." He extended a hand in my
direction. The others, except Dell and me, had been provided with legal pads and Department of the Treasury pens
and were getting themselves into position to listen and take
notes. Bottled water, Coke and Diet Coke, and an ice bucket
were lined up on the left side of a dark Formica refectory
table along the wall. Styrofoam coffee cups, a large vacuum
bottle, and a pint of ultra-pasteurized half-and-half were
on the other end of the table, as if to avoid cross-
contamination. Used cups and water bottles were already
in front of the participants. Dell got up and walked around
the table and grabbed two bottles of water. He handed one
to me and sat down. BlackBerrys, iPhones, and iPads were
arranged in differing but compulsively neat patterns
around the yellow pads. No one was more than a second
away from base, and I noticed English and Marks already
glancing down at flashing lights. I didn't know whether or

not to stand, and chose not to. I chewed my cheek and gazed upward, as I tend to do when I'm looking for inspiration, then got right into it.

Twenty-five minutes later I had stumbled to the present. The hardest part was trying to keep the events of the last week chronological, unembellished, and unedited. I might have been long-winded, but I was into it. Everyone sighed and fidgeted a bit as I took a brief break before adding, "That's how it happened. I'm convinced the whole thing means a terrorist event in the next few days."

English broke the silence with a word.

"Where?"

"I don't really know. Obviously, New York, but I don't know where." I felt like that was a dumb answer or at least not the answer they wanted, and they were testing me. The faces around the table were not laughing at me, but they could have been. I felt defensive enough to explain my reasoning. "The port of entry has always been Kennedy. All the practice runs came through there, even though it may be the most secure airport in the country. Air transport was used repeatedly, even though our borders, north and south, and our ports are like sieves and truck or ship would have been easier and carried a far larger payload."

"So that means what?" English again.

"Well, it means that the target is New York City. It's less than an hour from JFK. Neither bags nor people are routinely examined at the port of entry, and the city has nothing more than a patrol car and a cop at bridge and tunnel entries, and if you take a look at those guys, they're too busy texting or making calls to discourage anyone. My take: It's New York, and it's anthrax."

Panopolous was bouncing the spring end of his pen on the table and moving his head to some inner tune. He had our attention when he finally spoke. Actually, he had our attention when he was thinking.

"Are we all agreed this is not a classified substance matter?"

"Drugs?" someone asked. It was a rhetorical question.

"No, not drugs," I said. "They would go broke pushing such small quantities past customs. The infrastructure and the losses would cripple them. Look at the people involved; there are red flags all over the place. This is al-Qaeda."

Panopolous nodded in agreement. "I agree with the good doctor."

I was as sensitive about that good doctor bullshit as I was about doc. A false tribute about as meaningful as "my fine feathered friend." "I agree with my fine feathered friend over here . . . though he is surely a babe in the woods." But lots of silly, unimportant things annoy me. It may help explain why I live alone.

"This could be the real thing," Panopolous continued. "We have had intercepts sent up over the last three months that now make sense, but there is no humint to back it up. I need to bounce this back to the CT desk."

Ben Marks interrupted. "Any chatter heard in your shop, Harriet?"

"Nothing that fits this. We hear mostly Stateside stuff. By the time the combined task forces are given intel to consider, it has been through the filter. This is raw stuff. Not our meat."

"Figured that," Marks said. "Dell?"

"Nothing. I heard all this first from Wendell, made some calls, talked to the secretary, who knew what Constantine knew and gave us the green."

"Okay," Marks said, assuming the role of team leader and taking charge of the meeting. I half-expected him to go around the table pointing fingers. "What do we know about Ms . . . Dr. Withers? Where is she, and how does she tie into the big picture? Doctor?" Panopolous lifted an eyebrow at the power coup. The others either didn't notice or let it slide. I had a little rush of anxiety before realizing I had already read him chapter and verse of all I knew. Maybe this was a good way to force us to focus, and I was all for that.

"I haven't a clue," I answered. "I think she's on our team, I mean, I'm pretty sure she's on our team, but her behavior doesn't square with the rest of the story." I heard my response meld into my private doubts. "To answer your question directly, I have no idea how she fits in." I stopped talking and looked at the inexpressive faces across from me. No one was rushing forward with information or letting me off the hook.

"Dell?" The headmaster moved his gaze a few degrees to my right, taking in the quiet agent, the only man in a business suit. He was sitting comfortably erect, taking it all in. Dell kicked his chair back from the table and folded his hands across his chest. "We have made inquiries through several channels. We know her background is MI6, just as she told Wendell. They refer to her as Alison Withers, which does not mean that's her name, not that it matters. Their people, pretty high up the chain, claim no knowledge of her whereabouts, which we tend to believe. This is not the kind of thing one deludes an ally over. We can count on the Brits to do whatever they can to defuse this, but they still may be skirting around giving up an asset. Whatever. We kicked the inquiry up to the very highest level. Let's see if anything comes back."

"Do we all agree this represents a real threat?" Marks seemed to be looking for a show of hands. There was none. English nodded, followed by Dell. Marks skipped by me. "What about you?" he asked, looking at Panopolous.

"Ben," Panopolous snapped back. "With all due respect, this is our territory. We have procedures for situations like this. There can't be a criminal investigation in the U.S. Attorney's office without a crime or a suspect on American soil. So ease up."

If Marks was flustered, he didn't show it. His face reddened a bit, but he barreled on. "Got it, so let's lay it out."

"No, no. You don't understand. At this stage you are an observer. I hope to God we will need you for legal opinions and prosecution, but right now, let us do our jobs." Which struck a nerve.

"Hey, if I'm not needed here, why did you fuck up my Sunday?" Now he was seriously red in the face. Marks had that look that only hypertensive, obese men can muster . . . two or three seconds of hyperventilation and apoplexy.

"Ben, get a grip. Let me do what they pay me to do. The secretary requested DOJ presence. Me, I think the action will start and end at Kennedy. That would be the U.S. Attorney from the Eastern District, unless I am mistaken. Correct?"

New York City is divided into two federal judicial districts, the Southern and the Eastern. Each district has its own roster of federal judges and a U.S. attorney. John F. Kennedy Airport is located in the Borough of Queens. And Queens and Brooklyn are in the Eastern District. If anything legal went down, Benjamin Marks would be bypassed, and the case would go to his colleague in the less publicized, very busy Eastern District. Marks was a smart guy. It could be a career-changer and he wanted to stay in the game.

Panopolous was in charge. It also looked natural on him. He was the gritty, working-class, tough guy at school, who instinctively did the right thing, put himself on the line, then disappeared into the crowd. Now he ran with the ball. "How will this attack go down?"

Dell interrupted, "Are we all convinced there will be an attempt?" That was a bit more optimistic. The show of hands was unanimous. He deferred to Panopolous, who was bouncing his pen again.

"I think we should all thank Dr. Black here for his great work." He showed his upturned palm my way. "Doctor, you have done the nation a great service." He stood and reached across the table to shake my hand and I stood to meet him halfway. The others provided a smattering of applause. I was being dismissed.

Dell rose as well. "Hold on, Constantine. Wendell is in the middle of this. We need his help. He blew the whistle. He knows the players."

"Dell, all kidding aside, we are professionals. Again, this is what we do. We will go to Dr. Black as necessary to check facts, and his ideas are welcome."

Dell responded, "Right, but he knows more of the technical stuff about anthrax than we do, and he is plugged into the medical establishment. He's also NYPD, and we have to include them soon. Very soon. Be nice to have as little town-gown agro as possible."

"Dr. Black, are you a toxicologist?"

"No." Duh. He knew I was a police surgeon, not a lab rat. "But I'm as close to an expert on weaponizing anthrax as anyone else, and I know more of the science than any of you. By the time you rally the people at Fort Detrick it might be too late. And this is no longer about weaponizing the bug, we're into the intervention phase, and I know the players better than anyone in this room." If the first part was an exaggeration, the second was true. Time was a-wasting. I had read a great deal on the subject after the anthrax attacks following 9/11. Most every doctor had. It had become virtually negligent not to have a working knowledge. I forgot a lot of it, but I could get up to speed quickly. It wasn't all that complicated. I went on. "There was nothing a couple of microbiologists and a bunch of un-trained terrorists couldn't learn from the Internet. Obtain some spores of *Bacillus anthracus*, which was still a disease to be reckoned with in much of the Third World. Grow it in an enriched medium, deprive it of enrichment so spores form; dry the hardened spores and grind them down as close to one micron each, about one-twenty-fifth the thickness of a Kleenex; add bentonite or silica to neutralize the electrostatic charge on the spores so they won't stick together—and bingo, you have an aerosolized biological weapon. Inhale the spores, allow them to sprout in the lungs, which, by the way, are a perfect place—warm, moist, and rich with nutrients—and the anthrax bacillus is reconstituted from its spores, infects and destroys the lungs, and in short order you have a 90 percent fatality rate among untreated cases."

Panopolous listened intently to every word. "I stand corrected," he said. "Please stay with us." I knew I liked the guy.

38

On the way back to the apartment, I made a stop at the Dog House, retrieved my better half, and made for Central Park. The cab driver spoke English and didn't complain about Tonto. I opened the window a crack as he sat almost calmly beside me, having his head scratched and watching the people in the cars around us watch him. I smiled. We both smiled. Things seemed normal again, at least for a few minutes.

No beauty is more unexpected than the park materializing amid the bricks and mortar of New York City. A fresh breeze tickled the tops of the lazy old trees, still very green and still some weeks from turning. What a miracle. An 843-acre oasis that made Manhattan Island fit for humans. Dogs, too. On a Sunday it was wall-to-wall beasts. Where did all those dogs come from? Tonto was in sniff heaven.

I was preoccupied and worried. How were they going to cover the bases? The counterterrorism divisions of every agency had been alerted to the heightened security risk, but for the moment, no public announcement would be made beyond the present Level Orange. The others at our meeting had gone to base to mobilize forces. Panopolous planned a quick turnaround to Washington to brief the secretary, who, in turn, would carry the message to the National Security Council and bear the burden of deciding at what point to alert the president of the United States. The government G-4 was scheduled to touch down at LaGuardia at nine this evening, with Panopolous and his crew, and we would reconvene at nine thirty. The NSC, the cryptographic service branch of the armed forces, and the Middle East and Pakistan desks of the CIA were probably alerted by now. New intercepts from the area would go highest-priority, and analysts would be scrutinizing old messages with a new focus. Great Britain was added to the list. MI5 and MI6 would be enlisted to sift through intelligence from agents on the ground who had infiltrated into the ranks of the radical Muslim underground in every British city. A full-court press would be instituted.

They would be looking for a clue to the time and place of the strike. What was not in doubt was the nature of the attempt. Anthrax. All this didn't give me a feeling of confidence, since no one knew better than I how flimsy the information leading to that conclusion was.

Tonto and I meandered across Sheep Meadow and then the western limb of the park drive, which was closed to automobile traffic on weekends. We crossed the meadow again, to the east this time, and finally exited the park at Seventy-second Street and walked the ten blocks home.

It was nearly six when we arrived, and Tonto and I were both famished. He banged his metal bowl around the kitchen until I got the point. I served up a bowl of enriched, scientifically formulated, dry dog food, full of organic, natural goodness, and topped it off with two shredded slices of American cheese. Processed cheese food, whatever. Tonto loved it. So did I. What could be more soothing and reassuring than a grilled cheese sandwich?

I found four relatively fresh slices of packaged white bread, unwrapped four more slices of American cheese, and fried the two sandwiches in butter. I usually salve my conscience by frying in olive oil, but what the hell, who knew if there would be a tomorrow? The coffee maker sounded about the time the frying pan was getting a little smoky. I managed to slice the sandwiches into triangles, which is the only way to attack melted cheese, pour out a mug of coffee, top it off with Skim Plus, and get everything to the table without a disaster. There were newspapers and mail to glance through, and dinner passed pleasantly. Tonto played it smart and sat by my side. There was no way I could finish both sandwiches, and the remainder disappeared between his gentle jaws. He licked his chops and did a little hip-hop. It was a toss-up as to who was more satisfied.

I kicked my shoes off and lay down on the sofa with the paper, fully aware that there was no chance of getting through so much as the front page. An incessant ringtone brought me back an hour later. I did the "where's the phone" routine and quickly recognized the sound of the little black alarm clock. It was no less annoying, and I had confidence in its doing the job.

The hot shower felt good. I brushed my teeth, tossed the clothes from the bathroom floor into the hamper, and put on fresh chinos and a blue oxford shirt. I grabbed my phone, wallet, and badge case and stuffed them into the pockets of the tweed jacket hanging on the doorknob. Tonto got a few words of apology for being left again, but he was already snoring. I was out the door and in a taxi by eight forty-five.

The conventional wisdom is that taking a break helps one clear the mental clutter and see things more clearly. It didn't seem to have helped me. Just then I realized that I hadn't called Deuce to report on the big meeting. He answered his cell on the third ring and didn't mention that he had been waiting for my call. The ploy was perfect, and I wanted to spill my guts out to gain forgiveness. Instead, I simply said, "I'm in a cab going back for round two."

"Who was there?" Deuce asked. I looked ahead at the driver, who did not appear to be paying particular attention to my conversation, but I decided to err on the side of circumspection.

"Bureau, DOJ, and Homeland." No names or titles. Deuce caught on.

"Nobody from the job?"

"Nope."

"There will be. Something like this can't go down here without the NYPD. No chance of the feds going it alone. Rule number one, 'Make preparations to share the blame if anything goes wrong.' Got to have NYPD and the Port Authority boys."

"We'll see. Nobody said anything about them joining us."

"So you're on the task force?"

"Apparently, but only just." He laughed at that.

"Call me later . . . when you can talk. Don't forget this time."

"Will do."

39

I arrived at the conference room fifteen minutes early, which was probably a good thing. Security at the FBI offices was tighter than it had been earlier. My ID and gold shield were hung over my neck on the standard NYPD tape.

"May I see your identification, sir?" It wasn't really a question. I slipped the tape over my head and handed it to the stiff Hispanic woman in an equally stiff dark blue federal uniform. She looked at the identification for longer than I thought necessary. There was just so much information in a picture, a name, family name first, a shield number, and NYPD gibberish. But she was letting me know who was boss. My face gave me away. "Just orders, sir. Be another moment." She checked my name against a list on a computer out of view, typed something in, and waited for a response before looking up at me. "First elevator on the right, sir."

I tried to act like an adult and said, "Thank you."

A less intrusive version of the procedure was repeated at the executive floor before I was shown into the conference room we had met in earlier. By nine thirty all ten seats at the table were taken and a full rank of chairs along the wall were occupied as well. Another few minutes and it would have been back bench for me. The only familiar face among the new members was the police commissioner. We had met several times before, but he showed no sign of recognition and I didn't feel like sucking up. Someone else would do the honors at the right time. There were two uniforms at the table. One was the chief of Port Authority police, and the other was an army general with a chest full of ribbons. I wondered if he was trying to impress us or trying to show he belonged. It didn't take long to realize that neither was the case. He was in charge of U.S. Army counterintelligence, and he was probably the smartest guy in the room.

Marks's counterpart in Brooklyn and Queens represented the Eastern District. A petite fiftyish woman in a severe blue suit, she made a point of sitting beside Marks and chatting conspiratorially. He appeared only mildly interested, and I had the feeling Marks didn't share well. Every agency important enough to have initials was at the table: DOD, DOJ, DEA, ICE, FBI, NYPD, and probably others that I missed. The back-row people had already started whispering into the ears of their masters, and the meeting hadn't even been called to order. Panopolous didn't waste a moment before making it clear who was in charge.

"Ladies and gentlemen, thank you for being prompt. At 1800 hours today, my boss, the secretary of Homeland Security, was ordered by the president of the United States to assign the highest national priority to the potential crisis at hand. Full cooperation by every agency—federal, state, and local—is required. Absolutely no territorial bullshit

will be tolerated—my words, not his. None. Is that perfectly clear?"

There were murmurs of agreement. Half the attendees
didn't know if they were senior enough to respond, and the
other half agreed but were not accustomed to being spoken
to so bluntly. There was a new alpha dog.

"We believe the courier, the mule, will arrive at Kennedy Airport within the next twenty-four hours, thirty-
six hours at the outside. This is based on information
provided by Dr. Black, over here"—he offered a palm
across the table. I had been here before. This was his
dance. Disarming but not embracing. I knew to take it as
a simple fact, no more than that. He went on, "As well as
information secured by the British intelligence services
and passed on to us this evening. Based on accumulated
information, we believe the target will be the New York
City water supply."

That surprised everyone, myself included. The buzz in
the room was distracting enough to make Panopolous
pause. "Here's why. After the success of 9/11, any minor
incursion would be a blip. They can't follow it with something smaller, less impressive. The biggest hit possible
would be contaminating the water supply of a large city.
Which, in this case, has to be New York. It's a real problem.
Anthrax spores are not simple, susceptible microorgan-
isms. They become dormant, and the spore coat protects
them until circumstances favor germination. The spores
can survive the standard chlorine concentration of drinking water, which is one milligram per liter. The spores also

cling to pipes and pass through most existing filters. This has the possibility of becoming a crippling event."

Commissioner Carey raised his hand and spoke up. Half-schoolboy asking to be recognized, half–top cop reclaiming his ground. "We could turn off the water supply and hyperchlorinate. It's not like the scenario hasn't occurred to NYPD counterterrorism. We have the details in our playbook. It doesn't have to be a disaster."

"Right. And how long do ten million people have to live on bottled water? And who gets Cipro prophylaxis to prevent the disease, since there is not enough available to treat the entire population? Who is left to die? Maybe the city should be evacuated until the water supply is safe to drink. One milligram of chlorine per liter kills most of the crap that lives in drinking water. But anthrax spores aren't your average bugs. Over at the Aberdeen Proving Ground in Maryland they figured out you need ten milligrams of chlorine per liter of water to kill 99.9 percent of anthrax spores. That's like drinking from a swimming pool. Any way you look at it, the economic toll would be enormous, which is exactly what the bastards want. Let's not even talk about the loss of life. If they manage to do this, the fallout is not going away anytime soon. It could cripple our economy and destroy our morale."

Carey had no response. We were all silent. I'm not sure what possessed me, but I blurted out, "It's too easy."

Panopolous snapped his head to his left and cast a withering stare in my direction. It wasn't one of those "who farted?" moments where you could stare at other people to shift the blame. I was it, so I continued.

"You can cut off access to the watershed. It's doable and they have to know it. The water supply sounds like a red herring to me." There was a bit of buzzing, but no one murmured approval or disapproval. There was certainly no groundswell.

"Thank you for the benefit of your years of security experience, Dr. Black."

The room became unpleasantly still. Everyone froze and waited. Fuck him, and the horse he rode in on.

"No need to be nasty, Panopolous," I said. "Your guys don't exactly have a sterling record interpreting intercepts. Let's be grown-ups here. We all have something to offer, and we should all have the same goal. I, for one, don't have to cover my ass."

"Yeah, well I'm not exactly covering mine being so cocksure. So, let's start again."

I knew I liked the guy.

We spent more than three hours free-associating. Despite a chest covered in fruit salad, General Pearson was the best of us at shedding his ego and thinking like the enemy. He and Panopolous batted ideas around the room, and pretty soon we were all chiming in. The Secret Service had no specific antiterrorism mandate within Homeland Security, but Dell had a broad experience, and once we stopped standing on ceremony, his insights were helpful. There were endless devastating possibilities to consider, and the NYPD Counterterrorism Bureau, which I actually knew something about, provided a wealth of information on targets and strategy. Once the turf-protection nonsense was behind us, we had become a very high-level functioning unit.

The good news that we came to understand was that, given time to prepare, we could contain most anthrax attacks. The bad news was that we didn't know what we were preparing for. Water supply, subway system, indoor gatherings, special events. Aerosolized anthrax spores were an effective all-purpose killer, and I made it my business to keep that tidbit on the table.

By the time the meeting was wrapped for the evening, a reasonable delegation of duties was established under Panopolous.

"Best-guess flight route is LHR to JFK. That's what they have been practicing; that's what they will do. We know they used Virgin at least once. That was the flight Dr. Black was on. They are familiar with Terminal 4. Best guess is that is where they will land. We have Virgin Atlantic, Continental, Delta, and Air India all landing at Terminal 4 from Heathrow. Isn't that right, Port Authority?"

The superintendent of the Port Authority deferred to the uniformed chief at the table. Panopolous didn't seem to know either of their names. The chief responded.

"Correct. Four is our primary international hub. It's the old International Arrivals Building. Brought us into the twenty-first century. It was rebuilt about ten years ago and keeps evolving. We have seventeen gates and forty carriers operating out of Four, and Delta has pretty much moved all its international operations there from Three. Virgin has the most flights to Four from Heathrow. Five a day, I think." He fished a pair of steel-rimmed glasses from his shirt pocket, set them on his nose, and scanned a form in front of him. "No, six a day from LHR. First one arrives at 1220 military, last one 2010 military. That's 8:10 p.m. So we have six flights over approximately eight hours."

"Thank you, Chief Zanko." Panopolous surprised me again.

Heathrow was on high alert. Every flight on every airline destined for JFK would be scrutinized closely. There were enough body-scanning machines at Heathrow to handle the traffic. The problem was encouraging scanning without causing a panic. Profiles were developed around what I had observed on the flight and the information given to me by Tahani. Genetic Asian males dressed like females, exhibiting female secondary sex characteristics. Breasts. Scans would be far more effective than pat-down techniques.

Whatever was going to happen would take place in the forty-eight hours beginning with the 12:20 flight tomorrow afternoon. There was no plan beyond that, which was okay with me. Some general once said that great plans are adhered to until the first shot is fired.

Panopolous organized us according to our expertise. With no particular skills to offer, I was assigned to the anti-bioterrorism group comprised of two other doctors, one from the New York State Department of Health and another from the army. Talk about having nothing to offer. These two were experts. But at least I was still in the game. We were expected to meet with our little committees and then present our ideas and information to the group when we next convened at ten, tomorrow morning. My new play-mates and I decided to get some sleep before scratching our brains. We would meet at seven at the FBI building.

It was almost midnight, and I had had enough for one day. Probably everyone had. I just wanted to sleep. But be-fore I could do that, I had to call Deuce and fill him in. Nothing secret had transpired, and if Deuce had been of rank and unit, he would have been with us. I guess what I meant was that he wasn't excluded; he just wasn't included. Talking to him wasn't leaking secrets or talking out of school. Anyway, until a few hours ago he knew more about it than most of the people running the task force. I sent him a text to alert him to the impending ring of his phone, and I dialed thirty seconds later. The great detective answered on the first ring.

"Hey, thanks for the alert. You gave me enough time to slip out of bed. Amy seems to think she has a right to a full night's sleep on Sundays. What's shaking?"

"Same old shit. Panopolous thinks it will be somewhere in the watershed area in the next twenty-four."

"No way. What do you think?"

"I actually agree with you. Too easy. And too easy to defend, or at least stall. Too many countermeasures. Costly ones, but countermeasures."

"Yup. Panopolous still in charge?"

"Yeah, but we got a green light from the big guy. The really big guy. City agencies are quietly going to red alert, so by morning every cop in town will be decked out in Kevlar and hassling taxi drivers. Panopolous is a fucking steamroller. Takes no prisoners, and he's really tough on himself. Anything new in the outside world?"

"Word is starting to filter through the ranks. Probably won't be a surprise tomorrow. How do the experts think the heightened alert will affect the bad guys?"

"Force them into a now-or-never posture. Make them rash and sloppy. I hope they're right."

"Amen. And for what it's worth, I agree."

"That's a bad sign. What do you think would be a more likely target than the watershed?"

"Are they sure it's anthrax?"

I hesitated for a second. "Yeah, they are, but it was pretty much based on what I told them. So guess who may end up being the goat of the century?"

"Oh, man. That makes me laugh. Rodriguez and the other jerk would love that. They still buy this as drugs. Rodriguez called me right after you did, around six. He was still trying to get a line on you and Alison. He is really on your case."

"What case? Is he that fucking dumb? How in the world can he still suspect me when Homeland, the commissioner, and the bureau credential me?"

"Nobody's perfect."

"Good night, Deuce." I smiled at the jokes, but the Rodriguez business still disturbed me.

By the time our short phone conversation ended, I was close to home. It was Sunday night again, and New York City was like anyplace else in the world. The streets were deserted, and traffic flowed swiftly and painlessly. It seemed as though I barely had time to close my eyes when the cab stopped in front of my apartment building. I paid the driver, saluted the doorman, and stepped through the open elevator door. Upstairs, I waited to hear Tonto before putting my key in the lock, but I heard no shaking, pawing, or sniffing. Unusual. A bit unsettled, I worked both locks as quickly as possible and swung the door open. Tonto was unconscious on the sofa with a smiling Alison happily scratching his head.

40

Coming home to find Alison and Tonto in the living room would have been a heartwarming family scene if it hadn't been so bizarrely out of place. I was too dumbstruck to speak, so I just stood in the entry and stared. Alison broke the silence.

"Shhh, don't wake him up," she said, the picture of maternal happiness. Astounding.

"When did you get here?" I asked, probably with an appropriate edge in my voice.

"Can't you do better than that? If you don't want to kiss me, at least say hello." She was dressed in jeans, a black T-shirt, and a thin, dark blue cardigan, and looked great. She always looked great. I walked into the room noisily enough for Tonto to raise his head from Alison's lap and look at me. He wasn't about to move. Smart dog. His sleek, black tail wagged twice in greeting, flopping against the cushion with a smacking sound.

"Hello, Alison," I said grudgingly, knowing I was losing the battle. I walked to where she was sitting, put my left hand on the back of her head, and kissed her lightly on the lips. She tasted faintly of strawberry lip gloss, which, I assumed, she had recently applied. The truth was, I really wanted to take her right there. One kiss, the minute my tongue found hers, she would be wet, and it would all spin out of control. I made my way to the comfortable club chair near the arm of the sofa, sat heavily, leaned forward, and asked, "Where have you been? Everybody but the pope has been looking for you." I left out that she had skipped out on me as well, the city was on crisis alert, and she was somewhere near the center of it all.

"Yes, I know. Sorry. I had some things to clear up. Professional things, you know."

"No, I don't know." I answered loudly enough for Tonto to take the hint and scamper away. "And you apparently were not doing your professional things for your British secret intelligence services. The folks at MI6 deny you are on assignment. In fact, your MI6 people have been looking for you. And Rodriguez is on search-and-destroy. Obviously, this is more complicated than you let on, so let's try the whole truth. It seems like it's always the same issue with you."

I was no longer tired, and I wasn't in a forgiving mood. We were racing against the clock to put the puzzle together, and Alison probably held a few of the critical pieces. She had me figured out perfectly and didn't attempt any diversionary tactics. She asked for a drink. I poured out two generous measures of Jameson's, handed one to her, returned to my seat, and prepared to listen. What follows is a summary of Alison's tale. Forget about the false starts and attempts at trying to extract information about how much I knew, or how tight the noose around her neck had become. I was not forthcoming. Still, after a bit, I fell into the rhythm of her view of things.

"Alison, the more you bullshit us and play hide-and-seek, the more they see you for this. They're getting closer. I promise, they're getting closer."

She sipped her drink and didn't speak. I waited.

"How do they see this going down?" she asked.

"Alison, tell me your story." I wasn't about to volunteer any more information.

"It isn't all that complicated, love," she said without smiling. "I think you get my problem with the Firm. We had an honest difference of opinion, and I am doing what I feel I must. It really is as simple as that." When her pause became silence, I said, "That's not enough, Alison. Start from the beginning."

She took what seemed like an exaggerated deep breath, exhaled, looked away from me for a few seconds, and spoke.

"I have been a low-level operative with the intelligence service for years. Very low-level. For a doctor with good scientific credentials, good manners, and a nice appearance, it was easy to find my way into interesting scientific circles in Europe, the Middle East, and the States, wherever I was posted. I already told you all that."

"You were specifically sent to infiltrate what?"

"No, no, nothing like that. Mostly, I went where my interests took me. They didn't play much of a role in the choices. My job was simply to make influential friends who might come in handy along the way. From time to time a few crumbs fell from the table, which I collected and reported. Early on, I managed to confirm some work being done on an important biotech project in Iran. That kind of made my bones. But my time was spent becoming a plastic surgeon. I worked and socialized and kept my eyes and ears open, but mostly it wasn't out of the ordinary. Months went by without contact from Vauxhall Cross, and finally I contacted them about resigning. The financial support was helpful, but by this point I could do well without it. We had had talks the last time I visited home."

"When was that?"

"Maybe six months ago. Last winter."

"And?"

"And nothing was decided. There, as here, resigning means different things to different people. If one were called upon for an assignment even after ceasing to draw salary, few would decline. No decision was made, and I stayed in the service. But then Farzan confided his suspicions to me, and it got interesting."

"And when was that?"

"About three months ago."

"Three months ago. I had no clue," I said. Alison didn't act surprised or contrite.

"It was about drugs. It wasn't part of our life."

"Why would Farzan talk to you about that? It makes no sense."

"Farzan knew about my connection to the Firm, and he asked me to bring his suspicions to the proper authorities."

I left that alone and allowed her to go on. "My superiors didn't believe that sort of investigation was within the scope of our franchise and suggested the Metropolitan Police. I was busy. I had no interest in functioning as a messenger and no interest in being endlessly detained by their inquiries, so I let the issue drop."

"What did Farzan say?"

"I didn't tell him. Then all this happened so quickly, and poor Farzan was killed. I . . ."

That was a conversation-stopper. I said nothing and waited for Alison to regain her composure.

"You know the rest. I began to see this as a far more dangerous issue. I contacted Vauxhall repeatedly. They stonewalled me. I couldn't get them to open their eyes, so I made some contact here. That bounced back, and they called me in. I turned a deaf ear, which was not at all appreciated. All of which makes me a bit of an outcast. Worse than that, a rogue agent."

A rogue agent, meaning she had disobeyed orders and was no longer credentialed.

She and Farzan had been in closer contact than I had been led to believe, but I didn't bother weighing what that meant. He was dead, bad shit was happening, and I couldn't sweat the small stuff.

"I was frightened. I tried to piece together what Farzan's murder and Tahani's disappearance meant. The long and short of it was they were unimpressed or unwilling to help. Or maybe unwilling to confide in me that something bigger and more crucial to British interests was happening and the powers that be did not want it derailed by my interference. That was not unheard of, but I couldn't ignore it."

Finding her apartment inexpertly tossed had made the wild shooting on Forty-ninth Street a more obvious message from someone to lay off, so she checked out of one hotel and into another. Not quite certain of my allegiance, she continued making fruitless calls. Finally, unable to enlist official help of any kind, she decided to take a chance with me.

I assumed she meant I would be able to square things with the authorities. But she had no such idea. Her brilliant conclusion was that we would go it alone, which was not going to happen.

There wasn't much new insight until Alison said, "I think they have contacts working at Heathrow and JFK, which would explain how they were able to finesse security and exit the airport unseen."

"But what makes you think that?"

"It's just too easy for them to repeat the process. You have to believe most people would think once is enough. Change locations. Maybe even change styles for each run."

"True, but how do you know they are running the same play?"

Alison shook her head as if I were too dumb to know my fingers were on my hands. "Because of what Farzan and Tahani said. They have a system of recruiting indentured Asians working in Arab countries and shipping them off to London with the promise of surgery. They have a routine.

Same mules, same doctors, and they must have the same operatives at each airport. Think about when you fly. How many Muslim workers are at the airports?"

"Alison, Muslim doesn't mean terrorist. There used to be mostly Italians, and after that Latinos . . ."

"Right," she interrupted, "before that there were a lot of Italians, and the Italian Mafia controlled the crime at the airports, and guess what, most of the complicit workers were Italian. Does that make me a bigot?"

"That was different."

"It was not. Who do you think the mafiosi could relate to and bend to their will, the Irish? Give me a break. In this case fundamentalists find other fundamentalists, terrorists find almost terrorists, or wannabe terrorists. It's obvious."

I guess it was. From there, our discussion became more concrete.

An hour later, Alison was asleep on my arm. We had undressed and fallen into bed and to sleep without so much as a good-night kiss. About three, all the coffee and Diet Coke caught up with me. My right arm was numb from the pressure of Alison's head, and I slipped it free without difficulty. Alison was comatose. Standing over the toilet, I resolved to call Deuce and alert him to the reappearance of the mystery woman, and let the chips fall where they may. I finished up and pulled the old blanket off the back of the chair by the window and stretched out on the sofa. I felt disloyal contemplating dropping a dime on Alison, and I was still annoyed at her behavior. It was more comfortable alone.

When I awoke, it was fully light and looked to be about seven. My neck was too stiff to turn, and my legs felt like they were permanently fixed in the semi-fetal position. With Alison still deeply asleep, I congratulated myself on my resolve to keep my distance, though she had missed the whole episode. I shaved and showered, and while I dressed, the coffee was dripping through. I poured the thick, hot stuff into my old mug, added the usual Skim Plus, and sipped at it standing in front of my desk scanning the morning's *Times* on the laptop. Then I did what I should have done last night and texted Deuce and told him Alison was with me, and filled him in on her theory. I took Tonto for a twenty-minute walk, even though he would be picked up shortly, deposited him in the apartment, and took off for FBI headquarters. On the way, I called my office and told Mrs. Black that I would be out for a few days. Apparently, she was more plugged in than I, and said, "Do your duty for our country, Dr. Black."

41

The meeting of my subcommittee was like a study group in medical school. We were the reserve nerds. We all knew the basics of anthrax bioterror. The drug of choice for prophylaxis and treatment is Ciprofloxacin—Cipro—and the availability of large quantities of it had been greatly facilitated by the rash of attacks in 2001. The stores of the drug could be quickly mobilized by state health authorities, but none of us knew the actual extent of the supply or whether the expired drug was regularly rotated out and replaced. The state health commissioner was a little embarrassed by that and texted the appropriate subordinates for answers. We established a triage paradigm, which, like all medical triage plans, established sorting centers to separate the salvageable from the hopeless. Primary trauma centers would be alerted. State medical personnel would be alerted. Amazingly, there was no seriously high-tech medical bioterror alert system in New York State. Once, under Governor George Pataki, in the years after 9/11, an attempt at an Internet-based alert system for all doctors was begun. It was a good idea but got lost in influence-wrangling with the medical societies. Individual hospitals then instituted systems to alert staff, and that would have to do.

The tasks to be performed could easily be handled by the staff of my federal and state colleagues. Mostly, they had protocol in place. Anthrax was an old story that had already been told. It was no surprise that I was left with little to do but offer the following summary: "We know how we will respond to an anthrax attack, but we don't know where and for whom."

My cell phone had vibrated three times during the meeting. I elected to ignore the calls, giving my full attention to the problem at hand. Sitting on a bench in the sun at the end of the sterile, green corridor giving on to endless conference rooms, I keyed up my voice mail. All three messages were from Alison. The first, personal and endearing, made me want to kick myself for letting my annoyance get between us last night. The other two were obviously immediate response to thoughts about the mechanics of imminent terror strikes. Neither were revelations, and both were directed at the likelihood of inside conspirators at both ends of the flight. I saved all three messages and walked down the sunlit corridor to the meeting.

The conference room looked like Monday morning. Wastebaskets were empty, fresh pads and pencils were in military formation on the table, and the sideboard was stocked with water bottles, soda cans, ice buckets, and vacuum pump carafes of coffee, decaf, and hot water. A pile of pastries and cookies sat undisturbed beside the coffee.

Polo shirts, chinos, and blue jeans were gone. Suits and ties had the day. Everyone in the cast appeared a lot more serious, or at least a lot more grown up. Constantine Pano- polous looked like he had already put in a full day. His necktie was pulled three or four inches below his unbut- toned shirt collar, and the jacket of his gray suit was draped over the back of his chair. He was still bouncing pens, but he wasn't talking.

Most of the faces were the same, and we greeted one another and chatted like old friends. There was even some laughter. Panopolous called us to order and all conversa- tions stopped. In Harriet English's place sat Edgar Hum- phreys, the director of the FBI. That was impressive. Harriet sat along the wall behind him, though the quick demotion in rank didn't show on her face. Humphreys was a tall man. I'm guessing nearly six-seven. Thin as a distance runner, he had long, skinny fingers, a beak nose, a perfect row of white teeth, and deeply lined gray eyes under a thick wave of mostly white hair. The collar of his blue button-down shirt was tight around his neck, and he wore a muted, red- and-blue-striped bow tie. He was well put together and confident.

I can't remember exactly when Humphreys was not a fixture in Washington. He had been in his current position through two administrations, and he was deputy director before that. Humphreys regarded his politics as his own business. If not always liked, he was universally respected. Under most imaginable circumstances, leadership of the group would automatically have been ceded to him, but he graciously looked to Panopolous, which reflected either the will of the president, or good manners, or a prearrangement—or all three.

"Folks, let's start by introducing Director Humphreys, who has cleared a busy schedule to be with us." He nodded toward Humphreys, who seemed reluctant to smile but ultimately found some common ground between what was expected in a social situation and appropriate solemnity. Panopolous went on. "Our people have been in contact with sister intelligence services around the world. I'm sorry to say there isn't much to pass on. Here's what little we learned. Despite an increasingly contentious relationship with the ISI, General Kahn has given us assurances that the Pakistani Intelligence Service is not aware of information pertaining to an impending attack upon the United States. I have to believe he understands how seriously we would consider being misled. The general also offered the opinion that homegrown English-Pakistani nationals have no known affiliation with Iranian operatives in Britain. He denies all knowledge of involvement with al-Qaeda of the Arabian Peninsula. The close relationship between al-Qaeda in Pakistan and radical elements in Great Britain is well known, a fact that the general did not deny. But according to the general, no information from his assets with the cells indicates any link to the current issue. All of which means absolutely nothing to me. Remember, these are the same guys who had no idea where Bin Laden was hiding.

"On the other end, our friends on King Saul Boulevard

think the link is definitely AQAP, Yemen, with financing from the Saudis, not Iran. The Israelis have a sixty-year head start on us in dealing with these birds. Their intel has kept them alive. Our humint is challenged at best, so we have to take them seriously. So here we are.

"We don't know who our enemy is, and it's too late to worry about it." He bounced his pen a few times. I kept waiting for it to fly across the table, but he was in a zone and the repetitive action was hypnotizing and remarkably well timed. "As I said, we expect them at JFK in the next day or so. So, at the very least, we're looking for a gay guy with big boobs . . ." There was spotty laughter around the table, and Panopolous wore a big, Cheshire Cat grin, then more laughter. "Not PC, and my apologies to the ladies." He bounced his pen again and almost regained his composure. Even Humphreys smiled broadly. "Okay, okay, not a joking matter, but imagine the headlines. The *Post* will have a field day.

"We do know that the only mule so far identified was an Asian partial transsexual, though the fine points are beyond my pay grade. I think that once the sex-change surgery begins, the transsexual designation is appropriate. The persons involved are believed to be domestic workers employed in Saudi Arabia or the Emirates. We have no reason to assume this pattern will change. In fact, there is evidence that it will continue. We assumed there was an Iranian connection. But the nature of the potential attack has al-Qaeda written all over it. Particularly agents allied to the AQAP bunch in Yemen.

"More pressing than knowing the mastermind, we need

to figure out who to look for and where they are heading. I still believe the water supply is a great method to distribute anthrax. Deaths aside, and there could be hundreds of thousands, the chaos and economic upheaval would be unimaginable. Even with the new filtration system for the Croton branch, there is no assurance it would filter effectively enough. If we close the entire system and raise the chlorine content, there is no definite all-clear date for the water. Even if nobody dies, the fish are gone and we're fucked. I say it's the water, and we can't let it happen.

"Among other good guesses this morning was Grand Central Station. Just drop a bag of anthrax and walk away. You don't just sweep it up. That would be a good one. Any indoor arena would work the same: thousands of people in a confined space is where anthrax attack is most effective. The American Banking Association has its fall meeting at the Javits Center starting on Thursday. That would be symbolic. Then, there's the big target: the United Nations. The opening session of the General Assembly begins Thursday. One hundred and ninety-two heads of state will be in town. The commissioner tells me his security detail is virtually the entire New York City Police Department, and Dell says the Secret Service pulls people from all over the country for the event. For the moment, it is only at the ambassadorial level. All that changes in seventy-two hours. The only way that target is feasible is an inside job. Somebody on the staff of a delegation. Dell, fill us in on that."

Panopolous had been speaking without interruption, without notes, and without a filter. Battlefield conditions, and he did it well. Dell took a sip of coffee from the paper cup in front of him, and stood. He fidgeted and straightened his red necktie before beginning; obviously less at ease than Panopolous, he was no less confident and organized.

"Good morning," said Dell. "Not too much to go over here. We have responsibility for protecting visiting bigwigs. Heads of state, foreign ministers, people of diplomatic status. You all know the drill: black SUVs with D.C. plates and guys in suits with automatic weapons hanging out of the windows on high alert while the president of the Ivory Coast speeds to the Four Seasons for dinner. Nothing we can do about it. But internally, at the missions and in the UN, and in the private cocktail parties and meetings, we are on the outside. Nobody frisks heads of state, ambassadors, counsels general, and deputies, and their assistants get a free ride as well. We are definitely outside the delegation. They are simply above the law. The NYPD lines the streets, keeps the traffic going, provides sharpshooters and anti-terror squads, but it doesn't get inside. We are inside restaurants, stores, and nightclubs, all the public places, but not diplomatic functions.

"People living anywhere near the UN can't even get home. Security is that tight. But that's for outsiders trying to get in. Without a tip or blind luck, there is no way we would be able to contain an inside effort." Dell stopped speaking and scanned the room. He remained standing, anticipating questions, and the varied pitch of all the voices starting simultaneously was the human version of an orchestra tuning up. Humphreys was among the speakers. The floor was yielded to him the moment his voice was heard. It was impressive. The tall man did not bother to stand. Dell quietly took his seat.

"I would like to take a step back, if I may." He did not look to anyone for permission. "There is a Homeland Security office at every international airport in Europe. And there are backscatter or millimeter wave scanners at every airport as well. Particularly Heathrow. There are about thirty flights a day from Heathrow to New York. How hard would it be to be all over them for a few days?"

"What about flights from Gatwick or Stanwick and flights to Newark Liberty?" asked the chief of the Port Authority Police. His question turned a few heads—for interrupting Humphreys, if nothing else. Humphreys raised an eyebrow and seemed to be framing his response when Panopolous spoke.

"Forget about Gatwick and Stanwick, chief. Those flights are mostly charters cheapies, not business flights. They're for working-class Brits, usually ticketed long in advance. It's Kennedy because that is what they know. Newark Liberty? Who the hell ever used that name? Jesus." That brought more smiles.

"They pay my salary, Mr. Undersecretary."

"You got it, chief. Newark Liberty," said Panopolous, yielding to Humphreys, who observed the exchange without apparent amusement.

"Mr. Panopolous is correct," Humphreys began. "The pattern is Heathrow, and it should be easy enough to blanket. It may require that every passenger is screened, patted down, and interrogated, but we can stop this. We can ensure that no passenger with breast implants boards any of the flights in question. That's easy enough."

The civil rights argument was quick to rise. Not necessarily in support of the inevitable ACLU stance, but aware of it. I have to admit I couldn't give a shit what they said. Inconveniencing a small number of people to save tens of thousands of lives is a no-brainer. Humphreys felt similarly. "I will take responsibility for whatever inconvenience the screening causes," he said, to the nodding of heads.

"Director Humphreys," I said. "I'm Wendell Black, a police surgeon with the NYPD, sir. I think we all agree with your position on screening, but if airport personnel are involved in the cell, then screening won't be enough. We need a system to check the screened passengers against every person on the plane. And that has to be after the doors are closed. Otherwise we have no assurance that they haven't gone around us." I thought I was restating the obvious, but apparently Humphreys didn't dismiss the thought. I figured I was on a roll, so I continued my stream-of-consciousness remarks. "And if we can ensure compliance, how seriously do we deal with protecting possible targets?"

"The water supply?"

"Among others, yes." Panopolous tapped the director's sleeve for attention. Humphreys raised his eyebrows as if he was surprised to have been touched. "Constantine, what's on your mind?"

"Sir, if I may respond." Panopolous rose. "We have to

work on the theory that they can elude us at the airports. Or possibly change their port of entry. I do not think we can effectively protect the enormous city watershed from the Catskills to Croton to the Bronx. The rivers and reservoirs are exposed for a hundred miles. Sure, we might be able to guard the treatment facilities in the Bronx and the pumping stations, but the rest is open territory. Think of how poorly we patrol our borders. We can make a show of restricting access to the watershed areas, and we can rely on minute-by-minute testing and prepare to shut down and dump chlorine into the system at a moment's notice and hope for the best. That's the best we can do. Then we make a list of other targets and do whatever we can to protect them. But the director hit the nail on the head. Our best efforts have to be spent on prevention."

A few minutes more and we began reentering the same circle, probably because we didn't know what else to do. Homeland, MI5, and the Special Terrorism Task Force would screen every passenger boarding flights to New York City from Heathrow. At our end, Homeland and customs would head a beefed-up welcoming committee, beginning with flights scheduled to arrive this afternoon.

Something still didn't seem right. It wasn't just the frustration of an unknown enemy. The target was too obvious, and we were too confident about being able to intercept the perpetrators. I felt very uncomfortable. But what it was about was too vague to express. It was just that—a feeling. Even in the face of intuition, whatever that really is, scientifically trained people think in logical sequence. I was sure some of the others shared my discomfort, but no one spoke up.

Two hours into the meeting, Panopolous laid out the plan for deployment of security forces, most of which he would oversee directly. Humphreys would manage relations with MI5 and MI6. Police Commissioner Carey would be on the horn with the chief of the London Metropolitan Police, 24/7, and General Pearson would be our liaison with the rest of the world. How often the head honchos would meet was undetermined, or at least not announced to the rest of us. We were issued new, plastic ID badges, complete with photos and bar codes, to be worn on fresh HS lanyards. Amazing how efficient we could be when we wanted to.

It was half past noon. I headed home to collect Alison and catch a bite. It was unclear how much I would share with her, but the reality was that the only new insight was based on the idea of airport workers' involvement, and that was her idea. I called the office before checking my messages. It took an effort not to scan the list.

"We are surviving without you, Dr. Black. The guys divided up sick call, and nothing pressing to report."

"Calls?"

"The usual. Rodriguez, sounding wild, and Lieutenant Secondi."

"Do I have to call them?" I was hoping for a no. Instead, I got "Rodriguez immediately, and Secondi whenever you can."

No surprise. Fucking Rodriguez.

42

The beautiful morning had clouded over with my mood.
Time was flying by, and the barriers to attack seemed like
a rake with broken teeth. I got to my building quickly
enough and stood outside, trying to get through to Alison
on my cell phone. When she didn't answer, I headed in to
the elevator. I must have been a bit distracted because I
missed whatever it was that the doorman was saying to me.
I had the phone to my ear and waved. Just then, the elevator doors slipped open, and Rodriguez and Griffin came out
at a full run. The big guy slammed into me as he tried to
take the corner around the concierge desk. He went low,
gracefully righted himself like a speed skater, and kept
moving. Rodriguez was ten feet ahead of him and shouting,
"Go right." And then they were gone. Not a word to me—I
was invisible. There wasn't much doubt about where they
had been, but I didn't know where they were going.

I lost my footing and fell back against the concierge desk,
using it to stay on my feet as both Griffin and Rodriguez
raced for the street. Instinctively, I followed. It didn't take

long to get up to speed. They split right and left. Predictably, I went left and found myself closing ground on Rodriguez. Pulling my shield from my pocket, I slipped the lanyard over my neck as I ran. It's hard to tell the good guys from the perps in street clothes. Particularly the way young cops dress. I didn't have a gun drawn—I didn't have a gun at all, and Rodriguez would know me anywhere. But he was a loose cannon. Identifying yourself as a police officer is lesson one in staying alive in street action.

At the corner of Fifth Avenue, he stopped, looked both ways, then again to his right when he saw me. I ran toward him, and he swung around, grabbed my shoulders, and tried to turn me around face-first into the limestone façade of the apartment building on the corner. Instinctively, I resisted.

"Don't fucking move. You're under arrest." He tried to wrestle my arms behind me, and then he reached behind his back for his handcuffs. This time I spun around, drove my left shoulder into his chest. As he staggered back, I put my left leg behind his knees, my hands on his shoulders, and pushed with all my weight. He went down like the sack of shit that he was, and I was all over him. I tried to pin him, but he was too strong. He couldn't reach his gun because I was sitting on his midsection and blocking his movement.

"Stop it, God damn it, stop it, stop it," I screamed in his face, but he kept squirming, and I was beginning to lose my seat on the bucking bull. I raised my butt a foot or so over him, and before he realized he was free, I dropped my full weight on his belly, knocking the breath out of him. Then I rose higher and quickly did it again, bouncing a hundred and eighty-five pounds on his midsection before he could inhale. As Rodriguez struggled for air, I levered the pistol out from behind his back and tossed it along the sidewalk to the building wall. I moved my knees to his shoulders, grabbed his throat with my right hand, and was about to go wild when my better judgment kicked in.

"I could kill you now. Don't make me do this. Settle down. I outrank you here, you dumb fuck. Don't forget it. You want to be a cop? You like being a cop? Then stop this shit." I might have been getting through to him, but the adrenaline rush was definitely over for me, and I was getting shaky.

"I'm getting off you now." I stood over him. "Get up slowly." Which he did, moving tentatively and looking for his gun. Before he could start scrambling, I moved to the wall and had the gun in my hand. Just then, Griffin came around the corner and was trying to process the situation. The pistol was in my pocket and Rodriguez was up and making exaggerated motions of cleaning himself and straightening his clothing, which was so grungy to begin with that it was difficult to tell the difference.

"Hey, Griffin? Your pal here just slipped on his butt. Better come and help him." Griffin seemed to buy it. No reason he shouldn't. He didn't come at me or pull his gun. I was watching every move, ready to react. Rodriguez was humiliated—that's the only way I can explain his acquiescence. He rubbed the top of his head and didn't mention his pistol.

"What are you guys doing here?" I asked Griffin.

"We know she was at your apartment, so don't be cute. I'm sure you wouldn't know anything about that." His tone was sarcastic, and he had every reason to be.

"No, I don't. Was she up there?"

"Yeah. She was there all right. At least, a woman answered the phone, but when we got in, she was gone."

"How did you get in?"

"Building manager. Where is she?" Rodriguez hadn't said a word. I wasn't accustomed to Griffin doing the talking. He hadn't said much since our first meeting. He was blunt and direct but not provocative, not even intimidating. The little guy, his partner, was the nasty bit of business.

"Did you have a warrant to enter my apartment?"

"Where is she?" Griffin snapped.

"Enough. Let's stop this right now. First, you have to show a warrant or good reason to suspect illegal activity, or a clear emergency, to enter uninvited. You know that. No warrant, no entry, and it's too late to document a line of bullshit. I'm not letting this go. I want some answers and some respect."

They were about to protest the technicalities of when police surgeons can pull rank, but I was more certain of my ground than they were. It lowered the pitch of the moment. I had my hands stuffed into the pockets of my sport coat, the right hand around the handle of what felt like a Glock.

I wasn't sure if it was ready to fire, and I had no intention of finding out. The good news was that Rodriguez was too embarrassed about losing his weapon to challenge me.

But I wasn't getting any answers. "Let's bring this matter to your captain. I don't like being accused, and I don't think you have any evidence to sustain invading my home and harassing Dr. Withers."

Griffin looked to Rodriguez.

"Get the car. I'll stay with him," Rodriguez said sharply. He was sounding like himself again. When Griffin's back was turned, I stood between him and Rodriguez, took the pistol from my pocket, and looked at it as I handed it over, barrel-first. It was a Glock. Nice weapon. Rodriguez took the pistol and stashed it in the waistband holster behind his right hip.

"That bitch is involved in this horse-dealing, and you know it."

"Listen, sergeant, this is not about heroin trafficking. This is about bioterror. Bioterror in New York, not some minor drug deal that you think you know something about. Try and get that through your skull, okay? Now I'm going up to my apartment. Get off my case."

"She's a bad apple, doc. Mark my words. We're going to get her, and you better not be involved, that's all I can say. You're obstructing a legitimate investigation, and that doesn't smell right."

Alison's position in this was fair game for suspicion, but like I told Rodriguez, there was a lot more at stake here than a simple drug bust, and I had to keep my priorities straight. I could no longer care about one more minor heroin scheme when the lives of millions of people might be at risk.

I was about to give the building staff hell for allowing the two goons to enter my apartment without a warrant, but having just reminded myself how unimportant this sideshow was, I decided to let it slide.

"Dr. Black, I was trying to tell you about your friends who . . ." The doorman was in midsentence when I interrupted and waved him off.

"Not important, Henry. See you later."

When I got to my apartment, I found the door wide-open. "Fuck!" I said out loud, to nobody, and walked in and looked around. Nothing was disturbed. "Alison, it's me, Wendell. You can come out." There was no answer. I kicked the door closed. And where the hell was Tonto? My question was answered soon enough. Tonto's leash was gone and the service door at the back of the apartment was unlocked. I rang for the service elevator. Thirty seconds later, our much-loved AA operator, who was probably fifty and looked seventy, greeted me with a smile. "How y'all, doc." Billy Joe's jack-o'-lantern smile was hard to appreciate. Usually I would look away, as though I was trying to see who "y'all" was, to avoid staring. But I wasn't in the mood for my own silly humor, and his smile didn't bother me all that much today.

"Seen Dr. Alison . . . Alice and Tonto, Billy Joe?"

"Sure thing, doc. Took 'em down a bit ago. In a big hurry they was. Doc asked me to say I ain't seen her. Which is what I done. Not two minutes later a couple of scruffy-looking bulls, you know, with gold badges around their neck, came tough at me. I done what the doc asked me to. She all right?"

"I'm sure she is fine, Billy Joe. You did the right thing. Saved us a lot of dumb talk."

Alison was gone again. It was becoming a habit. But this time she had Tonto, so I was confident she would surface quickly. Anyway, keeping away from Rodriguez was a good move. I plopped myself into my favorite chair with the *Times*, crossed my feet on the ottoman, and opened the paper full-width—a luxury and the best way to get the whole scope of the newspaper of record. But I could not relax. After glancing at the front page and the spread of pages A2 and A3, I tossed it on the carpet beside the chair, got up, and walked through the living room to the terrace door. I unlocked the dead bolt and stepped outside, and there, parading along Sixty-fourth Street, looking happy and normal, were Alison and Tonto. He was smelling around for evidence of friends, and she was perfectly willing to stand by as he peed indiscriminately on every vertical surface in sight.

I was overjoyed to see them, with the relief that comes of thinking the worst and being proven wrong. For a few seconds I was happy to be just another neurotic New Yorker. Alison looked like she didn't have a care in the world. How could she do it? I whistled three loud blasts, which was my "come" signal for Tonto. He became regally alert, stimulated, confused, and with no idea what was going on. He heard me, but he couldn't find me. Alison immediately looked to the terrace and began waving. After some pointing and calling, Tonto got the idea and barked twice in my direction. Probably all I deserved. For the time being, all was well with the world.

43

Instead of the pure happiness I experienced at seeing Alison evade the police, I should have been concerned with her equanimity in the face of that sort of challenge. Normal people do not take episodes like this in stride.

When she returned to the apartment, Alison seemed confident the police would not return, and she laughed about how easy it had been to slip out the back stairs and through the rear service door onto the street.

"Lots of the tenants must take their dogs out that way. Tonto was in heaven."

"That's true. All the dog walkers use it. Billy Joe knows them all. So does Tonto." I was becoming more relaxed as well. Just another family moment, if your family is dysfunctional, pursued by police, tangentially related to murder, drug smuggling, and intelligence services, and otherwise composed of two highly trained professionals in way over their heads.

I filled Alison in on the meeting. She was still adamant that the water supply was not the target. "Too obvious. Too hard to widely contaminate and not enough shock value."

"Think of the economic havoc," I countered, taking a position I stood against at the meeting.

"No. These people are unsophisticated. They believe in 'boom.' Look at every attack, successful or otherwise. Suicide bombers in the marketplace in Iraq, cafés and school buses in Israel, boom, 'look what we did.' Shoe bombers, underwear bombers, car bombers, and the destruction of the World Trade Center towers. Boom, boom, 'look what we did.' The anthrax mailings in 2002 were quiet terror. One of your crazies, not al-Qaeda. They plant bombs, blow people up, and dance around the chaos. They are fucking Neanderthals. Poisoning the New York watershed, as destructive as it might be, doesn't have enough bang for the buck."

I agreed.

"So, now what?"

26 Federal Plaza isn't exactly home, but I was beginning to feel fairly comfortable there. The new, bar-coded ID opened lots of doors, and simply bypassing the interrogation lightened the load at the security checkpoints. More than eleven hundred special agents are assigned to the New York City field office, which, along with Los Angeles and Washington, D.C., was overseen by a bureau assistant director instead of a special agent in charge, as in the other fifty-three field offices. Only a fraction of the special agents were performing the "gang-busting" tasks that made the bureau famous. Bank robbers were still apprehended, and organized crime confronted, but the days of Dillinger, Bonnie and

Clyde, and the Mafia had passed, of necessity, in favor of antiterrorism work. The bank robber Willie Sutton's succinct answer to the question "Why do you rob banks?" was said to be "Because that's where the money is." Which, in a nutshell, explains the reassignment of manpower within the bureau. Terrorism. That's where the action is.

Worth Street and Federal Plaza is just an easy stroll from Police Plaza. But, as impossible as it seems, the area is even less hospitable to normal life than our home base. Police Plaza is separated from Chinatown by the Chatham Green housing development. The area is dotted with old churches and the tiny Chatham Square Cemetery, the burial ground of the oldest Jewish congregation in North America. It pulses with the good and bad of humanity.

Federal Plaza, on the other hand, is all about Foley Square, the federal courts, and everything that services the courts. One could argue that it is upscale from the goings-on at Police Plaza. A look at the crisp white shirts and pressed suits in the corridors is all that is necessary to see that the scruffy New York edge has been burnished away. The federal grunts lived here. Correction, nobody lived there. But it is the home of federal law enforcement. Sterile, by the book, and I hope more efficient than we hear over at Police Plaza. Only a short walk separates them; the two buildings feel worlds apart.

After 9/11, the high command closed the streets surrounding Police Plaza to protect the building from terrorist truck bombs, or whatever. If they were isolated and forbidding before, this was the frosting on the cake. Still, the hustle and bustle within is real, and the place has all the energy of a subway car. Which brings me back to Federal Plaza.

It is clean. The floors are shiny, and it is quiet, which is why I am surprised to feel comfortable there. In the final analysis, it is all about the people, and this was a good bunch. It had better be. Millions of lives could depend on how good these people were at their jobs. We were all taking our responsibilities seriously.

I had a couple of hours before we reconvened, and though I knew I should be concentrating solely on the problem, as I expected the others were, I was revved up by the surprise visit from Rodriguez and Griffin. In truth, after hearing Alison's side of the story, I felt no more enlightened. I continued to live with the recurring thought that everyone knew more than I, particularly Alison. But I couldn't crystallize my suspicions. Did I think Rodriguez and Griffin were correct? Was she involved with the traffickers? I couldn't imagine that she was, but those guys were professionals, and they made no bones about their suspicions. That was an understatement. In a fairly benign way, I had questioned Alison on several occasions and I saw no benefit in challenging her and hearing yet another denial. Alison, meanwhile, was either turned on by the excitement or was playing to my weakness. Whatever the case, I responded as she sat cuddled under my left arm on the sofa and we kissed.

"Do you want to do it here?" she whispered, opening my pants and slipping her warm hand inside. "This is what I want."

Before I could tear myself from her delicious, moist lips to answer, Alison had eased off the sofa onto the carpet and had my erect penis in her mouth. Everything about me wanted to close my eyes and let it happen, I was ready to explode, but I managed to disengage and led Alison into the bedroom. I wanted everything: love, sex, and release. In the end it was worth the temporary self-sacrifice. I was at peace. My mind had not yet resumed churning, and Alison began to snore lightly as we lay spent and happy on the bed. Tonto had the decency to stay in the living room.

After a quick shower and a return to reality, I gave Alison a quick good-bye kiss and was off to Federal Plaza.

At three p.m., we reported to the conference room. Panopolous looked even more disheveled than he had earlier. I couldn't imagine how he would look after the all-nighter that we assumed was in store for us. We were in it. The time for hypothesizing had passed this morning and we were full-throttle into deployment. Panopolous had made the leap from treating the group on a need-to-know basis to what I am convinced was full disclosure, though one was always unsure what full disclosure meant to spooks.

The first concrete step taken was the deployment of the New York National Guard to police the watershed area. Panopolous reported the deployment less than enthusiastically, as it was unlikely to have much effect in the next twenty-four hours. The seventeen-thousand-member guard had been stretched to the limit. But a small force of uniforms with blackened M4A1 automatic carbines along the Catskill or Croton watersheds would go a long way toward showing we were serious. Unfortunately, it was impossible to provide a human chain-link fence of armed soldiers protecting the collecting lakes, ancient aqueducts, and processing plants that delivered the 1.2 billion gallons of fresh, clean water that New York City consumed each day.

An elevated terrorism advisory had been issued by e-mail to first responders and care providers on the pull side of a push-pull system. Meaning that though there still was no system for pushing information out to all concerned, individuals who had requested bulletins would receive them by e-mail, Twitter, and other social media outlets. Detailed information was not provided. The old system of color-coded alert levels had been abandoned in 2011. We were now operating on an ever-vigilant baseline with two possible bumps: first to ELEVATED, indicating a credible but unspecified threat level; and then to IMMINENT, indicating a credible and specific terrorist threat. The new DHS Counterterrorism Advisory Board would meet within half an hour of a newly uncovered threat, for interagency coordination, and within two hours a new advisory would be issued.

This time, it didn't exactly work that way. Most of the agencies involved had been in on the deliberations for twenty-four hours, trying to parse the presence of a threat versus the level of panic the IMMINENT threat alert would cause. In the end, the level was raised to ELEVATED, but specific details were withheld.

I couldn't see how that would help. Panopolous called it our "cover-your-ass mode." That I understood. So did everyone else around the table.

"We can't send every mother in America searching for Cipro. At least not yet," he added. "Of course, seeing soldiers on the Taconic Parkway ain't exactly SOP. But standard operating procedure or not, some of the troops would be deployed by evening. General Patrick, here, will give us an update."

The new uniform in the room stood. A tall and fit major general in battle fatigues, Patrick was impressive but looked very young. My first thought was, "How could this kid be the adjutant general of the New York National Guard?" He looked about my age. Of course, Dwight David Eisenhower was only a year or two older when he was Supreme Allied Commander in World War II.

Patrick might have had a trace of Boston in his voice. He was forthright and clear, and he might just as well have been addressing his troops. At least it sounded that way. All stiffness and pretense had dissolved among the rest of the core group, so this puffery, if that is what it was, was unexpected.

"I have issued orders for the immediate mobilization of the 42nd Infantry Division of Staten Island, the 27th Infantry Battalion, including the 69th Infantry Regiment, and the 1st Battalion of the 258th Field Artillery, as well as the 105th Military Police Company and the 2nd WMD Support Team stationed at the Bronx filtration facility . . ."

"Excuse me, general," Panopolous interrupted. "How many troops are already at station?"

"None, sir. The first personnel will be in place by 1800 hours today."

"Okay. Can you estimate our total troop complement by 0800 tomorrow?"

"By my best reckoning, 2,412, sir, inclusive of the Weapons of Mass Destruction Support Team."

Panopolous slid his chair back from the table. "Twenty-four hundred troops protecting a thousand fucking miles of watershed. Amazing. That won't cut it, general."

"Sorry, sir, as of 1200 hours today, that is all the manpower available for mobilization. Our troops are spread thin doing tours in Afghanistan. That is all I can offer."

"Sheeeit. Goddamn. Not your fault, general. Sorry. No offense meant."

"None taken, sir."

"Be seated. Be seated, general. Thank you."

The general was obviously unaccustomed to taking orders, and I would hate to be the aide sitting outside in his staff car. It was going to be a rotten day.

The first flights from London were scheduled for arrival within the hour. The Customs and Border Protection, the TSA, and the Port Authority police were on high alert with an increased presence everywhere. National Guard troops were stationed in the arrivals buildings, but fierce as they looked, they had no specific training for the job at hand. Panopolous intended to monitor the situation from the office he had commandeered on the twenty-third floor, just down the corridor from the conference room. It looked like a RadioShack in there, with newly installed electronic equipment on every horizontal surface. Some of it was sitting on crates stenciled with the names of army branches and codes. The two communications officers at desks within the mess were frantically busy and didn't welcome questions. Both were in shirtsleeves and neckties and wore antiterror crisis task force IDs.

Standard operating procedure dictates that every passenger and all luggage entering the United States or moving between airports within the country is scanned, wanded, or physically examined. Which, of course, does not mean that nothing slips by. No scan, no flight is the rule at Heathrow, and individuals in full burka who refused scans or body searches have been turned away. That assumes everything works properly. If there is complicity with airport employees, all bets are off. Any number of events can circumvent the system. There are other, safer ways to prevent suspect individuals from boarding.

Homeland maintains offices at major airports around the world. Their presence at Heathrow is well known and integrated into the security apparatus. By now they were on full alert, with a mission not quite as hopeless as looking for a needle in a haystack. The incidence of breast implants in the general population is not as low as one might think. In the U.S., more than 300,000 women undergo the operation every year. Over ten years that comes to 3,000,000 women in this country alone, and the operation has been around for fifty years, so maybe one in twenty to one in fifty women have breast implants. That works out to a reasonable possibility of several on each flight. Easy enough to scan—if they present themselves for scanning. And exactly how much do the scans tell us? Can a scan differentiate anthrax from silicone gel? The density of the substance determines its resistance to X-ray penetration. But you can't Google that question for a simple answer, and backscatter detects the implant, not its contents. But if the machine could be powered up, it might do the trick. For the moment I dismissed the outrage that would engender. One step at a time.

After daydreaming through some part of the meeting, I made my first real contribution since selling my hypothesis. I excused myself, went into the corridor, and called the chief medical examiner, where this mess was first discovered.

For want of a protocol, Benson had stored the intact, heroin-filled, second implant with the ruptured implant and the recovered heroin powder in a sealed container within a sealed locker. Benson knew the street value of the heroin in his care. He also knew how to handle and preserve evidence.

After a greeting and a modest interlude, I said, "We need a big favor . . ."

"Who's we?" Benson asked, but he wasn't negative right out of the box.

I explained about the anthrax threat and ad hoc group and ticked off some of the more impressive members.

"Anthrax. Jesus. And what, pray tell, are you doing swimming with those sharks?"

"Not much, truth be told. But I was the guy who stumbled into the whole mess, and kind of started the ball rolling."

"And now they think the ball has gotten enough mass to become a biological avalanche?"

"Maybe time bomb is a better description," I answered. "You can imagine what the hell is going on here."

"Call out the troops, doctor, call out the troops."

"Already have. Please don't talk about anything we just discussed. We're kind of holding it close to the vest until we figure out what to do."

"How close are you?"

"Not close at all. We really need to know the density of an anthrax-filled implant to see if it can be distinguished from a garden-variety implant by a backsplash or scatter device." The line was silent.

"Ben?"

"Yeah. I'm here. I'm not familiar enough with the units in use at JFK."

"It's worse," I interrupted. "We are particularly concerned with Heathrow. I can get the specs for you."

"Right. But let's take baby steps. You get all of that in order; I want to get an X-ray and MRI of the intact implant."

"I get it. Heroin powder side-by-side with saline- and gel-filled implants. That will give us the general idea."

"Righto. A word to the wise. If your level of suspicion is red alert, then stop everyone with implants. Don't let them board. Worry about the inconvenience later."

"Thanks, Sherlock, I'll pass it on to my masters."

Panopolous had been on that one from the first conversation. His position on everything was "Prepare for the worst." He had already been through extensive conversations with MI5, Scotland Yard, and Homeland at Heathrow. No one with breast implants was boarding. Not at Heathrow, not at Gatwick, and, with a bit more time to make the case, not at any airport in Western Europe. Meanwhile, outside the UK, it was IMMINENT alert and screen, screen, screen. If the terrorist cell had any clue that we were on to them—and they had to—the smart move would be to wait it out. We couldn't keep up this level of vigilance indefinitely. Symbolic moments aside, they could do whatever they planned to do anytime. Analysts at Langley were working on permutations involving important moments for the jihad, Muslim history, numerical symbols, and any other combinations that might offer a clue to some sort of timing imperative that might help pin down the date. So far, no luck.

By six, there wasn't a lot for me to do. The half dozen seats in the situation room were taken by the professionals, and I was an observer with nothing to contribute. But my sense was we were still not going at it correctly. That is, all the moves were correct and appropriate, but we were missing something. Something key. I didn't share my reservations with Panopolous.

As soon as I left the building, I called Alison. She answered promptly from my living room.

"Amazing," I said. "You're where you were meant to be."

"Hello, Wendell. I am meant to be in your home, is that it?"

"Not such a bad thing."

"Why, doctor, how romantic." There was that smile in her voice.

"Hmmm. Not a good segue, but how about meeting me in Chinatown for dinner?"

"Incurable romantic."

"But I am downtown, and I am hungry, and you are always hungry, and let's do it."

"We did earlier, you insatiable brute."

"A-li-son," I growled.

"What time and where?"

Then I called Deuce. There was no reason to check in other than wanting a sounding board for my thoughts.

"Hey, doc," Deuce said, reading my name on his phone.

"Don't call me doc. You know I hate that."

"All the more reason." The formalities completed, we got down to business.

"Deuce, I need to pick your brain on this terrorist thing, or at least share my thoughts with you. The whole thing seems to be playing out wrong."

"What happened?" Deuce asked quickly.

"Well, nothing happened. I just think it isn't going to go down the way the brass think it will. And we may miss the boat completely."

"Nah. Those guys are real pros. They have good intel, and they know how the creeps think. It's not our thing. We think street. That's our job. These guys are different. I don't mean the bureau hotshots. You know how I feel about them. But the CIA and Homeland people, they have their own rules, and they get shit done. Have faith." He seemed convinced, but I wasn't buying.

"I agree. They are impressive, but intuition counts, and these guys have not been on the ground. They're big brass, suits, whatever. The intel comes from blind sources. Something isn't right. Correction. Something tells me we are missing a catalyst."

"What does that mean?" Deuce interrupted.

"You know, something that accelerates a chemical reaction."

"What the fuck are you talking about? Bombs?" He was serious. Sometimes what seems like the most basic reference is actually professional jargon outside the frame of reference of others.

"No, no. Sorry. It's not about bombs. I mean we are missing some ingredient, and it's making us spin our wheels unnecessarily."

"Right. Why didn't you say that?"

"Deuce, I did." Before things degenerated further, I had the bright idea to invite him to join us for dinner.

"Yeah, sure. I would love that. Let me call home and tell Amy. Want me to pick you up?"

"No thanks. I'm still over at Federal Plaza. A stroll over to Chinatown will do me good."

44

Doyers Street is a nasty little one-block arc joining the Bowery with Pell Street. At the turn of the last century it was known as the Bloody Angle, after the murderous ambushes tong members met in the blind alley. The immediate area is home to some of the very special joints in Chinatown. Joe's Shanghai, a communal-table mecca of steamer baskets of hot, squirty soup dumplings, holds down the Bowery end of Pell Street before the alley. At the shoulders of the angle on Doyers is a little place dear to my heart. A savory child-hood memory called Nom Wah Tea Parlor. It was down at the heels then, and it hasn't aged gracefully, which is part of its charm. It has a tall young owner now, capping fifty years of family management. He is as American as an iPad, and he gets it. The food is great, the place still looks like 1950, and the little plates of dumplings washed down with icy Tsingtao beer are still a bargain. I'm not sure everyone enjoys it as much as I do, but I don't really care. Alison loves it.

"Take my word for it, this is a good place" was my only explanation. Deuce gave me the raised eyebrow and was about to begin another round of bitching when Alison arrived. He stood to greet her. They had met once before, and I was glad to see he was comfortable enough to accept a couple of European-style kisses on the cheek without getting red in the face and flustered the way big guys do.

"Nice to see you, doctor."

"And you, lieutenant."

"Deuce," he answered.

"Alison," she countered. "I hope you like this place as much as we do."

"The lieutenant was perusing the plastic menu and saying something which I will paraphrase as 'who can eat this stuff?'"

"Try it. If you don't like it, we can take you for a steak after dinner." We all smiled. I managed to convey our desire for water, tea, and three beers to a mystified waitress, and we got down to studying the menu.

"Anything you don't eat?"

Deuce shook his head. "I don't know what any of this stuff is."

I waved the waitress over and handed her the billet with a whole lot of choices checked off. Then we got down to business.

Alison was quiet during my summation. Deuce asked a few questions and finally said, "Why don't they put you in the field? You know Tahani and the guy who was killed, Farzan. You saw the mule, and you have more of a sense of them than a bunch of soldiers and feds."

"Sure, but where should I go?"

"Terminal 4 at Kennedy," Alison answered before Deuce could speak.

"I wasn't even thinking that," Deuce said, "but it is a damned good idea. Get you out there, maybe both of you, with a feel for the opposition. We can do the rest."

"Deuce, with all due respect, you are not part of this. They would kill me if I brought you in." I shook my head as if to emphasize what a bad idea that would be.

Two baskets of steamed shrimp dumplings arrived, and I served them out. I felt like the parent of a three-year-old. When Deuce struggled long enough with the chopsticks to be humiliated, I flagged down the waitress and got him a fork. Conversation was suspended as he followed instructions and added some soy sauce and hot mustard to the brew. He chewed, made some sort of noise, and smiled. "Wow."

"Wow, indeed. Glad you like it. Much more to come."

The food came fast and furiously, and talk was held to the essentials of eating until we had, all three, overeaten and were sipping hot tea.

"What would we do at the terminal—just hang out and look at people?"

"Pretty much," Alison said.

I considered it again. "Better than twiddling our thumbs," I agreed.

"I think she's right," Deuce said. "It might amount to something. A sighting, a face, something."

Alison spoke again. "It has to be tomorrow. It just makes sense."

"I'm glad you are so sure of yourself. I'm so frustrated, I could be convinced to go along with anything. Panopolous might have an issue with me going out there. I should check with him. The place is probably a military zone by now. We might not be able to get through the barriers."

"Your fancy new ID should open all doors," Deuce said, "assuming the guys down the chain of command have heard about the brain trust. I'll go out there with you. They can't stop an NYPD Homicide detective from doing his job."

That's how it all began. Simply and well intentioned. We agreed that we were too tired tonight, and anyway, by the time we got to Kennedy there would only be two or three more arrivals from LHR. Better to have a good night's sleep and go at it fresh in the morning.

I paid the dinner check; Deuce left a twenty-dollar tip on the table, and he gave us a lift to my place. We agreed to head out to the airport at ten in the morning, which would get us there in time to welcome the first flight.

"You still don't have wheels, right?"

"Right. We can go out with you, or I can rent a car."

"Are you on leave? If not, you can get a car and driver from the motor pool. This is business."

"Nah. Can't do that. I would feel funny. Anyway, the driver would waste the day sleeping in the car in front of Terminal 4, when he could be doing his job."

"Man, what a straight arrow. I'll pick you up at ten. If I get bored or called out, you can get a cab home."

Alison kept me company on the nightly walk. Tonto seemed to find it natural enough. So did I.

After strolling for a bit with Tonto's lead in my right hand, Alison slipped her arm around my left elbow and said, "We never talked to Deuce about Rodriguez and company."

"Funny. You're right. I wasn't avoiding the topic. You know that I spoke to him after it went down. I guess there was too much happening, and I simply forgot. Plenty of time to fill him in tomorrow."

We chatted as we walked the big nightly circle in the park, ending back at the door to my building. It was almost ten, and I had correctly assumed Alison planned to stay. Six weeks ago, she had claimed a foot of bedroom closet space, which seemed a small price to pay for her company. On top of that, she had been thoughtful enough to deposit her lotions and potions in the guest bath. The system worked for both of us, and I didn't feel hemmed in.

While Alison was in the powder room, I checked my e-mail and messages. There was a text from a number I didn't recognize. I scrolled through it quickly for the sign-off name. Tahani! Tahani. Apparently, he wasn't dead, if the message was genuinely from him. It had been received fifteen minutes earlier, three a.m. London time, if he was in London. Or did that mean it was sent at five past ten, which would indicate he was in the country, or at least in the time zone. I stopped diddling with the time issue and read the message.

"Thank you for your concern. My patient is now doing well. She can travel in the morning. Tahani."

I felt my body shiver from my head and neck down to my shoulders, chest, and knees, like a wet dog shaking off. Man. I was certain he was dead. And now he was back from the dead and sending me very important information. I sat on the edge of the bed to think it through. The message was real enough, based on the last question I had asked him, and the information was important. Very important. It meant everything, if it was true. Alison was right. Tomorrow was the day.

I scrolled through my BlackBerry for the encoded sequence to text Panopolous. Intelligence people were devoted to BlackBerry technology. It was the only self-contained system. It had its own servers and couldn't be hacked. Or at least was far more difficult to hack than iPhones. On top of that, all phone messages, e-mails, and texts went to the servers in the situation room, were encoded there, and forwarded in some manner that was far above my capabilities. All I knew was that direct communication between us was restricted to emergent situations. Messages of all lower priority were sent by secure electronic mail and distributed instantly.

"Following message received at 10:15 p.m. Please advise. Black."

The message was forwarded as received, including the time and routing information.

Alison was standing in the archway to the bedroom, wearing only a blue shirt of mine. Her arms were crossed under her breasts and she was watching me stare at the BlackBerry in my hand. "What?" she asked.

"You were right. Tomorrow is the day. Tahani just texted me." I scrolled back to the message and handed the device to her. She read it and continued to stare at the screen for a while, as I had.

"Super. God, I wonder where Tahani is, where he was all this time. Good for him. I had written him off. Hadn't you?"

"Definitely."

"Now what?"

"Now we wait. I just forwarded the message to Panopolous. Let's see what he has to say."

I brushed my teeth, washed my face, used the toilet, tossed my shirt and shorts into the hamper, and slipped under the covers next to Alison. Before I could get close to her, my cell phone began to vibrate on the night table. It was Panopolous. No surprise. "Black?"

"Yes. Thanks for getting back to me."

"Have you thought about why he contacted you?"

"Why he contacted me." That was an uncharacteristically dumb question, I thought. "Sure. I was nice to him in London, and I think he realizes what a horror show this can become. I think, basically, he's a good guy trying to do the right thing."

"And how do you account for his sudden reemergence?"

"I can't." I was hesitant to say "we can't."

"Interesting."

"Why, how would you look at it?"

"Well, you could postulate he was being held by the

forces of evil, maybe even tortured or dead, and his phone was used to disseminate disinformation. Did you speak to him?" Panopolous asked.

"No, I didn't try. I sent the message directly to you."

"Yeah, that was proper procedure. Well, we tried to reach him. The phone was shut down. No signal picked up by us or the Brits. Whoever sent the text probably pulled the battery so we can't locate the phone. Not usually the thought process of a helpful citizen."

I was silent. I looked over at Alison, who was sitting up in bed listening to my side of the conversation. She shrugged her shoulders, held up her palms, and made it clear she couldn't follow.

"That is possible, but what do we lose by treating it as the real thing?"

"We deploy our forces, cripple the airport, inconvenience several thousand people, and look like fools. Then they can play the game again, knowing what our response will be. Makes evasion a lot easier."

"All of that makes sense, but I don't think we can discount this as a real threat. Can't we keep our vigil? We expected tomorrow might be the day anyway. Do whatever you planned, don't call off any other exercises, and assume the information confirmed our guess. That way we won't take it as disinformation and lower our guard and risk having them slip past us tomorrow."

"You should have been a spook. For your information, General Pearson agrees with your assessment. That's the plan."

"What's the plan?"

"Take the message as another piece falling into place confirming tomorrow as the day. No extra activity beyond what is already in place. Everything according to plan. Good work." Panopolous was finished with the conversation, but I wanted another word.

"I would like to be on site tomorrow," I said, intentionally avoiding asking if he had any objections. Panopolous answered quickly.

"Sure thing. You're in the middle of this. We have an expanded field office at Terminal 4. Ask the TSA people for the Homeland officer. They won't know what the hell your ID means, so badge them and wait for Ted Philos. He's my guy. He'll be expecting you. And, Dr. Black, you can bring the girl."

That caught me by surprise. Why was Alison suddenly welcome? He knew more than I thought. It made me wonder how secure my phones and my home were. And this is how they treat the good guys.

45

There was one report of a passenger who was refused flying status from LHR. Four women on the first Virgin flight screened positive for breast implants. All four were detained at the Homeland office and re-scanned. Three agreed to physical examination by a nurse employed by MI5, as a condition for boarding. One declined and was turned away, despite a zero level of suspicion. The three cleared to fly had mature inframammary surgical scars. There were no periareolar or axillary scars. Breast implants can be inserted from around the areola or under the arm, but those routes were far less common. None had evidence of recent abdominal incisions or other possible routes of insertion. Two were returning American women, and the third was French. All were in their late thirties and had verified identities and reasons for travel. All three were in the air when we arrived outside customs in Terminal 4.

Panopolous was correct about my ACG ID being useless, and the TSA employee stonewalled me. Deuce wasn't having any of it. In less than thirty seconds, he had badged him and insisted on seeing a supervisor. A quick call and a

very brief waiting period, and we had an intelligent, coop-
erative thirtysomething woman guiding us to the Homeland office. She was informed of the mission, held the door
open for us, and asked if there was anything else she could
do to help. It felt like we were on the same side.

The office was decidedly unimpressive. It could have
been any government office, police station, or airport
lounge in the country. Lifeless lime-green walls, plastic
chairs, and veteran desks in their second or third incarna-
tion were the only furniture. The requisite flags stood
guard around photos of the president and the secretary of
Homeland Security. Otherwise, the three rooms that I could
see from the entry were unadorned. The far wall of the
main room was hung with CCTV screens, which I assumed
were trained on sensitive areas of the terminal. All the
desks held large, last-generation computers, which the
agents seemed to be ignoring in favor of tablets and other
handheld devices. The place was buzzing with activity.
Five of the six agents in the large room gave us the once-
over. The sixth was giggling on his cell phone, probably
planning a life after his shift. Two of the five were women,
and there were three female secretaries scurrying around.
All the secretaries appeared to be Latina. The agents were
all over the place. A handsome young Latino man in a
white Homeland golf shirt; a tall guy with deep-set, sad
eyes and a light-blond crew cut, in the same kind of shirt,
who appeared to be Eastern European; and the third man,
clearly Middle Eastern, dressed in fancy blue jeans and a
Versace T-shirt. The women were good-looking and in their

twenties. Both wore jeans and sweaters and could have been valley girls. I looked at Deuce and we smiled. It looked like the locker room at a SoHo gym. I guess that was the general idea. Fit in.

We had plenty of time to take in our surroundings because the "one minute" the secretary promised it would take to produce Philos had dragged on past twenty.

"If that prick doesn't show up in two minutes, we're out of here."

"Calm down, Deuce. Philos is on the firing line. Particularly today." Just as Deuce turned away from me, the door opened at the far left of the space that functioned as reception room and bullpen. A man every bit as tall as Deuce, but at least fifty pounds lighter, entered smiling. He was polished and handsome, with a ring of fair hair going gray, a tanned bald scalp, and a good-sized black mustache. Every bit of sixty, more presidential than cop, and hardly what Panopolous's term "Greek Mafia" brought to mind, other than an eye-snapping resemblance to the Greek president.

"Folks, please excuse me for keeping you waiting, I simply could not break free. This place is crazier than ever, which I hear is due to you. So thank you for that. I hope we do some good today. I'm Ted Philos." He extended his hand and shook mine firmly. He greeted Deuce the same way, and then turned to Alison, took her hand, and stared into her eyes. She all but melted. Philos had won us over by being himself, or so it seemed. "We thought since you both know Dr. Tahani, and the doctor who was killed, you might come across a familiar face during deplaning and customs clearance. We have excellent CCTV coverage of everything that goes on out there. You will be able to watch it all in real time over there." He pointed to the door he had come through earlier. "That's why I was detained. I was reviewing the digital recordings of the late flights last night."

"Reviewing as in viewing again?" I asked.

"No, reviewing the work done by my team. Extra eyeballs never hurt."

"What were you looking for?" I asked.

"The usual. Suspicious behavior and individuals profiled in our brief. In this case, Asian men, Asian men dressed as women traveling alone, and generally, people from the Stans and the Middle East."

"That covers a great deal of ground on flights from London, doesn't it, Mr. Philos?" Alison asked. It was a rhetorical question, and the first time she had spoken without having been asked a question.

"Yes. This is a busy posting for that profile, but my team is good at it. The best, I hope. Everything at the JFK port of entry is first-team." We were still standing where we had met, and Philos looked at us. "Why are you smiling?"

"The TSA people out front. What a joke," Deuce said.

"Not every employee is a rocket scientist, I will give you that. But the agency is only ten years old, and it's under Homeland now. All that will change."

"Great. They're still a bunch of idiots."

Philos laughed dismissively. "I understand the frustration people feel interacting with them, but they are the first line of defense, and they do what they are instructed to do, and not always perfectly. But there are fifty thousand TSA employees. We at Homeland haven't chosen the bulk of them, and it is not a high-paying or high-prestige job. These are the people who deal directly with the public. Our version of your traffic enforcement agents in the city. They represent the city, wear the insignias of the NYPD, and are the lowest common denominator among public employees. Lousy job, low pay, and the people attracted to the opportunity are not the best-educated people in the job pool. What do you expect?"

Apparently, Philos had had the discussion more than once.

Deuce said, "Yeah. We all have our problems." And the subject was dropped. In the silence, I thought about Mrs. Black, my secretary. Mrs. Black, about as gentle and well-educated as her job allows, always contended that doctors, lawyers, and bankers had no idea how to run a business. They deal with the public, depend on public perception, and still have the least experienced, and often lowest paid, employees answering phones and dealing with the public. Why not be represented by people your clientele can relate to. People with good manners. People who make an effort to speak the language. People who make an effort to be nice. It's not a big deal, just common sense. Philos would probably counter: "Civil service, unions, human resources." All the excuses for poor performance, and generally I agreed. When you run across a pleasant, intelligent TSA employee or traffic agent, they are invariably supervisors. I rest Mrs. Black's case.

"Now that we have settled that," Philos said, "let me take you through the sterile area." Alison and I shared a "huh" moment, but we followed him through the viewing room and out the other side into the vast immigration hall. We stood between the lines where the customs agents screened passports and the exit to the baggage claim and customs inspection.

"There are three points of contact between U.S. Customs agents and arriving passengers. Throughout the entire process, passengers are isolated from the outside. Cell phone use is forbidden, and reception is intentionally poor in the immigration hall. Since yesterday, we have been intercepting calls instead of jamming the circuits.

"The baggage claim area is isolated but not totally sterile. There are airline employees, baggage handlers, and porters milling around. They have all been screened, but I wouldn't vouch for them. The only exit for passengers is through the customs funnel, where two agents clear customs declarations and either pass people to the exit or assign them to an alley where luggage is inspected and passengers are further interviewed." Philos finished and was waiting for comments. Nothing he said was a great revelation if you did any foreign travel.

"What's the weak link?" Deuce asked.

"There is none. Nothing obvious. It's a pretty good system."

That seemed a bit optimistic to me. Deuce beat me to the punch. "Any place where the environment is unsterile is suspect. How many doors in and out of the baggage claim area?"

"Offhand, I don't know. But we watch everything."

"Like what?" Deuce asked.

"Like I said, everything. In that area we look for items handed off to personnel. Things that wouldn't get through inspection. It doesn't happen often. A rich guy trying to avoid duty on jewelry isn't going to entrust it to a hip-hop dude pushing a wagon. Profiling smugglers is about likely associates. Same goes for terrorists. Think 'it takes one to know one' and most of the time you will be right."

"Too simple," Deuce said. "Let's watch."

46

To say the day went slowly is to soft-sell boredom. There wasn't a comfortable place to sit, and milling around the immigration hall and baggage area got old quickly. People-watching was why we were there. That part was interesting and new to me. The waiting between arrivals was torture.

"Welcome to your first stakeout, doc."

"Fuck you too, lieutenant."

"Boys," said Alison, semi-seriously.

Trying to be unobtrusive in a huge, unadorned public space isn't easy. What made it almost possible was the endless stream of new faces. Without the turnover we would be made in minutes. Alison and I strolled together, trying to look like a couple waiting for their luggage. Periodically, one or the other of us would look annoyed at the inept baggage delivery system. Deuce looked like a cop.

After an hour, we adjourned to the CCTV viewing area and found seats. The initial immediacy of purpose was gone, but it was strangely easier to stay alert.

"Look at how many people on the non-U.S. passport lines are from Asia, the Middle East, or the Raj," Alison remarked. It was the first time I ever heard anyone use the term *Raj* in conversation. I thought it was one of those politically incorrect things people no longer said.

"You mean Indian and Pakistani?"

"Yes, of course. And their neighbors on the subcontinent, the other Stans."

I didn't want to sound bigoted, but I asked, "How can you tell the difference between people from all the Stans?"

Alison answered evenly, "Forget bias. Just profile the people you see. See if you can pigeonhole them. It's a game. Male or female, skin color, features, size of nose, type of hair, all the things you were taught to make believe you didn't notice. Typical phenotypic characteristics. Eye color is all over the map, you know that, but some things hold true: 99 percent of ethnic Estonians have blue eyes . . . so if we ever go to war with Estonia keep that in mind. The point is it's stupid not to use common sense. Look at how people dress. There are ethnic trends even when they think there aren't. People from Eastern Europe look like people from Eastern Europe. Look at shoes, particularly men's shoes. Shoes tell a lot about a man's social class and origins. More than women. Affluent women buy shoes from a few big-name designers, and down the line the knock-offs follow. Men don't see shoes as fashion. Pay attention to what they look like. Make snap decisions. You do it anyway, we all do, and now it can help us." Alison waited for a comment.

"Don't accuse me of being a bleeding heart—I'm not. But I've been on the job far too long not to see the abuses. Terry stops have been going on since the 1968 Supreme Court decision, I think."

"What are Terry stops?" Alison asked.

"Terry stops refers to a Supreme Court case under Earl Warren, which allowed stop-and-search by police officers when they have reasonable suspicion of an illegal act, or believe they are in danger, but have no actual knowledge that anything illegal has been done. Since then it has been used to harass generations of black and Hispanic males but also to arrest a lot of bad-ass, weapon-carrying perps. Point is, it has been amazingly well used and seriously abused. But that's ancient history. The Patriot Act makes Terry stops look like an ACLU invention."

"Do you really believe that?"

"What, that profiling is abused? Definitely. If you were a nice black college kid driving through town after a party with a carload of friends, maybe playing the tunes a bit louder than necessary, what do you think the chances of being stopped and searched by the police would be versus the same stop-and-search probability for white kids? And would you feel alienated, or would you say, 'Okay, most violent crime in cities is perpetrated by young black males, so thank you, officer, for the stop-and-search.' I doubt it. But I also believe it is a necessary evil. A reflection of the facts of life. If all cops were thoughtful, well educated, and secure, there would be no issue. But, sadly, most of them are human, and some are bigots and bullies, and some suf-

fer from mass mentality, which, combined with fear for either themselves or the country, puts civil rights in jeopardy.
If anyone has the right to curtail civil rights, where does it
end, and who will be the judge of that?"

"Wendell, I understand. I'm English; we pat traitors on
the wrist and wish them well. I've grown up respecting
civil rights and the right to dissent, to disagree. Now please,
just keep an eye out for nice people who look like they
might be terrorists."

"Jesus, don't you think that's what I'm doing?" I asked.

"After that lecture, I had a moment of doubt."

"Don't."

"Good. Our problem is not going to be individuals who
fit the profile. They are too smart for that. We have a leg up
knowing about the Asian male mules, but don't count on it.
Watch everything, everybody. Something won't be right.
A movement, a twitch, something won't fit. That's our
sign," Alison said.

"Don't profile?"

"No, do profile, but don't exclude anyone or anything.
These people know what we look for. A young guy with a
ratty beard and a bulky coat is going to be a red herring,
but we have to react. If we don't, one day one of them will
be carrying a bomb. We have to spend resources even
when our level of suspicion is low. In the long haul, that
has been one of their most potent weapons. Security everywhere, lifestyle interruptions, crippling expense. The col-
lateral damage is killing us, literally, and changing our
lives. We're only now learning how to play the game. Your

drones have been a great help in taking guerrilla warfare to the guerrillas. Much more effective than in Pakistan. Nothing has been more disruptive to al-Qaeda, AQAP, and their allies. Al-Awlaki is a great example. Now, I think we are looking at their response."

Six hours later there was nothing to report other than that we now knew our way around backroom security and the public areas. Things looked pretty much the way one would expect in the immigration and baggage areas. There was no unusual show of force inside isolation. Panopolous and Philos had made the hard decision that the courier was on the way whether or not we showed overwhelming force on site. The area was controlled, and no one could get out of isolation areas unless Customs and Homeland passed them. Outside baggage claim, it was an armed camp. The thinking was that once airborne, they couldn't turn the mule back despite whatever panic message was issued. On arrival, the mule had to be apprehended and would be, but maintaining a business-as-usual appearance in sensitive areas would allow authorities to trap the cell operatives at the airport. There was nothing to lose so long as the mule didn't get through.

Between arrivals, the hall was eerie. The plastic tape defining the immigration queues stood despite the absence of crowds. The occasional straggler still was made to drag hand luggage through the switchbacks to reach a bored employee in an ill-fitting uniform, assigning customs booths. The lack of consideration was both psychologically diminishing for the traveler and an unpleasant welcome to the United States. It also allowed the cameras more time to observe each and every movement.

Drifting toward four p.m., there was more activity at arrivals and definitely more behind the scenes. Customs inspectors, TSA, and airline employees made ready for the shift change. It all looked routine. The same number of uniforms came in as departed, but the demographics were decidedly different. Sharp-looking, fit, military-type personnel replaced the tired, stressed men and women unified by the chips on their shoulders and bad attitudes. Only the uniforms were the same. The new TSA inspectors were highly trained DHS antiterror operatives. The new shift of customs officers had the benefit of a detailed briefing from Philos, which didn't happen often, and they were on high alert. Law enforcement officials began to talk about food.

47

Being inside the guts of an airport was like anything else.
The wonder and magic were short-lived. Technical miracles
like tracking aircraft in flight and passengers on the ground
were briefly new, and then just another tool. The Homeland
guys had listening devices, jammers, intelligence networks,
and the finest weapons an unlimited budget could buy.
They were federal special officers sworn to protect the
country against its enemies, and then they were just another bunch of cops using different jargon.

Operation "Dust" was in its early stages, and an enthusiastic team spirit enlivened everything. The level of security employee skyrocketed noticeably as Homeland stood
in for TSA. It was SOP under suspicion of imminent attack.
Mostly, they were nice guys. A little intense for my style,
but they worked from crisis to crisis, and the stakes were
high. Right now, we were still getting to know one another.
It was dinnertime, and hungry people were more alike
than different. One of the feds, a thick redhead about
thirty, wearing chinos and a fashionably wrinkled work-
shirt, was holding court at a nearly clear desktop at the

periphery of the room. He was writing with his left hand, taking food orders on a lined legal pad with the Homeland Security logo at the top of the sheet. With the pile of cash in front of him and the steady stream of men and women dictating orders and dropping money, the place had the air of the ten-dollar window at Belmont.

"How about the finest. What do you guys want for dinner?" he asked.

"What's on the menu, J. Edgar?" Deuce asked.

"Gourmet choices. We're doing Subway. What'll it be?"

"We pass," Deuce said. "Thanks." He waved away my objections with a glance. His eyes said, "Trust me."

It was almost an hour and a half until VS009 arrived at 2010; 8:10 p.m. to us. Alison and I followed Deuce out the back of the Homeland office into the bowels of the terminal. He was doing double time, and his strides were longer than ours.

"Hold it, man. What's the hurry?" Deuce just waved us on and kept moving. How we managed to get from immigration to the departures area was a mystery, but Deuce halted in front of the Palm Bar and Grille, and gave us his best smile. "Ain't I good to you?"

"The Palm. The real Palm, in the airport?" I asked.

"You bet. It's the real thing. We deserve some decent chow."

In fact, Deuce was right. An offspring of the famous steak house, the menu boasted mouthwatering slabs of pure cholesterol. We opted for the fabulous hamburgers and greedily stuffed our faces and drank Diet Coke, which was too bad, since an ice cold Heineken would have been perfect. I was disappointed that my companions wasted great beef on burgers cooked medium. Mine was very rare and very delicious. I ate it all and was spiraling toward a protein-induced coma. Two cups of thick, old coffee were necessary to banish the fuzz. I picked up the tab for dinner. It was an expensive hamburger.

We returned to the command center a lot less alert and edgy than we had been an hour ago. The science disputes that food in the stomach and intestines causes pooling of blood in the abdomen, depletes blood supply to the brain, and results in sleepiness. My father believed it and regularly fell asleep in his green leather chair immediately after leaving the table and filling his pipe. Lunch or dinner, it didn't matter. He ate and he snored. Others indict elevated blood sugar and the release of insulin, though I'm not exactly sure how that makes you sleepy. Anyway, the edge was off, too far off. There were three more flights from LHR expected this evening, and we needed to be vigilant.

Deuce wandered off on his own, working two cell phones, which was something all the agents seemed to be doing as well. I watched the monitors and tried to imagine every step a traveler took from deplaning to exiting the airport. The territory was too unfamiliar, and I decided to walk the course. From the Jetway to customs was easy enough, and raised no red flags. Proximal to the Jetway was the tarmac and a no-go for the moment, but I wasn't worried about the subject jumping from a moving aircraft or rappelling down beneath the Jetway. There were too many eyes for that. I kept reminding myself that my presence here hinged on the possibility that I might recognize one of the players. I was not a detective, DHS agent, FBI special agent, or CBP agent. I was a doctor, a police surgeon, essentially a guest.

But the mission culture was inclusive. Once you were part of the team you were part of the team, and I was thinking like one of them. You didn't have to be a master sleuth to figure out traffic patterns. Open your eyes and observe. Observation is an experience-based science. Bombers are always nervous. They have no experience, since they only get to do that particular job once. But that doesn't necessarily mean facial tics and pacing. Maybe a bobbing Adam's apple indicating dry mouth, or nervous swallowing, darting eye movements, rapid breathing, or the telltale sign of all telltale signs, lips moving in silent prayer. The mules would be easier to identify. I tried to learn my lessons quickly and provide another useful pair of eyes. There was no quiz and no bell to end the session. Keep alert and keep watching.

Alison was very quiet and very intense during all of this. She was anxious to the very edge of jumpy. I wasn't used to seeing her that way. Deuce was talkative and amusing, but his eyes were constantly working. It was 8:10, and VS009 had been cleared to the gate. The immigration hall was empty except for the uniformed line monitors loitering together in three groups. There were more men than women, mostly black and Hispanic, and all looked to be under thirty. Conversations were animated, and there was a good deal of friendly pushing and laughing. Most were congregated at the point where the spillway from the gates emptied into the hall, talking on cell phones and texting. It was an area of robust cellular reception and quickly identified by the workers. It was also the most effective location for listening devices. Every spoken word was monitored in real time and recorded. The group, as a whole, made less than a great first impression of the United States. Ill-fitting, dark uniforms did little to upgrade the sloppy look. The women were generally overweight and favored long, imaginatively painted fingernails. The men were more unremarkable in appearance and visibly enjoying the break. Least expressive among the group was a tall, very thin man with handsome African features and very dark skin. His buttoned shirt collar hung like a wreath around a very bony neck and his coat sleeves couldn't contain his gangly wrists. He appeared uncomfortable and reticent, staying at the fringe of the core group while trying to belong. He was rarely noticed or included in the conversation; nor was he ostracized, which was good, because he was one of ours.

Embedding Manny—his name was Emanuel Brock— had been the initial move made by Panopolous after our first session. Young as he looked, Manny was an old-timer at DHS. Five years on the job after three as a street cop in Baltimore. He thought undercover was a stress-free way to spend the day. He was our eyes and ears among the workers on the floor. No one expected Manny to be privy to secrets after only two shifts, but he was closer to the action than plainclothes cops, uniformed CBP agents, or the rest of us hiding behind one-way mirrors and CCTV screens that everyone knew existed.

At 8:41 the first passenger entered the hall. A very tan man, fifty, maybe fifty-five years old, dressed in jeans and a form-fitting, glove-leather jacket. He was hurriedly pulling a brown wheeley dressed with tan leather piping, and taking quick, sure steps in hipster laceless red sneakers. He was easily fifty yards in front of the next arrival and showed no signs of slowing down. Entering the labyrinth, he began ducking under the plastic tapes, short-circuiting the switchbacks, and heading for the immigration alleys. Every eye in the room was on him. One of the guards entered the labyrinth from the opposite end to confront the man. The loud conversation echoed through the hall.

"Sir. You will have to stop right there. You can't go under the tape."

"Why not?" was the response, but the man never stopped making forward progress.

"Sir. Stop now." There wasn't time enough to register whether the order would be heeded before three armed DHS agents converged on the man. In seconds, he was restrained by two of the big men and quickly but thoroughly frisked by the third. When it was determined that he was not armed, the third agent spoke.

"You need to come with us, sir."

"Come with you—who are you? I have to get home." There were words passed and the flashing of badges and identification cards.

Aware of the serious motives of the armed men confronting him, he tried to excuse his behavior. "Why should I have to snake around the tape when the whole damned place is empty?"

The agents tightened their hold on his arms, and the decibel level rose. He was visibly upset but gave no evidence of being dangerously out of control. In civil society, the reaction is to soothe or defuse the situation. "Why are you so excited? We have these rules for good reason." But the response of authority is invariably confrontational, invariably a show of force to control the situation. In this case, overwhelming force, which was met with outrage and arm-waving as the man was hustled back to the Homeland station. The third agent pulled the wheeled suitcase in through the unmarked door to the interrogation room and closed the door behind them.

A minute or so after the door had closed, things settled down. For a second time, someone shouted, "Action. Immigration hall." I stood quickly, knocking my chair on its back. There was more scraping of chairs across the room. All seven people in the room moved directly to the battery of CCTV monitors and scanned the images. One of the views included an en-face picture of Brock. His eyes were fixed on arriving passengers streaming into the hall and only glanced over at the new disturbance infrequently, while he was doing his job. All other eyes in the room had been diverted to an escalating argument. Progress through the labyrinth had halted. The hall was in stop-action mode. Brock turned his head, following a small, dark Asian man, maybe Indonesian, who had been stopped at the head of the queue by a female TSA employee. She was signaling for assistance. Brock wheeled and raced toward the man as two uniformed CBP agents in the line of sight of the call for assistance scrambled out of their booths, freeing the restraining flaps on their holsters as they ran. Two others closed off access to the baggage claim, and four DHS agents materialized, pistols drawn, onto the working floor. Brock and the Customs and Border Protection agents arrived simultaneously, prepared to pounce, but the man had obviously experienced takedown before and had already dropped to the floor with his hands clasped behind his head.

The arrest and removal of the suspect to the interrogation area happened quickly enough to seem planned. In seconds, normal activity resumed. Brock returned to his post, but whether his cover had been broken during his quick response would remain to be seen. I was not invited to participate in the interrogation, but the sound feed and the scene through the one-way glass did not raise hopes of having found the mule.

The man appeared nervous and was nearly emaciated, but he did not behave with any sense of surprise. He carried a Malaysian passport in a full document case, a wad of Malaysian ringgit, five $100 bills, and a few twenties, and he refused to speak English. While the agents waited for a translator, they performed a thorough search of his clothing and hand luggage, finding another large stash of ringgit banded together in his duffel.

The Homeland agent standing beside me whispered, "Another fucking drug tourist."

"Drug tourist?" I repeated.

The agent looked at me like I was retarded. "Yeah, you know, people who come here on a drug holiday. Buy in and stay stoned."

"Why come here?" It seemed like a reasonable question.

"Malaysia is a Muslim country. Drug penalties are severe. This guy is an addict. He's been around the block. And he's carrying a lot of money. Real tourists use credit cards these days."

"Point taken."

In the adjoining interrogation room, the tan man was getting himself together, preparing to resume the process of reentering the country. Deuce turned to me. "Just a jerk in a hurry. Got my hopes up for a minute. You know, a disturbance to divert us from the main event. But no go. The junkie has nothing for us, either. Let's go back into the hall."

That was the extent of the action. Day one was a washout for everyone but me. I learned the basics of airport surveillance and made a new friend in a lovely drug-sniffing beagle.

48

Deuce dropped us at Alison's apartment. We went upstairs together, but she was uncomfortable with staying there. The place was still a mess. I flopped onto the bed and worked the remote, looking for the eleven-o'clock news while Alison packed a few things to take over to my place. I'm not sure what she needed so badly that wasn't already there, but it wasn't worth questioning. She opened, closed, reopened, hung up, put down, washed her face, and was ready to head out in almost half an hour. There was nothing on the local news about the terror alert, and my eyes were dropping shut.

The small bag was a pain to drag through the halls and streets. It kept flipping around on one wheel or the other, and I ended up carrying it like a suitcase, just like everyone did ten years ago. The doorman took the bag from the cab trunk, extended the handle, dragged it to the elevator, and turned it over to me. I lifted it again. Before I could set the bag down in front of my apartment door, the welcoming committee was working. Alison and I smiled at each other, and I unlocked the door extra slowly to make Tonto crazy.

When the door was cracked open enough for him to insert his snout, he did the flying wedge and was in full jumping mode.

"Sit, sit. No jumping. Tonto, SIT." That, of course, did no good. I had incited a riot, and now we had to endure the jumping, bumping, and licking. When a semblance of quiet was reestablished, I carried the suitcase inside the door and sent Tonto for his leash. He and I both knew that he had been walked, but we both faked it and headed out. Alison begged off.

"I'm too tired to take another step. Please excuse me, boys." She managed to yawn and tap her mouth a few times with her opened right hand. "Excuse me." She yawned again. This time it seemed genuine.

When we returned, I thought I heard voices from the apartment and entered quietly. Alison was just walking into the bedroom. She was still dressed.

"I thought I heard voices," I said.

"It was probably just me. I was answering some of my messages. Now for a quick shower." She headed for the luxurious limestone enclosure in the master bedroom, instead of the more spartan setup in the guest bath.

"I'm next." I was too tired to try working my way into a co-ed scrub. While Alison was in the shower, I undressed and waited. I checked my own phone. No messages or calls. We had both been on and off the phone and the Internet all day. How did these messages suddenly materialize? I thought about checking Alison's phone log. While I was pondering the ethics of snooping, the bathroom door opened. Alison emerged in a cloud of steam, wearing one of my shirts and a white towel wrapped around her hair. She looked great, and she was carrying her soiled clothes and her handbag. We passed at the door, looking like customers in a Turkish bath.

It couldn't have taken ten minutes for Alison to fall asleep. I listened to her rhythmic breathing and thought about the past twenty-four hours. If we were right about all this, tomorrow had to be the day. The information from Tahani was the cornerstone of all our theories. If he was misleading us, all bets were off and I would look like an ass. But that didn't mean an attack wasn't going down. There was no reason I could conjure up for Tahani to be double-dealing, or was it triple-dealing. Flighty and fucked up as he was, I had a sense of his inherent decency and I believed him.

I thought about Panopolous and what was or wasn't happening in the effort to protect the water supply. If we were right about the airport, the mule, and the weapon, the threat was still two steps removed from the attempt. If we were wrong, it could be going on now. Why couldn't the anthrax have arrived in Montreal and be safely hidden in a car tooling down I-87 to the New York Thruway, arriving at the watershed from the north. That's what I would have done.

"Terrorists follow orders. Normal people adapt" was how Panopolous dismissed my concern. "They will do it the way it was planned. That gives us a leg up. Don't over-estimate them. There will never again be an attack on our soil as dramatic and devastating as 9/11."

He was confident. I was not.

"We are alert and prepared. Not perfect, but prepared. We will get them." Which one of us was he trying to convince?

Once again I wondered what Alison was hiding. Who could she be talking to minutes before midnight—five a.m. in London?

My thoughts were interrupted by whimpering near the apartment door. The bedroom was flooded with daylight. It was ten minutes past eight in the morning, nearly two hours beyond Tonto's usual walk time, and the walker wasn't scheduled for today. I was it. I did my best imitation of jumping out of bed, pulled jeans and a thin sweater over my sleepy body, and headed out. The sky was bright, but there were high, thin mares' tails to the west. The weather was going to change for the worse, which would make protecting the lakes and reservoirs that much more difficult. Twenty minutes later, back in the apartment, I had a pot of coffee working, fed Tonto, and called the office.

"Dr. Black, ah do declare," Mrs. Black greeted me.

"I can do without the sarcasm," I said, a bit more sharply than I had intended. "Anything I need to know about?"

"No, just the usual. The chief of Ds came by, but I think it was about the flu. He didn't know you were on leave, and he was sniffling to beat the band."

"I'm not on leave. Why would you think that?"

"You aren't working, and you aren't on sick, you aren't on admin, and you haven't told me where you are. I assume something is wrong." Things had happened so quickly that I hadn't considered that my NYPD colleagues were in the dark.

"I am truly touched. You have my word that nothing is wrong. No personal problems. Nothing. I'm working up to my ears on that special project. Sorry if I worried you."

"Oh you secretive boys. Anything I can do?"

"Just don't worry. You'll know the whole story soon enough. Anything in the mail? Calls?"

"Nothing that can't wait," she answered, back in her matter-of-fact voice. "Hurry back to us. People on the job keep lining up waiting to see Mr. Soft Touch. Your pals Ginsburg and Walsh keep sending the poor babies back to duty."

"Tell them to keep up the good work. I should be back before the end of the week. I'll give you twenty-four hours' notice so you can fill the benches with smiling faces."

After a quick cup of very strong coffee laced with just enough milk to make it palatable, I brushed my teeth, shaved, and showered. Back in the bedroom, Alison was sitting up in bed sipping black coffee.

"Yuck. This coffee is awful." She was right. We were on a lousy coffee roll.

"And good morning to you." I looked at my watch. "It's eight-forty. We have to get going. You in?" I took the coffee cup from Alison and started for the kitchen.

"Yes. Give me twenty minutes." No chance. I called a car service and headed off to the second bathroom to shower. I have rarely used the guest bath. The soap and shampoo were foreign to me, and it felt like a shower in a mediocre hotel. I made a mental note to spruce things up a bit. No wonder Alison opted for the master bath. By the time I returned, Alison had her left foot propped on the toilet seat and was drying off her very attractive leg. Before I could comment, she squeezed past me and slipped into the flesh-colored bra and panties laid out on the bed. I watched as she pulled on jeans, a T-shirt, and a blue sweater.

"Better get moving. I'm ready," she said.

It took me half a minute to free a fresh blue shirt from the plastic laundry wrapper, shake it open, button down, button up, and jump into gray wool pants. I skipped the necktie, opting for comfort. The old cashmere tweed sport jacket was hanging on the doorknob. I grabbed it and we were out the door at nine, on the dot. Gus, the morning man on the door, led us out to the black Lincoln Town Car waiting at the curb. The driver was part of the Subcontinent mafia that dominated the legions of car-service drivers favored by New Yorkers, the alternative to the knee-knocking rattletraps masquerading as taxicabs throughout the city.

"Kennedy airport, please."

"Do you have a voucher?" he asked. The usual routine.

"No. I will use one of yours." The car had already started rolling as he handed back the receipt pad with a ball pen stuck in the binding. "No luggage?" he asked.

"No. No luggage. Terminal 4 please."

If the driver was curious, he didn't show it. Alison and

I held hands and said nothing until she said, "Did you remember your passport?"

"Yup. Right here." I patted my breast pocket with my right hand. "Always a good question." For the rest of the trip we behaved the way we thought travelers would behave. I was very self-conscious. Alison was into it.

"I can't wait to get away"—that sort of small talk, until the driver asked, "What airline?" I was caught short.

"Delta," Alison replied. Smooth. And good thinking, since Delta dominated Terminal 4, and it rang true. In New York City, taxi and limo work has long been the entry-level job of choice, and the ethnic groups dominating the trade mirror population shifts as a whole. In the last few days I had become acutely aware of the new demographics. There was no reason to believe that the driver was anything more than a hardworking recent immigrant doing his job, but we were sensitized. Made you think how difficult it must be to be Muslim in America these days.

The terminal might still have looked normal to the casual traveler. Look closely and the number of TSA people was significantly increased, and they were young, bright-looking, and alert. Not the usual "shoes off, no water, wait behind the line" people. Only the uniforms were the same. We headed for the Homeland office and banged heads with two sets of TSA gatekeepers. My ID scanned, and Alison was required to show identification despite my protests that she was with me. I expected to see my first British Secret Service warrant card, if there was such a thing. But Alison produced a New York State driver's license and a New York

State physician's photo ID instead. Apparently, she was on the list. The gates opened wide.

"I want to have a good look around the tarmac outside the gate. Want to come?"

"Sure," Alison answered, and we headed for the door beyond the immigration hall. For the first time, it was guarded. The bar code on my card opened the lock, and I was allowed to pass through. Alison was required to open with her own ID. The TSA guard was unwavering. I went ahead and Alison headed back to Homeland headquarters, looking for someone to pass her through.

There was nothing magic out there. Anyone who has traveled through southern Italy, the Sun Belt, the Caribbean, or wherever passengers are required to walk between terminal and boarding stairs knows the drill. The planes are big, you are small, and there are trucks and buses apparently on a mission to sideswipe you at any opportunity. Airports in colder climates insulate the traveler from the action on the tarmac. Usually, airline employees keep absentminded strollers out of harm's way. Today, I was on my own, and it was a little intimidating at first.

I walked the perimeter of the terminal, trying doors and poking my head into everything. Maybe the ID hanging around my neck was identifiable, but I doubted it. No one came close enough to get a good look, and no one seemed to care. Walk around like you belong, and you belong.

On the face of it, Terminal 4 is a slant-front, airy-looking, steel-and-glass structure. Basically, two overgrown stories, with the control tower looming like a mutant mushroom behind it. The central terminal houses the business end of airline travel, processes passengers coming and going, and is the only terminal in the airport with 24/7 customs control and Homeland presence. Stuck to the back of the terminal building are two limbs with a total of seventeen gates, which doesn't sound all that imposing. But consider that the $1.4 billion monolith sits on 165 acres and handles 10 million passengers annually, and you gain more perspective on how small I felt under the wings of 757s, ducking vehicles and poking around looking for who knows what.

The two sets of paired runways at Kennedy are laid out in a perpendicular grid. 13R-31L, at 14,572 feet, is the second-longest commercial runway in the country. At almost three miles, it is long enough to be a backup for space shuttle landings. The shortest runway, its mate, at 8,400 feet, was the first in North America to have an EMAS aircraft arresting system engineered to prevent overshooting of runways by the bigger birds. That was installed in the mid-nineties, when 8,400 feet was beginning to look too short to accommodate modern air traffic. The good news is that the airport was built on landfill in Jamaica Bay and had room to expand. The bad news is the sandy area on the far side of runway 4L is a great breeding spot for turtles, and on occasional June days, hundreds of terrapins come ambling across the tarmac to higher ground to lay their eggs, and they close down the runway.

The miles and miles of runway was what I had expected. The enormous infrastructure necessary to make it all happen wasn't. It seemed that as much of the terminal structure was devoted to mechanical functions as passengers. Most of the closed doors and the free-standing structures were clearly identified by building numbers and signage. Some remained a mystery.

A worker in sleeveless coveralls and an orange-and-green vest sat atop an open aircraft-towing rigs, looking at everything and tapping on communication devices. I walked over to his perch.

"Can I talk to you for a minute?" I shouted up at him.

He made an "I don't understand" kind of face and pointed at his headset. He was a big, athletic-looking guy, and he easily bent over to get within conversational distance without dismounting. He lifted one earpiece and pushed it back to sit behind his ear. I took the cue and did the same.

"What goes on in that building?" I asked, pointing to a mechanical monster that looked like a 1930s Charles Sheeler painting. The big-bore curved pipes whirring like man-size pneumatic tubes. Rust drips stained some of the areas where the massive pipes were joined, but otherwise they were solid and well maintained. The apparatus entered and exited a formidable, windowless metal structure and buzzed with activity.

"And who might you be?" he responded in a pleasant, West Indian voice. I slipped my ID over my head and handed it up. He studied it long enough for me to know it meant nothing in particular to him but was seriously official. He handed it back.

"Never saw this kind of ID out here. Are you investigating my men?"

"No. Not at all. Just routine government inspection. I never noticed that unit before."

"Been here twenty years. Long as I have. It's the strainer. All those pipes clean the water so the air-cooling works in the terminal. Pumps all day, every day. As far as I know, it's never been down."

"Who goes in there?" I asked.

"Mostly, nobody. Routine maintenance, but it don't seem to break down. Nobody been in there on my shift in a very long time."

"Thank you." I reached up to retrieve my identification card, and he shook my hand before handing it over.

"Nice to meet you, sir," he said, and went back to his crackling handheld device.

There was no handle on the outside of the metal door, just a keypad and two dead-bolt locks alongside a sign reading AUTHORIZED PERSONNEL ONLY. Just like everything else at the airport.

As I came around the building, the control tower loomed massive and ugly from the ground. Philos had that covered, and I didn't want to disturb the controllers or the security people visible at the head of the stairs.

From the start, I couldn't get past feeling that baggage handling might be a problem. Traditional security in the baggage area at Kennedy was nonexistent. On the air cargo side, theft was a $10 billion industry worldwide. Air-freight theft was an acknowledged Mafia-owned industry and had come under increasing scrutiny. Passenger terminal thefts were less organized. The terminal didn't handle valuable bulk cargo, like shipments of sable from Sweden, but electronics, cash, and personal goods were fair game. Baggage handlers and TSA employees have repeatedly been nailed in sting operations, and all kinds of nefarious behind-the-scenes activity takes place. The Port Authority police hold down the published crime rate by categorizing laptops and jewelry and the like missing from luggage as "lost items." The idiotic explanation is if the items weren't observed being stolen, then they were lost, and are therefore categorized as such. Sophistry rides again. No wonder people think the cops are as bad as the crooks.

Entering the baggage area is easy. The flow of bags and boxes from the bellies of the giant aircraft makes for traffic jams and too many employees to constantly scrutinize. Supervisors aren't exactly management, and the place is an unruly horror show. The handling of baggage resembles the old television ads for Samsonite, where gorillas bounce and stomp on suitcases. As a group, the baggage handlers are not gentle little fellows. The job is hard, the bags are heavy, and your maiden aunt can't cut it.

I hopped between the overloaded articulated carts and the belts and stood by for five minutes watching the inbound agents work. No one challenged me. Access from the outside was controlled, and Big Brother was everywhere. For sure, the CCTV monitors were being manned 24/7, and it was all digitally recorded. Baggage handling at Terminal 4 is still done the old way: 6,500 bags an hour, by hand. It's a big job, and there's an automated system in the works. Meanwhile, the noises of trucks, conveyor belts, and bouncing bags made the area seem more frantic than it was. No one was moving quickly. Over toward the cart entry, I spotted two Homeland ICE agents entering and looking around. They recognized me as foreign to the environment, split up, and headed my way. I held up my ID, but they kept coming. The first agent, a short, dark-haired woman, was walking purposefully toward me. She had her right hand on the handle of the pistol in her holster. Her eyes fixed on my card before we were in talking range and visibly softened.

"May I see your ID, sir?" she asked, and had her left hand on the card before I could answer.

"Special task force," she said, reading the laminated card. "Welcome, sir. How can we help you?" She had an attractive Southern accent.

"You are?" Two can play that game, and I was feeling important.

"ICE Agent Janet Kolson, sir. This is Agent Budzar." They both offered their hands. I shook Agent Kolson's hand first and studied her identification card. I did the same with Budzar before speaking.

"Is this your regular post?" I asked.

"No, sir. We are on our tour of the perimeter. See if anything unusual is happening and make our presence known."

"About how often is that?" I asked.

"Once or twice an hour. Our instructions are to come by irregularly. Keep 'em guessing." She smiled a bright smile lit by perfect, white teeth. Agent Kolson was very pretty when she wasn't threatening. Budzar was tall and dark-skinned, most likely Pakistani, judging from his name.

"What are you looking for, Agent Budzar?" I asked.

"Don't know, sir. Someone passing something, violating sealed baggage. Maybe someone who doesn't belong here."

I thought about what he said and was getting ready to leave when another question occurred to me. "Is this your regular beat, the airport?"

"No, sir," they answered in unison. "This is day two. Usually in the city."

"You work for Philos?" I asked.

"No, sir," Kolson answered. "We work for Mr. Panopolous." That meant a lot. These were definitely high-end people if they worked directly for Panopolous.

"Good man. I guess I'm working for him, too. See you later," I said, and waved as I headed for the exit out to the tarmac.

49

The early afternoon had passed quickly enough, and we began to gear up for the heavy traffic period when the bulk of the flights from LHR were expected. I found Alison in the surveillance area. She was sitting in front of the monitor bank with a notepad on her lap.

"Hi."

"Hi," I answered. She stayed riveted by the monitors as we spoke. "I guess you didn't pass the test."

"Correct. I could get out there if I tossed bags or waved magic wands at planes. But being a simple British agent, I couldn't cut it."

"Life is grand. Let's have lunch."

Alison stuffed the pad into her shoulder bag, and we headed out into the terminal.

"What were you looking for? You were glued to the screens."

"I don't know. You look, and you look. No plan, and when something is wrong, unnatural, you see it."

"Just like that?"

"Yes. Just like that. It jumps out at you, but only if you are observing normal, normal, normal . . . then bingo, abnormal. I can't explain it any other way. Do you see?"

"I do," I answered. "I mean I understand what you are saying, not that I see anything. I haven't had the experience. I haven't tried."

"Well, it is like surgery or any sort of medicine. You just know when something is wrong."

"But what were you fixed on? You couldn't be watching the entire immigration process, or maybe you could. But why would you choose that rather than anything else around Terminal 4?"

"That is where it is going to happen, don't you think?"

"I do," I answered. But it seemed too obvious. The anthrax would enter on—or, in this case, in—the person of the mule, and that person has to be slipped through customs. Too obvious. "I keep thinking that there must be a step that we are missing."

"Like what?" Alison asked.

"Like how they get the mule onto the plane. We have the boarding process sewn shut. We are X-raying people until they glow in the dark. We know everything. You want to see breasts, we got 'em. You want to see guys with huge equipment, we got 'em. I mean, we do actually know what is boarding every airplane headed to JFK from Heathrow."

Alison was silent. I couldn't tell if I had set her thinking, but I was definitely seeing a little light. Not too bright, but a light. I was excited.

"Alison," I said. "We have been looking at this the wrong way. Forget boarding procedures and customs. They found a way of bypassing all that. We need to look outside the normal procedure."

"Okay, but what do you have in mind?"

"I mean outside the boarding process. People with access. It has to be. It works. They have to have people at the airports. People behind the scenes. People we don't see. It makes sense."

"It could be," Alison said again.

"Think of it like a differential diagnosis. You try to think of one thing that could explain the whole package of symptoms. First you eliminate the most obvious diagnostic possibilities. You know, it can't be appendicitis if the patient has had her appendix removed. Something else is causing the pain in the right lower quadrant of the abdomen.

"People get on and off planes through boarding and customs procedures. But if you search every passenger and you don't find a mule, and yet you know the mule was on the plane, then they are outflanking us. It happens all the time. The French were certain the Germans couldn't get through the Maginot Line in 1940, because that was the normal route between the two countries and it was very well fortified. So they bet Paris on it. The Germans just went around them. Outflanked them. That's what they are doing here, outflanking us."

"Take me through it from Heathrow," Alison said, holding my shoulder. We were standing off to the side of the food arcade in the terminal, not a dozen steps from a busy kiosk.

"I will. Let's grab something and take it back where we can talk privately. Here," I said, picking two bananas from a bin, two pint containers of fresh orange juice from a cooler, and two bland-looking tuna fish sandwiches from the refrigerated display, and handing the lot to her while I reached for my wallet. "We should pick up a couple of sandwiches and a Coke for Deuce," I said and added two ham-and-cheese to the pile.

"Healthier than yesterday," Alison said.

"But not as tasty. Let's go."

We grabbed an unoccupied desk in the corner of the Homeland base. Deuce was still not around, so I put his food in the little fridge in the back room. Someone would eat it if Deuce didn't show.

"Okay, take me through it." Alison had begun peeling a banana before I spoke, and was playing with it in a distracted manner. One of the guys across the room was staring at her, smiling. His companion followed his eyes and was smiling, too. When she put the end of the banana in her mouth, we all laughed. Alison looked around and blushed. She said nothing and took a fierce bite out of the banana. Everyone looked away.

"They evaded detection each trip by moving the mule through the back of the terminal onto the plane. Maybe someone else went through security and passport control. Then, either en route to the aircraft or on board, they switched. Maybe they inserted the mule on the Jetway; maybe the mule was one of those people bringing wheelchairs to the boarding door or the gate. Maybe the mule was switched into the wheelchair between the gate and the aircraft. Or maybe the mule was part of the cleaning crew and stayed in the lavatory."

"Those are a lot of maybes."

"Let me finish. However they did it, they had a person or people working at Heathrow. That's the key. That's what we have to think about. It's easy enough to imagine how they enlisted help. Coercion, money, relatives in the Old Country, true believers, lots of possibilities. The mule gets on the plane. They land at JFK and the reverse process takes place between deplaning and customs."

"How?"

"They switch on board or after everyone else has deplaned."

"Deplaned. My God. You have been spending too much time here."

"That's the truth. Someone stays on the plane after the other passengers have gone. The ground crew comes aboard. They switch identities. The worker goes through customs with the passenger's documents, and the mule is whisked away through the employees exit. Not much security on the way out of work for cleaners, baggage handlers, and mechanics." I stopped and thought for a moment. "I haven't worked out the details. A lot of this may be just plain wrong, but the general idea is correct. Some variant of this is how they do it."

"Is it possible that the mule never goes through customs at all? Do they check deplaning passengers off a list?"

"Deplaning passengers?" I said, smiling.

"Sorry," she continued. "But do they check them off a list? Do they know if three hundred people boarded in London and two hundred and ninety-nine entered the U.S.? I never saw any evidence of a checklist. Immigration and customs are a free-for-all with passengers from various flights mixed together. The flight crew abandons ship on a run, and no one is counting heads. It could work. You could be right."

"I am right. I'll call Panopolous."

"Protocol is to speak to Philos—he can call Panopolous," Alison said.

My head was spinning with ideas, and I didn't register what she said. The activity level in the room had increased with the arrival of passengers in the hall. Chairs scraped and people stood at the monitors. Then Philos entered with a man in his mid-fifties, wearing a gray suit, neat white shirt, and a red tie held by a clasp with the presidential seal. He stood nearly a head shorter than Philos. I had never seen him before, but there was every indication that he was government and important. They were deep in conversation, or at least Philos was speaking. The other man nodded his head or listened quietly. Alison's suggestion popped into my head. Philos seemed to be briefing the visitor on the situation. He was treating him with obvious deference, so I waited for a break in the conversation. Several times, at pauses, I motioned and tried to get Philos's attention, but even when he looked my way, he was looking through me and making his case. I was about to call out to him when he guided his guest out of the room.

"Shit. I shouldn't have let him go."

"He would not have been receptive. He was obviously on the carpet."

"You think?" I asked. "That guy seemed completely out of the loop. Hold on a minute while I ask our friends over there"—pointing at a couple of the agents—"if they know anything about the visitor."

"What difference does it make who he is. You have to talk to Philos."

I shrugged and stepped over to the agents, exchanged a few words, thanked them, and returned to Alison.

"Congressman. They think the guy has some responsibility for Homeland appropriations. Hours of ass-kissing will follow the briefing. I do not think Philos will want to hear my theory about missing the boat. It's time to call Panopolous."

Getting through to Panopolous was easier than I expected. The deputy secretary answered the secure cell phone quickly and seemed less harried than usual. I dove right in. His questions were direct, and he digested my hypothesis as we spoke. His conclusion was that while it was a bit unlikely, it was worth looking into. Meanwhile, he was not about to plunge headlong into the belly of the airport. "I'll deploy a few more uniformed Homeland agents behind the scenes to make our presence known. Add some eyes and ears on the ground. Sometimes real-time CCTV surveillance isn't good enough."

"What should I do?" I asked, with no real agenda. I suspected I was going to follow my intuition no matter what

Panopolous suggested, but I wanted to hear how he would deal with my involvement.

"Don't underestimate yourself, Dr. Black. Your instincts about this have been excellent. Keep an eye out and work your side of the street. I'll tell Philos you need a body or two, and see what you see. Come to think of it, skip Philos. He has his hands full with Ryan. We need friends in Congress. That SOB is one pain in the ass, but he's our pain in the ass." Panopolous stopped speaking, probably wishing he hadn't confided the last thought. Then he added, "In the end we want the same thing: a safe America and a strong intelligence service." That was a better sound bite. "I'll get one of the ICE boys to lend a hand. Meanwhile, get your boys on board. That big cop friend of yours, is he around?"

"If you mean Lieutenant Secondi, he's somewhere out here."

"Yeah. I'll tell them he and the girl have free access. They can pick up task force IDs from Philos's office."

"Thank you, sir." I didn't bother telling him that Deuce would consider the ID an insult in his city. And he did consider New York his city. And the fact that the JFK was the territory of the Port Authority of New York and New Jersey meant nothing to him. So far, he had been right. No one dared deny him access, and with his street cop ethic, Deuce would be the last guy to suck up to the feds. And how about calling Alison "the girl." She wouldn't be happy with that.

I reported what little there was to report to Alison, neglecting to mention the reference to her as "the girl." She was delighted to be given full access, or at least the same level of access I had. We ate the sandwiches, drank the juice, and had some of the lousy coffee from the machine. We still had not seen Deuce. I called his cell and left a message. It was four ten p.m. Virgin flight VS045 had landed twenty minutes ahead of schedule and was being held on the tarmac while the gate was being made ready. Instead of joining the screen jockeys, we headed out to the immigration hall and baggage claim.

"Follow me." I swiped my card at the door marked EM-PLOYEES ONLY, and we entered the baggage-handling area. "Time to test the theory." I handed Alison a set of the sound-suppressing earphones I had pulled from the bin in the office. She held each individually to an ear and engaged the battery power. I did the same. The move had become automatic to many with the popularity of high-tech, sound-canceling audio headsets. But these were no $300 Bose beauties. Just functional pads, like the kind we both grew up using on the pistol range. They canceled the frequency of loud noises, like gunshots and jet engines, by producing waves of the same frequency at 180-degree opposite polarity, allowing sounds in the range of the human voice to remain unmasked. The fancy ones connect you to your music and keep out 70 percent of everything else. Most of the regular tarmac employees wore ear canal–fitted protection. Too many people were deaf at fifty to risk working without protection. I was once naive enough to go bare at a Stones concert at the Garden. No ear protection. I looked cool, and I heard nothing but high-pitched whistling for the next three days. I hear it now.

Outside, we headed into the disturbed air kicked up by a Boeing 777 making an unlikely right-angle turn into its berth. The giant bird wasn't close enough to worry about, but size and decibels overcame rationality. We would be hard to see from the cockpit, but from the ground we were far too easy to spot; two civilians wandering around the tarmac without visibility vests. I noticed that even the ICE people wore orange. It was dumb to stand out like that, but dumber to be dangerously invisible. I approached one of the ICE special agents standing around the baggage bay. I don't think I recognized him, and we certainly did not have the nodding acquaintance established with the people coming and going from the Homeland office. He correctly made a show of studying my card. Satisfied, he shook my hand and led us to a closet full of orange-and-chartreuse vests. I pulled one labeled MAINTENANCE. Alison got IN-BOUND BAGGAGE. She was swimming in the large vest, but nobody seemed to care.

No human movement was visible until the Jetway made its way to the door on the port side of the aircraft. Then there was lots of scurrying, both in and around the Jetway and on the ground. All of it seemed legitimate, but I had nothing to compare it to. No one climbed down from the Jetway, but I could see attendants trundling wheelchairs through the Jetway. A mobile conveyor belt was secured at the open door to the cargo hold in the fuselage, and a utility truck pulled a linked chain of empty baggage containers to the base of the belt. Collapsed fiber hoses two feet across were locked into female receptacles under the fuselage, preparing to flush air into the cabins. Maintenance people were everywhere. Cleaning crews arrived in separate vehicles and waited at the base of the Jetway along with catering trucks ready to remove the prefabricated meal units. There was no sign of anyone exiting the opened ports, and as yet, no one had boarded the aircraft.

The Homeland agent we were speaking to was assigned to the baggage area, and he did not follow as Alison and I wandered out toward the aircraft.

"Let me know if I can help," he said, giving us a friendly salute and turning his attention to the still-quiet belt and the men lounging around it.

The aircraft engines had shut down. Hand-signaling and directing had ceased, and flying crew and ground support were in the let-down period after mission accomplished. When the last passenger deplaned, the crew would be double-timing along the telescopic corridors and out through customs with their carry-on luggage. Crew waiting for bags along with the civilians had a different agenda and always earned a look-through by the inspectors.

The business of servicing the aircraft after 276 passengers had left was now in the hands of the JFK-based crews. They approached, boarded, backed trucks, opened hatches, attached hoses, extended accordion lifts, and began work. Two members of the incoming baggage crew climbed the belt and disappeared into the belly of the aircraft.

"Shit," I said, more to myself than to Alison. "Did you get a good look at their faces?"

"No. What are you thinking?"

"One of them might be switching identities with a mule in the cargo hold."

"Come on. She would freeze to death down there. And anyway, your mule was a passenger. Why would they change a system that works?" It was a legitimate question.

"They probably wouldn't, but we have to focus on how the mules—and I think they have all been males—get through to customs without scrutiny, and then pass," I answered.

"But I thought we determined that there is no scrutiny of landed passengers. And drug-sniffing dogs weren't likely to pick up a scent through sealed silicone, fat, and skin."

"Maybe. Just humor me."

I walked closer to the apparatus, which had not yet begun to operate. In less than fifteen seconds, the two workers, both burly black men, were back at the open hatch. One shouted down to the operator, "Ready in here. No animals. Roll." The belt began to rumble.

The cargo-holding areas of modern aircraft are fully pressurized and barely heated, to uncomfortably cold but not dangerous temperatures. This is primarily to prevent contents from freezing and water expanding and contracting. Pet crates are usually transported on a forward pallet nearest the warming apparatus. Unloading animals first was routine, and handlers, being human, bent down and peeked through the fence fronts of the crates, checking their cargo. They made welcoming, friendly sounds for the bewildered, stoned animals, and generally handled them

kindly. No pets had been stowed on VS045. In their absence, the process of tossing bags began. The first, nondescript, black bag hit the conveyor belt for the short,
forty-five-degree transit to the team at the waiting convoy.
I put the fingers of my right hand on Alison's back and directed her to the terminal. Nothing seemed out of order,
but, of course, we had no standard for comparison. It was
foreign territory, but not a very steep learning curve.

The trick was to find weaknesses in the security of the
system before we paid the price. We watched the terminal
end of the baggage-unloading process for a few minutes
more. It seemed endless, and we weren't lifting a thousand
bulging bags. Cleaning crews entering the cabin were
checked in by a Homeland agent, which was not routine
and definitely did not go unnoticed by the workers. No one
working in the guts of Terminal 4 was unaware of unusual
scrutiny. But it did not alter their routines. And it was not
an unusual occurrence. This was the drill every time an
unclaimed bag was reported in the terminal or alert status
was raised on "credible intelligence." It happened every
time a new, increasingly blatant series of thefts was reported, and it happened with every Homeland training
run-through. Nobody seemed to pay it any mind. I couldn't
help feeling how routine everything was.

"What's wrong with this picture?" I asked Alison. Well,
maybe I was asking myself more than Alison. It just did not
make sense. "Everything is so routine. Nothing edgy or out
of place."

"Well, if you are correct, someone is either oblivious or good at hiding their anxiety, or maybe they aren't here at all," Alison said.

"Which would make me wrong. And I am not wrong. The delivery will happen in front of our eyes, or at least where our eyes should have been. Let's go inside and watch the screens."

The CCTV room was crowded with agents. Too many agents from too many overlapping jurisdictions. It took on the look of a party with lots of healthy young people jostling for position at a bar, talking trash about people on the immigration queue instead of a football field. Underneath it all, the tension on our side was obvious from the smell of excitement all around us.

"Ripe in here," I whispered to Alison. "Or is it me?"

"Not you. Never. But these guys are ready for it to happen."

The corridor had emptied of all but staff. The 276 passengers, or something like that number, seemed to have formed lines behind the U.S. citizen and alien entry lines. Twice the computer alarm sounded in the room, and Homeland agents were dispatched onto the floor to interview incoming passengers. Both times for questioning of alien travelers. Both were young males. Both seemed bewildered by the process, and both were released and allowed to enter baggage claim without interrogation. Each time the CCTV room grew quiet, as if a silent alarm had spread the word that something might be going down.

The baggage area slowed to a halt as all incoming was loaded on two successive caravans, each carriage with protective side curtains held away and piled full by an irregular mass of predominantly black bags, with the occasional corrugated box tied with twine, backpack, or plaid piece breaking the monotony.

An accordion lift backed in to replace the baggage conveyor belt and was raised to the cargo hold. I had no idea what would happen next and just pointed Alison's attention to the screen and waited. We didn't have long to wait. In seconds, three men, accustomed to the task, wrestled a highly polished casket of dark wood by its brass handles onto the platform of the lift. I was interested and watched as a black SUV with ambulance doors pulled onto the tarmac. The operator lowered the lift to the height of the ambulance doors of the SUV. The driver exited and watched while the three baggage men and the lift operator grasped the brass handles and respectfully worked the casket into the truck. Damn!

"That's it! That's it. Stop them," I shouted. "Stop the hearse."

50

*And then all hell broke loose. Philos materialized from no-*where, trailed by two other men in suits. The muscle boys in the ICE shirts parted like the Red Sea for Moses.

"What have you got, doctor?" Philos asked, remarkably calmly after the alarm my excitement had sounded in the room.

"Stop that hearse . . . the SUV. That's the perfect place for the anthrax. It's sealed and safe, and even the baggage guys are handling it with respect. Don't let it get out of here."

Philos looked at me with obvious skepticism at first, then acceded with a little vertical nod of his head. He took a phone from the left inside pocket of his suit coat, and the musical notes of speed dialing filled the now-quiet room. "This is Command One. Isolate the tarmac until the all-clear from me." Then another series of electronic sounds and he was giving quiet orders again. "Send a car out to the funeral SUV at gate 12. Hold the car and all occupants."

"The baggage handlers. Stop them, too," I interrupted, with my hand on his arm. Philos did his version of a nod again, and said, "And hold the baggage handlers who low-

ered the coffin. They are . . ." He looked over at the CCTV
and added, "They are still at the hold. Detain the lift operator, too. Isolate them. Confiscate their cell phones. Nobody
leaves, and no communication with the outside. Understood?" He listened to a response for a few seconds and
said, "Isolate them from one another." Another pause.
"Don't tell them anything. Just get enough men out there
now. Right now."

Philos looked at me. "Interesting, Dr. Black. We shall
see." Then he spoke directly to the two men accompanying
him. "What do we know about the body being transported?"

"Nothing, sir," said one.

"Nothing, sir," said the other suit. Everyone in the room
could see Philos clench his jaw. His fists were tight at his
sides, and I thought he was going to explode.

"Get on the phone with the carrier. Find out what the hell
is going on here. I want to see the papers. Gilliam. Gilliam."
Now he was beginning to raise his voice. "Where the fuck
is Gilliam?"

"Here, sir." It was a voice from the archway between the
rooms of the suite.

"Get out there and find out what the fuck is in that fucking coffin. And then explain to me why the fuck we didn't
expect it." Philos was a cop after all.

Emergency vehicles materialized across the tarmac from
every fifteen degrees of the compass. The strobe lights on
the rooftop bars were annoying even on TV. I could barely
hear their sirens, but doubtless they were screaming for

attention as they were meant to. My inclination was to run out there myself, but everything was frozen until Philos calmed down and gave orders. Alison had disappeared, or at least I lost track of her. In truth, I wasn't looking for her. I was trying to figure out the best way to contain the danger.

In the next minute or two, Philos drifted away from us and made more calls, with his eyes fixed on the CCTV screens. He finished talking and held his phone at his side instead of replacing it in his pocket.

"Let's go," Philos said. I expected a stampede of agents, but no one moved. He was speaking to me, but I was frozen in front of the screen. "Now, doctor."

By the time I pushed through the agents, he had made half a dozen long strides and was headed out the back door to the tarmac. I ran the first twenty-five yards and was beside him walking quickly out to the aircraft. A fully lit Port Authority police car pulled directly across our path and stopped. Philos switched his phone to his left hand and held up an open badge case in his right. He started around the vehicle. Before the Port Authority officers could open the doors and disengage themselves, half a dozen Homeland people were all over them. Then Philos and I ran, more than jogged, out to the scene. The Homeland agents cleared a path for Philos, and I followed in his wake to the center of activity, which was the black SUV carrying the coffin.

"Cuff them all. Take the keys and put the driver back in the car. The others go to interrogation."

There was a flurry of activity. Philos and an agent he

singled out from the group approached the SUV. Philos opened the back door and seated himself behind the driver. He signaled the agent to sit alongside the driver. "Close the doors; I can't hear myself think," he said. I saw the driver through the window. He was a pale, Anglo-looking man in his forties, in a black suit, white shirt, and dark tie. As far from Middle-Eastern-looking as imaginable, which probably meant nothing. I glanced around at the other men being detained. All three looked vaguely familiar. Of course they did—I had been watching them work before it hit the fan. Their faces were already in my memory bank. They were the two black guys from the incoming baggage crew, and a grungy-looking Caucasian with a black Van Dyke beard and soul patch. All three were acting out varying degrees of fear and anger. None of their questions were being answered, which added frustration to the mix. Baggage workers and ground crew stopped working and followed the action in small groups. I hadn't heard an order being given, but two of the muscle agents in ICE shirts began to circulate among the workers and collect cell phones. Other agents were stationed in pairs at every exit from the tarmac. The concept of a quiet operation was history.

I waited for Philos. The conversation in the SUV was not audible from where I stood outside the front passenger seat. Philos had gone to his phone twice during the five minutes of questioning, which was carried out almost entirely by the agent in the front seat. I couldn't tell whether he was initiating calls or answering, but each conversation was quick. The first ended abruptly after Philos had the last word . . . the last sentence. He spent the second call listening. I wondered from how high up the chain of command that call had originated.

I began to think ahead. I had to think about containment. Assuming the coffin carried the biological bomb. How much anthrax were we looking at? Caskets are eighty-four inches long, twenty-eight inches wide, and twenty-three inches high—or about twenty-eight cubic feet in volume. That could hold a cataclysmic volume of anthrax spores. Too horrible to contemplate. Properly dispersed, that volume was enough to rapidly eliminate the population of a great city. New York City. I wasn't sure there was that much anthrax in the world or if it could be secretly produced outside of a professional laboratory.

Casket arrangements vary from country to country. An inner casket for burial, dressed in a fancy show box removed before interment or cremation, was a popular British option, and this box was coming from London. What I cared about was how far from the anthrax we would be. How insulated from danger were we? I didn't know the answers, but I was beginning to think of the questions.

Philos opened the left rear door of the SUV and angled his long legs out. All eyes were on him. He motioned two agents to him. They were the guys in suits. I edged closer. Out of earshot of the others, Philos spoke.

"Nobody knows anything. This guy"—he motioned with his head toward the driver of the SUV—"knows nothing. He has been driving for Frank Campbell's for six years. His dispatcher identified him. He is supposed to pick up the body of an eighty-one-year-old woman named"—Philos stopped and scrolled through his messages, then looked up—"Goodman, Ellen. Ellen Goodman. She died"—he looked at his message again—"almost forty-eight hours ago at the Connaught Hotel in London, and her family hired Campbell's to make travel arrangements. No one has seen the body. If there is a body. So we have to get this damned thing open ASAP."

I raised my hand to interrupt. I realized I didn't know Philos's first name, and I was uncomfortable saying "Excuse me, Assistant Director Philos, may I speak," so I simply raised my hand a bit for attention and said, "You can't do that."

All eyes were now on me, and I wondered which Philos was going to respond.

"You don't have to tell me that, doctor. I know the rules," he said calmly and evenly. "We can't pop the lid without permission, Patriot Act or not. But we can wall this thing off so nobody can get to it before we get to open it."

"I didn't mean that," I responded. "I think the first order of business is to protect everyone from anthrax exposure, including, actually, especially us. Who knows how much can leak out of that box? I doubt that it is anything close to airtight." Philos raised his eyebrows. Everyone in our circle waited for me to continue, so I did.

51

I laid out my plan. It was simple. Two steps. First: We wrap the casket, the whole thing, in thick sheets of plastic and heat-seal the edges. That would isolate the casket and its contents. While arrangements were being made to procure the proper equipment, we would use one of those commercial plastic suitcase-wrapping machines to add a layer of isolation. I had no idea how well sealed that system would be, but it was better than nothing until the real thing came along. Second: We run the wrapped casket through the baggage X-ray machine. Not the backscatter screener—the real thing, the heavy-duty machine used on baggage. That should tell us a lot. At the very least, we would see if there was a body in the casket and any opaque foreign substances packed around it. Maybe, if the exposure wasn't fixed, we could manipulate it for greater penetration and see what was inside the body. Failing that, we transport the casket to a nearby hospital and X-ray it there.

Philos agreed. "And we better talk to those guys," he said, looking over at the red hazmat truck and the small army of people in full-body, white, hazardous material suits and breathing devices. He took another brief call. "Let's wait here another minute or two," he said. We stood in place. The two baggage men had been taken to interrogation, and the driver was alone in the SUV with the casket. If he was worried about breathing anthrax-contaminated air, he didn't show it. He had rolled down the window and had lit a cigarette. With his elbow on the sill and his head in his palm, he stared out and smoked. A stillness had descended on the tarmac. There was none of the usual noise associated with the coming and going of aircraft.

"Quiet," I said.

"Airport is in shutdown. Nothing in or out," Philos responded without looking my way. That explained Philos's calls. He had not been idle. As if on cue, the *whoosh* of helicopter rotors filled the air. I spun around, trying to locate the sound, as a very obvious and very large marine VH-60N Night Hawk became outlined in silhouette by the low sun, in the process of setting down not a hundred yards west of us. The noise and turbulent air made conversation difficult, and the moment was thrilling. The big machine was quick to settle in and begin to shut down. It was the same model designated Marine One when transporting the president, and it had been the mainstay of VIP transportation for years. The three-man crew got ready for disembarkation. When the stairs folded down beneath the rotors, Constantine Panopolous, undersecretary for Homeland Security, emerged. Panopolous held the handrail on his right and virtually tumbled down the steps. His light gray suit was impossibly disheveled, and as usual, his collar was opened and his necktie pulled down a few inches. Philos was by his side before I realized he had moved. The two men shook hands vigorously, and Panopolous even laughed about something Philos had bent down and whispered into his ear. They were an unlikely-looking pair; tall, fine-tuned, tightly wound Philos, and the unkempt, tough little dynamo that was his boss, but there was an obvious bond. Panopolous had not always been an office guy, and I had wondered when and where they had been together, and how far he would allow himself to be separated from the operation on the ground. The answer to the second question was not surprising. Specifically, the Night Hawk had a cruising speed of 150 mph. The Wall Street Heliport on Pier Six in the East River was eleven nautical miles west of Kennedy Airport. The eight-minute flight took about as long as the lights-and-siren ride from Federal Plaza to Pier Six. Panopolous had been launched twenty minutes ago, just as all this fuss began. Not very far from the action at all.

Philos waved Gilliam over from the sidelines and sent him to collect me.

"Good going, doctor," Panopolous said, extending his hand. "Now let's hope you are right." Of course, I had thought of that. Once I had everyone committed, I thought of nothing else. But better a red face than a dead crowd.

"Thank you, Mr. Undersecretary."

"Oh, for Christ's fucking sake! Call me Connie. Mr. Undersecretary, Jesus." He was shaking his head pleasantly. It was obviously an old routine.

"I might be right. At least this was the only unexplained event in a day and a half of surveillance."

"Surveillance is about patience. A day and a half is just the warm-up."

"Right. What I meant was we are on a compressed schedule of twenty-four to seventy-two hours, and this was the first event. Better to react and apologize than not react and lose the patient."

"What patient?" he asked.

"Sorry, doctor talk. In the old days the rule was for surgeons to operate at the first suspicion of appendicitis. If 50 percent of the appendices you removed weren't normal, you weren't doing your job."

"Good for business."

"Yeah, but the point was if you waited and you were wrong, what should have been a minor operation becomes a major catastrophe. Now the diagnosis is made by scans, taking the doctoring, or the guessing, out of the equation."

"Nice analogy. I hope you are right. Let's get the box scanned."

Philos gave orders to Gilliam, who gathered some of his men around him and delegated tasks. This took far more time than it took to instruct him. Then Philos, Panopolous, and I walked over to the hazmat team. Having seen everyone casually approaching the site, they had removed their headgear and breathing devices. A lieutenant stepped forward to meet us. He was a man in his early forties, just under six feet tall, with a rugged face framing a large, sharp nose, which made him look stern. The Martian costume added to the impression.

Panopolous introduced himself, then Philos and me. The lieutenant was impressed. He stood at attention.

"Yes, sir. I am Lieutenant James Rizzo, New York City Fire Department." He went through the same drill for Philos and me. The guy was clearly ex-military and serious. It was a serious job.

"At ease, lieutenant," Panopolous ordered. Then Philos filled the lieutenant in on our situation. It was determined that the hazmat team would transport the casket to wrapping and X-ray. "And Dr. Black will be with you. Can you suit him up?"

"Yes, sir," Lieutenant Rizzo answered smartly. I didn't think it was so damned smart, and I had no intention of wearing all that silly getup. After a minor negotiation, it was agreed that I was qualified by training to act as on-scene incident commander, as required by code. In that position, I could be slightly removed from immediate exposure, unless—or until—it was deemed necessary for me to don a Level A protective suit with SCBA, what the hazmat people called the self-contained breathing apparatus, intrinsic to a Level A protective suit. The SCBA makes the entire getup seamlessly isolated from environmental bio-pathogens. Wearing the suit is a big decision. It is extremely difficult to work in Level A suits. They are heavy and hot, and the air supply provides for an uncomfortable twenty minutes of bottled and filtered air. It is no picnic. These guys are well trained and in great shape. I am neither. I was reasonably familiar with the gear. We used similar equipment in the air force; and in both the hospital and NYPD, hazardous material and re-breathing training was mandatory. But this getup was for a moon landing, and it would take a lot to get me to use it. For starters, the re-breathing apparatus alone would be fine, so long as I wasn't handling the hazardous material. I knew enough to give anthrax a wide berth. I could probably handle it safely in the lab, and I had Cipro on board, since the possibility of coming face-to-face with the nasty little buggers had become real. I was covered, and I wasn't worried for myself.

Clearing the passenger terminal was impractical if at all avoidable. The ensuing panic would spread through the city in minutes. I argued for restraint. Philos considered the conservative position to be evacuation, which was probably correct, but we had time for that. Right now we could seal the casket from behind the scene. The closed SUV was another layer of protection for everyone but the driver, and he seemed to take everything in stride, even as he was about to be hustled off to detention.

"Isolate the driver, and start everyone who has been in contact with the casket on Cipro immediately," I said to Philos, before our own driver, in a Level A protective suit, was installed at the wheel of the SUV. For starters, we had the hundred tablets that I had brought from home that morning. That could provide blood-level protection for a dozen people with casual contact. All bets were off for overwhelming respiratory inhalation. Right now we were dealing with casual contact, but if the source was liberated, it would be hard to tell where casual ended and inhalation began.

The idea of sending men into the terminal to explain to a low-level civilian employee the need to commandeer his bag-wrapping machine would be beyond imagination. But as it turned out, Philos's people simply flashed badges, had hands on pistols, pushed the machine onto the arms of a forklift, and ran it out behind the terminal with the wrap operator in tow. No explanations. They kept it on the lift and moved close to an electrical connection, still out in the open air. The operator was suited and gloved and was almost too panicked to move. Instantly upon seeing the Level A suit, he had begun to shake, and his shirt became transparent with perspiration. When the ambulance doors of the SUV were opened and he saw the casket, he began speaking very quickly in a language I took to be unintelligible Hindi. Then he turned to leave. Two agents took his arms as he attempted to stumble away. It didn't take long for the poor man to gain control of himself and grasp what he was being asked to do. The casket was fed into the wrap machine and the entire box was done up like a mummy. I doubted the need for further wrapping and heat-sealing, but it was my idea, and I had learned that indecision and waffling were destructive to the mission. I wanted to remain on top of this.

Getting the casket through the X-ray machine was easier than I had imagined, though it required several passes. Ultimately, three sequential frames covered all the ground necessary. It was like creating a bizarre triptych. There was, in fact, a body in the casket. A slight female with osteoporotic long bones and no evidence of breast implants. Nor was there any evidence of foreign substances packed in with her, a fact verified by the TSA supervisor assisting the search. My first thought was relief that there were no implants, because I hadn't followed up on the relative density of silicone gel versus anthrax powder in an image. I was so absorbed by my oversight and relieved at not having been found out that the meaning of the false alarm had initially escaped me.

I studied the X-ray images as the casket was passed through the machine yet again and stopped the belt every foot until the situation became obvious.

"We're good, everybody. Nothing here." My anxiety was met by nothing but relief.

"Good job, doc," someone said. The hazmat suits were being unzipped before the exchange was complete. I called Panopolous. He answered on the first ring and seemed truly relieved.

We were returning to the SUV with the plastic-wrapped casket when the Night Hawk lifted up over us. Panopolous was off site.

The letdown among the Homeland people was palpable, and I shared it. Either Philos or Panopolous had immediately lifted the traffic freeze, and jumbo jets were already taxiing out to line up for takeoff sequence. Alison was in the Homeland area when I returned.

"Where have you been? You missed all the action."

"I know. I was watching the terminal. I wanted to see what was going on in the crowd waiting for arrivals."

"Smart. Anything?"

"No. Nothing but annoyance. The sound suppression in the terminal is so good that they didn't register the absence of engine noise. Nothing was posted, so I don't think they were aware of the freeze. Nothing to report."

"Did you just get back? I was looking for you out there. Might have needed a consultation," I said. Then I gave her the short version. Apparently, she had heard much of it in the buzz around the room.

"So actually, we have gotten nowhere," I added.

"Not so," she replied. "Now every airport employee knows we are on high alert. It will be interesting to see if they abort."

"Abort? Aren't you giving them too much credit? They are on a mission. Doing God's will. They won't abort."

"No, they will not, not in that sense," Alison agreed. "But they may push the timetable back, which makes it far more difficult to intercept the operation."

That was food for thought. Still, my sense was that the process was in motion, and nothing could alter the sequence.

52

The 20:10 ETA for VS009 would be the last Virgin arrival of the day. It was bracketed by Delta, BA, Continental, and American flights, all originating at Heathrow. But I was fixed on Virgin. It was the airline of choice for the drug runners, and if we were correct about someone being on the inside, then they would have to stay with what they knew. The Homeland team was all over every flight, not only Virgin Atlantic. You had to respect them for that. They were diligent and alert, and it had been a long day. I was beat and more than a little self-conscious about leading the charge to nowhere. Things quieted down, and I became less the center of attention as arrivals resumed and scrutiny continued. That was some relief.

Philos assigned a team to match up three sets of passenger numbers: the number checked in at LHR, the number of occupied seats before takeoff, and the number of disembarking passengers. The first two were readily available, as every airline controlled those numbers as well as identification of checked-in passengers against checked luggage. If one hundred passengers checked luggage onto a flight, and only ninety-nine boarded, they knew it. If one hundred passengers checked in and only ninety-nine seats were occupied, they were supposed to know that as well. But once the aircraft landed, the danger of in-flight incident was past, and there was no procedure in place to count heads. Philos put a team on it.

Philos was a professional. More often than not, leads went nowhere. That was the cost of doing business. Clean up and move on to the next one. He gave no evidence of holding my actions against me or of any loss of confidence. It said a lot about my ego that my mood went to black over being wrong, when nobody even looked at me cross-eyed. I was pretty much sick of the airport, and it was nearly three hours until the last Virgin flight of the evening.

I paced the baggage area for a while, but the hideous, sickly pastel paint, the industrial floors, the sounds, and the smell had become oppressive. I was looking for any reason to call it a day. Alison had gone out on another walk-about, and there was no one to commiserate with, not that I would have been honest about either the self-doubt or the growling of the black dog. I headed back into Homeland headquarters and stood under the screens a few steps apart from the others when the big arm of the man in the tan suit draped across my shoulder. Deuce was back.

"Hey, man. Where you been?"

"Around. Maybe they let you sign out and play *federale*. Not me. Homicide is a real job. Remember those days? People keep killing each other. You know how it is."

"Yeah, well, you didn't miss much," I said.

"Not what I heard, bro."

"Yeah, well, it all made sense, until it didn't. The casket was unexpected, and the timing was perfect. I didn't think we could let it go."

"No question about that. You did the right thing. The fucked-up part is no one else thought to check it out. That scares the hell out of me. Fucking feds." Deuce was loving it, and he made me feel better in the bargain.

"I just happened to be there. They would have stopped the SUV at the gate," I said.

"Bullshit," Deuce countered, more emphatically than necessary.

"Don't get worked up. They know their jobs as well as we do ours. We don't exactly have a zero-defects police force." Deuce made a few faces and fidgeted a bit. We had worn the topic out.

"You going to be here for a while?"

"Yeah," Deuce answered. "Till the last flight. You?"

I gave him my Virgin speech, and he seemed to agree with the logic. I asked if he would give us a ride home, but he said he was going to stay through the schedule.

"I don't get it," I said. "You just agreed that the Virgin flight is the only one that made sense, and then you say you'll hang around after it clears. What's that about?"

"I have a bad feeling that we are missing something."

"Deuce," I said loudly, "we are missing everything. Where have you been?"

"No, not just the threat. The whole package doesn't make sense to me. Maybe if I hang around, I can make some sense of the parts."

"Like what?" I asked.

"Ah . . . I'm not ready to say. Not yet."

"Jesus, man, you can tell me. I just had a hunch and screwed up air traffic in half the country for nothing. I won't laugh at you."

"Nah. Not yet."

I wasn't curious enough to press the issue, and I needed alone time for thinking. I don't really mean alone—it's impossible to be alone at JFK—just away from people I knew and situations with the potential to stir up conversation. I was all talked out. I knew I wasn't quite myself, and wandering alone was good therapy. It had always been that way with me. I was never able to follow my train of thought interrupted by civil conversation. It was a minor disability, but it probably made me seem either dumb or aloof. Some switch in my head couldn't be thrown tightly enough to shut out the noise of conversation for me to follow an idea through to the end.

Despite the best intentions of the developers, Terminal 4 is terminally boring. It's the nature of the beast. Airports are about convenience and conveyance. Anything that serves thousands of occasional travelers in a hurry cannot serve the needs of the constant occupant. At Terminal 4, the Transit Authority partnered with the operators of Schiphol Airport in Amsterdam to build and operate the steel-and-glass behemoth, in a deal financed by Lehman Brothers. If that trifecta doesn't sound exactly promising, imagine spending all day there. I couldn't look at another Euro-luxury alcove peddling junk they couldn't sell in the city.

Magazine covers began to look alike. Fast food smelled like it tasted. Amazingly, I wasn't hungry at all. Maybe the whole list lumped into a diagnosis I wouldn't like to hear, but I was a little down.

I zoned out and began a time line in my head. I imagined a chalkboard within reach, and I could add and erase like a math teacher. I might even have been waving my hands and talking to myself. As I made the turn around the central seating area, I thought I saw a familiar face in the passing crowd, but it was difficult to separate from what was playing on the screen in my head. A man in a hat, a baseball cap. I followed the back of his head for some seconds but couldn't crank up the proper synapse. Either he didn't want to acknowledge me, or he hadn't known me, or maybe he didn't see me. Traffic on my side of the seating was sparse, and I must have stood out as the only man strolling along without luggage, sporting a plastic ID around his neck, and clearly in his own world. Whatever had clicked disappeared equally quickly as I lost sight of the man in the hat.

The moment was ruined, and I couldn't get back to my chalkboard. I did another lap in vain and couldn't recover the mood. I was drawn back deeply enough into the real world to notice the Häagen-Dazs stand a few steps to my right. True to my normal state, I bought a lethal-looking coffee bar with chocolate praline coating. I got very little change back from a $10 bill, and I made up for the outrageous price by loading up on napkins. I scanned the area and sat in the closest, relatively clean seat with no immediate neighbors. The process of opening the ice cream bar consumed my attention, and the first bite was fabulous. Actually, the second was equally enjoyable until a large section of chocolate coating took flight, evaded my patchwork quilt of napkins, and landed square and flat on the front of my gray pants.

"God damn it."

"God damn what? Baby made a mess?" I hadn't noticed Alison, who was standing in front of me, laughing.

"Shit." I took another very aggressive bite—the damage had been done—and handed the ice cream stick to Alison.

"Have a ball. I need to clean up." I did a poor job of prying the large chocolate flake off my pants, smearing the melting edges into the fabric. Alison held the stick daintily, her right pinky finger extended like she was drinking tea. She started nibbling away at the remaining ice cream while I went off to the men's room across the hall. I folded over one of the crude paper towels from the washroom roll, soaked it with water, pumped a shot of hand soap in the middle, and did the best I could on the chocolate stain. Then I headed over to the rank of urinals. My father was always heading off to the men's facility—that's what he called it—saying, "A smart man never passes up the men's facility; you never know when the next opportunity will come." I was becoming my father. I rearranged myself and zipped up, and saw the enormous wet spot covering the front of my left upper pant leg. I considered undressing and holding my wet pants up to the hot-air hand-dryer, but that was way too geeky to contemplate, and I decided to bite the bullet and face the stares. As it turned out, no one cared.

53

And then the lightbulb flashed. "Alison," I said. "*I think I* saw Rodriguez out on the concourse. At least it was some guy that looked a lot like him. He was wearing a dark blue baseball cap, and I couldn't be quite sure. I just didn't expect to see him here and didn't make the connection in time."

"I didn't see him. Why would Rodriguez be here?" Alison asked.

I didn't have a good answer for that. In fact, I had no answer, so I let it slide. Alison looked around, doing a complete three-sixty.

"Maybe it wasn't him," I said. "I'm not sure."

"I would wager that is the case. And he surely would have seen you as well and had something to say. Forget Mr. Rodriguez. The man is a bad memory."

"Amen," I said. But I wasn't convinced.

We walked slowly back through the concourse, both of us keeping a sharp eye out. We walked through the disorganized mess of drivers and relatives outside the automatic doors separating it from the insulated world of customs.

From there into the Homeland station. There was very little going on and nearly an hour before the next arrival. Deuce was nowhere in sight, and the agents in the room were more concerned with eating than watching the screens. In truth, there was nothing happening. I had an attack of heavy eyelids and needed to nod off for a few minutes. Sometimes the only alternative to sleep is a sudden jolt of adrenaline. When the roadside grass and trees meld into a blur of green, nothing will prevent sleep. And the first rumble of a tire on the shoulder jolts you to full alert, and the adrenaline cures any further sleepiness. Or you could stop driving, pull over, and fall asleep. I was there. I pulled out one of the uncomfortable metal chairs around the table, kind of slid down into it, and was snoring before I could readjust my feet. I was unconscious for better than ten minutes when Alison kicked my shoes.

"Let's do it. The 009 is coming in early."

"Oh . . . thank you. Man, I fell off."

"Indeed you did. Rise and shine."

I stood, stretched my arms overhead. With a little bit of difficulty, I touched my toes three times, readjusted my jacket, and smoothed down my hair. I must have been pretty disheveled, but my pants were almost dry.

Most of the base group moved to the screens and watched the 747-400 dock gracefully at gate 6 in concourse A, and then came the stampede to the arrivals hall. In the end the passengers would still wait for their bags. Philos had had two men pulled off the arriving baggage crew to give his people extra time to mingle and examine the irate passengers, and there was no reason to rush. In reality, there never was. We followed their progress on the screens as they snaked through the corridors, down the stairs, and into the hall.

"Let's go and see them," I said. Alison agreed without speaking. The remainder of the Homeland and ICE people had gone off to their assigned posts, and we wandered onto the floor of the hall. We were on site for fewer than three minutes, and both lines were already beginning to take shape. I was as focused as I could be, knowing that this was an exercise in futility. They would not be risking interrogation and search. They were going to go around us.

"There's nothing here for us. Let's go onto the plane."

"Why?" Alison asked.

I had no explanation and no patience. I just knew I should go there. "Stay if you want to. I'm going onto the plane." Alison hesitated and then reluctantly followed me out of the hall, reversing the steps taken by the disembarking passengers. Initially, we were swimming upstream as the stragglers, three and four abreast, were working their way to the arrivals hall.

"Excuse me, pardon us. Sorry." The last significant cluster was older people walking slowly alongside as their companions in wheelchairs were pushed by attendants.

"Stop," I said. Holding up my identity card in my left hand and making the universal sign for stop with my right. A single chair had passed us, occupied by a bent older woman with wisps of unnaturally black hair protruding from the sides of a baseball cap. There was an eight- or nine-year-old girl at her side. I followed their progress with my eyes. When they continued past us not stopping, Alison made a move to go after them, but I restrained her. Watching and waiting did not seem much of a risk to take, especially since I really didn't know what had clicked for that brief moment.

We focused on the remaining chair-bound passengers and their attendants. There were five in all. They did not question our authority, and we did not interrogate them. In fact, we didn't speak to them at all. Just systematically took stock of what we were dealing with. With one exception, the passengers were Anglo and appeared infirm. The exception was a man in his forties, bearing a long leg cast on the extended-left-leg platform of the chair. From the look of it, the cast was relatively new. It was clean and white and free of graffiti. He wore an unpolished black shoe on his right foot, black pants, a long black coat, and wide-brimmed black felt hat. His beard was untrimmed and barely speckled with gray. White fringe, which I took to be religious apparatus, was visible at his waist. He eyed us warily and made a halfhearted attempt at a smile. The attendant behind the chair was young. No more than twenty-five, dark, and maybe Indian or Pakistani. I didn't like the way this looked. Alison made her way behind the wheelchair attendant while I dismissed the others. Orthodox apparatus was a not-infrequent ruse in Israeli suicide attacks, and it wouldn't get a free pass here.

We waited until the others were out of earshot, and I approached the man in the chair. "Good evening, sir," I said. "I am with the special Homeland Security Task Force. I would like to ask you some questions. May I see your passport?"

The man made a quick motion with his right hand into his black suit coat. I reached forward and grabbed his arm before he could withdraw it. The attendant made a move toward us, and Alison closed in from behind, spun him around, and pushed him, face-forward, into the long, gray wall decorated with WELCOME TO AMERICA. She quickly had his arm twisted unnaturally toward his scapula, and he yelped in pain. He was effectively neutralized, and she turned her head around so she could watch the action.

"Take your hand out of your jacket very slowly," I said, working my way behind the wheelchair. The bearded man did as he was told. He withdrew an empty right hand from within his jacket and raised both arms over his head in the position of a supplicant. I ran my hands over his upper body and hips, then reached into his left inside coat pocket and removed a United States passport. Working it open with my fingers, I matched the picture to the bearded face of Richard Alan Sheinbaum. Entry stamps were confined to the U. S., The Netherlands, Israel, and the UK.

I circled the chair and returned the passport.

"When did you injure your leg, Mr. Sheinbaum?"

"Yesterday, no, now two days ago. A little fracture and a cast, so I can't walk. Stupid, very stupid, but the doctors in London are very nice. And it's all free. We should take a lesson from them."

"What is your business, Mr. Sheinbaum?"

The fact that Sheinbaum didn't have an accent kept throwing me. Somehow I continued to confuse fundamentalist and foreign. These were fundamentalists, my coreligionist fundamentalists, and I was only slightly more comfortable with him than any of the other religious extremists.

"I am a diamond dealer. You can see from the passport, and these." He began to reach into his waistband and I tensed again. He sensed my reaction.

"May I?" he asked. And without waiting for an answer, he brought out a small velvet sack with a snap closure. He held it out to me. I took it in my right hand. "Open it." I did. "Shake them out." I did. Half a dozen beautifully cut, lively, sparkling diamonds tumbled into my hand.

"Wow. Beautiful." Alison craned her neck to see what was going on, without releasing the pressure on her captive. I replaced the stones, handed the bag to Sheinbaum, finished patting him down, apologized for stopping him, and did the same to Alison's captive.

"Hey, man, I know what's going on. Just doing your job. Me, too." He was smiling at us and massaging his shoulder.

"Let's get going," Sheinbaum called out to him, and they began to make their way down the long corridor. We had spent fewer than five minutes in the exchange with Sheinbaum, but that was all it took for the corridor to clear of passengers. Airline staffers were standing on the Jetway near the aircraft door. The flight crew was long gone. In fact, two of the flight attendants, probably the last two, passed as we were questioning Sheinbaum. They never broke stride. See no evil, and get to town. A three-man cleaning crew pushed past us, dragging trash bags and supplies, wearing headphones, and paying no attention to us, nor, apparently, to anything but their music. We followed them to the aircraft door where we were stopped by airline ground crew. I showed my identification, as did Alison, but the woman, a slip of a person with a stunningly working-class British accent, would not let us pass.

"Sorry, guv, this plane is out of service. Crew only."

Explaining our mission to deaf ears got us nowhere.

Alison took over. "Listen up, you dumb tart, I order you out of our path," she growled, and pulled a nine-millimeter Beretta automatic from behind her back.

"Put that away," I ordered. I was thinking "Where the hell did you get that?" but didn't say it. I read the nameplate on the woman's uniform. When I looked up at her face, there were tears in her eyes, but she was not yet audibly crying. "Sorry about this, Peggy. Please call your supervisor and advise him that two Homeland Security Task Force agents request permission to board the aircraft."

"Her," Peggy snapped, trying to regain self-importance. I was ready to tear her goddamned head off.

"Just call her. I am losing my patience."

"Step back please, sir."

We did. And she keyed her radio. I turned my back to her and faced Alison. "Why didn't you tell me you had a gun?"

I was angry. It wasn't simply carryover, I was furious with Alison for deceiving me yet again. "And how did you get the damned thing in here?"

"Wendell, relax. I am acting in my capacity as an anti-terrorist agent. This is what we do. I am trained and competent."

"Bullshit. Put it away and keep it away. You're not anything but a visitor here, and you got in on my ticket. Do not try to tell me you have a carry permit here, and I don't fucking want to know how you got it through security. It gives me a bad feeling." I hadn't noticed that Peggy had stepped aside to allow our entry. Her radio began to crackle again, and she "Rogered" something I couldn't hear.

I left Alison standing where she was and entered the cabin. I turned left into the first-class section. It was empty except for the cleaner, picking up trash from between the seats. He had already filled half the black plastic bag he was dragging back from row one. I made a quick visual check to be sure the area was empty and checked the lavatories, which had not yet been serviced. Then I headed to the spiral stairway to the small upper deck, where I did the same. Empty. Downstairs again, to the enormous main cabin. There were 393 seats in business and economy. Empty of passengers, it looked like a thousand. At the far end Alison was checking the lavatories, leaving the doors open behind her. The cleaning people were systematically working to the back from the galley amidships. I looked to Alison. "Nothing," she said.

"Let's go," I said and turned around and headed for the door. Several other ground employees were outside the door with bags of supplies that looked like in-flight magazines and paper products. They were in no rush to enter. Peggy was gone.

I guess I was disappointed not to find anything out of order, and maybe a little relieved not to have to confront it if I had. On the way back to the Homeland station, we stopped at both the arrivals hall and baggage. Agents were everywhere. There were at least half a dozen whose faces I recognized, and I don't know how many others that I didn't. They no more than glanced at us, gave no sign of recognition. It was clear that we were meant to do the same. That much even I knew. Same as every prior flight today. Our presence seemed gratuitous, at least mine did, but I needed to stay and watch for a while. I tucked my ID into my shirt and did my job. I saw nothing out of the ordinary beyond generally eccentric human behavior. People are weird and annoying as hell. From outside looking in, they made a zoo seem dull.

Back at base, the crowd around the CCTV screens had thinned. Most of those remaining had been assigned to the task. I got a cold Diet Coke from the mini fridge and a water for Alison. I handed it to her without speaking.

"Thanks," she said, smiling. I wanted to smile back, but I was still pissed. She rolled the wet, cold plastic bottle along her forehead, then wiped the moisture into her hair with her right hand. She struggled with the twist-off cap but got it opened before I offered to help. She took a long, exaggerated slug and replaced the cap. We watched silently. Nothing happened. Twenty minutes later, the arrivals hall was empty of all but agents and employees. A Delta flight was expected in less than half an hour, and the same coverage was in effect. Panopolous had agreed that the attempt would be on Virgin, but he refused to take the risk of ignoring the others. At least, I think he agreed. On the other hand, he still believed the terror attack was going to play out in the watershed. Different strokes. I stared at the screens, hoping they would show me something special for believing, but I was losing faith. Finally, the four cleaners exited the aircraft door. They tossed the bags of refuse out onto the tarmac and followed down the stairs with their equipment. That was it. The plane was empty, arrivals had been cleared, and only baggage claim remained. Damn. It had to be today. There was no second chance.

I turned to Alison. We hadn't actually spoken since the pistol incident. "Let's look at baggage—this is done."

"I know. Sorry. I thought we were on it, but when the cleaners left the aircraft, it was a big letdown. Like 'Ciao, it's over.'"

"Right," I said. Then, "The cleaners. Alison . . . how many cleaners were on the plane with us?"

"Three."

"Fuck."

"What?"

"Four cleaners just went down those stairs."

"Are you certain?" she asked. "Let's have them play back the last couple of minutes."

"No time. I'm sure. Shit. Let's go." I tossed my Coke into the wastebasket and started out. Then stopped and called to the agents manning the screens, "Call Philos. Tell him to keep an eye on me and send a team."

Before they could ask questions, we were out the door.

54

I ran blindly through baggage claim, slipping on the first turn around the carousel and landing hard on my left knee and hand. I was up again and running before anyone could assist, and by now we were attracting attention. I didn't bother signaling the agents. It would take forever to get them to leave their stations, but for sure someone would see what was going on and report it. And it was on CCTV. I kept running for the door. Alison was nowhere to be seen, but in truth I didn't look back. I slid my ID through the sensor and opened the door to the arriving baggage area and the tarmac just as Alison caught up. A few men were working. Most were waiting. I stopped, looked around, no cleaners.

"Anyone see the cleaning crew?" I shouted at two men sitting on the edge of a cart looking out onto the field.

"Which cleaning crew?" a tired-looking, middle-aged black man asked, as he wiped perspiration from his brow with a bandanna pulled from his back pocket.

"Off 009. Just now." He looked out onto the tarmac.

"No, man. I wasn't looking."

I waved and ran out in the direction of the big plane. Alison followed. It was still light, but only just, and I had difficulty adjusting from the brightly lit terminal to the autumnal dusk. We stopped running when we arrived under the wing, just short of the mounting stairs. The area was deserted, at least at ground level. The 747-400 was grounded by wheel chocks hoses and huge electrical cords, and looked eerie in the twilight.

"Check every door to the terminal. You go left. Use your card. Just check. Nothing else. Call me if you see anything. You have your phone?"

"Yes."

"Okay. Do you have me on speed dial on that thing?" I indicated the mobile phone she had in her hand. Alison nodded. "Call me for anything. You have to keep in touch. Understand?" She nodded again. I ran to the right. I ran hard for about fifty yards and found myself facing the back wall of the terminal. Back where I started. Farther to the right was the massive industrial piping of the HVAC building. Beyond that was the tower. It wasn't going to be the tower. Too much security.

The HVAC building. HVAC and anthrax. My imagination soared. Oh my God! That was it. For starters they could kill every person in the airport. Everyone breathing airport air. Every breathing thing. Shit. I wheeled and headed for the building. I remembered the general position of the door and saved seconds of searching. It was no longer obvious in the early evening, and when I found it, it was secured. There was no way to know whether the dead bolts had been thrown. Steel molding prevented slipping a credit card along the jam to check. I leaned forward and angled the bar-coded end of my ID into the scanner. Ratchets clicked and the tongue of the automatic lock retracted. I took a deep breath and pulled the handle down. The door moved noiselessly inward for an inch or two. Time was pressing, but I was not ready to enter. A hum—or maybe it was a vibration—came from within. I eased the steel door closed until it reseated firmly in its frame. I stepped around with my back to the building. I took my phone out of my pocket, hit the A key for Alison, and was shocked as the musical calling tones began to sound. The noise surprised me. I hit the end button quickly and scrambled to silence the tones and redial. I wasted ten precious seconds. The first call must have alerted Alison because she answered before I heard the phone ring.

"Why did you hang up?"

"Call Philos and tell him to bring people over to the HVAC building near the tower. Tell him to get here quickly. Very quickly, stat." I ended the call before she could ask questions, for fear of being overheard, and turned toward the door again. They had to be in here. Just the fact that the dead bolts on the second lock hadn't been thrown meant someone was in there. I took a deep breath, exhaled, and eased the door open enough to slip in. It was dark. The floor was hard and smooth. A few searing shards of light appeared like crossed swords from left and right, where rooms came off the entry foyer. I closed my eyes tight and stood still against the closed door, waiting for my vision to accommodate to the dark. I waited several seconds, then looked away from where I remembered the light sources to be. The room was large and sharp-sided, possibly square. It was tall and both deep and wide, but the center was consumed by enclosed machinery giving off the rhythmic hum I had felt, more than heard, outside. Coming from the top of the box were the huge turned pipes that I had seen hugging the outside walls of the building after they exited the box. I could not make out where they breeched the walls. That had to be part of the air-conditioning apparatus. As I approached it, with my hand against the steel container for stability, it was cold to the touch, and I could identify the hum as rushing water, part of the straining apparatus that kept the water in the system clear. Behind it were the first three steps of a wide steel staircase. The wedges of light had nothing to do with doors or windows, and I could see they were white, pinpoint safety lights identifying the edges of the steel landing.

Making my way along the wall and heading for the staircase, I took exaggerated strides—high-stepping, slow steps—trying to avoid unnecessary noise. Nearing the corner, I extended my upper body to sneak a look, but as I did, my right foot lost its purchase and slipped forward. It was all I could do to avoid falling against the wall. My hand slapped the steel, but there was no noise beyond the continuous, muffled rush of water. The oil or grease underfoot was unexpected. The place felt surgically clean. I heard nothing unusual. Two more careful steps and I rounded the corner, then I lost footing again and my right foot shot forward. My arms were flailing, and I was about to complete a full split when my right foot wedged under something solid and I fell forward, my fall broken by another person.

My hands were suddenly wet, and I pushed forcefully against the bulk. I tried to get up. I wanted to apologize, but the person didn't move. I was on top of a body, a recently dead body. Still warm and covered in fresh blood, the same blood that I had slipped on seconds ago. I got to my knees and took stock. It was a man's body. About my size, maybe an inch or two shorter, and beefy. A working man in a baggage-handler's uniform. All but the very side of his reflective vest was covered with blood. I touched the pooling blood again. It was warm and not coagulated. He could not have been dead for more than minutes. I quickly tried to feel for his carotid pulse to be sure. There was none. His head was bent away at a grotesque angle, almost gone. His throat had been severed with a very sharp blade wielded with the force of a powerful butcher. Ear to ear. Both carotids and his jugular veins were laid open. His trachea was cut through, and the bones of his neck were shining through the gaping muscles. It would have taken no more than a minute for him to bleed out, seconds to lose consciousness.

My fingers were stuck together with blood. I stood up and wiped my hands on my pants. I spread my fingers and wiped between them, one after another, again and again. I tried to think. How many were there? I had no idea. There was no way to know. They were in the building, that was certain, and the best I could figure they would probably

sacrifice the mule—this wasn't going to be a surgical implant removal. It would be fast and dirty and inhumane.
And then the real damage would be done. One death, two
deaths, ten thousand here, and maybe the watershed next.
There was enough anthrax in those implants to cripple the
entire metropolitan area.

I took the metal stairs two at a time. Twelve long strides
and the wall of steel doors appeared at the landing. I listened at the first and heard nothing. There were four in all,
and something inside me didn't want to find the one that
opened to the mayhem that was in store. Then there was a
noise. It sounded loud and disturbing, and for a moment I
thought the man at the foot of the stairs was moving. I
looked for cover, but there was none. Instead, I held fast to
the darkest spot along the wall. I tried to see what was
going on, but it was too dark. The ambient light up here
had reversed my night vision. I was blind to what was
going on beneath me, but I wasn't deaf. Whoever was moving down there was doing nothing at all to mask the noise.
All I could think of was to wait at the top of the stairs, then
spring from the dark, hit him with my shoulder, and hope
he went down the stairs. But then I would have to run. No
chance of going undiscovered with the noise of a body
bouncing down twenty-four steps. Two, three, four foot-
falls on the stairs. The sound of metal against metal. The
sounds were very close. I bent into a football lineman's position, balanced on the fingers of my right hand, and prepared to launch myself. And then a barely audible
"Wendell? Wendell, are you here?"

I stood. "Shh. Up here." I listened to, more than watched, Alison as she approached. She had the Beretta in her right hand and still held the metal railing with her left. That much I could see.

"Did you see the body?"

"Yes."

"They're up here," I said, edging toward the doors, when a single, terrifying scream filled the cold space. Then it went quiet again. Dead quiet for seconds before I could make out muffled male voices. No need to guess about what was happening. "Let's go in. You cover me." I didn't wait for an answer. There was no time. No time at all.

I lifted the heavy metal lever, and the locking mechanism disengaged smoothly. Despite what we had heard, I managed to maintain some caution and entered slowly. The industrial space was well lit by gangs of fluorescent bulbs hanging ten or twelve feet above the floor. The long wall across from the entry housed evenly spaced louvered metal fins, behind which mechanical elements were visible. The floor between where we entered and the wall was clean and clear of debris. It was painted light gray, and the reflection of the lights was dazzling. I took a second to squeeze my eyelids closed, then reopened them, squinting against the light. There was a neat tool station along the left wall, and a clean metal worktable was bolted to the floor a few feet in front of it. The room echoed the lower floor and bent around the central condenser. I motioned Alison to stop, and I tried to look around the corner without being seen, which didn't matter. The carnage in front of us had run from the work-height metal table onto the floor. A figure, nude from the waist, was fastened to the surface by encircling coils of gray duct tape. The head was extended at an unnatural angle over the end of the table, and the neck had been brutally slashed, like that of the body downstairs, No more than a minute had passed since we heard the scream, and the arterial spurts of blood had already stopped. Two slash wounds were on the chest where the breasts had been. Bright blood painted the flanks, and darker red pools were forming on the steel.

Even without the implants, the body could just as easily be assumed to be a female as a hairless, slight male. A fast glance at the ghostly face didn't offer a clue, and it didn't matter. They had the anthrax, and they were about to use it. Alison and I were icily clinical regarding the body and did not even utter any of the very human clichés. Instead, we bolted through the open door at the other end of the room and started to mount another tall flight of steel stairs. An orange reflecting vest flashed around a corner at the top of the stairs and disappeared.

"There," I said, and began running up the stairs. There were two of them in reflective vests. They moved purposefully to the face of a vibrating sheet-metal duct that consumed the entire wall. They were not yet aware of us, and neither looked back. When they did turn, the reality of the situation became clear. Both were wearing gauntlet-type rubber gloves covering their arms to the elbows, and re-breathing masks. They faced each other, and we could see them clearly in profile. Their faces were science fiction anteaters with plastic eye shields. The man on the left was working a heavy-duty electric bolt wrench, removing the fifth of a series of ten screw-fasteners holding the six-foot metal door in the duct. The other held the breast implants, one in each outstretched palm, in the manner of an offering in a pagan ritual. I didn't see a bloody knife or a pistol. They held nothing dangerous except five hundred grams of the deadliest bacterial weapon known to man.

55

The man holding the anthrax-filled implants turned to face us with robot-like movements. He moved his head as though the re-breathing device had fixed it in place. He stepped forty-five degrees to his right before alerting his companion to our presence, all the while holding the implants out and away from his body. He did not threaten us with them. He did nothing but stare at us. When the other man saw us, he looked away, then at us again, then at the anthrax, as if to be sure we got the picture, and resumed removing the last fastening bolts from the window in the duct.

Weighing the odds of stopping the attack, or even surviving this confrontation, was paralyzing. I froze. They froze. The whole ballet could not have taken ten seconds, but it was a lifetime. Then the sheet metal door from the duct crashed to the floor. The racket was deafening. Everything was back in motion, but the speed was wrong. We had forever to make our moves. They were going to break open the implants and dump the infectious powder into the air-distribution ducts. The window in the main duct was well beyond the HEPA filters and the cleansing system. Nothing could stop it. Huge volumes of forced air would carry the spores through miles of ductwork, contaminating every cubic millimeter of air in the entire airport complex. Mothers and children, bartenders and pizza-makers, cops, customs agents, voyagers, welcomers, ticket sellers and taxi hustlers, every person who breathed the comfortably climate-controlled air was doomed.

I turned to Alison and pushed her back to the staircase. "Go. Go," I shouted. "Let's get out of here. Hurry." I had the framework of a plan, but I had surprised her and she did not know how to respond. I forced her back, and she hesitated, trying to regain her footing while backpedaling onto the first step. I grabbed the handrail and flew downward past her. I looked up to see that Alison had dropped to her left knee and smoothly brought the Beretta to combat position in both hands. She fired off two rapid series of three shots each. The deafening noise made me stop in my tracks. I was halfway down the stairs, but it was easy to see what had happened. The first volley blew away the entire skull-cap of the man holding the anthrax. The shots instantly splattered the remains of his brain onto the bright steel wall. She pumped a second close grouping into the chest of the other man as he struggled to free a large knife from his belt. He went down to his knees, and then onto his face, with the knife handle still in his fist. It was good shooting.

Alison remained in the firing position staring at what she had done. I stumbled back up to her. I could see one implant on the floor. It appeared intact. The other had to be under the body. Maybe broken open, maybe not. I grabbed her hand and pulled her to her feet.

"Now! We have to leave now. Listen to me, please," I said loudly, almost unable to coax her from the scene. "Come on. Don't breathe. Exhale only; don't inhale. Hold your breath and run." When she was halfway down the first flight, I released her hand and hurtled downward as fast as I could, falling down at least as many steps as I navigated. Alison was right behind me. We ran around the body on the floor, and just inside the door, I threw the light switch, opened the door, and pushed Alison to safety. I was beginning to feel the need to breathe. I could hold out for another fifteen seconds, but my mind was playing panic games. Then I saw it, right where I remembered it to be: chest-high on the tool wall. I ran to the far side of the bench. My lungs were exploding. I flipped the steel safety door open, grabbed the horizontal handle, and threw the main power switch down. The quiet was instant, the compressors and fans stopped humming, the sound of running water ceased, and the air stopped blowing. The room was dark again. Lights from the terminal twinkled through the open door. I followed the lights and ran outside, pulling the door closed behind me.

Alison was crouched against the exterior wall not far from the door, trying to get her breath. I don't remember having exhaled, but my lungs were collapsed and running on empty. The first few breaths almost hurt, and then they felt good. Really good.

"You surprised me," I said to Alison.

She nodded, still breathing deeply and not looking at me. "It had to be done." That may have been true. That was true. No time for negotiation, but we could have made a run for it, turned off the power, and let the team deal with two trapped terrorists and five hundred grams of anthrax. That was not in the cards.

"You did great. Quick reaction and really good shooting. You saved the day, and a lot more than that."

"Thank you," Alison said, still sitting on her heels.

I was starting to dial Philos when I saw the emergency vehicles. There were a lot of them making a noise-and-light show. They were visible from a mile away. If I was in a normal state, I would have seen them the minute I opened the door, but this wasn't normal. Anything but normal.

The hazmat unit was not the first to arrive, and none of the responders exited their vehicles until the fully protected hazmat team pulled up, exited their truck, and dressed us in isolation suits and surgical masks. We had become part of the problem. Philos was at the end of the parade. I had already told most of my story to Rizzo, the hazmat lieutenant, when Philos began debriefing me like a suspect or, at best, an underling.

"Why were you in that building? Under whose orders?" He had only begun to wind up.

"Hey, man," I said, stopping him in mid-sentence. "We just saved the whole fucking airport, so don't give me any attitude." Philos was thrown by my response. He was meant to be. But to give credit where it is due, he recovered and smiled.

"Well, since you put it that way, sorry, and thanks." His smile was broad and genuine. "Now, it's important that you answer my questions. Yes, we are on the same side, and yes, you have been key to preventing the apocalypse, but we have accumulated a lot more background intelligence than you need to know. My questions need to be answered the way I ask them. I can't worry about hurt feelings or being PC. Understood?"

"Understood."

Representatives of every imaginable agency were on site, but none rushed to stake out turf. No one was comfortable with the possibilities, and a little knowledge bred wholesale fear. Once it was determined that we had not had direct contact with the anthrax source, the isolation suits were abandoned. In the unlikely event that we could have inhaled anthrax spores, we were ordered to begin a course of Cipro, which was gingerly handed to us without making contact. I swallowed the big white pills without water and offered my thanks without telling the team I had been self-dosing for days.

Philos picked out three members of his team, who disappeared into the red truck, emerged suited up in protective gear, and were dispatched with the hazmat team into the HVAC building. Alison was standing two cars away. She had gained control of herself and was speaking in a very animated fashion to Homeland examiners. Every once in a while I glanced over. This time her movement caught my eye as she surrendered her pistol to the agents. It was protocol after a shooting-related incident—justified or not—and they carefully bagged and identified the weapon.

As it turned out, we were questioned for barely ten minutes, which was ten times the duration of the event. Then they did the musical-chairs bit. We stayed in place and the interrogators switched. There was no opportunity for us to speak to each other. It was good policy, but it made me laugh. There was really nothing whatever to laugh about.

The government has a protocol for everything. After the anthrax attacks a decade ago, a decontaminating procedure was spelled out for every situation. In this case, there was no evidence that we were contaminated, infected, or otherwise compromised. The disease, anthrax, is contracted through breaks in the skin during direct contact with the infective agent. That didn't happen. Pulmonary anthrax, potentially the most lethal form of the disease, is contracted by inhaling anthrax spores. I don't think that happened. Human-to-human transmission is virtually unheard of. It requires significant surface contamination, followed by one of the previous two situations. That wouldn't happen, either, but decontamination it was. In its simplest form, this entails disposing of potentially contaminated clothing and showering. Not too onerous a procedure.

The events of the evening still had a pulse of their own, and Philos and company were not about to send us home. The options for showering were a make-do arrangement in the hazmat truck, the locker room in the terminal, or the airport medical facility. But that was as public as transferring us to any of the local hospitals ten minutes from the airport. If they were going to control the flow of information, it had to start with limiting the circle of information.

With all the preparation and training, there was no accommodation for a proper clothing wardrobe, particularly for women.

Alison and I were escorted back to the terminal by two babysitters. All incoming and outgoing flights had again been put on hold, and Terminal 4 was in lockdown for the second time in four hours. This time it had been evacuated . . . totally. Shop clerks were not given time to lock up, food was still on steam tables, newspapers were there for the taking, and breaking news on television was seconds from being obsolete. The arrivals hall didn't look all that different from the interval between planes, but the undercovers weren't in character. They were manning posts and watching doors. The Homeland office was a beehive of activity. All the buzzing around stopped precipitously when we walked into the room. No one backed away, but no one rushed up to high-five us or shake our hands. All conversation stopped. Every voice disappeared in mid-sentence. I could feel the eyes on me, and the only voice was the incessant Wolf Blitzer on CNN, and then all hell broke loose. My ears were ringing with congratulations. The enthusiasm of the feds for the NYPD would be short-lived, but this was our moment. I looked around for people on the job to share the glory. No foot soldiers, no suits, no brass, no Deuce.

Alison had a sweater with her bag, and one of the female agents contributed jeans and sneakers that looked right. She wore a men's T-shirt under the thin sweater, but there was no disguising the braless look, and we both knew that would change what the boys were chattering about really quickly. The men's locker room had the look of a second-hand clothing store, and I had my choice of a dozen shirts and nylon jackets, as long as I could live with being a walking billboard for Homeland or ICE. Finding pants that fit was easy, and I was all set. Our clothes were bagged and tagged by our hazmat keepers. Wallets, badges, money, phones, anything that was not conceivably a resting place for floating spores, remained private property. The rest was bound for the incinerator.

Alison grabbed her leather-trimmed canvas shoulder bag from the cubby in the office where she had stowed it, and we were ushered into Philos's office. A videoconference with Panopolous was already underway. Philos made it clear that the private portion of the conference was over by announcing our presence.

"Here they are now, Mr. Secretary," which made my ears twitch, since he usually referred to his boss as Connie. Panopolous sounded weird. He was anything but spontaneous, which was unlike him, and I was surprised that he wasn't already en route. I felt like a winning quarterback getting a congratulatory call from a president who had been rooting for the other team. There was no reason I could think of for this sudden formality, unless the conference was being recorded, in which case everyone in government was always in CYA mode. Panopolous finished with serial platitudes, also very much unlike him, and thanked us for our service to the country. I was waiting for the bit about the gold watch. It was that bad. He wasn't my boss, and I liked the guy enough to call him out on his peculiar behavior, but those were the same reasons I decided not to push the issue. We accepted the thanks of a grateful nation and the offer of a ride into town, but I had already called for a car and I needed a drink.

I told Alison my plan, and we headed for the eerily deserted gate area. We strolled slowly and quietly through our private terminal, making nearly the entire circuit in twenty minutes, looking for a suitable bar. The big laugh was Panopolous, a restaurant at gate A5.

"Do you think he knows?" I asked Alison.

"I was thinking about one of those dopey sports bars without the sports or the dopes, but we can't pass this up."

"Why do I think we might regret this?"

"Come on, it's just a drink."

The place was more a restaurant than a bar, but the cocktail lounge was adequate, and with the lights low it wasn't particularly unattractive. I had fun working the bottles with Alison sitting across the bar. From the bartender's vantage point, it was easy to see why she would get instant service. I poured an ice-cold Pinot Grigio from the fridge and set about the elaborate ritual of shaking up a martini for myself. I filled the bathtub-sized glass with ice and water to give it a chance to frost up while I added a few drops of vermouth to the filled shaker, swirled and discarded it, added a generous pour of Belvedere over the ice, capped the shaker, and lifted it over my head.

"Twenty-five shakes. Pro-style," I said, smiling. At nineteen my hands were frozen to the shaker and I quit.

"Wimp."

I rimmed the cold glass with lemon peel, filled it half-way, and admired my beautiful creation. "Here's to you, Annie Oakley."

"And you, partner. Good work."

"Good work."

56

At eleven the terminal reopened and flights resumed. I had
no more than three or four sips of my drink. That was
enough for the medicinal effect I needed. I did not want to
lose my edge, not yet. Alison got through most of her white
wine, and we were sitting side by side on reasonably comfortable bar stools when the restaurant manager returned.
He was surprised to see us. He was a slick, middle-aged
restaurant type and figured pretty quickly that we had to
be official. He told us we were his guests, and we had about
half an hour while they closed up around us. There were
two guys with the manager. I took the other men for bus-
boys, based on their quiet demeanor, Hispanic features,
and the fact that they did all the work. We stayed a few
minutes longer, but the mood wasn't the same. We both
thanked our host effusively and headed out.

Coming up on midnight wasn't the busiest hour for air
travel. The only crowds were at gates servicing late-night
flights to Europe. The nine- and ten-o'clock flights had been
delayed, so there were pockets of action, but it was still an
airport at midnight. I stopped at one of the television

monitors we were passing just in time to hear that the airport had been shut down, and Terminal 4 evacuated in response to a bomb scare. No mention of anthrax or the shooting. I wondered how long that would last.

We went out front to look for the car. Even at that hour the curb was lined with black Lincoln Town Cars. Some had signs with the car number on white plastic boards bearing the name of the service; other drivers were standing at the exit trying to hustle fares. It did not appear that any of the cars in the first rank were privately owned vehicles; nor were any from Empire Limo. I had to find the number for Empire on my contact list, which consumed my attention. Alison had her phone out as well and walked under the canopy away from the terminal exit. Though I saw her wander off, I have to admit it simply didn't register danger.

Maybe it was the screech of tires that brought me back, but for the second time tonight I saw Alison assume a combat position with both hands around the grip of a pistol. It looked just like the Beretta 84FS automatic that had materialized earlier. My mind was fixed on how she got another gun and not why she had that gun drawn and was prepared to use it on the arrivals drive of John F. Kennedy International Airport. A black SUV had turned and skidded to a stop, nose to the curb. The passenger door swung open and a man exited low, using the open door as cover. He was wearing blue jeans and a dark hoodie and was firing before his shoes hit the pavement. Not much of him was visible. He looked white, and he was professional. Alison returned fire, each of four semiautomatic muzzle flashes followed by the peculiar thud of lead into a hollow steel door, and the tinkling of ejected shell casings on the cement. Then the head went very low, and the pistol nosed around the bottom of the door.

"Alison, low," I shouted. As I said the words, two shots rang out and Alison dropped to her knees in slow motion. I knew immediately that she was done, even as I began to run to her. The way she was hit in the chest and the way she folded. It takes a devastating injury with a large-caliber weapon to stop a human cold. It was bad. I hadn't taken three blind steps when I heard shouting.

"Drop it. Drop the fucking gun, Rodriguez. Now." The voice was Deuce's. No question. Before he could say it again, the SUV sped off, grazing the front fender of a parked car and leaving Rodriguez, the man in the hoodie, in the open. He raised his pistol to fire. He was completely exposed, unprotected, and undisguised. It was over, and he began firing wildly. Two more shots rang out from behind one of the parked Town Cars. Rodriguez spun out and wobbled along the driveway. Another shot and another hit somewhere on his upper body, and he began to cry.

"Don't shoot, don't shoot. I'm hurt. Don't shoot. Call a bus, call a bus. I'm hurt."

"Drop your weapon," Deuce commanded. Rodriguez threw the pistol down and raised his hands.

"All right. All right. Call the bus. Can't you see I'm hurt? Please. Officer down. Officer down."

"Fuck you," Deuce shouted, coming out into the open.

Deuce had his pistol on Rodriguez, and as he approached, I thought he was going to fire again, but he didn't. Before Deuce could cuff Rodriguez, I was on the ground with Alison, but it was more for me than for her. Her face was peaccful and beautiful, but there was nothing left.

She was dead. I lifted Alison's head onto my thighs and stroked her hair. I cried. I didn't make a sound. I just cried and stroked her hair, and cried. And when her face was wet with my tears, I said, "You done good, kiddo, you done good."

EPILOGUE

It was more complicated than I had expected. Isn't it always? Bear with me, and I'll tell you what I know, which probably isn't everything. It has been a month now, and I feel more attached to the memory of Alison than I should. That's the way it happens. I was never sure I was in love with her when we were together, but I'm mourning her like I was. Maybe I was. Worse things have happened.

There was no time for boredom or banality in a relationship with Alison. She was mysterious, brilliant, and beautiful. She was warm, and hot, and she was a criminal.

Panopolous and Deuce were on to her before I had an inkling. I never really suspected anything until she pulled that handgun at the airport and was so quick to kill the two terrorists. Not that it was a bad thing, but it was not a natural reaction. That is, not unless you had been involved in drug-smuggling with them and couldn't afford to have them taken alive.

Deuce actually worked it out first. There had to be a New York connection. A doctor to remove the breast implants. They couldn't simply kill the mules. That might work in the final play, but as an ongoing business, the NYPD would take serial murders very seriously. Alison was the one. She was a perfect fit for MI6, and they put her into the case. At first it was just information-gathering, and she used Farzan to facilitate it. She was doing her job. Then she became the New York connection. She removed the implants and handed them off to Rodriguez and Griffin. Two bent narcotic cops. Two wealthy, bent narcotics cops. Rodriguez bought her act in every way. Alison became a partner until she wanted out. Rodriguez thought MI6 was his partner. That made him feel safe. Then Alison must have found God. She broke with them some time before she took up with me. At least I think it was before. The dates get fuzzy in my head. Anyway, Rodriguez played rough, and Alison was frightened. When the terror connection surfaced, they all wanted to distance themselves from it. Alison was a dangerous loose end. Rodriguez set the stage by dropping hints about her involvement. It all looked like it was going to break right for him. Alison had been quick to off the two baggage handlers. They were American-born and true believers, and they were the last two people who could have connected her to the drug ring. That could look bad for her. And even the shootout that eliminated her might have made Rodriguez a hero.

But then there was Deuce. He and Panopolous were isomers, mirror images, and once they got used to it, they made quite a team. They were smart, rough around the edges, secretive, and well connected. Between them, they had half the English-speaking world looking for Tahani.

He was the key. And when they pulled him off a flight to Tehran, he gave Alison up. It was Deuce who convinced Panopolous to let her tag along on the airport operation. I have no idea who else was in on the secret, but I wasn't. I'd like to think that Deuce was joking when he said he wasn't sure of me, but I wouldn't blame him if he had doubts. He was missing for much of that final day and a half, trailing Rodriguez. It was a one-man operation. Good as it is, the NYPD has more leaks than a rusty faucet. The only way to run a quiet sting on a guy on the job was to hand it off to Internal Affairs, and no street cop would do that. Especially not Deuce.

In the end, Alison just wanted it all to go away. She was certainly no terrorist, but self-preservation came first. Probably always did. She may have loved me. I'd like to think so, but it didn't matter. It was over.

Funny thing was, Alison was meant to go to London with me, and damned if I can remember if it was her idea to take that flight home or mine.

AUTHOR'S NOTE

This book is a work of fiction. Wendell Black is a fictional character, as are all others in the story. Great liberties have been taken in portraying the hierarchy and members of the NYPD. Neither the procedures nor the behavior of the characters are meant to represent actual events. This is simply a story, while New York's finest remain just that—the finest police force in the land.

Police surgeons are well-trained professionals who perform critical work and are integral to the functioning of a police force 34,500 strong. Details and locations of their work have been frequently altered to serve the story.

While the functioning of security agencies, in this era of terrorism, has been fictionalized, every effort has been made to present the science accurately. Any errors are mine, and mine alone.

Thanks are due to many who have helped this project along. Binky Urban, agent extraordinaire, has been in my corner for every project, and is always available with good advice, well-considered criticism, and practical help. Claire Wachtel, at HarperCollins, encouraged me from the start, and added editorial magic to nurture whatever is good about this book. Thank you. I would also like to thank associate editor Hannah Wood for her invaluable help in the preparation of the manuscript.

Beyond the writing, it has been a tradition to thank a diverse band of close friends who bounce ideas around and offer no real help or support. Jerry Della Femina, Michael Kramer, Andrew Bergman, and Jeff Greenfield, thanks for being there on Wednesdays. Joel Siegel, thanks for getting us together. We miss you.

My wife, the designer, entrepreneur, and filmmaker Cathryn Collins, has endured the ups and downs, the expletives, and the deadlines, all in fairly good humor. Thank you. And to the early-stage readers and listeners, my sons, Peter, Jason, and Gregory, thank you.